Sons of Heaven

Brenna

Lyons

Angel-Wing Saga

Fireborn Publishing
Copyright Statement

Sons of Heaven
Sons of Heaven: Beldon
Copyright © 2010/2017
Sons of Heaven: Unexpected Mates
Copyright © 2014/2017
by Brenna Lyons
Print ISBN: 978-1-946004-82-6
Print Publication: Match 2017

Cover Artist: Brenna Lyons
Editor: Kathryn Lively
Logo copyright © 2014 by Fireborn Publishing
and Allison Cassatta
Licensed material is being used for illustrative
purposes only. Any person depicted in the
licensed material is a model.

PUBLISHER

Glossary of Sakk Terms:

Appamora- akin to an apprentice on Earth, an appamora is trained in a particular trade by a master craftsman on Sakk

Bio bed- a bed that contains medical apparatus, designed to code *bio chains*, to do baseline medical tests, and to communicate with a *bio tracker* to perform continuous monitoring on a medical patient

Bio chain- ullium chains that mated couples wear; they are coded by a *bio bed* to the genetic signatures of the mated couple in the mating ceremony; they are the most basic type of *bio tracker*; they are worn for life, even if a spouse dies and a female remarries and gets a new bio chain, unless severed after being found guilty of a crime

Bio crib- see *bio bed*; a crib-type *bio bed* for infants and young toddlers

Bio tracker- usually contained in a medallion, sometimes decorated with a *Kieta*, this is a continuous monitoring medical device; it is worn by all members of the royal family and by those with medical problems who would benefit from continuous monitoring

Bionette- see *bio bed*; a *bionette* is a small cradle or bassinette *bio bed* for use with newborn infants, especially those with medical problems

Cazta- a female's clothing, usually wrapped around the body and secured with metal clasps

Cu-wrap- a male's informal clothing, worn around the waist not unlike an Egyptian *schenti* or a wrapped towel, secured with clasps; the *cu-wrap* is typically only worn for bedtime or for going to and from the showers on board ship or at the consulate

Cuzta- a male's clothing, usually wrapped around the body and secured with metal clasps

Eight-turn- a Sakk week, which consists of eight turnings (the Sakk term for a solar day)

Kahdi- a potentially-dangerous condition that affects Sakk females in the latter half of pregnancy; it is typified by violent movement by the baby in the womb, often occurring at night; it is treated most effectively by soothing sounds and motions, carried out by a Sakk male the mother trusts; untreated, *Kahdi* can result in bruising and tearing of the mother's internal abdominal cavity; at its worst, *Kahdi* can result in the death of the unborn child, death of the mother, or sterility of the mother

Kieta- a family crest

Sa- a term of respect in the Sakk language, used to refer to a master general

Sa-sen- a unit of time akin to an Earth month; a *sa-sen* lasts roughly twenty-four earth days

Sakkan- the main deity of the Sakk people, Sakkan is the first winged human on their world; known as the son of Sky and Earth, he was sent to the surface of Sakk and there married into the Sakk royal family and became progenitor of the modern Sakk race

Sakkra- the title used by the second son of the Sakk emperor; no one but the prince's family and mate may use his given name

Sakkraas- the joint title used when addressing a couple or group of princes and/or princesses

Sakkrettieff- a godchild of the Sakkrel (Sakk emperor) or Sakkriel (heir apparent); a *Sakkrettieff* is raised by his or her own parents but is otherwise treated like the children of the emperor, including quality of medical care, food, education and training, and preferential treatment in choosing a mate at adulthood

Sakkrel- the title used by the Sakk emperor; only his mate may use his given name

Sakkriel- the title used by the heir apparent to the Sakk throne; only his mate may use his given name

Sakkrit- the mate of a *Sakkrel*; the Sakk queen/empress

Sakku- a princess in the direct line of the seated emperor or who is mated to a prince in that line, but who is not mated to the heir apparent; since there is often more than one princess with this title, it is often used in conjunction with the given name of the princess in question to differentiate them in conversation

Sakku Yalu- a term of respect for an infant or toddler Sakku

Ses-time- a unit of time akin to an Earth hour; a *ses-time* lasts roughly seventy-five Earth minutes

Tova- soft, silky material used for most Sakk clothing; *tova* resists stains and most scents, but they are still washed daily for reasons of sanitation

Uba nut- a medium brown nut native to Sakk that resembles a chestnut in taste and consistency

Ullium- an element not found on Earth but native to Sakk; it is gold in color and very difficult to break or cut; it is used to make royal clothing and *Kietas, Kietas* for master generals and highly-decorated military men of lower ranks, *bio chains*, and armor

Yan- the Sakk equivalent of a year

Zadek bajou!- a Sakk phrase meaning 'Damn it all!'

Zhick- a Sakk swear word that pertains to a feeling of great disgust with a situation gone wrong

Zuda- a Sakk card game, played by a single player

In the Beginning:

Beldon

Introduction

From the Journal of Priest Ulan of Seed World 4, otherwise known as...Earth

The religions of the seed world invariably contain traces of us. Some worship us. Some vilify us. Amusingly, some do both. But—despite the redac spray to cloud the minds of the natives who stumble upon us, our shields, and our stealth—we never leave a world untouched.

There is no technology to completely wipe the minds of others, thank Sakkan. Even if there was, I highly suspect the stories of us...or of some entity like us, would exist. I still suspect advances in their technologies and cultures would flow to the natives, in our wake.

Every less advanced race dreams of flying; they all reach for the stars. Do they reach for the stars because they wish to evolve? Or do they reach out because they instinctively know those with the power to evolve their race sail the darkness of space, seeking worlds to seed and advance, selfish though their reasons for doing so might be?

Being a seed male myself, I long to continue the evolution. So far, none on Earth have come to a close resemblance of our seed creators, but I feel confident they will.

In the solitude of my chambers, I gaze at my reflection and imagine a descendant, fully-winged as the master is winged. I ask to check the readings on his bio tube just to see his majestic form on the sensors for a moment. I have basked in his shadow only once in my life and likely will never see him stir again. But, my sons and daughters...or their sons and daughters, will.

Perhaps one of my descendents will be blessed enough to welcome his needing length at his waking. Perhaps one will become the master's chosen mate. I would be honored to know that it was so.

In the interim, I smile at the quaint stories of the natives. They call the master an angel. They call his kind, fallen to Earth, devil or demon. They call us Sons of Heaven, drawn to the Daughters of Man, and say we lay with them to create the monsters of old, but we do not create monsters. We create hope for a dying world and advance this world in the process.

Chapter One

Beldon stirred, his mind and body coming to functionality at a maddening pace. His link to the sensors cleared first. He searched for signs of battle and relaxed at no such input.

There were only two reasons for the priests to wake him. If they didn't require his protection, they wished for him to evaluate one of the young and advise them on their progress toward suitable matches.

He sighed. So far, the breeding on this planet hadn't produced a close enough match. Beldon was starting to doubt it ever would, though saying it would be paramount to treason.

The priests had woken him countless times, and he hadn't found a match yet, close as they'd been. Still, he took solace in the soft bodies of those brought to him to be evaluated. The priests and the young expected it of him, and it was the least he'd earned.

How long has it been this time? How long since they've woken me? It might have been one generation, or it might have been ten. The longest so far had been ten.

The answer from the sensors sent his heart skittering. The bio tube suddenly felt too tight. He beat at the locks, shouting for the priests to manually release them. The wait for the computer was intolerable this time.

Too long. It's been millennia. Sakkan! What went wrong?

Without a doubt, something or someone had forced them to seal the tube for so long. What would have caused such a choice?

It couldn't have been battle. His bio tube was coded to wake him automatically for battle. He was, first and foremost, left here as protector to their seeded young.

They could have succumbed to disease; their first thought would have been to shield Beldon from it. They could have died in a cataclysm his bio tube had shielded him from.

Were they all dead? There was no answer from the tube, as if the systems were having problems understanding the question or identifying the answer.

Beldon cursed his shortsightedness in putting his bio tube under their sole control. He'd trusted the priests would wake him whenever it became necessary. In hindsight, that had been foolish.

What had woken him now? Was it a condition the priests had set? Was the bio tube breaking down? Surely, his Sakk brothers hadn't waited nearly three millennia to search him out.

With that, he struck the locks again. What if they wouldn't open? What if the bio tube *was* breaking down? Dying of dehydration wasn't a pleasing thought.

Strange tonals reached him through the tube's loosened seals. Beldon tapped at the translator circuitry, but he only succeeded in spurring sporadic translation.

"Wait...open..." An ancient curse followed.

Two of the locks snapped open. A cry of pain and a second curse identified the speaker as female.

Sakkan breathes! Where are the priests? Why was a female opening the tube?

He pleaded silently with the sensors, compiling all the data they could provide of the situation outside the bio tube. Whoever the female was, she was the only being within sensor range, which was highly unusual. There should have been hundreds of priests and young in range, if it was working properly. Even the basic sensors would cover the entire habitation areas of the temple, but Sakkan alone only knew what three thousand *yans* had done to the circuitry.

The final bit of information stopped him cold. The shields were down. If the generators were operational, only one of Sakk blood could open them, and there was only the unknown female in his proximity.

Was she one of the young? If so, where were the others? Was she human? If so, what was her purpose here?

Or were the generators broken and he defenseless? *Or, defenseless with young to protect? Sakkan, not that.*

Three more locks opened, and the computers took over, taking the last seven in a rush of air and the creak of untended pistons. The moment the opening was large enough, Beldon launched to the top, seeking the height advantage for possible battle.

She fell back with a cry of fear at the

movement, her pale skin going summer cloud white at the sight of him. Her dark eyes scanned up and down his body, stopping at his extended wings. Her breathing went ragged, and she collapsed to the dirt floor, her eyes slipping shut.

Beldon laughed harshly at that. Humans and the young bred in the temple were frail creatures. More than once, the young brought to him had fainted in his presence. Even more amusing were the battle-hardened human soldiers who'd loosed their bladders when pitted against him in battle.

He dropped down beside her, sobering. On closer inspection, it seemed the female was injured. Her clothing was ripped and stained in dirt and blood. Her head was discolored along the temple and cheek, as if she'd been struck...or had struck something else with formidable force.

Certain that he had time to spend, Beldon assessed his surroundings, his heart sinking. The temple was all but indistinguishable from the caverns in which it had been built. Whatever calamity destroyed it had been long ago.

A scan for biological traces told him roughly what he'd expected it to. The remains of the priests were the stuff archeologists and treasure hunters dreamed of finding. They were dead. All of them were, male and female. Nothing Sakk had moved here for almost as long as he'd slept.

There'd been no active breeding measures since then. There'd been no reports to Sakk. Beldon wasn't sure there was a home to return to.

What did that mean to him? Stranded on this alien world?

The female moved, a moan escaping her lips. Her shoulder-length hair feathers picked up red sand that nearly glowed against black curls.

Answers. I need answers she might have.

* * * *

Jannie hurt from the tips of her hair to her toenails. Her head was just one more pain in the lot, though it was the most troubling to her, since it was most likely to affect whether or not she found her way back to camp.

She wanted to believe the fall had been accidental, that the rope had been frayed or the clips faulty, but there was no denying the truth. The rope had been cut, and Edward was going to play this off as an "unfortunate incident in the field." *All for a little personal glory.*

By all rights, the fall should have killed her. Even now, Jannie couldn't identify what she'd hit. It had been smooth, warm, dome-shaped... She had slid down its side, landing hard at the base...of nothing.

The dreams that followed were even more bizarre: touching strange raised markings with blood-soaked fingers, wandering through half-lit caves she couldn't identify a light source in, a man trapped under the rock, vivid glyphs on a stone vault...and an angel.

"What dreams may come," she breathed.

No. That wasn't accurate. Jannie hurt too

much to be dead.

But I will be dead, if I don't find a way out of here.

She forced her eyes open, her breathing hitching at the apparition leaning over her. Deep blue eyes in a fierce face surrounded by waves of golden hair couldn't hold her attention when compared to the blinding white expanse of his wingspan.

Jannie swallowed hard. "Am I dead?"

After a moment, he smiled...then laughed, but he offered no answer.

Attempts at movement sent shards of pain down her shoulder and arm. She groaned. "Nope. I hurt too much to be dead," she reminded herself.

His brow furrowed, and he retreated to the stone vault. Now that her vision was clearing, Jannie realized light was emanating from inside it.

He returned with a metal cup and offered it to her. Jannie took it with a nod, hoping it was water. She couldn't identify the drink, but it was tasty and wet, so she drained it, then offered a word of thanks. He set the cup aside and settled on his knees, staring at her.

"Do you know a way out?" she asked.

He cocked his head to one side, his eyes narrowing.

Great. No English.

He understood enough to laugh when I asked if I was dead. "Do you understand me?"

There was a momentary pause. Then he tipped his head in response.

"Great. Can you show me the way out?"

No answer.

"Either you don't understand everything I say, or—"

Another tip of his head.

She groaned, scrubbing a hand over her face, then winced at the complaints from her bruises. "Of course. Whoever said angels spoke English?"

A hand touched her throat, and Jannie staggered to her feet. Her vision blurred, and she collapsed into his arms.

A series of dizzying movements later, she was surrounded by bright light, laying on a surface as smooth as glass and warm as bath water. A buzzing not unlike static electricity teased at her skin.

Jannie forced her eyes open, staring up at the angel. He pushed buttons etched with symbols not unlike those she'd seen on the scrolls. He did it by memory, his attention riveted to a glowing read-out of the same sorts of symbols. His fingers went still over the keypad, and one eyebrow rose in what she'd term surprise. His gaze panned from the readout to her face, and a smile lifted one corner of his lush mouth. For some reason, that expression made her distinctly nervous.

* * * *

Beldon stared at her, his heart warming at her naivety. She tensed as if to flee, and he placed a restraining hand on her uninjured shoulder.

"Calm, young one."

It was a given that she didn't understand Sakk, but she relaxed all the same.

Beldon looked around at his wings in surprise, noting how they'd curved around the tube in an unconscious move of protection and comfort. The move was instinctual; a young one was frightened, and he was sworn to protect her.

He'd denied his base side so long, the response shocked him. He was a soldier, not a caregiver. There had been nest parents and priests for that, but they no longer existed.

One hand came up, and she stroked at his primary feathers, murmuring something that didn't translate. He bit back his instinctual response to that. The young one didn't know what a Sakk male would expect after such a touch. Adopting a stern expression, he guided her hand away.

Her cheeks darkened, and she chewed at her lower lip. Her gaze flicked to his wings, then away, and she tipped her head in agreement.

That settled, Beldon moved on to his evaluation of her injuries. To his relief, they were minor. The young one would be unsteady on her feet for several weeks, and she'd require herbs to minimize the inflammation and ward off infection, but she'd heal well, he was sure.

She tried speaking to him again, but the only two words that translated were

out and *home*.

"Home is waiting for you, young one." He kept his tone soothing, needing to comfort her in the only way he could.

Her eyes drifted shut, most likely due to the *yosha* root he'd given her to drink before he moved her. In moments, her breathing was deep and even.

Beldon traced a finger along her lower lip. They'd done it. Priests or no priests, forced breeding or no, the match had been made.

He reached across her and started punching in the code to alert Sakk of their success.

Sakkan only knew what would happen next. Did Sakk still exist? Did they think Beldon dead? Would they leave him here, or would they take Beldon and the young one home?

Only time would tell.

Beldon froze, startling in the realization that he was humming Sakkan's Night Song to her. He hadn't even known he remembered it. What was happening to him?

Chapter Two

Jannie snuggled into softness and warmth. Something tickled at her cheek, and she jerked away. Arms encircled her, drawing her to a muscled chest. Levering her eyes open, she looked up into the face of the angel.

She sat, reclined against his lounging body. His wings surrounded her, cocooning her in a blanket of downy white.

He raised a cube to her lips. Jannie smelled it, tasted it, then took a bite and savored the strange concoction. More of the drink he'd given her the day before followed. By the end of the meal, sleep called to her again.

The angel helped her to a newly-unearthed chamber that contained a rudimentary bathroom and offered her a knee-length tunic to change into. When she was finished, he carried her back to the glowing vault.

All the while, she wondered at it. Archeologists lived to discover the truth behind myths. Here she was, in the presence of a living myth, seeing how he survived but with no more answers than she'd ever had.

This wasn't how he was meant to live, she was sure. What and where was his true home? How did he get here? Where were the others?

She sank to the glowing surface, stroking a hand over the wall. How long had he been trapped inside it? Why had he been?

There was no way to know.

Unless we learn to communicate with each

other.

Curiosity ate at her. Jannie touched his chest, drawing his eyes to hers. There was something enthralling about his gaze.

He looked at her hand, then met her eyes again, questioning her silently.

"How do I ask your name? How do I make you understand me?"

He cocked his head to one side, as he often did when she spoke to him. His hand covered hers. "Beldon."

"Beldon? Your name is Beldon?"

He tipped his head. His hand settled around her cheek, stroking lightly at her skin. He waited for her reply.

"Jannie. Jannie Reynolds."

His smile returned. "Jannie."

She yawned, her eyes slipping shut.

"Sleep, Jannie."

And so she did.

Chapter Three

Beldon woke to the most delightful sensation imaginable. It had been so long since he'd felt a woman's touch, he could hardly contain himself. He kept his eyes closed, savoring it a little longer.

The young one was in his lap, where he'd gathered her when the *yosha* root had sent her to healing sleep. Her hands were busy at his wings, tracing the lines of bones, smoothing feathers and arousing him in the process.

I shouldn't. She's so young and innocent.

Young was undeniable, but nothing Jannie did spoke of innocence.

I was promised the first. It wasn't why he'd agreed to take this post. Beldon had planned to step aside and give his promised to a younger male. What would a young female want with a battle-hardened Sakk master general late in his prime?

She wiggled against his rising cock, seemingly answering that question for herself.

Beldon opened his eyes, watching her pleasure him. Her skin was flushed, her breathing quick and uneven.

Jannie met his gaze. One smooth hand left his wing and trailed down his body to the ridge of his cock. When he didn't stop her, she sought out the edge of his *cuzta* and slipped the hand beneath, caressing his length directly.

That simply, his choice was made. He'd been promised this. He'd been separated from his world and people for five thousand *yans* and had no clue what he'd return to, if he could return at all. This little temptress was his, and he would claim her as his mate.

* * * *

His expression hardened, and Jannie's heart sank. He didn't enjoy what she was doing.

Beldon's hands closed on her hips, and he lifted. Just when she thought he meant to set her aside, he turned her to face him. Jannie shivered in delight, spreading her legs to straddle him.

He dragged up at her tunic and tossed it away. He took her visual measure, then started touching, pausing at her most sensitive erogenous zones as if mapping them for future reference. Beldon drove her crazy when what she really wanted was him driving into her.

Questions of why she was so aroused by him niggled at her, and she pushed them away. Everything about him drew her: his calloused hands, his mouth, his body...even his voice.

Jannie buried her face in his chest, her hands seeking out the fasteners she'd found at his shoulders. The front of his outfit peeled away, revealing chiseled muscle, crossed with a smattering of scars and dusted in gold and white fluff too soft and...feathery to be hair.

Feathers. They're down. She ran her fingers through them, eliciting a groan from Beldon.

He positioned her over his cock and thrust up, filling her in one savage movement. The down on his chest and abdomen teased her with every breath they took, and she started grinding down on him, moaning at the matching down around his cock, stroking her intimately.

Grumbled language she didn't understand left his lips. Then he was controlling the event, his hips rising and falling while he positioned her to take him.

Jannie sought out his mouth. At first, he pulled away. Then he returned, his lips parting to invite her in. At the first stroke of her tongue against his, he took control of the kiss as well.

With his cock and mouth working her hard, climax was close at hand. He growled against her tongue at the first contractions of her building release. Her scream was muted in his mouth.

Her hands tunneled through his hair, but it wasn't hair. The feathers were long and curling, millions of tiny wisps on each soft quill that teased at her palms.

His wings closed around her, fluttering lightly, most likely in excitement. Beldon went still, buried to the hilt in both her mouth and her core, his cum expanding into her.

His climax went on for what seemed like dozens of minutes, his cock jerking against her inner walls, his cum filling her, then overflowing, matting down the soft fuzz surrounding the base of his cock. All the while, he ravaged her mouth.

When his climax abated, Beldon stayed inside her, his mouth still meshed with hers. In the end, he didn't go flaccid. Instead, he eased back from the kiss and stared at her.

* * * *

What in Sakkan's name is this? Beldon groaned at the continuing call to the young one. By tradition, he knew what should happen next, but leaving her body to accomplish it was loathsome.

As if she agreed, Jannie moved against him. His cock erupted in aftershocks, and she cried out in pleasure.

I have to bind her. That thought in mind, he slid out of her body.

She clung to him, little whispers escaping her lush mouth. Beldon resisted the urge to taste that mouth again; if he did that, he'd be inside her. There were things he had to accomplish before he allowed it.

Beldon rose, lifting Jannie with him. He settled her atop the bio tube, then stripped off the last of his clothing. She shivered, and her eyes pleaded for more of his sex.

He pushed away the urge to indulge for the moment, reaching past her into the drawer he never thought he'd open. The *bio chains* felt warm to his touch, most likely a reaction to the pheromone and hormones coursing through his body.

The first locked on his wrist, he gasped at the force of his erection. Taking Jannie's hand in both of his, he closed the matching chain. Her body convulsed at the click of the lock, and she arched against him, offering herself.

"Not yet, young one."

Beldon climbed into the bio tube, lifting Jannie in after him. The order entered, he settled back to allow the chains to code to each other and their wearers.

Once coded, they could never be removed, save by a legal entity. A widow would wear her first chain, even if she also wore the chain of a subsequent mate. Only wanton prisoners were denied the chain.

Beldon would be able to track Jannie anywhere she went and vice versa. Any bio tube or bio screen would allow them to read the physical condition of the other mate at any reasonable distance.

His young mate took advantage of their positions to taste his body. Her lips and tongue played havoc with his thinking mind.

In desperation to stop her before she started something inappropriate to the coding cycle, Beldon used what little space they had with two in the bio tube to maneuver her beneath him, her back to his chest. He stroked at her body, denying them both what she was blatantly offering. The effects had them sweat-soaked and trembling, on the edges of a powerful joining.

When the end of cycle toned, Beldon straightened. He planted Jannie's hands on the top edge of the tube and drove up into her sweet body. Like the first time, he was fierce, the claim of a female and nothing less. The end was as explosive as he remembered, and he lay, rigid and ready, inside her long after they'd climaxed and she succumbed to sleep.

I should seal us in. His duty to his mate demanded that Beldon dress them both and set the bio tube to wake them when Sakk answered his call or in one *yan*, whichever came first. His actions after that would be dictated by what woke them.

The less rational part of him wanted a few more turnings with his young mate. *Just a little more time before I close us into oblivion. At least enough time to teach her a few words of Sakk.*

Chapter Four

Jannie met his eyes from across the distance separating them. She fingered the feather he'd given her, smiling as he tensed slightly. Beldon didn't move toward her or order her to him, which meant he wanted her to tease him.

She ran the feather along the line of her jaw, licking at the edge. His cock came up against his outfit at the offer.

Jannie stroked the feather down her throat, teasing her nipples through the fabric of the tunic. Beldon licked his lips, but he held his position.

Taking the lead, he unfastened his outfit, took his cock in his hand, and stroked himself. Jannie raised her tunic, dipping the feather between her thighs. Beldon never lasted long when she did this.

He growled her name, but she held her ground, stroking at her clit until her knees shook. He'd come to her soon...or he'd order her to him and sate this maddening arousal that hadn't abated since the first time they'd had sex.

The shifting of sand announced his approach. Jannie watched him marching toward her, stripping off his clothing as he came. When he reached her, she had no doubts that there would be no more teasing. He'd position her and take her in whatever way appealed to him, and she'd love every minute of it.

A piercing sound cut through her still-healing head. Jannie dropped the feather, clapping her hands over her ears. Beldon took off at a run, reaching for her, shouting her name.

Jannie took the hint and bolted for him, coming up hard against something solid but clear. She searched the surface frantically, blood from her split lip dotting an otherwise invisible wall.

Beldon reached the other side, slamming a roughened fist against the obstruction. His eyes scanned the space behind her, and he motioned. Jannie turned, noting a pile of rubble.

She didn't question his orders. In moments, she was pulling down rocks, trying to reach whatever was behind them.

The panel was half-smashed. Several keys were gone entirely, revealing colored tubes inside, some lit and some dark. Hopefully, there was enough of it left to open the wall.

Jannie moved aside, looking back at Beldon for some indication of what she should do next. His expression crumpled, and his body followed suit. He slumped against the wall in apparent misery.

There's no way to shut it off.

Beldon touched the wall, flattening his hand against it. Jannie ambled to him, matching the movement.

* * * *

His nerves jumped in agitation. The shield

should have turned off four *ses-time* after the last sensor contact. Either the equipment was faulty, or someone was actively trying to find a way around the shield. One way or the other, Jannie was trapped outside his shield with no supplies or protection and had been for well over a turning.

He couldn't even be certain she was protected as well. There were three shield wall layers. He knew that the sensor line to the outer two wasn't functioning. He couldn't be certain they were intact.

I hope they aren't. I have to get her to the outside, to the humans...if I can.

His heart aching, Beldon started drawing a map in the sand floor.

Jannie watched him, tears welling in her eyes, then falling. She shook her head, pleading with him silently, then with sobs. Beldon motioned to the tunnel she needed, praying the rest was intact. Then he did the hardest thing he'd ever done; Beldon turned his back on his mate and walked away.

He didn't look back at the thumps of her fists against the shield. He didn't show compassion when she vented cries, though his hands fisted in fury and frustration.

Finally, the air was still and silent. Beldon used the bio tube's sensors to assure himself that she'd gone before he turned to look. The only signs of her left were the blood smears and footprints in the sand. Even the feather she'd begged him for was gone.

Beldon vented a howl of loss at the shielded

sanctum, cursing himself. *We should have been sealed in the bio tube. She's gone, and it's my fault that she is.*

I'll find her. I'll find a way.

That resolved, he started programming the bio tube. If the Sakk contacted him, he'd wake. If the shield dropped, he'd wake. As an afterthought, Beldon entered one more possibility. If Jannie returned to the shield, he'd wake to see her...no matter what torture that was.

* * * *

Jannie slid in the semi-darkness, tumbling down a steep incline, striking her leg on a rock. She lay at the bottom, aching in body and heart.

He told me to leave. She sobbed at that. Beldon had refused to look at her when she'd begged him to.

He had to. Some rebellious voice insisted that Beldon had a reason for this. He had to make her leave; he just didn't have the words to explain it to her.

He'll come for me. The chain around her wrist seemed to warm at that idea.

Grasping the feather, she tried to stand. Blinding pain stopped her halfway to her knees.

One look up the slope confirmed that she couldn't make it back to Beldon in this condition...at least without a splint, and where would she find the wood and cloth she needed to make one? Like it or not, Jannie had to follow his directions and hope there was a way out.

The last two tunnels were slow going, accomplished by way of a modified Army crawl, excruciating because of her injured leg. If she had to backtrack, she was going to have a hard time of it.

As she feared, the tunnel dead-ended. Jannie collapsed to the ground, shivering in pain and defeat.

Lights flashed around her, and she raised her head, staring at them blearily. The same alarm that had separated them sounded. Before Jannie could react, an icy spray hit her full in the face. She gasped, and it chilled her throat and lungs, making her cough in response.

The world went gray...then black. Pain pierced the nothingness, then was gone.

* * * *

"Jannie! Jan!"

Hands pulled at her, and she batted ineffectually at them.

"What is she wearing?" a man she vaguely recognized asked.

"Worry about that later," a woman snapped.

Jannie tried to open her eyes, squeezing them shut at the assault of the blinding sunlight. She shifted her aching body, crying out at the lance of pain up her left leg and the throbbing that followed.

"Don't move, Jannie. Bryan will splint it."

"Eve?" Jannie's voice was rough, and her throat burned.

"I'm here, sweetie. Do you remember how you

did this?"

She tried, but there was nothing past the scrolls...fighting with Edward over those damned scrolls. "No." Even that single syllable exhausted her.

"Where have you been, Jannie?" Bryan asked.

"What do you mean?" She'd been in the caves. Where else would she be?

Silence fell around her, and Jannie forced her eyes open. Eve and Bryan stared at each other across her body, their expressions unreadable.

"What?" she asked again. Jannie rubbed her dry tongue around her mouth and winced at the bitter taste she couldn't identify. She was thirsty...ravenous.

Eve recovered enough to speak, before she could ask for food and water. "Jannie...you've been missing for twelve days."

She searched for answers, but there was nothing coherent she could latch onto. One moment, she'd been arguing with Edward. The next... Swirls of gray played in her mind.

"Look at this," Bryan called.

Jannie focused on the feather in his hand, and images exploded in her mind...wings fluttering hard, deep blue eyes, bright lights...and...

And nothing. Her breathing went ragged, and the world slipped away.

Chapter Five

"...can't explain it. Whatever this is, it's a new element."

Jannie forced her eyes open, taking in Dr. Abrams and Bryan. Over their shoulders, the camp physician, Dr. Hall, shook his head in apparent confusion.

She was in the camp hospital, reclined but not flat in the bed. But what was she doing here? What were they talking about?

"What is?" she ventured.

Jannie started taking inventory, grimacing at the cast on her ankle. "Hope this is a walking cast," she joked. It would be hard enough getting around the compound with a walking cast. Crutches would be nearly impossible...hazardous.

Abrams sighed. "Where did you get the bracelet? Can you tell us?"

She searched out the thin gold chain with the interlocked crescent moons, her head spinning in the vain attempt to draw any memories of it forth. "Wish I knew. It's...beautiful." It was. It was fragile, something she didn't indulge in, as a rule. Anything would snap at the first catch on rock was useless, in this line of work.

"It's also impossible to remove," Bryan reported.

She looked for a catch, but there didn't seem to be one. It was too small to slide over the heel of her hand. "Don't be ridiculous. If it went on, it has to come off."

"You'd think," he replied acidly. "Look at this." He passed a tool into her hand.

Jannie considered them for a moment. "So. These are just simple tin snips." They used them for opening sealed containers from the states.

Bryan pointed to several scars on the metal blades. "We can't cut the chain."

"You tried to cut it?" For reasons she couldn't understand, that thought chilled her...panicked her.

His eyes narrowed. "Well, we can't. It looks like gold, but whatever it is, gold isn't it. We can't even get a sample of it to test."

Jannie passed the tin snips back, lost in thought.

"Where did you get the clothes, Jannie?" Abrams changed the subject smoothly, to another she had no memory of.

"What clothes?" Something told her he didn't mean her climbing gear. He turned, then came back with a long tunic of metallic silver cloth.

"Well, at least it came off," she quipped.

"I'll take it you don't remember this, either?"

Jannie started to answer in the negative, then hesitated.

"What is it?" Hall inquired.

"Soft. I don't know why, but...soft...comes to mind. Is it?" She wanted to reach out and run her fingers through the fabric, to see if it matched the faint memories she had of it.

"Like silk," Abrams confirmed, "but it doesn't rip or soil. You came in covered in dirt and blood, sweat-soaked, and the garment was as clean and sweet-smelling as it is now."

"Definitely strange," she agreed.

"And you have no idea where you got it." He didn't question it.

"Unfortunately, none."

"She remembered the feather," Bryan reported. "Or...it sparked something, at least."

"Feather? It probably reminded me of the scrolls I found. They indicated a bird-man god figure...fairly common in many ancient cultures." *Beldon...* Blue eyes danced before her suddenly-fuzzy field of vision...an intense stare from a warrior's face. There was something distinctly Greek in his looks, like statues founds in ruins there.

"What did you say?" Abrams pounced on something she couldn't name for a long moment. "Jannie? What was that word?"

"Beldon," she breathed. "His name was Beldon."

He was abruptly at her side. "Whose name? What did you see? Where did you find that name?"

She was falling...screaming...sliding down a dome-like structure... No handholds... She crumpled at the base, broken... Hurt... Betrayed...

"Jannie?" That was Hall.

"I don't know. I have...bits of memories but nothing that makes sense." The rope was cut... *Cut!* She'd fingered the smooth end and shouted at—

"Jannie?" Bryan, she noted.

"Edward... He—he cut the rope...I think." It

was better not to make solid accusations she couldn't back up. Jannie knew it was true, but how could she—

"We know." That was Abrams, and he was furious. His eyes were narrowed and hard as steel, his face crimson. Jannie was sure if she touched his cheek, it would be scorching against her skin.

She stared at him, struck mute by his reaction.

"He tried to hide it...moved the ropes...frayed them. He didn't count on Bryan knowing the difference. We never did find your descent point."

Jannie nodded, relieved that he'd been found out. "Where is he?"

There was a moment of silence. "Where do murderers belong? The US authorities may get him back...eventually. I'm sure the consulate is working on that."

The thought of anyone—even Edward—in the local prison system turned her stomach, and she swallowed down a sour wave.

Hall cleared his throat. "There's another thing we have to ask, Jannie."

"I seriously doubt it can be freakier than the rest. Hit me."

The three men cast uneasy looks at each other, and Bryan executed a hasty retreat. The door closing behind him punctuated the move.

"Okay. Maybe it can get worse." She tried to calm her pounding heart, but adrenaline was pumping.

Hall met her gaze, his entire frame tense in

some unnamed emotion. "Did Edward...assault you?"

"You mean besides cutting my ropes? We argued, but I don't remember—"

"Sexually?"

That one word hung between them. Her blood ran cold, and her stomach rioted.

"Or even something consensual?" Abrams offered. "It happens in close quarters sometimes."

"Not to me." She swallowed in a vain attempt to wet her dry throat. "What exactly are you saying?"

Hall shot another unreadable look at Abrams. "There was semen. By the time we got to decent equipment... I can't begin to guess when it—"

"*Inside* me?" A sick headache took root.

"And on you...on your inner thighs. That alone would indicate it wasn't... Wasn't that long ago."

She buried her head in her hands, leaning forward, taking slow, deep breaths that did nothing to calm the whirling top in her skull.

"You have no memory of it?" Hall asked.

A wild flapping of wings played out in her mind. Deep blue eyes riveted on hers. She'd never seen eyes quite that color before. *Nothing that makes sense.* "No. I wish I did...I think." Something that smacked of *Agnes of God* certainly wasn't helping.

"Understandable," Abrams replied gruffly.

"Then we'll have to test," Hall spoke over him.

"Edward?" she guessed.

"Everyone," Abrams insisted. "If it wasn't Edward, I want to know who it was."

She nodded. There were other women on the team. Eve, Abrams' wife, was on the team. "Do it." But what was she going to do, when they had an answer?

Chapter Six

"How's that leg, sweetie?"

Jannie smiled at Eve over the computer terminal. "Can't wait for this cast to come off. The sooner I'm back in the caves, the better."

"A few more days, according to Hall."

She sighed. "Plus time to strengthen it." Abrams was sure to stretch that out as far as he could. He'd been loath to let Jannie out of sight for more than a minute, and he'd insisted that she carry a radio with her everywhere, even in her own quarters or the showers. It was a good thing they were water-resistant.

When she did return to the caves, Abrams had ordered teams of three. With no match for the semen, the consensus was that there was a rogue element in the area, and Jannie had played victim once, though she still had no memory of it.

The feather drew her gaze and then her fingers. It was a strong feather, one seemingly designed for flight.

It remained unidentified. The size, color, and density matched no known avian form. She was certain the biologists would like more than the samples Abrams had given them, but the idea of losing it had sent Jannie into a panic. In the end, Abrams had let her keep it, since she took comfort from touching it.

It did more than comfort her. The feather brought a calming surety that she was protected...along with disconcerting arousal. She stroked at the edges of the plume, her body going wet and needing.

Eve's voice dragged her back to the present. "A couple of weeks...tops. Jacob wants you back in." She turned, offering a wrapped sandwich and a travel mug that probably contained juice. "In the meantime...lunch, since you never stop to go get it for yourself."

"Why should I? I know you'll bring me one," she teased. Jannie snagged the offered food, unwrapping the sandwich. She was ravenous, and it seemed she had been for days. "What's on the menu?"

"Uh...chicken, I think."

She dropped the sandwich on the work table, her head spinning. The feather was under her hand, and she closed her fingers around it reflexively. Her stomach tightened, then lurched, and Jannie dragged the waste basket over, just in time to upchuck into it. A cold sweat coated her body, and she groaned...then launched into another bout of vomiting.

Eve's hand pressed to her forehead, and she grabbed Jannie's radio off the table. "Hall, I need you. It's Jannie."

* * * *

"Feeling better?" Hall asked.

Jannie managed a weak smile. "Yeah. Stomach flu, I guess." She disliked the term Montezuma's Revenge, and since she'd never suffered it before, it didn't make sense that she would now. After all, the water purification systems should negate the possibility of it.

He didn't look up from the chart in his hand. "Doubt it."

Something in his tone sent her head back into a spin. It took a long moment and his droll stare for her to lock onto something else that caused nausea and dizziness. "No. Oh, no."

"Unfortunately, yes." There was nothing comforting in that confirmation.

Words failed her, then returned in a slightly manic rush. "Damn it, and I don't even know who to inform he's about to be a father." It was a weak joke, at best.

"You don't have to," he suggested.

"Have...to?"

Hall's gaze bored holes into the chart, then returned to her, panning up slowly. He tucked the chart under his arm. "You're pregnant to gods-know-who and gods-know-how, Jannie. No one would blame you, if you're not up to this."

She let his words sink in. On one level, they comforted her. On another, they made her stomach squirm like a pit of snakes.

Jannie closed her hand on the feather she'd brought with her, clutched in a shaking hand. What if she remembered and it was a horrible memory? Would she still be able to see this through?

The feather brushed her cheek, and a fractured memory half-formed in her mind. The kiss was hard and hot, breath stealing. She wanted to scream in pleasure, but she didn't want to leave that kiss.

"Jannie?"

She blinked her eyes, focusing on Hall. What was that? Was it real? Her body's reaction to it was real enough.

"Should I contact—"

"No." Jannie pressed the feather to her lower abdomen. "No. I won't do that."

"Are you sure? You have a limited amount of time to make this kind of decision."

She nodded. *It wasn't rape. I don't know what did happen, but I agreed to it.*

More than that, she knew she'd enjoyed it. For now, that was enough.

Chapter Seven

Jannie paused, gasping at the unexpected sensation. It was sharp, akin to an erogenous zone, and—like many of the other changes in her life—new and unexplainable.

She ran a hand up her abdomen, shivering at the feel of tiny hairs. Using a hand mirror, she tried to see them, but they were too fine and light to see. Her pubic hair, leg, and arm hair had always been the same: barely there, so much so that ex-boyfriends often believed she shaved them. Jannie had no such need.

She'd enjoyed that anomaly. This one set her teeth on edge. Jannie traced the line, from her pubic hair to just below her breasts...a fraction of a finger wide. She'd heard women sometimes developed pigmentation there during pregnancy, but there was no sign of it. She'd heard older women often developed coarse hairs below their navels, but these were soft.

Still, they made her skin crawl. Jannie pulled out the razor she used on her underarms, the only body hair dark enough and coarse enough for her to bother with shaving it. She shaved the offending hair, taking breaks to still her trembling hands.

Relieved, though she couldn't say why she was, Jannie crawled into bed and fell asleep to a haunting tune she couldn't name.

* * * *

46

"They finally identified the drug in your system," Abrams informed her.

Jannie looked up from the sand-dusted carvings she'd been studying, her interest piqued. "That's good. If it's that rare, it'll be easier to track to a distributor and a buyer." *And, ultimately...to the father for my baby. To a man my dreams say was the hottest ticket I've ever cashed in bed.*

Of course, her dreams were frustratingly scarce on other details...like a name for him, how they'd ended up together, how they'd come to be separated, and where he was now.

Abrams offered a hand, pulled Jannie to her feet, and guided her to a camp stool. The two young archeologists with her moved a couple dozen yards away to nothing in particular, giving them space to talk in peace.

Jannie watched them go, her heart pounding. "This doesn't bode well."

It could be nothing. Few of the other team members wanted to talk about what had happened to her. It was too raw, too frightening in a place where cave ins and local animal life were usually the most pressing dangers.

But, something told her it wasn't that simple this time. Maybe it was Abrams' stiff posture. The man wore his emotions on his sleeve, for the most part.

"Left to ourselves, we never would have identified it," Abrams imparted. "Hall sent our readings and a sample to a botanist he knows, hoping for an herbal match."

She groaned. "Which means it's

untraceable." Her hopes of finding Mr. Orgasm deflated that quickly.

"Worse. It's an extinct form of flora used in religious ceremonies thousands of years ago."

"Extinct?" *You have got to be kidding me!*

"They've got chemical traces on altar tools and such from this general area, but it doesn't—"

"There's a patch somewhere," she interrupted him. "They think it's extinct, but there's some hidden away in the mountain range."

"Jannie..." He sighed.

"There has to be," she insisted, letting her stubborn streak have full rein.

"Maybe. I guess it's possible." But his voice and expression said he wasn't convinced.

"When you eliminate the impossible, whatever is left, no matter how improbable, must be so."

"Paraphrasing Sherlock Holmes?"

She ignored the question. "What's the impossible? Time travel? Either someone has a superbly-preserved stash of this stuff, or there's a plant still in existence. The former...less likely. The latter is most probable."

He nodded. "Stranger things have happened, I suppose."

There was a tense moment of silence between them. The air seemed to crackle with something unspoken.

"Yes?" Jannie prompted him.

"Hall wants to do a sonogram."

Her heart stuttered. "Something wrong?"

She'd thought she was settling into the pregnancy well, despite the fact that meat made her queasy. Surprisingly, she tolerated beef better than most.

"You said you're feeling movement?"

Feeling it? She could see the baby moving some days. "It's not unheard of for over four months." *Unusual but not unheard of. Okay, seeing movement at this stage is, but I'm not about to share the weirder side of things with anyone.*

"You're running big for four and a half months," he countered.

"Hall thinks I'm further along?" Did he think she was lying about not knowing who the father was, as well?

"Hall doesn't know what to think."

Jannie stroked at the feather she'd woven into her hair. "Okay. But give me a few days."

Abrams' hand closed over her shoulder. "You have all the time you need."

A niggling whisper in the back of her mind insisted that it wasn't true. She was running out of time.

For what?

There was no answer to that.

Chapter Eight

Beldon came to consciousness with a jolt.

What woke me? The sensors returned an answer that both chilled and thrilled him. *The Sakk.* It wasn't an answer from them; it *was* them...in the flesh and bone and feather.

He accessed other sensors, noting that the shield was still up. Five *sa-sen*—more than four Earth moons—had passed, while he lay trapped in the bio tube.

"Five?" The shields hadn't dropped in five *sa-sen*? Jannie had been without his protection for a quarter of a *yan*? His shock was so deep, he didn't realize the locks had disengaged until the pistons started pushing the lid away.

Beldon launched from the bio tube, ignoring the tones signifying an override of the shield. "Jannie." All that mattered was his mate. He punched in the code that ordered a track of her location.

She was close. *Still within the range of mountains easily, unless the topography has changed significantly.* His heart easing, he tapped up her physical condition.

Beldon straightened so quickly, bones shifted and cracked in his shoulders. Old scars ached, reminding him that he was a man of war...and an elder general at that, a master and honed in the great wars.

Thanks to Jannie, he was much more. She carried his son. He would retire from war to care for them, live as he'd lived with her those

50

few precious turnings. It was Sakkan's reward among the living to be so blessed.

Five Sakk warriors marched from the tunnels, offering a curt bow in unison. Beldon turned to them, taking in their longer *cuzta* and the *uza* armor in little more than passing interest. The time for serious study of all he'd missed would come later.

The leader went down on one knee. "Master Beldon, praise Sakkan you live."

The greeting pleased him. Even in his own time, Beldon had been something of a legend, which was why he'd been trusted for this mission.

Still, that was a concern for later. "I'll take time to praise Him properly when Jannie is in my care." Beldon strode past them and into the tunnel they'd exited. "I require armor." His own had been lost in the long sleep: to the rock falls, hidden by the priests, or taken as spoils of war.

They rushed to match his stride. "Master, we have created matches on other seed worlds. One match female is of no great importance to us. Our orders are to—"

Beldon turned to him, grasping the young commander by the throat. He raised his chained arm and rotated it before the young one. "It is of paramount importance to *me*. Jannie carries my son, and I will have her beneath my wing."

There was no hesitation. "Yes, Master. As you say."

He released the other man and led the way

toward the waiting shuttle. "We track."

* * * *

Jannie closed her eyes, trying to pretend she was anywhere but on the exam table with a gelled wand pressing to her abdomen. The sonogram machine had been intended for very different purposes than what it was currently being put to use for. With all her heart, Jannie wished it was still being put to those uses and not to her.

A flurry of movement made her stomach shift uneasily.

"I wish he'd stop doing that," Hall grumbled.

"He?" Her heart skipped a beat in excitement she hadn't realized she'd feel.

"If the baby would stay still long enough, I could be sure."

"And you wonder why I feel movement," she quipped.

Abrams took her hand. "No one doubts you, Jannie." He squeezed, then released her.

She nodded, her nerves jumping nonetheless. It seemed the baby agreed. If Jannie had to guess, she'd say he was doing cartwheels inside her.

Jannie placed her hands under her abdomen, humming a tune she couldn't quite place. The baby settled in response.

"That's better," Hall sighed.

She kept humming, drifting between sleep and waking. "What in the—"

Abrams' voice overpowered Hall's. "My gods."

Jannie forced heavy lids up and stared at them, more asleep than awake. "What is it?"

There was no answer. Both men stared at the screen, wide-eyed. Hall pressed a button, then set the wand on the edge of the table, no doubt focusing on a single recorded image.

She levered herself up on her elbows, her heart hammering. Sleep deserted her. Jannie strained to see the screen, but it was turned slightly away, making an indistinct gray blur of everything on it. "What? Damn it, Hall—"

Hall stared at her, seemingly shocked into silence. He pressed another button and stepped back, giving her a clear view of the larger facing screen.

At first, Jannie couldn't make sense of it. Details came into focus slowly: the face, tiny arms and legs, fingers and toes, the penis standing proud. She smiled widely, but the smile disappeared as the final features took shape—wings.

A memory exploded in her mind. He was tall and chiseled, a golden god-man. His expression was fierce, his touch demanding, but his voice kind. She was his, held to his body, full of him, surrounded by his arms and wings.

"Beldon," she breathed.

Abrams turned to her, his eyes manic. "We're not talking about an ancient deity here. Remember impossible and improbable?"

Jannie eased off the table, wiping the gel away with a hand towel. She took her time, straightening her clothes, while her mind rioted in search of an answer to that.

"You're right," she agreed. "I don't think we are." She knew Beldon wasn't a story.

More memories unfolded: laughing, teasing, bathing, feeding each other on strange cubed food... *Oh, he's real.*

The lullaby... He'd hummed it to her the many times she'd slept on him. Was that why their son responded to it?

Our son... She backed to the counter, grasping it in one hand as the future played out. Each scenario was more gruesome than the last: a fight for "ownership" of the winged deity child, the search for and capture of Beldon, labs, freak shows... Or would they want to destroy and study the baby's corpse?

"Jannie, we need answers here," Abrams barked.

She focused on him, easing away along the counter. He was strung tight, and though she'd never have suspected he could be a violent man, Abrams looked as if he might erupt any moment.

"What?" She forced the word past numb lips.

"Gods mating with humans being the sort of fantasies one human tells another as a cautionary tale or to explain the unexplainable... What is the probable answer here?"

Her fingers strayed to the feather, still unidentified. "A living being that the myths were based on."

"You're postulating," he accused. "Badly, I might add."

She motioned to the screens. "Does that

look like I'm postulating?" There was an edge of panic in her voice, a rising fear she couldn't control.

Abrams took a moment to study the screen facing him, his expression changing so fast it made her head spin. "A society of winged creatures? Is that what you're suggesting?"

Her stomach clenched at the word *creature.* Beldon wasn't a creature; he was a person. "Nothing in the snips of memories I have suggests more than one, but I *can't* remember, so your guess is as good as mine."

High winds buffeted the building. Windows rattled, and trees struck the roof as if seeking a way in. It ended as quickly as it began.

"What was that?" she asked, her unease with the situation more acute.

Abrams ignored her and forged on. "Where has the creature been hiding?"

"I don't know. In the caves somewhere, I'd guess. It's a labyrinth down there. Even imaging doesn't reveal more than a few layers of tunnels."

"Are you suggesting Jules Verne?" There was more than a hint of disbelief in that.

What happened to no one doubting me? The change hurt, but she stuffed it down, needing her mind not her emotions. "I don't remember a world like that," she offered calmly.

"What do you remember?"

He took a step closer, and Hall took a step away. That was a clear enough sign that she was on her own.

"Rock...sand...carvings... Ruins maybe..." She remembered a tub; it hadn't been a natural pool. "Light sources I can't account for..."

"And?" Abrams challenged.

"Beldon." Admitting that was easier than she'd thought possible. "I remember him. He cared for me, fed me when I was hurt. I was injured in the fall, as the tests showed." The early x-rays had revealed a crack in her collarbone, well toward healed when she'd emerged from the caves.

"Do you remember *that*?" He motioned to the large screen without taking his gaze off of her.

"A little. It's surreal...disjointed."

"She was drugged, Abrams," Hall reminded him.

Her face heated at the reminder. Nothing in her memories indicated she was incapacitated while they'd had sex. If she had to guess, Jannie would say that came later, but now was the wrong time to admit it.

Abrams stepped toward her, too close for her comfort. Jannie retreated, backing herself into a corner.

"How does it survive, if the environment is rock and sand? Where does it get food and water?"

The stone vault and food cubes raced through her mind, but she had no clue how the systems worked or where the raw materials came from. "I don't know how *he* survives." Beldon wasn't a creature, an "it" to be sneered at. *He's a warrior.*

"How did you? You were missing twelve days, yet you came back injured but fairly hydrated and well fed."

"Beldon cared for me." It was the only solid fact she could state.

His voice rose a few octaves. "How? Where did you *get* the food and water?"

"I don't know!"

He grasped her arm, squeezing down on the wrist circled by the gold chain bracelet. Jannie's heart pounded so hard she felt lightheaded.

His mouth opened, no doubt to make some threat or order she wouldn't like. The words never left him.

The door burst in, and decisive movement drew her gaze. The armored man slid, right shoulder first, then left, through the doorway, spreading his wings once he'd cleared it. His blue eyes burned from within a golden helmet—no doubt made of the same metal the chain was. Even with his upper face covered to the lips, save the eye slit, she recognized him.

"Beldon." It came out a gasp of pain, thanks to the tightening of Abrams' hand.

He moved in a blur of motion. At the end, Abrams had been wrenched around to face him, and Beldon had a sword pressed to Abrams' throat. There were no words between the men. There were none needed. Abrams released her arm.

Jannie hurried to Beldon's side, and his wing curved around her.

Beldon looked down at her. "*Ka tu, yanata.*"

"*Shee ma-tee.*" The words slipped from between her lips without plan or reason. They felt right, and she used them.

Beldon's smile was answer enough. His free hand sought out hers, and he guided her away from Abrams.

"What did he say?" Abrams demanded.

"He ordered me to come with him." *And yanata is a pet name for me.* How she knew that was a mystery to her, but she did.

"And what did you answer?"

"Yes." That wasn't true, she knew. It was an endearment of some sort, but she couldn't remember what either *yanata* or *shee ma-tee* meant.

Beldon started to turn, keeping Jannie on the far side of his body, in relation to Abrams. He stopped, tensed, and his gaze locked on the image of their son on the large screen.

"*Sa Beldon!*"

Jannie peeked around his wing at two more armored angels. They peered at her, tipping their heads to acknowledge or greet her. She offered a shaky return of the movement and sank back to Beldon's side. At her retreat, his wing closed around her fully.

A quick exchange of their language followed. There were sounds of a struggle and protests from Hall and Abrams.

"Don't hurt them," she requested. Her breathing hitched. Did Beldon understand her? Or did he only speak his own language?

His wing folded back, revealing an empty room. Beldon wrapped an arm around her, raising Jannie chest-to-chest with him. She hesitated, then lifted his helmet off.

Beldon surged toward her mouth, parting

her lips, sealing them together. In a few heartbeats, the kiss rivaled the first she'd remembered: hot, hard, their bodies pressed tight and moving sensuously.

She buried her free hand in his hair feathers, his mouth mastering hers. She let the other arm relax down his back, clenching her fingers when his helmet started to slide away.

He settled her on the edge of the exam table. Jannie felt sure he meant to make love to her there, that he couldn't wait a moment longer.

Instead, Beldon looked up at the screen. Something nurturing softened his features. It was an expression she'd wager only she'd seen.

His hand stroked at her womb, and a cooing sound whispered from between his lips. Jannie gasped at the fluttering against his big hands, their son. Beldon chuckled, then straightened.

He fingered the feather in her hair, his expression heating again. "*Yanata,*" he breathed. "Jannie."

She nodded, and he lifted her into his arms, cradling Jannie to his chest with his helmet in her lap. His gaze strayed to the screen again, and his jaw tightened. Beldon carried her outside, his wings drawn back proudly.

His men stood in the setting sun. As a group, they bowed to Beldon.

Unsettled by the display, Jannie looked around at her kneeling team members. "No, Beldon. Don't hurt them." She prayed he understood her, because there wasn't a doubt in her mind that Beldon would have killed Abrams if she hadn't been there. Of course, if she hadn't been there, Beldon would have had no reason to kill Abrams.

His lips pressed to her jaw, and soothing tones warmed her skin. If she ever knew what they meant, she didn't now.

The other angels moved. Two returned to the main building. The other three advanced on the human captives.

Jannie tensed, and Beldon captured her lips in another kiss. Part of her argued that he was making a show of their relationship in challenge. Another argued that he was distracting her from something very unpleasant happening to her friends and coworkers. Both were drowned out by pure sensation.

A hissing sound invaded her thinking mind, and she eased out of the kiss, chancing a look at the others. The angel-soldiers were spraying some sort of mist into the crowd instead of cutting them down with weapons.

Beldon guided her face back to his, his breath hot and fast against her lips. Jannie tipped her face up and met his lips, flattening her hand against the breastplate of his armor. No matter what message he was trying to send, she'd agree to it.

One of the others addressed Beldon, and he straightened, leaving her gasping in the wake of his passion. She peeked around at the other humans, expecting shock...maybe animosity.

They were unconscious, sprawled on the ground but still breathing. "What did you do to them?" she asked.

Beldon didn't answer. Instead, he marched into a waiting craft of some sort...the sleek lines of a space shuttle with three ski-like supports. Beldon settled onto a thin-backed chair, drawing Jannie onto his lap.

His men crowded in after them, and the door closed. At the bark of command from Beldon, the craft started to move.

Chapter Nine

"Destroy it," Beldon ordered.

The vision of his son on their sensors, coupled with the human man's attack on Jannie's person, had brought out the worst of his battle sense. Had she not pleaded for their lives, he would have killed them all as threats to his mate and son.

As it was, the knowledge they had was too dangerous. Using the redac spray, destroying the captured technology and treasures of the temple, and destroying logs they had on hand was necessary.

They'd wake in a decimated camp with no memory of what had caused the blast. If they remembered anything of a winged child...or the warriors who'd taken the young one who bore him from them, it would likely be attributed to hysteria.

The temple itself would be destroyed, reduced to a solid glass sphere within the mountainside. There would be no more trophies of Sakk culture captured by adventurous natives.

The shuttle soared through the upper atmosphere, out of reach of any humans with a mind to pursue or destroy them. Jannie calmed in his embrace, her breathing and heart slowing, her trembling subsiding.

The first stroke down the knuckle line of his wing nearly brought him off the flight chair. He started to censure her for so blatant a show in public, but her expression stilled the rebuke.

It was a comfort to touch his feathers; it always had been for her. He'd allowed Jannie such freedoms with him in private, but he'd never thought to teach her proper etiquette in a crowd.

There'd been no time!

Still, he had to discourage such displays before other men. Already, those situated in a position to see it were pretending not to notice what she was doing. Beldon didn't question that they were all aroused by the show.

He guided her hand to the feather in her hair, urging her to stroke it instead. Then he added a sharp look at the other men, hoping she understood what he meant by it.

Her eyes questioned him, but Jannie did as he'd bid her. It was still suggestive, but it was less so than the other.

One of the young warriors turned to say something, then stopped to gape at her. Beldon growled a word of warning, and he looked away.

"We dock in a quarter *ses-time*, Master."

"Sakkan be praised. I cannot wait to return home," he breathed. He only hoped he would recognize his home world when they arrived.

The time passed quickly, and the door to the ship opened all too soon.

Beldon didn't deliberate over how to introduce Jannie to his people. She was his mate. A bold statement had to be made.

He stood her beneath his left arm, the corresponding wing curved only slightly around her to show his growing son and the helm tucked under her left arm. Beldon guided her right hand to his sword belt and closed her fingers around it. Finally, he grasped the hilt of his sword, bringing their *bio chains* close together in emphasis of their bond and his intent to defend it.

Jannie scanned her gaze over their positions but didn't question him. Beldon stepped through the airlock door, holding Jannie to his side when she moved to ease behind him at the sight of dozens of Sakk warriors.

"Master Beldon," the general in charge greeted him. He offered his hand.

Beldon didn't take it. "My mate," he replied by way of explanation. "Jannie."

The general bowed to her reverently, then met Beldon's gaze. "Do you require a healer for her?"

"After we've rested and eaten. I have not held Jannie in five *sa-sen*."

Jannie laid her head to his side, most likely exhausted by the events of the day. Beldon released his sword and lifted her into his arms, curling his left wing tight around her. In her half-sleep, he heard Sakkan's Night Song rising from her lips.

The general's lips curved in a knowing smile, and he turned smartly, leading the way to command-level living quarters...if the layout of the ship was roughly as it had been in Beldon's day.

Lower-ranking warriors bowed to him, staring as he made his way to a bath and bed. Whispers wafted between them after Beldon passed with his pleasant bundle.

The rooms were larger than even a commander or visiting general would have had in Beldon's day, indicating that a command-level warrior had been ejected to make room for them. It provided a space comfortable enough for two, so Beldon was glad for the sacrifice he'd made, whoever he might be.

Beldon nodded his thanks, then requested a meal of whatever the cooks were preparing. To his surprise, the general gave him three separate choices. Beldon ordered all three. Even if he hadn't been starved for the foods of his home, he was anxious to learn what Jannie liked best.

In the wake of the other man's exit, he settled Jannie on the wide bed and started to remove his newly-acquired armor. Her gaze went hungry, and she reached to her upper covering, unfastening it. There was a second layer beneath, and she discarded it as well, baring lush breasts and the upper swell of his young son.

Beldon worked at his *cuzta*, encouraging her silently to continue her disrobing. Jannie toed off her foot coverings and went to work on the legged lower coverings. She took them and the soft foot coverings off together. He slipped his sandals off, motioning her to leave the last layer of her own for him to remove.

Jannie leaned back on her elbows, spreading her legs to reveal the damp fabric covering her sex. It was an invitation, a tease.

He extended his right wing, stroking his

feathers over her warmed slit. She arched up to him, her breathing going ragged, her eyes closing in pleasure.

"Beldon, please. I've waited so long."

He startled in the realization that the ship's translator circuitry was giving him a full translation. *They've scanned Earth media and made a catalog.* With that, he could teach Jannie Sakk much more effectively.

The time for that was later. For now, his mate was asking for him.

A mate that didn't have the luxury of sleeping away our time apart. A niggling of guilt ate at him for her suffering.

Beldon went to his knees between her spread legs, running his hands over the beautiful womb that held his son. He stripped away the last bit of fabric covering her, feasting his gaze on what lay beneath.

It was nearly perfect. He'd hoped she'd display dame's down, but show or not, his son grew in her...a winged son. He laid a kiss and moved on, stroking his lips up her body, tasting her breasts and then her throat.

Jannie touched his wing, then drew back, darkening. Beldon wondered at that. She knew she was free to touch his wings when they were intimate...or when she was hinting that she wished to be. He'd always encouraged it.

Beldon guided her hand to the wing, cursing the fact that the ship's translators weren't made to work both ways. Jannie hesitated, then started working the wing. He groaned at the sensations he'd feared he'd never feel again.

Her legs circled his hips, fumbling for the position she'd learned to find easily. Was it her pregnancy or disuse?

That question in mind, he eased back on his knees, lifting her hips to position her. Jannie shifted, riding the crown of his cock restlessly, her head rocking back on her slender neck.

Beldon eased into her when he wanted to thrust. She was unused, carrying...potentially fragile. Until the ship's healer evaluated her, he would have to be cautious.

Her sounds were sweet torture, little mews and coos mixed with moans and sharp cries. He lifted her, settling Jannie belly-to-belly with him, her breath teasing at his throat, her body clenching and releasing his length in the precursors of climax.

His wings jerked and fluttered in a combination of her attentions and his matching crest. Jannie clasped one hand on his shoulder, levering herself up and down his cock, speeding him. It was too much; Beldon captured her lips, emptying into her in a rush, his shout of climax mingling with hers over their dueling tongues.

Jannie pulled away, gasping for breath, burying her face in his chest. He thought it was in exhaustion, until the first sob wracked her body.

Terror lit in his heart as Beldon had never felt it before. Had he injured her? Was it the babe?

Her translated voice made his heart stutter.

"How could I forget this? Even for a minute,

Beldon... How could I?"

Forget? Had she believed he would never come for her? Had she sought out the company of another man in his absence? Perhaps the one who'd attacked her? Had that male believed the child his own and been proven the fool?

No, this was something else. This wasn't guilt. It was a trauma or— "Redac." He hadn't told her about the automatic systems. They'd escaped his memory in his grief that he was sending her away.

Tears dotted his chest, and her sobs became more frantic. He had to calm her. Carrying or not, this bordered on hysteria and was unhealthy.

Beldon eased out of her body and gathered the sheet around her. Jannie stared at him in misery, probably believing he meant to leave her. Again, he cursed the lack of proper communication between them.

He dressed quickly, leaving his weapons and sandals where they lay. On board ship, he had no need of them.

Jannie snuggled into his arms, her face pressed to his shoulder. One small hand gripped his neck and one foot extended past the sheet. Beldon set off for medical, barking orders to have the healer meet them at the first young warrior he passed. Thankfully, he took Beldon's need seriously and scurried to the nearest comm board.

She clutched at him, fighting Beldon's move to place her on the *bio bed*, though it was a close relative of the bio tube he'd used to check her healing daily. Jannie's wracking sobs and pleas made him heartsick.

She doesn't remember. He didn't question that anymore.

"Hold her on the bed," the healer ordered. "It can separate you for the purposes of evaluation."

Nodding, Beldon eased up onto the surface. Jannie stopped fighting him, shooting him a look of misery. She wrapped herself around him. It was an indecent display of their union, but if it helped calm her, he'd bow to it.

He healer didn't comment on it. He checked her gross physical condition and administered a sedative, as Beldon knew he would.

Jannie's muscles unknotted, her grip easing and then falling away, leaving her a pleasant quilt over him, much as she had been at the most pressing moments of her early healing. He didn't move her. With his nerves as rattled as they were, the comfort would do them both good.

The young healer scowled at Beldon. "I will attempt to make no assumptions, Master. Explain your mate's state."

"Jannie..." He sighed. "She complains of memory loss. I'd seen the signs of it, but I'd thought it simple disuse, since she remembered so many of the things we'd shared."

"Redac spray?"

"Or injury. I cannot be certain which. She had a mild head injury when we found each other but nothing I would have... I have little practical knowledge of the bred matches' physiology," he admitted. "Perhaps she is frailer than I'd anticipated."

The healer tipped his head and motioned for silence. "I will evaluate her condition." He went to work, his expressions starkly serious. "You have been separated..."

"Five *sa-sen.* We were together for eight turnings before that."

"So short a time," he mused.

Beldon tensed. "Not nearly enough," he agreed. "But enough to mate and claim...and produce a strong young warrior."

"Obviously so." The healer went back to his work. "Yes. I can see the lingering effects of the head injury you describe...and her shoulder and arm. You cared for her well."

He bristled. "Of course."

"I meant no disrespect. It was a compliment."

Beldon's muscles unclenched, slightly mollified.

"She's suffered mildly in your absence."

"Abuse?" Visions of the human man fired his battle sense again. *If he harmed her, I will return and gut him.*

"No...a fall, I'd wager. A broken leg, but the natives set it well."

Beldon gathered her closer in a vain effort to shield her from hurts he couldn't...hurts she'd suffered due to his inattention and dereliction of his duty to her protection.

"There are no injuries that left a lasting stain," the healer reported.

"Can you test for redac?" Beldon didn't know enough about the chems to be sure. He knew a simple blood test or scan would reveal it in the first two turnings.

"At five *sa-sen*, the testing would be extreme...much more than I would suggest for a carrying female. And it is unnecessary."

Beldon took a calming breath. "What do you mean?"

"General Zedin ordered a full load of all remaining logs and readings. If I can access data from the time of your mate's loss, I'll know if she triggered the protective systems."

He nodded. It was a sound plan, one he might have considered himself, if he was in a less scattered state. "Do it. I must know what caused this."

The healer turned to a terminal and started scanning for what he sought. "Ah...yes. Five *sa-sen* and four turnings ago, the shields activated. A turning later—"

"The redac," Beldon guessed.

"Yes." He paused. "I cannot guarantee the effectiveness of the counteragent, at this time. It is meant to be administered within the first *eight-turn*. It may return all of her memories. It may return a fraction of them. It may return none.

"If she has some memories of you, she has already been recovering them. It is a testament to your bond and the power of the memories that they are not easily buried. And..."

"And what?" Beldon prompted him.

"Proximity may unlock more of the memories. Little things you share now may bring back related links to old." The healer turned to him, a speculative expression on his face. "Yes, that may happen."

"That's good," he breathed.

"Perhaps not."

Beldon stared at him, the feathers at the nape of his neck and the line of his spine rising in warning.

"Even good memories may overwhelm her," the healer cautioned.

"And bad ones?"

"They could prove a trauma."

Beldon considered that. "But Jannie may remember them, with or without the counteragent?"

"Precisely."

"Do it. Return as much as you can now, healer."

He started preparing a mist mask. "My name is Oben, Master. You may have need of me again. Ask for me, if you do."

"My thanks, Oben."

The healer applied the mask to Jannie's serene face, then motioned for Beldon to take it. His gaze panned over her, then shifted away before Beldon could take offense to it.

"She has no clothing but what she arrived in," Oben guessed.

Beldon shook his head. "None."

"Then we will arrange some for her."

"On a troop ship?" Beldon asked, incredulous.

"Some of the men have wingless younger sisters or mothers that they purchase finery for. I am certain someone has a serviceable outfit to offer for such a pressing need."

As long as the male doesn't believe it gives him any other rights to her.

Chapter Ten

Jannie shifted in half-sleep...warm, cocooned, lazy. Beldon's hand massaged at her back, and she groaned in relief. The whisper of fans and breathing, coupled with his heartbeat beneath her cheek, wove a soothing auditory tapestry.

Without opening her eyes, she knew his wings were closed around her. "I love when you hold me," she whispered.

Soft sounds puffed at her hair, words she couldn't understand.

"Will we ever understand each other?"

Beldon's wings parted, and he cupped her face up to his. He didn't kiss her; instead, he stared at her for a moment, then nodded.

"You understand me, but—"

He placed a finger over her lips, silencing her. Beldon rose from the mattress, lifted Jannie, and carried her, still wrapped in the bed sheet, to a table with a screen and keyboard set on it. Beldon settled in a chair, placed her on his lap, and motioned to the machine. She stared at it, trying to gauge his meaning.

"I don't know how to use this." She didn't know what the symbols meant any more than she did his spoken language. "I hadn't managed a translation yet. There's no Rosetta stone for your language." *Thank goodness!* She cringed inwardly at what Abrams would have done if he'd known—

I remember. Jannie tested her faculties,

blushing at the carnality of her days with Beldon. *And I seduced him. How could I forget it?*

She opened her mouth to ask that question, but Beldon's expression stole her breath. He sat, still as stone, his brow furrowed in confusion. His face smoothed, and he nodded. Beldon tapped at the symbols, then waited. After a moment, he tipped her chin up, so she focused on the screen instead of the keys. The message on the screen was in English...stilted but readable.

WE WILL UNDERSTAND BOTH. THIS. FOR NOW WHILE YOU LEARN SAKK.

She read it aloud, marveling that he'd found a way to communicate. Beldon chuckled, his muscles easing beneath her hand.

"I'm learning Sakk. Why won't you learn English?" A rebellious streak raised its head at that thought.

His expression was one of disbelief. She started to protest, but Beldon started typing again. Jannie focused on the screen, counting a silent ten and reminding herself to hear him out first. She blushed at the answer.

ON SAKK NO ONE SPEAK YOUR LANGUAGE. TRANSLATOR LET US HEAR YOUR WORDS. NOT MADE TO LET YOU HEAR SAKK.

"That makes sense, I guess," she conceded. The only way she would understand them would be to learn their language. Otherwise, she'd need one of these terminals to communicate.

It's not as if we can go back to Earth. Jannie shivered, pulling the sheet further up her shoulders. No, if they went back to Earth, who knew what would happen to them? Especially to their baby.

She took a deep breath, steeling herself for a long, hard road of learning a new language. "How do I use this?"

Beldon smiled and then tapped a sequence of keys. An English keyboard—in QWERTY—appeared at the bottom of the screen, and he motioned to it.

"Touch screen?" she inquired.

He paused, cocked his head, then nodded.

Jannie stared at the screen for a moment, considering it. "I have to start somewhere," she mused. *Simple words. She'd start with the basics.*

Reaching out, she typed in "man." Nothing happened, and she met Beldon's eyes. He reached for the screen and pressed a yellow triangle. Two of his symbols appeared beneath what she'd typed.

She chewed at her lower lip. "I can see how I'm supposed to learn *written* language," she agreed. But written and spoken were very different processes.

He reached out again and touched the blue triangle. A voice pronounced the foreign sounds. Jannie pressed a fingertip to the blue triangle again, hoping it would repeat the sounds, if she did.

"*Ma-tee*," the masculine tones repeated.

"I know that word." Jannie knew it was part of the endearment she used for Beldon. "Does this translate phrases and sentences, as well as words?"

Beldon tipped his head and waved her on. At the first letter she pressed, what went before disappeared and was replaced with the new query. She typed in "my man," then pressed the yellow triangle.

Jannie glanced at the three symbols and stopped, her mind working fast. "Your language is read right to left?"

An expression of surprise settled on his face, and Beldon offered another tip of his head.

She pressed the blue triangle. "*Shee ma-tee.*"

Jannie snuggled into his lap, warming at the thought of it. "My man."

* * * *

Beldon forced his breathing to even. The thought of her claiming him as her own, coupled with her body so close to his, left Beldon with nearly as little control as a pre-prime trying to settle his mating instincts.

She looked up at him, smiling. Slowly, her smile faded. Jannie shrugged the sheet off of one arm, baring her chest and swollen womb to her hip.

He licked his lips, his mouth watering to taste her. Still, he tarried. Their loving had sent her into hysterics, and he still didn't know how much she remembered. Rash moves could do her harm.

His hands unsteady, Beldon coded in the question. Jannie peeled her gaze from his and read the English message on the screen.

"Yes... I remember." There was a moment of

silence. "Why didn't I remember, Beldon? How could I forget? How did I remember again?"

His heart aching, he considered how best to explain it. *Keep it simple for her. Don't frighten her with the concepts.*

He tapped the keys slowly, weighing each word. In the end, Jannie read his answer aloud.

"Accident. You set off security system that uses...forget spray?" She pressed her fingertips to her mouth. "Is that what you did to the others?" Her head swiveled around, and she stared at him, waiting for an answer.

Beldon nodded slowly, praying to Sakkan she wouldn't hold it against him.

"Did you know? Did you know I'd...forget you, when you sent me away?"

He shook his head, wishing he had the words to tell her how sorry he was that she'd suffered it.

"And now..." Her chest hitched, and she started again. "Did you use something to reverse it? To make me remember?"

Beldon nodded.

For a moment long enough to make him nervous, she didn't respond to that.

Then she was astride him, facing Beldon, planting kisses on his face and neck. The sheet gaped open around her body, tempting him. Beldon took advantage of it, reaching between their bodies to stroke his thumb over her tender little nub.

Jannie arched her back with a mew, her body leaking hot female musk down her thighs and onto his.

Taste her. The need to sate himself on her sweet sap was maddening.

Beldon lifted Jannie and took her to the bed. The mattress was soft and inviting, and the linens smelled of Sakk-grown spice.

He sank to the surface and positioned her over his mouth. She gasped at the spear of his tongue, and her hands fisted in his hair feathers.

Memories of the first taste he'd taken taunted him. They'd been in the bath, and he'd lifted her to the side and spread her legs. Jannie had doubtless thought he'd intended to bury his cock in her tight little body, and his tongue and lips had drawn happy squeals from her.

That in mind, he feasted, reveling in her sounds and the tightening of her fists in his hair feathers.

On one level, it was greed that drove him. Beldon had been five *sa-sen* without her unique flavor. Though he'd slept most of it away, just the knowledge of how long it had been was maddening.

On another level, it was an apology of sorts, repayment for her time without him. He was certain she hadn't taken a human lover in his absence, lack of memories or not. She'd been denied, left hungering for what he could offer her.

Jannie didn't deny herself or him. She moved against him, guiding him to where she needed his suckling and licking mouth most acutely.

"Beldon. Oh, I missed you."

At his breaking point, he turned her to her back on the mattress and drank from her long and hard. Taking the superior was her undoing. Jannie shouted again and again, her thighs tightening around his head, her sheath spasming against his tongue.

Beldon eased away, his body aching for more. *No. This is for her.*

At the moment, there was no clear indication what Jannie wanted from him. She lay on the bed, her legs parted, her eyes squeezed shut in the aftermath of her climax.

He levered himself up beside her, smiling. It made a man feel good to see his mate so lost in passion. It was a greater accomplishment than all the battles he'd won combined.

At the first sign that she was recovering, Beldon trailed his fingertips up her inner thigh and played them inside her slit. She rose against him with a mew, her nipples tightening in the room air.

I will pleasure her until she sleeps in my arms and then again when she wakes.

His move to thrust his fingers inside her ended at her plea. "I need to taste you."

His heart hammering, Beldon started to protest. This was for her.

And she wants to wrap that lovely little mouth around my cock. Sakkan, yes.

* * * *

His stillness was so complete, Jannie was certain he hadn't heard her. She opened her mouth to repeat it.

His nod was slow and measured. Beldon

thrust two fingers inside her, bringing her off the bed. He removed them almost as quickly and sucked them into his mouth, leaving her gasping for breath.

If it was a challenge, it was unnecessary. Jannie fully intended to suck him down and not stop until he was begging for more of her.

She turned on the bed, well aware of what she was offering him. Though she'd sucked him without positioning herself for his mouth before, she knew he liked sixty-nine, and something told her he wanted this today.

Beldon didn't move to take her up on it immediately. He lay there, whispering words that made no sense to her, while she took the broad tip into her mouth and sucked gently at his saline and spice fluids.

Jannie took him deeper, moaning at the length and girth filling her mouth. Her memories confirmed that Beldon enjoyed slow suckling, very little movement and a lot of change in suction.

"Sakkan, *ul tren.*"

Her mind provided the translation. He was pleading with his god for strength.

That a given, she suckled harder, wringing a shout from him. His hips rose, forcing his cock deeper. He was close. She could feel it, taste the increase in his musk production.

Her own musk seeped down her thighs. Why was he waiting? Why wasn't he between her thighs already, using that talented mouth?

Jannie parted her thighs, rocking her hips toward him. Beldon's fingers eased along her slit, and she groaned. Something she was sure was a curse left his lips, and Beldon went at her like a man starved.

Beldon turned over her, a careful motion that kept precisely the amount of his cock in her mouth she'd been working on before. It was also a move that put him in control, a place she admittedly loved him being.

His tongue swirled and dipped, a slow torture that made it more difficult to concentrate on what she was doing to him. That wasn't a problem. Beldon's cock jerked against her lips, and his cum poured into her mouth. She swallowed, determined to show him how much she'd missed him.

His sounds were harsh, his tongue soft and teasing. The control it took to continue eating her while he was climaxing was staggering.

She couldn't do the same. Her body screaming for more, Jannie pulled back.

She bit at her lower lip, grinding against his mouth.

His hands tightened on her body, positioning her where he wanted her. He was relentless, driving her toward another release, demanding it. Her body wasn't her own when he touched her, and Jannie loved every minute of it.

The second climax was less frenetic, a soothing warmth rushing over her nerves. Beldon kissed and nibbled, keeping her in the corona of pleasure.

She sucked his cock in again, bobbing her head. He hardened for her.

"Jannie." His whisper filled the

conspicuously empty space between her spread legs.

She released his length. "Promise me anything."

Beldon turned, covering her with his body. A spate of his language left his lips. There were few words she understood in the mix, but *yes* was definitely one of them.

Chapter Eleven

Beldon stared at Zedin across the lounging space, sipping at the *usha* ale the general had offered. They'd traveled two *eight-turns*, and Beldon had yet to have time to speak with the commander of this vessel. It was time to change that, time to get the answers he needed, before they reached Sakk.

"Why was I left on Earth? Was a search ever mounted?"

Zedin shifted uncomfortably. "It was our dark time, Master Beldon. According to the records we've found of the events, we received four messages from Sakkan's priests on Earth that were of any importance in answering your question."

He hesitated, seemingly ordering his response. After a drink of his own ale, he started piecing together the lost millennia of Beldon's life.

"The first two spoke of a great cataclysm. Rather...they spoke of a series of them. Over the course of several centuries, there was massive flooding that forced the priests to move the young ones and much of the equipment to the upper reaches. Many of the young fell ill. A shocking number perished."

"And they feared losing me." Beldon didn't question it.

"Or the warriors that would come to retrieve you," he confirmed. "Until the plague was eradicated, the priests couldn't chance any Sakk coming to aid you...or them. They declared an exclusion zone."

"A sensible choice," Beldon admitted. Any disease brought aboard a warship might have infected all aboard...then the home world, killing off an already-struggling race. "And when the plague was eradicated?"

"The flood waters receded in time, and the sickness passed. The young ones were repopulated with promising results. The priests were hopeful the matches were close."

Beldon smiled wryly. Obviously, the priests had created stronger stock than they'd known. Had they woken him to test, chances were his acceptance of a young one would have been more than ceremonial. He might even have sired a young warrior on one...or a young match.

But, then he never would have found Jannie. Such a life was inconceivable to him now that he had.

"The next cataclysm came before those young were old enough to present to you. It was an explosion...magma forced up and crust plates shifting...centered on the peak to the north.

"The message was chilling. The initial blast killed more than half the priests. The young ones that were lost were poisoned by gasses and suffocated by ash. The priests shielded the rest. They lost a full third of the temple caverns on the side facing the eruption.

"One of the blasts..." He darkened, averted his eyes, and drank deeply of his ale.

At first, Beldon thought it was in upset, but the sound of Jannie padding to the water room indicated another cause for Zedin's unease.

Women were not, as a rule, visitors on board Sakk warships. When matches were transported to Sakk from seed worlds, they were to be housed in secured nests with a nest pair to see to their needs. The soldiers were not to be permitted access to them, save in emergency situations, and the mated nest mother was as sheltered as the unmated young were.

She returned, and Beldon turned to watch her. He didn't question why the males weren't typically permitted near females that were not their own. The sway of her hips beneath the *cazta* provided for her, accentuated by her full and pregnant profile, was enough to make any soldier starved for a woman hard. A few without self-control might consider the unthinkable...or commit such atrocities.

His hand fisted and his jaw clenched at the thought of someone harming Jannie that way. It was the reason they never left their quarters. It was the reason Jannie was kept secluded in the curtained bed when another male was in the room. Only the fact that he'd ordered her to see to her bodily needs had drawn her out this time.

Jannie slipped through the bed curtain and returned to her studies with a smile for him. She was an avid student, and they tested her command of Sakk every evening.

Once she was safely hidden from view, Zedin continued. "One of the blasts damaged the controls for the outer layer of shields."

"Leaving the priests and young in an unprotected area...and yet they didn't wake me to protect them." Beldon ground his teeth at the thought. He'd been stationed on Earth to protect them; his own life was hardly worth more than all in his care.

"They no doubt feared your loss. Some of the humans... They came to the ruins of the temple, believing the priests had caused the destruction... Or perhaps they followed some childish dream that the priests had the ability to stop it. They killed all but one of the priests. That one fled with two of the young to a newly-restored and shielded cavern."

"And the rest of the young?"

Zedin paused. "He found only one dead female."

"Taken, then." Perhaps one of them was the one Jannie had descended from.

"We assume so. They were healthy, young females at a time when many women and children had died. They would have been prized catches."

Beldon took a sip of his ale. "And the three?"

Zedin winced. "The final message begged removal, but the Sakk were in the midst of a civil war. No warship was sent for them."

Beldon tried to digest that. Even when females were all but extinct, they hadn't resorted to that. "It's not our way. What caused the war?"

"Females. The first of the matches from seed worlds started arriving on Sakk. We'd managed not to war when we had to rely on females from our own world, but with the addition of even a trickle more... A thousand men for each female arriving," Zedin spat. "A thousand *desperate* men."

He shook his head, drank deeply of his ale, and poured himself another. Zedin took his time, composing himself slowly. "By the end of the war, there were only six hundred vying for each female. Strict rules were agreed upon, rules that favored those of rank and age but still young enough to produce strong young, rules that provided willing widows or widows that hadn't produced two viable young to their first mates to other men."

"Nearly half of our population?" Beldon demanded, trying not to focus on the idea of Jannie being forced to take another mate, if he died before she'd given him two young.

"Unfortunately so. It began over females. It ended over a single one."

Beldon couldn't form words at that. When he forced his voice out, it was rasping. "They killed a female?"

Zedin shook his head sadly. "One was stolen from the compound they'd sequestered the matches in. When news spread, all in-fighting ceased, and the hunt was on for the one who'd done it.

"When they found him... He'd raped her...repeatedly, drugged her to accomplish it...and claimed her. They say the other males tore his body apart. It was *yans* before the young one he'd injured chose to allow another male..." He took a deep breath and drained the second ale.

"Sakk has changed, Master. Nearly every

male has military training, even artists and poets."

"But why?"

Zedin met his gaze, seemingly searching for words. "Even with the success of the seed worlds, there is a shortage. All other factors being equal, males fight for the right to claim a female as we did in our barbaric root *yans*."

Beldon shook his head in wonder. His home world had degenerated to such a system again? "And females, mated females...? Are they safe on Sakk?" What would he do if the general said they weren't?

"Very safe. At the first sign that a female is mishandled, the death of the one responsible is quick and decisive."

He relaxed at that. Every male acting the part of protector was acceptable.

I was supposed to be a protector. He had to know. "What happened to the final three?"

Zedin seemed to backtrack the conversation to the point Beldon had returned to. "The logs retrieved from Earth did give a bit more information about the final three. The priest mated with both of the young, producing with them. Since the logs ended, we assume he perished."

"And the young?"

"No word. We assume they fled the ruined temple and tried to join the native population."

Beldon glanced to the curtained bed. "It is a given that some of our young survived and produced young with the humans. It may have been those taken...or those impregnated by the final priest. It may have been both."

"Which means there may be others," Zedin agreed, a look of calculation on his face.

"Yes, but not raised of a mind to accept us."

"Your mate did."

"Jannie is an exceptional woman, and our situation was unique."

Zedin scowled, then nodded his agreement.

* * * *

Jannie smiled at the sound of the curtain parting, anticipating Beldon's touch.

He knelt to the mattress and pressed his lips to her bare back. "*And what have you learned today?*" His Sakk was slow and smooth, encouraging Jannie to learn it.

She called the string of sounds to mind. She'd practiced the phrase countless times, wanting it to be perfect.

"*Wi walna yatee.*" Jannie held her breath, hoping for a response and not a correction.

Beldon grasped her hips and turned her to face him, one eyebrow raised in challenge. "*Yatee walna?*"

"I obviously said it right. I want you." Jannie repeated the phrase in Sakk.

He pulled her to his chest, parting her lips in a fierce kiss. His hand traced the lines of her womb, and she recoiled from the intense sensation, gasping, trembling, wrapping her arms around herself in an effort to cover the line of hairs that had grown back in.

Beldon stared at her, his expression cycling

between hurt and concern.

She wanted to reassure him, but she wasn't certain how to explain it. "I have to shave."

He cocked his head to one side, indicating that it hadn't translated. She'd been afraid of this. As far as she could tell, the Sakk didn't grow facial hair to shave.

Jannie reached for the terminal, typing in the sentence and adding slightly more detail. It provided a translation, broken by buzzing that probably indicated English words with no corresponding word in Sakk.

Predictably, he still seemed confused.

His hand cupped her womb, and he swept the pad of his thumb over the hairs. She batted at his hand, panting out a plea for him to stop.

Beldon's smile returned and widened. "*Be still,*" he ordered.

Jannie watched in shock as he lowered his head. His breath fanned the hairs, and her nipples came to hard points. Her sheath was wet, and she reached for his wing automatically, wanting him as crazy as she was.

He captured her wrists in his hands and guided them to the mattress, holding them down. His next stream of air traced the line from her pubic curls to her breasts.

Realization that the Sakk considered this a form of sex play made it through the mush that was acting as her brain. After that, everything was sensation.

Beldon teased at the fluff, ignoring her spread legs and her pleas for more. He blew at it, stroked it with his cheek and chin, tangled his hair feathers in it. He licked at a portion along the line below her breastbone.

Jannie wrapped her legs around his chest, searching for friction. He denied her. Beldon went at the fuzz along the line of her pregnant womb more avidly.

She felt the orgasm coming moments before it crashed over her. Jannie came with a scream, her entire body alive to sensation.

He moved abruptly, thrusting deep inside her spasming body, every movement stimulating the line further. His grumbled curse mixed with her second scream.

There was nothing gentle about what followed. Beldon's wings folded back as if he was in a dive, and he took her like the warrior he was, claiming what was his.

His roar echoed off the walls, and his cum scorched against her already-heated core. Jannie's head spun pleasantly.

Beldon brushed a kiss against her forehead. "*You will not be* shaving," he informed her.

Jannie groaned, unable to form the words in either language to agree.

Chapter Twelve

Beldon smoothed the dress over Jannie's womb, smiling at her shiver of delight. She'd never seen him so gleeful, but he was now. It seemed dressing in the finery the captain had delivered to them after they'd docked had changed his entire attitude, lightened it somehow.

The dress was unlike either the *cazta* she'd worn at the temple on Earth or the one she'd worn aboard ship. Beldon told her it was the design worn by women who carried at formal events. It was deep purple with a triangular panel of silver, the apex of which rested between her breasts. The panel accentuated her very pregnant form. It was longer than the knee-length *cazta* she'd worn before, coming to a point halfway down her shins.

She wore silver gloves that reached to above her elbows, and the sleeves of the dress overlapped with them. As she understood it, no men but Beldon and doctors were permitted to touch her bare skin.

A bracelet not unlike the bio chain was clasped around her wrist, outside the glove. Since the bio chain was too tight to fit the gloves beneath and could not be removed, it was a reminder that she was another male's woman.

Beldon had arranged her hair in a cascade of curls with a cream that reminded her of fresh fruits and golden combs that matched the bio chain. Though he'd apologized for his lack of finesse, when compared with a woman, Jannie thought it looked wonderful. The only glaring departure he'd not only allowed but encouraged was the feather she'd bound into her hair.

The entire outfit was topped off with a matching purple cape. Though it was light, Beldon assured her it would keep her warm, even in a frigid wind.

His outfit was little different than what he wore daily. The *cuzta* was a bit longer than it usually was, and there were ropes of the same golden material as the *cuzta* was made of.

While she watched, he donned his armor and helm, then strapped on his sword. A medal on a golden ribbon settled over his shoulders and lay against his armor. The entire outfit was topped off with a golden cape, fastened with a bird in flight clasp.

Jannie looked down at herself and saw that her silver clasp matched it.

Something about that warmed her.

She reached out and touched the medal he wore, straightening it. "What does this mean?"

A smile curved his lips up. His Sakk was smooth and rich. "It means your mate has fought many battles, to the glory of our family and Sakkan."

She traced the clasp with one glove-clad finger. "And this?"

"My family *kietia*."

Jannie nodded, certain that the strange word meant some sort of crest.

He continued. "My family sent it, along with the clothing and jewelry. It honors all to have your first step onto Sakk celebrated."

That stated, he guided her to a chair and settled her on it. Beldon unwrapped a cloth bundle and lifted out two pair of gleaming black boots. They were knee-height and decorated in buckles, silver for her and golden for him.

Beldon pulled hers on and fastened the buckles. Jannie curled her toes. The lining was the same silken material the dress and gloves were made from.

Once hers were in place, he donned his own. He rose to his feet, and Jannie's heart skittered in excitement. He was a formidable man.

And he's mine.

Beldon offered his hand, and she took it, coming to her feet at his tug. He stared down at her, seemingly stunned.

"You will stay by my side, Jannie."

She managed a shaky agreement.

He hesitated, then sealed his mouth to hers. His scent wrapped around her, drawing her in until Jannie collided with his armored chest. Beldon drew back, his breathing harsh. His eyes remained closed.

"Just like that," he whispered cryptically.

"Like what?" Her voice was thready and low in arousal.

Jannie winced at the mess she'd made of his outfit. She hurried to make him presentable again.

His chuckle was dark in promise. "You will see when we reach my ancestral home."

* * * *

Beldon kept his wing extended behind Jannie, walking slowly in deference to the bulk of his son within her. General Zedin glanced back at them, nodded, and slowed his step to match them.

He paused at the docking ring, and Beldon did the same, pulling Jannie to a halt beside him. There was no question what Zedin was about to do, and Beldon wanted the general to revel in the glory this day would bring him. According to the tales of Sakk he'd heard, this might even win the general his own mate in the near future.

General Zedin strode into the reception room, and the noises of the crowd tapered off. "Sakkrel and esteemed brothers."

Beldon tensed at that. The king himself had come to greet him? Was such a thing done these days?

The words repeated in Jannie's language and then translated to Beldon again. They were translating for her? He'd never heard of such a thing.

I have not set foot on Sakk in five thousand yans. *Who knows what has changed in so long a time?*

Zedin continued. "In our darkest hour, Sakkrel's ancestors chose twenty of our finest generals for a mission to save Sakk. One by one, we lost the esteemed ones. Not one of them returned to us...until now. I give to you, Master Beldon, protector of Seed World Four, and his mate, Jannie."

Beldon took her hand and drew Jannie toward the opening. He hesitated with one leg on each side of the barrier, watching her step over cautiously. It wasn't until he raised his head and spied the shocked faces of the closest officers that he realized the crowd had gone from hushed to silent.

Straightening, he led her down the golden carpet toward the dais where the royal couple sat. There was a disconcerting separation in the crowd. The officers closest to the door they were emerging through were without mates. The ones closest to the dais had mates and sometimes nursing babes with them. Between them was a line of guards that were undeniably royal and priest class warriors. Taking the unmated males as a threat, Beldon settled his hand around the hilt of his sword.

Jannie looked around nervously, then moved closer to Beldon. Her grip on his hand eased slightly as they reached the mated couples.

Her step slowed. Jannie peered at a chubby short-flight baby in a nursing sling, her expression going soft and wistful. Her gloved hand stroked at her own womb.

Beldon took a moment to marvel at her. His hand left the sword and covered hers, and their son wriggled beneath them.

"Master Beldon?"

He turned toward the voice, startling at the fact that the king and his mate were descending the dais to them. Beldon folded his wings and bowed to them. Jannie executed what was probably a sign of respect from her world, though her legs wobbled a bit in her gravid state. He wrapped his arms around her, steadying her.

To his surprise, the king bowed to him in return. Then his mate did the same. The former offered his hand in a warrior's agreement, and Beldon took it, momentarily tongue tied at the turn of events.

"A five thousand *yans*, Master. Truly, Sakkan has blessed me to see such a thing."

"As you say," Beldon deferred to him.

His gaze slid to Jannie. "And your mate. Unbelievable that she found you."

Beldon realized a translator was supplying the king's words to Jannie. "Yes, Sakkrel. It was Sakkan's hand alone, I am sure."

The king's gaze lingered, and the hair feathers on the back of Beldon's neck rose in warning. Just when he tensed to pull Jannie behind him, the king looked toward the crowd.

"Young match," he addressed Jannie. "I understand that women of your...culture would be unwilling to submit to the normal matching procedures."

Jannie snapped a look of confusion at Beldon. Her words came slowly, carefully chosen he suspected. "There are many cultures on Earth, but no... Women of this time would be unlikely to welcome kidnapping and being forced to mate with a man she didn't choose."

His jaw tightened. "It will have to be handled diplomatically then."

Jannie's hand closed on Beldon's arm, and

she moved closer to him.

Beldon shot a look around, assuring himself that no one was closing on him. "Sakkrel, what will have to be handled diplomatically?"

"Gaining mates from...Earth." He tipped his head to Jannie, as he forced out the foreign word.

"You can't," she protested, before Beldon could stop her. "Being descended from Sakk genes doesn't mean you own them."

A murmur of discord started rising from the crowd, and Beldon curled his wing around Jannie, his hand stealing to his sword again.

The king raised a hand and motioned for silence. Beldon prayed that it was a good sign and not one that he meant to have them both arrested. When the room had gone silent as a cold pyre, he spoke again.

"I trust your assessment, but you misunderstood my intent, young one." There was a moment of tense silence. "When your young warrior is old enough to travel, I would like Master Beldon and yourself to approach the...Earth..." He managed it a little better that time. "government."

Jannie hesitated for a heartbeat. "For what purpose?"

"Voluntary testing to find other matches or close matches. If a woman does not wish to be tested, she need not be."

She pressed her cheek to Beldon's arm. "Promise it."

Beldon winced. "Sakkrel is bound by his word, Jannie. If he has said it, he has already promised it." It was treason to question the king.

To his surprise, His Majesty chuckled. He bowed his head to Jannie. "You have my vow, young Jannie. Will you aid us?"

Her nod was slow coming. "If it means that much...and if Beldon agrees, I will."

He didn't take his gaze off Jannie. "And do you accept this station, Master?"

Beldon considered it carefully. In the end, he met Jannie's eyes, noting her near-pleading expression. "With men enough to secure my mate and son, I will."

Chapter Thirteen

This is madness.

Beldon straightened as the three human delegates and their guards started across the meadow and toward the conference table Jannie had had the Sakk request.

It was madness to do this. He wanted his mate and child as far from Earth as he could take them. *At least, as far as Sakk.*

Though Jannie had agreed to this—insisted they do it—Beldon still believed she'd done so with the mistaken idea that the Sakk would take the women by force, if she refused. Her understanding of the breeding measures was limited, at best.

She'd worked diligently with the king and his advisors, revising the leader's plans to something palatable to human sensibilities. Jannie had sifted through the whole of the breeding program and Beldon's presence on Earth and decided what to say and how to say it to avoid the impression that they were an aggressive race who'd invaded Earth once before.

The native races had willingly given them the first females they'd used in the breeding program. Even then, the Sakk had been unwilling to kidnap and rape to meet their needs, though they would have purchased females on Earth as they had on other barbaric worlds, if it had come to that.

While Jannie had been planning the diplomatic side of the mission, Beldon had been schooling the soldiers under his command in ancient tactics, long forgotten. In return, he had been educated in technological advances in weaponry that he incorporated into his plans to safeguard his family.

"*Sa Beldon?*"

Strange how his primary language had started to sound alien to him. He'd spent so long learning English from Jannie and practicing it with the soldiers he was training, Beldon couldn't remember how long it had been since he'd indulged in the Sakk language.

"*I know. It is time.*" He started down the slope, six high-ranking officers at his back. It was a safeguard he'd insisted on personally, but he didn't like it. It felt weak, and weak was something Beldon had never been.

The human delegates stopped a mere body's length from the table. They stared, and one took two shuffling steps backward.

Beldon smirked. Humans watched entertainment vids of monsters and insectile aliens, but winged humanoids terrified them.

The young male delegate regained his composure and started toward the table again, passing by the still-gaping elders. They didn't sit, which displayed a modicum of battle sense. Their guards stood between the delegates and the Sakk, handling weapons the sensors said were readied but for the flip of a switch and a pull on the trigger.

Beldon stopped on the Sakk side of the table and offered a tip of his head to the humans. "Who is your spokesman?" he inquired. He knew the highest ranking man among them already, but Jannie had explained the misdirections her countrymen often perpetrated to protect the leaders they valued. This was likely no exception.

"I am," the center one attested.

One of the generals at Beldon's back imperfectly masked a sound of disgust. Beldon pretended not to notice it, though the warrior in him screamed to call them out as cowards.

"Of course. With your indulgence, Representative Odan—"

The man paled a notch.

Beldon bit back a laugh at his shock. "We have a shield we would like to raise. It will protect us all from long-range attacks."

Odan opened his mouth to protest, and Beldon hurried on.

"Your guards may stay, of course. As may your..." He glanced at half a dozen camera lenses. "media."

"Absolutely not."

Beldon's jaw tightened at the implication that *he* was untrustworthy, when they'd blatantly lied to him. "Very well. We will depart for deliberations with one of the other nations who have agreed to meet with us. Good day to you." He turned, taking a step toward the spearhead behind him.

"Wait!"

Beldon glanced back in surprise, focusing on the true leader of this little band of politicians. So, he'd decided to speak. With exaggerated care, Beldon faced them. "Yes,

Representative Ellwood?"

He cleared his throat. "Being locked under your shield is an incredible risk," he reasoned.

"Chancing our representative unshielded, when you possess the ability to kill us at a distance, is a risk I will *not* take." It took all Beldon's self-control not to snarl at them.

Ellwood hesitated. No doubt his guards had ordered him not to take chances in deliberation, but it would be a sign of weakness to admit such a thing. A leader must be leader, at least where adversaries can see it.

This man wasn't schooled in hiding his unease. He deliberated so intently, it was written on his face.

Odan snorted. "I assume that means you could kill us within the shield and be safe from reprisals."

Beldon glared at him. "If I intended to kill you, we could do so now. The shield would come up and protect us from your...reprisals. Reason it. Why would we want you dead?"

Odan gaped, and his guards shifted their weapons nervously, no doubt in the realization that, in any confrontation, they would die quickly.

Beldon motioned for silence, though no one was talking. "You have my vow as a Sakk warrior. We mean you no harm. Successful or not, if the negotiations end with no aggressive show on your part, they will end peacefully." It was the only vow he would make.

Still, Odan pressed him. "Shield or not, our forces will—"

Beldon's strained patience snapped. "I could raise the shield without your consent, but our representative counsels me that you would interpret seeing to our own protection as an attack of some sort. It is out of courtesy I ask." He paused a moment. "If you are not so courteous as to agree, we will take our leave in peace." It had taken him days to learn that speech. As Jannie expected, he'd needed it.

"Raise the shield," Ellwood decided.

Odan turned to him, wild-eyed. "They could—"

"Someone has to show trust first. We have the home court advantage. It is time for us to be gracious."

Odan looked as if he wanted to argue, but he held his tongue.

Beldon offered a bow of his head in respect and appreciation. "As you say, Representative Ellwood. I guarantee you will not regret this magnanimous show."

He motioned to his men, and one of the generals activated the shield with a handheld control. Once it was up, Beldon made a show of removing his helm and setting it on the table.

All of the cameras focused on him.

* * * *

"*The shield has been activated,*" one of Jannie's personal guards reported to her.

She wanted to run to Beldon, but that wasn't the plan he'd laid out for them. Her guards would prevent her from doing it, if she tried to. Until

Beldon signaled, she was to remain inside the ship.

Still, she peeked around their shoulders. At last, she saw it. *"Beldon's helm is off. It's time."*

The general in charge of her guard grunted his agreement. He waved the rest into formation around her. Even with the shield in place, Beldon had insisted on this show of force.

The human delegates watched her approach. From yards away, Jannie saw the Sakk warriors stiffen as if their interest in her was a threat.

The ranks of soldiers protecting Beldon parted, allowing Jannie and her guards to step between. She walked to the table, laid a hand on Beldon's arm, and offered the humans a smile.

"Gentlemen, please sit," she invited.

Ellwood eased past the soldiers protecting him and reached his hand across the table to her. Beldon yanked her back, and the Sakk closed ranks, reaching for whatever weapons they carried. The soldiers reacted in kind.

"Stand down," Jannie ordered. She repeated it in English. Men on both sides froze in mid-motion.

She took a calming breath. "Please, pardon this misunderstanding. I should have had my guards explain before I approached the table. In Sakk culture, no man may touch a woman who isn't his, unless it is an emergency. The offer of a handshake was perceived as a threat to me."

The human soldiers glanced at each other uncertainly. One looked at Ellwood over his shoulder. "Sir?"

He laid a shaking hand on the soldier's shoulder, urging him aside. "Are there any other cultural idiosyncrasies I should know about before we continue?"

Around him, the soldiers lowered their weapons again.

She took her time, lowering the hood that covered her hair. "Staring intently at me or raising your voice will put the warriors on edge. A civil conversation would be best."

Ellwood sank into a chair, then placed his hands flat on the table where her guards could see them. "My apologies for the offense."

Jannie moved to take her seat, and Beldon tightened his hold, growling her name.

"*Beldon, I must sit to negotiate properly.*"

"*If he reaches for you again, I will gut him and every guard who tries to stop me.*"

She smiled. "*They wouldn't dare. Not this way.*"

His arms loosened, and she took a step away from him. Jannie didn't have to look back to know Beldon was scowling.

"Problem?" Odan asked.

She settled in the seat next to Beldon's helm, taking the time to arrange the long skirts Beldon had insisted she wear. "They seem fierce, I know... Well, they *are* undeniably fierce. But they mean well; they are protective of me. Just remember, no matter what they look like, they aren't a Thanagarian invasion force."

Beldon grumbled a curse in Sakk.

Jannie laughed and shot him a teasing look. "He *hates* that comparison," she confided, hoping to break the ice.

Odan and Gorse joined Ellwood at the table.

Gorse overcame the shock that had sent him shying away at Beldon's approach. "You must have studied our culture for years." There was a note of suspicion in his voice.

"You could say that," she offered delicately. "I grew up on Earth."

Odan worked at words that didn't emerge.

Ellwood recovered first. "America, by your accent. New England?"

"Pennsylvania," she corrected him.

"You've been spying on us," Odan exploded.

She didn't question that the sword tip resting on the table to her left was Beldon's. Odan stared at it, swallowing hard. The human soldiers watched but didn't respond.

Gorse sat back in his chair. "Keep it down, David. Nervous men with weapons. Not good."

Odan unglued his tongue. "Right. Down." He pressed his hands hard to the table, glancing up at Beldon.

The sword tip eased back, but there was no sound of Beldon sheathing it.

Jannie met Odan's gaze solidly. "I was no spy. I was born and raised on Earth."

"You're human then?" Ellwood asked.

I thought I was. That would be counterproductive. "May I explain?"

"I wish you would."

Beldon moved a step to one side and then closer, so Jannie could feel his heat against her shoulder.

"Five millennia ago or so, the Sakk had a

settlement on Earth." There was no sense in telling them about the breeding program. They wouldn't understand it; at best, they would think it was slavery. "Over the years, the two species...mingled."

"Interbred you mean," Gorse guessed.

"Precisely. You must have wondered where the stories came from. Angels... Sons of Heaven mating with Daughters of Man."

"And siring the heroes of old," Ellwood quoted.

"I wouldn't know about that."

"And then?"

"You've heard about the great disasters and plagues of old. Floods, volcanoes erupting, sickness... Many of the Sakk were killed in them. More were killed by the neighboring villages. It was the usual story. Looting for food and other necessities."

No one asked a question, so she continued.

"In the end, there was another shortage. Women. When there was nothing left to fight over, the native humans killed to take them."

Ellwood winced at her blunt interpretation.

"You asked what I am. I am a crossbred descendent of Sakk and human."

Odan was more restrained this time around. "And *how* did you end up with them instead of on Earth?"

It was a fair question and one she'd anticipated. *Keep it simple,* she reminded herself. "A year and a half ago, I was working on an archeological dig, a dig that had uncovered the Sakk settlement. I became separated from my team and injured.

"Before the catastrophes that destroyed the Sakk settlement, one master general had been sealed in stasis, in case attack came. The eruptions and quakes damaged equipment, and he remained in stasis, oblivious to the death of his people. There was only one thing that could release him from the tube, and I provided it. A person with Sakk blood had to touch the controls."

Jannie gave them time to digest that much.

After a few moments of silence, Gorse tried again. "So you would be listed as missing somewhere?"

It was a test, Jannie was sure. "Most likely dead. I'm certain you have some sort of Internet access with you."

Ellwood pulled a Pocket PC from his jacket, punched a few buttons, and waved her on.

"Janice Ellen Reynolds. I was working on Doctor Jacob Abrams' dig."

"*Janeese?*" Beldon asked.

"*Jannie is a love name,*" she explained.

"*And who gave you that love name?*" His voice held a warning that someone—not her—might face his blade.

He's jealous. The fact warmed her. "*My parents,*" she soothed him.

"*Acceptable.*"

She bit back a laugh at that.

Ellwood worked on his handheld, and Odan did likewise. The tension in the air was thick and potent.

At last Ellwood looked up. He opened his

mouth to speak, but nothing that made sense emerged. His hands shaking, he turned the Pocket PC to reveal a picture of her, taken after she'd been separated from Beldon.

Jannie reached up, touching the feather she still wore in her hair.

"The memorial page your friends maintain is lovely," Odan offered dryly.

She scowled at him. "I imagine it is."

"They have no memory of your disappearance. There was a series of explosions. All of the research, aside from what was sent off to the university for study, was destroyed. The entire dig was destroyed."

Beldon answered before Jannie could. "There were technologies we would prefer not to leave in the hands of...those who have not even mastered interstellar travel." The snub was unmistakable.

"And the memory loss?" he persisted.

This was one discussion she'd loathed having to engage in, but there was no way around it. "That is difficult to explain."

"Try."

"Oh-kay then." Jannie sighed. "Rather than killing people, the Sakk have the ability to...sever the links to memories over a finite period of time."

No one replied to that.

"It is used when someone poses a threat to the Sakk."

"I notice *you* had memory loss," Odan inserted acidly. "Or did you forget at all?"

"I accidentally dosed myself. I set off the defensive systems that were still intact in the settlement."

"And you remember this how?" One of his thin dark brows went up in challenge.

"It can be reversed. In part, at any rate."

Ellwood nodded. "You were pregnant when you disappeared. The reports say you were raped."

He stopped short as Beldon's hand closed on her shoulder. Grumbled threats in Sakk rose from his guards and hers. Jannie raised her hand, ordering silence.

She'd never told Beldon what her team members had believed. That was a mistake. "It wasn't rape, but with no memories, Doctor Hall and Doctor Abrams *assumed* it was rape."

They gaped at her, their color draining away.

"Maybe a break of an hour would be best," she suggested.

"Y-yes," Ellwood stuttered out.

Jannie rose and turned toward the ship. The warriors scrambled to surround her, save the ones that would guard her retreating back. Beldon's wing closed around her, and she pressed to his armored ribs.

* * * *

Beldon stood behind her, one hand on Jannie's shoulder in a show of both possession and protection.

The questions were slow coming, indicating that an hour hadn't been long enough to recover from the shock that Jannie had chosen to give herself to him. The delegates were pale and nervy.

Ellwood cleared his throat. "Why are you here?"

Jannie clasped her hands beneath the table. The tension in her shoulders set off Beldon's battle instincts.

"Long ago, the Sakk home world was attacked by an enemy. While the warriors were fighting elsewhere, the major cities were attacked with a chemical weapon." She wiped at her eyes, crying as she always did when she discussed the mass murders.

Jannie fisted her hands. "It killed non-combatant males, the elderly, women, children... Most of the women and children had gathered in the cities to defend themselves in case of invasion. There was no invasion. The enemy attacked from space."

Not even the abrasive Odan spoke. It seemed they understood the gravity of the situation.

She continued, her voice subdued. "Imagine an enemy annihilating every major city on Earth and their suburbs, while half the male population was gone...more than three-quarters of those of the age to take a mate. What would that do to a species?"

"Good God," Ellwood breathed. "Society could collapse under that pressure."

"It nearly did."

Beldon indulged himself, squeezing his eyes shut for a moment. He shook off the brutal memories of wailing, his younger sister's dead body in his arms. Now was the wrong time to succumb to the anguish of that fateful homecoming.

"Nearly?" Gorse inquired.

"There were riots, wars over the few remaining women."

Odan let loose a sound of disgust. "The irony is staggering. You're left with few women and kill more in a war."

Jannie answered before Beldon could protest. "One. Tens of millions of Sakk men died in that war...and one woman.

"In more than three thousand years, there have been only four murders of women and only three rapes on Sakk. Every perpetrator was punished with death within eight days of the attacks. I hardly need to remind you that most countries in the world can't say that about a month. Some not about a week or a day."

The guards closed ranks at that comment. Beldon drew Jannie closer to him. Why had she never shared those statistics with him? It was horrifying. How many women were raped and killed on this world every day?

"You want our women," Odan grumbled. "Don't you." It was an accusation, not a question.

"No. We don't," Jannie answered calmly.

All the human delegates stared at her as if in disbelief.

"The first few generations of human women who mated with Sakk males on Earth required a good deal of medical intervention to do so. Our men need mates, not lab rats."

Ellwood stared at her. "And that means?"

She took a slow, deep breath. "We want to

find strong crossbred women like I am." She raised a hand to still the rising protests from the humans. "A strictly voluntary program. Women willing to be tested would do so."

"And then?" Gorse asked.

"They would meet a group of our men, choose a mate, and go to Sakk with him."

"No one will choose to do that," Odan prophesized.

Beldon bit back a wince. It was what he'd feared.

Jannie shot the delegate a bland look. "Of course, they will. Archeologists, paleontologists, linguists, sociologists, biologists...members of certain religions... Not to mention the alien chasers. If you allow them to, a fair number will line up to be tested."

"Without knowing what life will be like there?" he scoffed.

"Some will. Some will want to be among the first to chronicle Sakk. Some will watch the videos I've brought with me and the media coverage. Some will refuse outright." She shrugged. "Voluntary is voluntary."

Ellwood motioned for her attention. "And if the women change their minds?"

Jannie reached back, and Beldon grasped her hand.

She sighed. "I'm afraid the Sakk mate for life. The women can mate again, if a first husband dies. The males never do. The good news is, if you are Sakk or a strong crossbred human-Sakk mix like me, the drive to mate for life is coded in the genes."

"Are there other women we could speak to?"

"On Earth? No. The only reason I'm here is to act as a representative of the Sakk, because I was born and raised on Earth. The Sakk do not risk their females."

Gorse spoke up again. "What sorts of things are Sakk women permitted to do? Or not?"

"I admit those who volunteer to come from Earth will have vastly different choices than those mated on Sakk do. Sakk women are raised with certain...expectations. It's rather like living in a country with arranged marriages.

"The strongest males with an interest vie for a particular female's attentions. The winner—the strongest only—is allowed to marry, but only if the female accepts him as her mate.

"Mated females largely live in leisure. Entire families live together in ancestral homes. The women and children share in the work, which leaves much of the day free for pursuing interests, learning new skills, relaxing, reading, and enjoying the pleasures of family."

Beldon smiled at her description of life on Sakk. Perhaps once the treaties were signed, they would have time to do just that.

Jannie continued. "Women who come from Earth, on the other hand, will meet males here. Still the strongest, but the choice to approach a male will be her choice. There will be no contests for the right to approach a woman. No Earth-born female will leave the planet without making that choice and mating formally...marrying.

"On Sakk, those with professions they wish

to continue may do so. Those who choose to live as Sakk women do may do so."

The three human delegates traded looks Beldon couldn't begin to comprehend.

Apparently, Jannie could. "A break until tomorrow," she suggested.

Ellwood tipped his head to her. "I believe I have several people to speak to."

Odan looked past them toward the ship. "Will we be permitted inside?"

Beldon's stomach squirmed uncomfortably.

Jannie hesitated, but she didn't look to him, taking his instruction about giving the appearance of leadership to heart. "We will allow a small number of unarmed observers and media inside...with Sakk escorts, of course. I apologize, but we cannot and will not allow soldiers inside the ship."

Beldon stroked her shoulder, communicating his agreement with her plan.

Odan considered it, then nodded. "Tomorrow?"

"Agreed," she stated.

Chapter Fourteen

"Halt, please," Beldon requested.

The humans came to an unruly stop in the entry corridor. The results of the scans barked from the comms, and Beldon motioned the officers around him into the crowd.

At the first move to take a weapon, Odan shouted a protest and drew away, shuffling on his bandage-wrapped ankle.

Beldon raised a hand, requesting silence as Jannie had taught him. "Any man who refuses to release his weapon to the guards will be escorted out."

"This is not a weapon," Odan insisted, motioning to the cane supporting him. "I twisted my ankle."

"There is a blade sheathed inside the metal tube." Perhaps he thought they were as limited as humans were, their machines confused by placing one bit of metal inside another.

Odan's face paled. He didn't bother to deny it.

Ellwood whirled around to face his fellow, wrenched the cane from Odan's hand, and handed it off to one of the younger Sakk warriors. "Remove him," he ordered, jerking his head toward Odan.

"Jack," Odan protested.

"I told you yesterday. We're playing this straight." Ellwood motioned to him. "Please... Remove him. My apologies for this breach of trust. I will not support subterfuge."

Odan shook off the warrior who grasped his arm and stomped out, proving his injured leg was a lie. Beldon considered pointing out that their medical sensors would have proven that, if asked.

"Who else?" Ellwood asked.

Before Beldon could speak, one of the media representatives pulled out a small blade and handed it over with a chastised expression. "It's for repairs. I swear it."

To his surprise, Beldon believed him. "You may stay." They were showing trust; Beldon had to do the same.

"Thanks. My editor would kill me if I screwed this up." It was an exaggeration, Beldon was sure.

"Any others?" Ellwood asked.

Beldon glared at Gorse. Something told him the delegate was simply young and foolish, that he didn't mean harm by bringing a weapon aboard.

His face going deep red, he pulled out a projectile weapon smaller than his hand and offered it to the closest warrior. "You people scare the bejeezus out of me," he admitted.

Beldon chuckled, a smile pulling at his face. "A good sign, I suppose. You call us people...men." He considered the young man. "You may stay."

Gorse looked up at him in surprise. "Thank you. I didn't expect it after Odan."

He didn't reply to that. Offering his thanks and the admission that he wasn't worthy of trust was proof enough that the young human had learned a valuable lesson this day.

Beldon turned and led the way deeper into the ship. He patiently showed them the controls—they couldn't possibly understand the drive, the weapons panels—likewise safe, medical, food preparation, eating areas, and sleeping quarters for both high-ranking officers and low.

The questions were numerous, and more than once, he had to resort to the translators to understand the query being posed. In one instance, he'd had to comm Jannie to explain a question posed in idiom he didn't understand personally.

At last, they came to the conference room, and Beldon swallowed a sigh of relief. Jannie would handle the delegates from here.

His smile at the sight of his mate faded, and he launched toward her with muttered Sakk curses. The priests parted to allow Beldon to reach her side.

Finding his voice to protest was difficult, but he finally managed it. "*Jannie, how could you do this?*"

She darkened slightly, but her smile never faltered. Beldon reined in his frustration. He'd promised to trust her judgment in dealing with the deliberations, but he hadn't anticipated his son being part of her plan.

Jannie turned their son on her lap, so the infant faced the humans. "This is our son, Jalen," she announced to their guests.

Cameras that had never seemed to point the same direction, save the moment he'd removed his helm to signal Jannie, were focused on his son. Their single-minded attention made the feathers at the back of Beldon's neck rise in warning.

Jannie broke the silence. "Only one in two hundred Sakk males is blessed enough to hold a child he sired in his lifetime. Only that one will ever have a woman of his own to love and protect."

Jannie twisted on her chair and placed Jalen in Beldon's hands. Their son patted Beldon's armor with a squeal of delight, probably playing with his own reflection in the *ullium*. Jalen bounced, his dark gold hair feathers curling and flying wildly. Beldon smiled, then laughed outright, his heart light.

"If even a few women prove compatible, it means less suffering for the men of Sakk. It means smiles in the place of misery. It means the laughter of babies in a household dying for lack of them. There is no such thing as an unwanted child on Sakk. Even the fiercest warriors are kittens in the face of a young child."

Beldon smiled down at her. Though it irked him to be described as a wriggling fluffy ball of infant mammal, he loved that she saw him that way.

Ellwood sank to an open chair, staring at Jalen. "Whatever I can do," he vowed.

As if in answer, the child waved a little fist at him and smiled.

* * * *

Jannie watched Beldon as he laid Jalen in the cradle and covered him with a light blanket. His wings curved in a protective show.

It was coming. Whatever discussion was brewing about her decision to bring Jalen into the deliberations was sure to be intense.

As if Beldon was listening to her thoughts, he turned and straightened, looking more the tiger than the kitten she'd painted him earlier. Jannie led the way to their bedroom, her heart pounding in apprehension at the sound of Jalen's door clicking shut.

Beldon didn't speak. He wrapped an arm around her shoulders and pulled Jannie into a searing kiss. The bio chain warmed against her wrist, and her reasons for bringing Jalen to the table were buried in the cascade of arousal his touch brought.

His free hand went to work on the fasteners on their outfits. In a few half-remembered moments, they were chest to glorious male chest. Her head spinning, she started stroking his cock.

He lifted her at the waist, and Jannie released him, bringing her legs up and out to hook them around him. Beldon was lodged inside her a heartbeat later. There was something desperate in his movements, something that claimed her as his own all over again.

Jannie wanted to soothe him. She wrapped her arms around his neck, smoothing his hair feathers. Grooming was always soothing, whether it was also arousing or not.

His sounds rose sharply at that move, and he thrust harder. She brushed her lips over his throat and jaw, enjoying the tang of his musk in her mouth.

The end was kinetic, a tapestry of shouts, starbursts of color. Beldon staggered to the bed and collapsed to the surface, closing his wings around her.

"One in two hundred," he whispered.

His meaning wasn't lost on her. "I knew you would have scanned for weapons, and there were guards and priests everywhere. They wouldn't have been able to hurt us."

"I waited thousands of *yans* for you and our son, Jannie. Do not return me to the misery and steal my smile."

"I promise."

His kiss was slow and sweet. When Beldon pulled away, his lips curved in a sensual smile. "You did it. Every Sakk male in existence thanks you."

"Not yet. But after today, I'm certain we will."

"You will. Sakkan alone brought you to me."

Jannie nestled her cheek to his chest. She could spend the rest of her life sleeping in his arms, and Sakkan willing, she would. "Sakkan gave us each other."

The End

Section One:
Asylum

Meredith and Jarem

Chapter One

"May I help you with your young one?" a Sakk warrior offered with a tip of his head.

I hope so. God, I really hope you can. Otherwise, this entire mad escapade has been for nothing. Meredith shifted Alice on her hip and focused on the imposing specimen who had made the offer. She forced a smile for him. "Would it be possible to speak with one of your doctors?"

"Do you have a medical referral, ma'am?"

"No. I..."

Alice picked that moment to look up at him. She clapped her little hands in glee, and her wings started flapping under the oversized cape-style coat she wore.

Meredith glanced around at the crowd, wincing at the attention Alice was drawing. The absolute *last* thing they needed right now was attention. *Not until we're inside the consulate. Technically, we're still at the gates.*

A blinding white screen blocked her view, and Meredith gasped in surprise. He'd extended his wing around them.

"May I?" he offered, his hands out to take Alice from her.

She handed the wiggling baby over, and the warrior unfastened the coat. He removed it carefully, and Alice's little wings flapped furiously.

A smile curved his mouth into a lush bow. "Your daughter is beautiful," he complimented her. "And fully winged. We haven't encountered any native young born winged until now, let alone fully winged."

Meredith swallowed a lump of fear as she rubbed at her forehead. *She's not my daughter. I wish she was. If Alice was mine, none of this would be necessary.* "Yes. She is."

Murmurs rose around them, reminding Meredith that time was limited. "I do need to speak to one of your doctors." *Quickly. Before they figure out we're not where we're supposed to be and come here looking for us.*

His smile faded into a look of horror. "Is the young one ill?"

"I don't know," she admitted. "That's what I've come here to find out." It was an accurate statement. *I hope to God I'm right. If I'm not, I'll go to jail for the next decade for nothing. Going to jail would be worth it, as long as I'm right.*

"Then there is no time to waste." He turned with Alice in his arms, his extended wing guiding Meredith with him. "A hole!" he thundered. "A hole, please."

In the distance, other warriors passed that command along. A line of armed and armored Sakk men waded into the crowd and widened the area between the rows for them to pass through.

Her heart hammering, Meredith hurried into the main consulate building. *And to safety. I hope.*

****

Jarem played with young Alice's toes, laughing at the babe's squeals of delight.

In the distance, Meredith waited for the healers' determination. Her hands were clenched in the young one's coat, her face tense.

The dame bore little resemblance to the babe on the *bio bed*. The former had hair as black as deep space and eyes the color of *uba nuts* at harvest. By comparison, her young one's hair was the color of cooling embers and her eyes a vibrant green.

Alice must resemble her sire. Jarem tried not to obsess over the question of where that male might be. What sort of man wasn't at his child's side in a medical emergency?

"I see no cause for concern," the healer decreed.

Jarem breathed a sigh of relief. The idea of a young one at risk was a difficult thing for any Sakk male to cope with, their own or those of other Sakk.

"You're certain?" Meredith asked urgently.

"Very certain."

"Then Alice needs asylum."

"Asylum?" Jarem asked. Even with his grasp of English, the term made no sense to him.

Meredith turned his way. "Your protection."

"She has that."

"Here in the consulate. She has to *stay* here in the consulate," she insisted.

"I do not understand," the master healer admitted.

Meredith visibly calmed herself and started her explanation again. "If you let them take her out of the consulate—"

The doors opened and Master Beldon marched in, sword drawn and armored for battle. A half dozen warriors followed in his wake, similarly armed.

Jarem stared at them, at a loss to comprehend this turn of events.

"Protect the young one," the master ordered.

Four of the six warriors surrounded the *bio bed*, and Alice startled at the rush of bodies. Jarem lifted her into his arms and let her fuss against his chest.

Master Beldon took another step toward the babe's mother. "Meredith Mallory, will you come with us peacefully?" he challenged.

She took a calming breath. "If you promise Alice asylum, you can take me away, hand me over, and I'll spend the rest of my days in a prison cell without complaint." Her eyes pleaded for his agreement.

"You cannot legally *ask* for asylum for this young one. You are not her dame."

"I'm the closest she has."

Master Beldon's wings ruffled in offense. "You abducted this child. The rightful authorities are waiting to take custody of her, and I will return her to them." It was a blatant warning that Meredith should not stand in his way.

"What?" Jarem protested. His arms tightened around his wriggling bundle. *Abducted? Alice's parents must be frantic to find her.*

"She's an orphan," Meredith countered. "She's a ward of the state."

Beldon didn't seem to understand the latter half any better than Jarem did.

"She has no parents. They died. Or rather... Her *mother* died. We have no clue who her father is."

Beldon questioned her. "She has been...adopted? Those are her parents if they have adopted her. You still have no right to—"

"She. Has. No. Parents. The government is raising her. Do you understand?"

He didn't seem to.

"You need to understand. They're going to surgically remove her wings. Today. They said it's for her health, but it's not. Your doctors have confirmed that Alice is healthy *with* her wings." She motioned frantically with one hand. "If you give her back to the government officials asking for her, they will take her wings away. Do you understand *that*?"

Jarem curled his wings around Alice. She was perfect, and someone wanted to maim her? His fury uncorked. "Who will take her wings? Why would they do such a thing?" *I will kill them if Master Beldon does not get to them before I do.*

"It's...complicated. There are three agencies that oversee orphans like Alice. They asked the courts to allow them to do this and were granted permission. I was ordered to take Alice to the surgery, but I couldn't do that without knowing there's no other way.

"Now, please...I beg of you. I did this, knowing I would go to jail for it. All I'm asking is for you to meet me halfway. My job... My *former* job was advocating for children like Alice. God knows, I tried to do that. I argued to stop this. If what I've done legally isn't enough, you'll have to advocate for her while I pay the price of stepping outside the law."

"In what way?"

Jarem startled at the sound of Ambassador Janice's voice.

Meredith focused on her. "I'm not Alice's family. I wish to God I was, but I'm not. Genetically, she's more Sakk than human."

Janice nodded. "You're saying we are the closest relatives Alice has."

Words seemed to fail her. Meredith nodded, a tear escaping her eye. "Please. Grant her asylum."

"Arrest her."

Meredith's throat bobbed, but she managed a shaking nod. The two remaining warriors strode toward her, and more tears splashed to her cheeks. They shackled her wrists in front of her but used soft restraints in deference to the fact that she was female, Sakk or not.

"Should we hand her over to the human authorities?" one of the warriors asked.

"Yes," the master rumbled.

"No," his mate ordered.

Beldon snapped a look of disbelief her direction.

Janice sighed. "Ms. Mallory has abducted a Sakk child. I believe the Sakk have questions for her."

Beldon stared at her for a moment, then nodded his agreement. "Cell two. Jannie and I will speak with her."

"Make sure to feed her," Janice added.

Chapter Two

Meredith sat on the cot, her legs snug to her chest.

Overall, the Sakk prison cell was more comfortable than the human cell she'd envisioned for herself. The food she'd been given had been tasty and plentiful. Not that she'd managed to eat much of it with her stomach tied in knots. The cot was twice as wide as most prison cots she'd seen, thick and soft.

Wings. They built it for the housing of winged prisoners. The beds had to be set to minimum standards for their comfort.

It won't last long. Eventually, the Sakk would turn her over to the local police. After that, there would be no comfortable beds for a long time.

Will they hand me over to the local police? They might hand me to the feds. Meredith wasn't entirely sure whether taking Alice onto Sakk sovereign soil equated to leaving the country with an abducted child. *That decade might turn out to be a lot longer.*

A speaker crackled to life. "Ms. Mallory? Are you prepared for questioning?" It was Beldon, she was sure.

"No time like the present, I suppose," she answered in return. She winced at the truth. The longer they waited to interrogate her, the longer she could stay in the comparative lap of luxury.

Master Beldon entered the room first, followed closely by Representative Janice.

Another warrior brought a chair in for Janice, then left and closed the door behind him.

Once she was seated, Janice started speaking. "The child protection authorities have confirmed that you were supposed to be taking Alice to surgery. They tried to dodge the question of what kind of surgery it was, of course."

Meredith breathed a sigh of relief. "Then you'll give Alice asylum?"

"With someone threatening to take her wings for no good reason? There's no question. If I returned her to them, I would have a riot on my hands at every consulate on Earth. Believe me, that is not something I want to risk. Sakk warriors are well trained." Her smile said she was making light of the situation, but Meredith didn't doubt she wasn't lying about it.

Beldon tipped his head. "I do not approve of the *way* you conducted yourself, but I cannot fault your drive to protect the young one."

"Still," Janice continued. "We do have questions."

Meredith nodded. "You need information about Alice's situation to fight them," she guessed.

"And to decide what to do about you," she countered. "I'll be honest. A lot of people out there want your blood, but I'm not comfortable with you spending the rest of your life in prison for doing what was right. In essence, for doing your job more completely and professionally than any of your coworkers or bosses did."

A bloom of hope lifted Meredith's spirits.

"But there must be *some* punishment," Beldon informed her.

That toned the hope down a notch. Meredith looked around at her current accomodations. "If this is an example of the Sakk prison system, I don't mind telling you I'd rather this than a prison on Earth. Well...unless it was Halden, but then again, I don't speak Norwegian or Danish, so I guess that wouldn't work."

Beldon seemed confused by the observation. Janice nodded in agreement.

She answered the unspoken question. "The problem is...the Sakk don't typically keep female prisoners long-term. And... Well, we checked you, using the bed."

Meredith looked down at the mattress, confused by that pronouncement.

"It's a *bio bed*, designed to keep track of the health of prisoners. We tested you, using the bed. You're not Sakk-descended. At least, not close enough to be a match. If you were, we'd be able to apply Sakk law without consideration of local laws. You being human, by our standards, means our hands are tied. You *must* be considered a foreigner on Sakk soil."

"Wait. You don't keep Sakk women in prison long-term. You're saying no women on Sakk commit felonies? Or whatever the Sakk call that type of crime?"

"Oh, a rare few do."

"Then what do you do with them?" It seemed as if Janice was talking in circles.

The representative cleared her throat. "Female prisoners are given a choice in their own punishment."

I'm not going to like this. "Go on."

"They can donate eggs to be used in aiding genetically-inferior women in carrying young for their mates. If they make that choice, they are also choosing humane termination for themselves afterward."

Meredith swallowed down a sour wave. She wasn't Sakk, so donating eggs wasn't happening, and at least life in prison meant life.

Janice kept talking. "They can also choose a life of prostitution. Any children they produce are sent to seed worlds to be raised at two years old, unless they are fully-winged daughters, in which case they are taken in by families on Sakk to raise as their own."

A life of prostitution didn't sound much better. *Keep going, Janice.*

"The final choice would be serving as a sexual servant to the priests on a seed world. Children born would be raised by their mothers on the seed world, and female young would go to Sakk at adulthood to be matched."

That broke Meredith's silence. "Prostitution, prostitution slash slavery, or death? That's some system you have there. No offense, but I'll take door A...Earth prison, if it comes to a choice."

Janice winced. "I would have to agree. It is only imposed for the most severe cases. Women who kill or attempt to kill their husbands or children. *Any* children." She seemed to come to a realization. "We wouldn't impose that on you! Surely, you know that."

"I didn't, but thanks." She took a calming breath. "So what will you do with me? If you don't want to hand me over to the authorities outside the walls and you don't want to impose Sakk justice for felonies on me... For that matter, whatever you do, I can never leave the consulate again, or I face the laws outside." Funny how she'd never considered that before.

Janice seemed to consider that. "Well, you *could* leave the consulate, if you went to Sakk or one of our seed world colonies. But the question is, what would you do there? You wouldn't be much use on a seed world. No offense."

"None taken."

"Nest parents are couples, and they train for years for what they do. Going to Sakk... We have a law that only mated women can be transported to Sakk from Earth. Not even female journalists are allowed to visit. The males on Sakk are..." She glanced at Beldon. "Well, they are better behaved when a woman is under the protection of a particular male or group of males."

He grunted his agreement to that statement.

"Which brings us back to what you intend to do. With no children in the consulate, it's not like you can give me community service in my own field. I'm hopeless in a kitchen, and I'm about as far from a green thumb as you can get. You should know that. I suppose I could be useful as a secretary or part of a cleaning crew." There had to be some punishment they could give her.

"Well, there *is* a child in the consulate. Children, to be precise. Our son Jalen is here...and Alice."

Beldon's wings ruffled at the mention of their child.

"I'm not going to kidnap your son, I assure you." *You'd kill me if I even thought about it.*

He didn't respond to her.

"You need a babysitter for them?" she asked Janice.

She smiled. "Jalen might benefit from a play date with Alice, but..." Janice sighed. "To be honest, Alice doesn't know me, which means she doesn't trust me. Jarem handles her well, but it is not considered appropriate to have an unmated male caring long-term for a child who is not his own."

Meredith nodded. "I can do that. I...I adore Alice, if you want to know the truth. I wish she was mine. I really mean that." But what were the chances of that? Meredith wasn't Sakk-descended, and for her safety, Alice had to be adopted by a Sakk family.

"This is long-term," Janice warned. "The nest parents who will transport Alice will not arrive for at least two months. Possibly three."

"And after they take Alice?" Her heart sank at the thought of it. *It has to happen.* "What happens to me?"

Beldon spoke up again. "We have several months to decide that. Do you accept this form of service as partial punishment for your crimes?"

Meredith considered it for only a moment. "Yes. Of course I do."

Beldon helped Janice to her feet, and the representative issued her orders.

"A room has been outfitted for you and Alice. Before we call Jarem to bring her to it, I would invite you to check it and tell us what else you need for Alice. Or for yourself, for that matter."

Meredith's senses spun at the turn of events. "Right away."

****

"No, I'm afraid you *don't* see," Jannie challenged the panel of men sitting across from her.

Behind her, Beldon shifted, no doubt on alert at the slight rise in her voice.

This particular group included two of their federal liaisons, the state governor, and three representatives of the local child services and social services offices involved in overseeing Alice's care, as well as several of their lawyers. *I've always hated lawyers.*

"I'm afraid it's you who doesn't understand, Mrs. Beldon," one of the social services lawyers insisted.

"It's Ambassador Janice, thank you," she corrected him. "And I disagree. Your entire case is founded on the idea that Alice is an American citizen, under the protection of the state and federal governments *of* Virginia and the United States of America."

"She *is*," he pressed.

"Not quite. You admit that the consulate area is Sakk sovereign soil, but you seem to have neglected to take Sakk laws into account. Unlike other foreign entities who have consulates, being Sakk is more than a matter of nation of birth, nationality of parents, and proclaimed allegiances. The Sakk are a separate species. The fact that we intermixed with humans aside, being Sakk or Sakk-descended is a matter of genetics, not a matter of place of birth. Born within the United States and in the state of Virginia, Alice is both American by the locality of her birth and the nationality of her mother *and* Sakk by virtue of her Sakk genes. She possesses dual citizenship."

She paused to let them digest that much. Half the panel gaped at her in disbelief.

One of the other lawyers spoke up. "You're saying all Sakk attached to the consulate should have diplomatic immunity? Or maybe that all persons with Sakk blood do?"

"Is this a case of diplomatic immunity?" she countered.

"Well...no, but..."

"You're correct. It's not. It is a case of a Sakk minor and the responsibility the Sakk have to her care and protection."

"That's *our* job," the head of the local fostering program complained.

"Then you have faulted at your position," Jannie informed her.

"Excuse me?"

"You heard me. You sit there and expect the Sakk to turn a blind eye to the mutilation of one of our children? Absolutely not, I assure you. Alice is a Sakk child on Sakk sovereign soil, and we will not permit such a sacrilege...such an atrocity to occur. To the Sakk, wings are sacred, a sign of the gods among mortals. Removing those wings is against everything the Sakk hold sacred."

"It is for her health."

Beldon answered before Jannie could, inserting himself into the proceedings. He rarely interrupted her when she was playing the part of ambassador for the Sakk, so it shocked her to hear it.

"You lie. We will willingly share our reports on the health of young Alice. She came to us with no medical problems, save normal childhood injuries associated with learning to stand. Certainly nothing that would indicate removing her wings. Were it truly a matter of her health and safety, we would remove her wings here at the consulate, with much less pain than human science is capable of."

Jannie nodded solemnly. "It occurs to me that those who testified in court to these *supposed* health problems have perjured themselves. That might be something you'll want to look into, Governor." She tipped her head to him, noting his darkening complexion in satisfaction.

"So you're just going to...keep Alice?" the woman from child protection asked.

"I see no reason not to allow her to find a Sakk family to raise her. They will certainly appreciate the innate beauty of a winged child like her."

"And they'll also give her to a man she's never met before to marry," the CPS representative countered. "Great plan for protecting her."

"Do you suggest that other countries on Earth who practice arranged marriages are abusing their daughters? Sakk girls are not married off to their husbands until they are legally adult, *and* they are able to refuse males who are less than acceptable to them outright. It seems that asylum is granted in the United States to women whose countries practice ritual female mutilation...sometimes. But not to women escaping arranged marriages. Considering this situation, it amazes me that you claim the opposite is what Alice should be subjected to."

Coleman, the elder of their two federal liaisons, half-hid a laugh in a fake cough. "We understand your concern about the wings."

"Then kindly understand this," she requested. "Not only do we intend to see to Alice's care... And if that doesn't sit well with you, we can certainly leave the United States and wash our hands of this entire country until you mature." Jannie let the threat hang between them.

No one spoke, though the representatives from child services and the foster care system looked like they wanted to take her up on that offer.

"Not only will we protect Alice, at all costs, we would like to arrange several new initiatives."

Brady, the younger liaison, spoke up. "Of what sort?"

"The first is very similar to your laws on surrendering infants and toddlers to the state. If a child tests as being Sakk-descended, we will allow surrender to us of that child, up to the age of two. Both parents must agree, if both are named on the birth certificate, save in cases of the death of a parent. Since this is Sakk sovereign soil, we have the ability to make such a decree as you do, state by state."

He nodded. "I can't see how we could stop it. And?"

"If a child is orphaned and is a ward of the state, we would like to test them routinely."

"To what end?" the woman from the foster system inquired coolly.

"Giving them a home outside the overworked and overrun state systems."

Coleman seemed to consider it. "That would have to be worked out, state by state. Some may insist that only children with no living relatives may be tested, and some may simply not approve it."

"Understood."

There was a moment of silence. Everyone except the liaisons started packing their paperwork and heading for the door.

When they were gone, Coleman sighed and pushed a hand through his heavily-grayed hair. "Have you had a chance to consider the extradition paperwork that was filed with you? I don't mind telling you that there are a lot of people out there steaming for a shot at Meredith Mallory's head."

"It is denied."

He gaped at her. "Seriously? This is not going to go down well."

Jannie wished Ellwood was here. He wouldn't have argued this with her, she was sure. "She *did* abduct a Sakk child, and she was captured on Sakk soil."

"I'm really starting to loathe the consulate rules," he admitted.

Brady piped up. "We'll have to check on her. You don't mind, do you?"

"Of course not. But do be aware that we will not return Ms. Mallory to you unless she asks to face your justice instead of ours."

"Fair enough," Coleman decided. "We can play up the fact that she's facing justice there."

****

Meredith looked up from Alice's diaper at the sound of a knock. "Just a moment," she called out.

"At your convenience, Meredith," Janice replied.

She rushed through putting on the fresh diaper, dropped the soiled one in the waste unit, then wiped her hands on a cleansing cloth the Sakk had provided for the chore. With Alice on her hip, Meredith made her way to the door and opened it.

Her smile faded at the sight of what appeared to be two human—and very official—

men. Her heart pounded out a warning. Had they decided to turn her over to the human authorities after all?

Why? What have I done? She'd been caring for Alice for three days, and there had been no complaints Meredith was aware of.

Janice covered Meredith's hand with her own, squeezing lightly. "May I present Representative Ellwood and Representative Gorse? They are two of our liaisons. It is their job to check on you and report whether or not you are being treated well in your confinement."

"Of...of course." Meredith backed off a step and waved them to the sofa. Then she placed Alice in the playpen and offered her the Sakk version of a spill-proof training cup.

With no further excuses, she took the last remaining open chair in the living room area.

The two liaisons were busy, looking around the room she shared with Alice. The older of the two—*Ellwood*—had one eyebrow raised as if he meant to challenge something.

"Not a cell, then? I know there are cells here at the consulate."

Meredith replied to it, though she wasn't certain if the question had been intended for her or for Janice. "I was in a cell for a while, but now I'm here." She hesitated and then offered the rest. "There are two guards on the door, so I guess it's a more comfortable cell."

Janice cut in. "The Sakk do not believe in long-term incarceration of females, unless it is a case of capital crimes. The guards are posted for the safety of Ms. Mallory and of Alice. When they do have reason to leave the room—to visit the garden or to go to the clinic, the guards accompany them. The guards also deliver whatever food items Ms. Mallory requests for herself and Alice."

She motioned to the curtain that separated the living room from the bedroom. "We have provided clothing, food, comfortable shelter, and even medical care. I dare say Ms. Mallory is better cared for here than she would have been in a stateside prison."

"Medical care?" Gorse asked.

Meredith managed a weak smile. "I slipped on a wet stone in the garden and cut my knee. It was just a little cut, but the guards demanded I go to the clinic and have it tended to."

Janice nodded her agreement. "Sakk warriors take protecting a woman or child very seriously."

Ellwood jumped into the conversation again. "The reason she's caring for Alice?"

Janice cut Meredith off at the pass. "Ms. Mallory is someone Alice knows and trusts. Since she brought Alice here, it seemed best to use her community service to provide the continuity of care a young one needs."

"Your proposed punishment is community service? I don't mind telling you there are people involved who will not feel that is an adequate exchange for the crimes they believe she has committed." The tip of his head toward Meredith let her know he didn't agree with it, but he had to play political games.

"That's one *part* of her punishment."

"And the rest?"

Meredith's heart pounded in apprehension. They hadn't discussed that further since Janice brought it up.

"That has not been decided yet, but it will be a Sakk-appropriate punishment for her level of crime."

Gorse shook his head. "Meaning what?"

Janice smiled. "We will give Ms. Mallory a choice. We will not impose a punishment on her she doesn't feel able to bear."

Considering the punishments she'd heard of so far, Meredith wasn't sure that was going to be a choice she wanted to face.

Chapter Three

Two weeks later

He was back again, and even Jarem couldn't state why he kept coming to see Meredith. He tried to convince himself it was Alice he came to see, but he knew that wasn't true. While he played with the babe, his attention often strayed to the female in question.

It made no sense that he could fathom. She wasn't a Sakk-descended woman. She wasn't a woman who could give him sons to save his dying family line.

But I want her. There was no question of it. His sights were firmly fixed on Meredith Mallory, and his libido demanded a taste of whatever she would grant him.

This isn't intelligent. I have to focus on finding a mate who will provide children for my family. He was the last hope of it. If Jarem failed to make a match or failed to produce at least one son with a mate, his family was doomed to extinction.

The guards offered a curt nod, and one knocked lightly at the door for him.

Meredith opened the door and smiled. She whispered across the opening, "Alice is already asleep."

Disappointment lodged in his chest and he nodded, preparing to withdraw.

Her smile dimmed. "Of course, if you'd like to come in and spend time with me while she sleeps...?"

"Yes. I would."

One of the guards scowled, but he didn't comment. Jarem ignored him.

Her smile was radiant, and his cock complained about the niceties of society.

Sakkan take it. I want her in bed.

Meredith backed off, and she waved an invitation. He ambled into her quarters. There was something nearly indecent about that move, entering a female's room without guards and without the veneer of being there to see Alice.

She leaned down to scoop up a toy, and Jarem's gaze locked on the curve of her ass pressing against jean shorts. The sight was enough to drive a horny male insane.

Especially Meredith's ass.

She dropped the toy in the playpen, oblivious to his interest in the view.

Halfway across the room, Meredith stopped and stretched her back, rubbing at a spot in the lower right quadrant. He was at her back in a heartbeat, his hand a whisper from her body.

Reality smacked him hard aside the head. He couldn't do this without her permission. "Do you mind?" he offered.

"Not at all."

His heart hammering against his ribs, Jarem started rubbing her back. Meredith moaned and dropped her head to his shoulder.

She turned minutely, murmuring instructions for where she needed him to rub.

That brought her hip into contact with the length of his erection.

They both went still, and he prepared for her outrage. Surely, she would tell him to leave. If she allowed him in again, it would only be to interact with Alice.

While I want her. Sakkan damn it all.

Meredith turned toward him slowly, her color high. She didn't say anything. Not an order to leave. Not an invitation to more. Jarem shifted toward her, a testing move intended to spur her to speech, one way or the other.

I must know, so I can move on.

She didn't speak. Meredith rose on tiptoe and brought her lips to his. Jarem chanced wrapping his arms around her, and she didn't protest.

Careful kissing led to more. In moments, they were crushed together, mouths meshing, parting to explore, and returning.

The bed beckoned, but Jarem thought better of it. Alice's crib was in the sleeping area. It wasn't going to be a bed for them.

He nibbled at her ear and whispered to her. "Can you be silent?" The last thing he wanted was to bring the guards with a scream or wake the baby before they'd finished.

Her negative response came out half eclipsed in a gasp.

Jarem considered their options and led her to the bathroom. He started the shower flowing to drown out their sounds. Since the consulate reclaimed and purified all their waste water and produced clean energy, it was a minor draw on the system and not a huge waste of resources.

He drew Meredith into a kiss, moaning at the feeling of her unbuttoning her shorts and pushing them away. The swivel of her hips against his cock fired a lust not unlike what he'd felt in his pre-prime settling period.

But now I am I man, and I know well enough how to please a woman.

Jarem lifted Meredith to the wide edge of the tub, urging her back onto her elbows. Her legs were spread, which worked well for what he intended.

He went to his knees and started to feast between her legs. Nothing encouraged a female to invite a male back faster than a male who was skilled at this form of pleasure, human or Sakk.

And I have been proven skilled. In fact, he'd asked the wanton prisoners who'd handled his settling to teach him, as part of their service. *I always knew this would come in handy.*

****

Pleasure knifed through Meredith, and she started to push further to sitting. Jarem pinned her in place with one hand without breaking stride. His tongue danced over her and inside her.

It was difficult to remind herself to keep quiet. For that matter, it was difficult to think at all. That established, she gave herself up to sensation and rode it to climax.

Jarem wasn't finished yet. He rose to his feet between her thighs and started stripping off his clothing.

Meredith watched his body appear, hungry for more of him. *Hungry for that beautiful cock.* She peeled off her t-shirt and unhooked her bra, making a show of taking it off and dropping it to the floor.

Jarem's expression was potent. He pushed her thighs wider and eased inside her, seemingly savoring every inch of her stretching around him.

Not that she *wasn't* enjoying it. Meredith couldn't imagine any heterosexual woman who *wouldn't* enjoy what Jarem was doing. Still, there was something enchanting about Jarem's expressions.

There was nothing rushed in their sex. Every motion was painstakingly planned. Or so it seemed to Meredith. She held to him, her head swimming.

"Come for me again," he requested.

Meredith didn't argue that she would. She couldn't have stopped that from happening if she'd wanted to. *And I don't.*

In moments, she was coming, her back arched. Breathless little cries escaped her throat.

Jarem followed her over, his teeth clenched shut on whatever sounds he wanted to vent. His heat flooded her, causing Meredith to gasp in surprise.

Realization calmed her. *He's Sakk. Between the difference in our biology and the Sakk medical advancements, there's no reason to use a condom with him.* And why did she find that so appealing, when she'd never found it an intrusion with human men?

A smile softened Jarem's face. "You enjoyed?"

Meredith groaned. "You know I did."

"I suspected it," he teased.

"What now?" Cuddling on the sofa with him sounded like the perfect way to drop off to sleep to her.

Something told her his look of deep consideration was feigned.

"I say we make use of this shower. Since it's heated now."

"I'll wash your...whatever, if you wash mine."

He lifted her with a wide grin, still impaled on his length.

Chapter Four

"You asked for me, Sa Beldon?"

The master general offered a warning look and waved the corporal working nearby away. In moments, they were alone in the office Beldon shared with his mate.

The hair feathers on the back of Jarem's scalp rose in warning. "Is there a problem?" he asked.

"Ms. Mallory's guards raised...concerns."

He swallowed a lump of true fear. If Beldon felt he'd mistreated Meredith or Alice somehow, he could be stripped of his right to win a mate. *And my family will die off as a result.* That couldn't be allowed to happen.

"As a result, I had the healers call her to the medical bay for tests. She thought they were tests on Alice, but they were tests on Ms. Mallory."

"I have not mistreated them. I assure you, I have not."

"You realize Ms. Mallory is not a Sakk female," Beldon countered.

"Of course I realize that." His heart ached. After the sex they'd had the night before, that was a painful reminder. Jarem couldn't imagine a female he'd want as a mate more. *And I can't have her.*

"Then you realize she is not a wanton prisoner who has chosen prostitution as her punishment?" It was a challenge.

His stomach cramped at the blunt question. "I would never treat Meredith that way."

"Would you not?"

"Never," Jarem repeated, his blood boiling at the insinuation. "Meredith and I shared consensual passion. There are no rules or laws against it. A formidable number of the Sakk males on Earth are having sex with human women."

"But this is a female under the protection of the consulate."

"It was consensual," he reminded Beldon. "Did anything the healers found indicate otherwise?"

The master didn't answer that, which gave Jarem hope he could fight his way out of whatever sanctions Beldon was envisioning for him.

"What are your intentions toward Ms. Mallory?"

"What intentions can there be? She's not Sakk-descended." Every time he said it, Jarem raged at it. How could Sakkan be so cruel as to give Jarem the perfect woman and simultaneously make it a woman Jarem couldn't hope to claim? "If you've read my file, you know my situation well enough. I must have a son. My family will die without one."

"And you're comfortable with that?"

"What choice have I?" He bit back several curses in English and Sakk, and he knew his anguish came through in the question.

Beldon was silent for a few tense heartbeats. "I see."

"Are you ordering me away from Meredith?"
Please, don't.

"I see no reason to."

Jarem nodded his thanks. "Is there anything else?"

"I believe your companionship is beneficial to Ms. Mallory and young Alice and your intentions meaningful. You may go."

He offered a tip of his head and went back to his work, his mind rioting. The only thing that was clear to him was that he would be returning to Meredith at his earliest convenience.

****

Meredith didn't question that the knock on the door was Jarem. After the night before, she didn't question that he'd choose to stay, even though Alice wasn't in the room for him to visit with.

She smiled at him across the open door. "Alice is spending the next two hours with Jalen. Would you like to come in?"

He tipped his head and made his way past her. "I would. Thank you."

She closed the door and crossed the room to him. There was no play at conversation, no hesitation on either of their parts.

The kiss turned to more in the blink of an eye, and Jarem guided her toward the bed, clothes dropping away as they moved. By the time they flopped to the mattress together, only her shorts and underwear remained.

Meredith worked at the button and zipper, while Jarem palmed a breast, licking his lips.

She smiled up at him. "I swear Janice knows about us," she informed him. The offer to give Meredith a few hours off at the time Jarem was returning from his daily shuttle run seemed to indicate either that or one heck of a coincidence.

His scowl made her heart stutter.

"What?"

"She does, but I would not be concerned about it."

"Clearly, if she's giving us time together." Still, it felt like an intrusion of their privacy. *Does he feel the same? Was that what the scowl was for?*

He hesitated, seemingly torn. "You do know I would give you all I have to offer, were that possible?"

The rising happiness hit the wall of reality. It was pillow talk. She'd heard her share of it. "I know."

After a moment of stillness, Jarem started working her shorts and underwear down her legs. Meredith lifted her hips to help him.

She consoled herself with the truth. He was Sakk, and he was from a family that had no other sons. Jarem's duty to his family would always take precedence over any other concern. It had to.

But I'll have the memories. They were excellent memories, and unless she somehow met and married a human man who was willing to accept her endless lockdown in the consulate, those were all she had hopes of.

Jarem raised his head, seemingly questioning her, and Meredith threw herself whole-heartedly into another kiss. If this was all she had—the time before Jarem found a mate, she wasn't going to waste a moment of it.

Chapter Five

Five weeks later

"Meredith?" The knock on the door repeated.

She rushed to it, opening it to Janice.

Beldon's wife smiled. "Would you be willing to come to the medical clinic with me?"

Meredith looked back toward the playpen, torn.

"I've already sent for Arya. She will be here with Jalen in a few minutes, and General Lea will watch over Alice until then." She motioned to the hulking general who led her personal guard.

Meredith nodded, and Lea slid past her and into the room with Alice. As usual, the baby greeted any winged newcomer with happy shouts.

She let herself out into the hallway, closing the door behind her. Janice led the way, trailed by four Sakk warriors. Meredith fell into step beside her.

Halfway down the hall, Meredith finally spoke. "What is it?"

"We've found two more babies. Their mothers want to surrender them. A baby boy is being flown in from Pennsylvania tonight. The other— another girl—is being surrendered here."

"Okay. So why do you need me?"

"I've been wracking my brains, trying to figure out what to do with you. No offense."

"None taken. You've been more than fair so far."

"We owe you a debt of thanks." It sounded like an admission.

"I did what I knew was right," Meredith dismissed her.

They made the turn toward the clinic. "Too many people didn't."

"I agree."

Janice stopped to look at her. "We need someone with your qualifications."

"You do?" Meredith wasn't sure what she meant. She didn't possess any special qualifications.

"Come with me."

The baby in the middle of the clinic was no more than a few months over a year old. Her face was screwed up, tears reddened her cheeks, and wails echoed off the walls.

Janice leaned toward Meredith to impart an explanation. "Her mother didn't even wait for the formal paperwork. The minute the tests came up positive, she handed the baby's birth certificate to the healers and walked out the door. The screaming started within a minute and hasn't stopped since. If we can't figure out how to stop her, the healers are going to sedate her, but we'd rather not do that."

Meredith gaped at her for a moment, trying to grasp at so unfeeling a monster. What kind of mothering had this child had up until now?

Not good.

She grasped the basket of toddler toys and made her way to the center of the room. The baby wailed louder.

"What's her name?" Meredith shouted over the din.

"Samantha Grace Norton, but her mother called her Sammy," the healer reported. "She is fourteen months of age."

She nodded and started setting out toys. Offering them failed. Backing away from the basket failed as spectacularly. Any reach toward Sammy made her scream louder and flail her arms at the interloper.

Finally, Meredith looked up at Janice. "Has anyone tried feeding her?"

The doctor motioned to a tray.

Meredith took stock of it and shook her head. It was a rice and sautéed vegetable mix with an open cup of the fortified almond milk the healers preferred for use with Sakk children. "I need a plate of the cookies the cooks make for Alice and a *bottle* of milk."

"But she's more than a year old," Janice started to argue.

She shot the representative a hard look. "Trust me. This child hasn't eaten well. She's had convenience foods and hasn't been moved to a cup. A mother like that... She did whatever was easiest, most likely."

The healer cleared his throat. "That would explain the condition of her teeth," he confirmed. "We will have to do some reparative work on them over the next few weeks." He tipped his head and went to the comm board to relay her request.

The tray showed up, and Meredith took it and placed it at her back. She lifted a cookie between herself and Sammy, and the child stopped screaming abruptly. Her lavender eyes were red-rimmed, and her white-blond hair was in complete disarray, matted and knotted, as if she'd pulled at it during the tantrum.

"That's better," Meredith crooned to her. "Come get the cookie, Sammy."

The toddler pushed to her feet, took the four steps separating them, snatched the cookie, and retreated to the far end of the clinic with it.

Meredith noted her responses...and how thin she was. "What did her medical tests show?"

"She is underweight," the healer reported. "By the human charts, she is no more than the fifteenth percentile in weight but nearly the ninetieth in height."

"I expected that. How's her nutrition? I'm betting she hasn't been eating a balanced diet."

"I can guarantee it. Her mother also reports that Sammy is always sick, that she often vomits after eating. She displays no food allergies, though."

Janice appeared at her side, sinking to the floor beside her. "What do you think?"

"I think, when I hand her the bottle, she's done eating. Sammy will drink her calories rather than eat them."

"Is that why the bottle is behind you?"

"You've got it." Meredith considered their options. "We're going to have to ease her into real food."

"What's your plan?"

Sammy finished the first cookie and peeked at Meredith. When she raised another and held it out, the toddler ran over, grabbed it, and retreated again, half tripping over shoes Meredith guessed were too large for her feet.

"Can your cooks make little baby-sized pies filled with fruits and vegetables?"

"They can make anything we want."

Meredith considered what she knew about Alice. "I take it it's normal for Sakk children not to eat eggs and meat. We noticed early on that Alice didn't eat anything but fish and tofu proteins...and the occasional chunk of cheese."

"That's typical," Janice confirmed.

"Have the cooks ever tried to make soy burgers and soy chicken nuggets?"

One of the healers ruffled his wings at the suggestion.

Janice shot him a quelling look. "I think I see what you're getting at. Convenience foods. The mother could tolerate meat and eggs. She was trying to feed Sammy what she ate, but Sammy wouldn't tolerate it."

"She was hungry enough to eat it," Meredith corrected. "She just couldn't keep it down."

The healer gasped. "She was feeding the young one...fowl?" His horror at the suggestion was impossible to miss.

Sammy appeared again, rocking her back foot. She stood on tiptoe, probably searching for another cookie. Meredith raised it but didn't extend her arm. The toddler walked to her calmly, took the cookie, and sat just more than an arm's length from Meredith's feet to eat it.

"That's right. A few days of eating food you don't puke up, and you may actually trust me."

Janice sighed. "I knew you were the right woman for the job."

"What job would that be?"

"What would you think of being mother to these three babies?" After a moment of hesitation, she continued. "In fact, I believe I've found the perfect punishment for your crime."

****

Meredith paced the floor of the large suite she now shared with all three children.

Alice and Sammy had matching cribs on one side of the combination nursery and library, and Todd's crib was along the opposite wall. A changing table sat between them, stocked with Pull-Ups and two sizes of diapers, wipes, and pajamas for all three children. A large wardrobe near the door held clothing for all three.

Two highchairs were pushed close to the dining room table, and one of the chairs had been outfitted with a booster seat for Sammy. Alice's playpen sat in the center of the living room, a smaller playpen was nestled next to it for Todd, and a wide variety of toys were scattered around the floor for Sammy.

And more toys arrive every hour. It seemed each of the warriors at the consulate wanted to give the children a toy. *Or a dress for one of the girls.* Meredith guessed that the vans the Sakk warriors took to shop in town were full on every run.

The large screen on the wall would play practically anything Meredith asked for, thanks to the generosity of the Sakk consulate. So far, she'd learned that Sammy liked *Caillou, Bear in the Big Blue House*, and the *Sesame Street* sing-along specials. Meredith hadn't been desperate enough to attempt *Barney*; that would have been a last resort, and thankfully it wasn't necessary.

"It looks like a fricken day care center," she muttered.

Not that Meredith minded having the three children around. She'd always promised herself a big family. She just hadn't expected to get it this way.

Three children under the age of eighteen months in one fell swoop.

And then there was the rest of Janice's plan. Meredith could hardly fathom following through with it, though she'd already agreed to it.

Unless Jarem is willing to be part of it. That wouldn't be a hardship at all. But what were the chances of that?

Not good, she wagered.

In fact, she wasn't sure any of the warriors were willing to follow through, though Janice seemed certain at least a few would be interested. Despite her assurances, no warrior had announced his intentions yet. *And they've had half the day.*

A light tapping on the door announced that Jarem had arrived. Meredith steeled her nerves and went to answer the door.

****

Jarem shifted from foot to foot, excited by the news. Word that two more babies had been located—and that Meredith was caring for all of them—had reached him shortly after he returned to the consulate that afternoon.

Meredith opened the door and waved him inside. He hesitated, noting how worn she looked.

She is caring for three babies. That must be hard work.

He located the cribs and examined the three sleeping children. They were as different as could be. The new little female had wispy hair the color of snow, and the infant male had hair as dark as Meredith's and skin that seemed to be naturally deep beige. Alice was the only winged babe in the group.

Based on their relative sizes, he guessed the new female to be the oldest of the group and the male to be the youngest, with Alice somewhere between the other two. Jarem cursed the fact that he hadn't been exposed to babies. He had little idea of their ages or what they would be able to do at their respective sizes.

He turned to Meredith, his excitement bubbling over. "What are their names?" he whispered.

She pointed toward the females. "Sammy." Then toward the young male. "Todd."

He committed the names to memory. Since the nest parents they'd rerouted wouldn't arrive for more than a month, Jarem would have ample time in their presence to get to know the babies before they went to permanent homes.

"The families who choose them will be very fortunate. They are all beautiful."

Meredith winced, and the hair feathers at the back of Jarem's neck rose in warning.

"What is it?"

She hesitated, then waved him toward the sleeping area. When they were closed behind the heavy curtain, Jarem still had no clue what was bothering her.

"Meredith?"

"Janice decided that it would be traumatic for the surrendered children to spend three months with the nest parents and then go to other parents when they reach Sakk, especially Alice, after spending all this time with me."

Words fought emerging. "The nest parents have agreed to keep all three babies?"

"Not these ones. And they won't care for the babies longer than it takes to get a pair of adoptive parents here, unless they agree to take on the next set permanently."

"I assume *someone* has agreed to care for these babies permanently."

She swallowed hard and managed a tight smile. "I have."

"On Earth?" That made no sense. Representative Janice had argued that, for legal reasons, the young had to leave the planet within three months of surrender, at which point, they would be legally adopted by their Sakk parents.

She shook her head.

"You're going to Sakk?"

Meredith nodded.

"Alone? I mean...unmated?" No female was supposed to leave the planet without mating first.

"No."

His stomach dropped out. "And who will be your mate?"

Meredith shrugged, her entire body quaking.

"No." He wasn't giving her up. Not now. Not ever.

His family would accept an adopted son, if that was the only choice they had. His sire had demanded Jarem save the family name, not the family's genetic code. That had already been saved, thanks to his female cousins.

****

"What?" His tight-lipped fury and that single-word answer made no sense to her.

In the next coherent moment, she was pressed to Jarem's chest, his lips parting hers. Meredith moaned into his mouth.

At last, he pulled away. "Do you wish another male?" he challenged.

She shook her head. It was the last thing she wanted.

"Then you and all three babies are mine to claim."

"You want—?"

"I intend to claim you before any other male has a chance to. Will you accept the *bio chains*, if I lay them?"

Her breathing went strangled, and Meredith nodded frantically.

He looked at the comm board beside the bed, glaring at it.

Realization made her gasp. "I know how to call for them," she admitted.

One eyebrow went up in surprise. Or maybe challenge.

"Janice told me how. She said...When I chose a male who was willing to adopt all three babies and...and everything else, I could call for the chains."

"Everything else?" There was a warning couched in that.

"She said no family would accept the situation unless I carried a child created with a donor egg and my...my mate's sperm. That way, he'll have a child of his own as well as the adopted children."

A sly smile curved his lips and he pulled Meredith into a kiss. "I think it's time to call for those *bio chains.*"

"You'd accept that?"

"Have I been less than straight-forward in my interactions with you so far?"

"Well...no, but we both thought that couldn't go any further."

He sighed and pressed a kiss to her lips. "We are sexually compatible. We have interests in common. The babies, for one thing. The Sakk have the technology to make sure we can have children together. Don't you realize that most Sakk mate without knowing if they are sexually compatible or if they share any interests at all?"

"And?" *Does it really matter if he has feelings for me? Most Sakk don't consider that in mating.* It was unlikely any male she chose would have feelings for her.

His next kiss was fully carnal. When he broke away, Meredith pressed a hand to his chest, trying to find her elusive balance.

Okay, a marriage based on that kind of sex wouldn't be such a hardship.

He smiled, most likely at her reaction. "I won't let you choose another male if you have any interest in me at all. That must tell you I have very definitive feelings for you."

Yes, but those feelings could be possessive or something warmer. She managed a smile that felt natural.

His expression softened. "I told you long ago what I wanted to give you, were it possible. It *is* possible, Meredith."

Her heart started pounding at the memory. *It was pillow talk. Wasn't it?*

"Promise me." He was starkly serious. "Promise me two children, if you are capable of carrying twice. And promise me that you are not choosing me as the lesser of evils."

"I promise...as long as we wait until Todd is at least a year old. There are only so many babies I can handle at once."

She expected him to argue it. Instead, Jarem laughed heartily. "As you wish."

"I'll give you more children," she hastened to add. "If the first two are girls... I know you want—"

Jarem's mouth closed over hers in a searing kiss that made her head spin. When he pulled away, she was boneless in pleasure, and every muscle in his chest and arms was strung tight.

"Get the chains. Let me place them."

Meredith made her way to the comm board on shaking legs. She entered the code and pulled the chains from the drawer that opened. She tried to hand them to Jarem, but he shook his head.

He raised his right wrist between them. "Clasp mine on."

She had to hold them up to see which was the larger chain. That established, she pulled the male chain around his wrist. "How do I—?" She gasped as the chain snapped together without her working a clasp.

Jarem's gasp echoed hers.

"Are you all right?" she asked, concerned.

"More than all right." He smiled. "You'll see." He took the remaining chain from her hand. "Do I have permission to lay the *bio chain*?" There was an air of formality to the question.

Meredith nodded and offered her wrist. The chain clicked shut, and the arousal washed over her body, causing her to shudder in the abrupt influx of sensation.

"That's right," he breathed.

In the next moment, they were engaged in deep kisses, and Jarem was guiding her to the bed. It wasn't enough. Meredith reached for his clothing, intent on getting him naked and inside her.

He pulled her hands away from the clasps with a sound of censure. Then his tongue was buried in her mouth again.

He pulled back abruptly. "Kneel on the bed."

Meredith followed his instructions, and Jarem did the same. His wings spread as they had when he'd shielded her from public view the first time they'd met. She gasped, awed by the show.

"Stay there."

She trembled in need. There was something sinfully appealing in taking his orders. "Okay."

Jarem took his time, stripping her clothes off and then his own. A tone sounded, and his smile widened. "You're mine now."

"Already? But I thought—"

"Oh, we will consummate it. Never fear. We will."

He pushed lightly at her shoulder, tumbling Meredith to the mattress and coming down over her. She spread her legs, offering herself to him.

Jarem groaned. In the next heartbeat, he was lodged deep inside her.

Meredith stifled a cry behind closed lips, trying not to wake the children. *Not yet. Not before we have a chance to finish.* She reached for his shoulders, needing something to hold onto, something to anchor herself with. Her fingers tangled in Jarem's wings.

He pulled back and thrust again. "Touch my wings, Meredith." It was a plea.

She did so, her heart fluttering in excitement at his gasps and the jerking of his cock inside her. Inspiration made her smile. "Later, I am going to climb into your lap and make you come just by doing this to your wings."

His thrusts speeded, and he whispered something in the Sakk language.

"You would come like that, wouldn't you?" she teased.

"We'll find out. Won't we?"

Meredith made a concerted effort at rubbing and combing his wings. He grabbed her wrists and pinned them down.

"Not this time."

Another order. Her body reacted fiercely every time he did that.

"And now, I claim you."

His thrusts made it clear he wasn't content with anything less than that. Meredith suddenly understood how Sakk women could stay with a single mate until he died. If this was how intent they were, she could easily imagine staying with Jarem that long.

That was the last coherent thought she managed. The rest was overlapping sensation. His heat sent her spiraling over the edge, and Meredith screamed.

She winced at the thought that it was sure to wake the children.

"Shhh," Jarem soothed her. "They have to learn to sleep through our sounds as all children do." He stroked a fingertip across her lips. "I plan on doing a lot of this. If it wouldn't distress you."

Meredith purred at the idea of more sex like this.

As if arguing his idea of what children needed, a piercing cry split the air.

Jarem levered himself out of her, then rose to his full height beside the bed. He glanced around and locked on the off white bundle placed on top of her bedside table. "Is that my *cu-wrap*?"

Meredith nodded. He'd left one in her quarters, so they could lounge in comfort after Alice's bedtime. "I wasn't sure if...if you would be coming back."

He chuckled. "There will be a lot more of my belongings here. Tomorrow." Jarem grasped the wrap and fastened it on.

Meredith pulled the nightshirt from the bedside table over her head, smoothing it over her thighs. "You might want to let me. That's Sammy, and she's...difficult."

He raised an eyebrow in challenge. "What do humans call a sire?"

"We have a lot of words for it." Why was he asking? Besides the obvious that he now was Sammy's father, of course.

"What do babies call their sires?"

"Usually Daddy."

He nodded and headed toward the cribs.

Thankfully, Alice and Todd had proven they could sleep through one of Sammy's fits earlier in the day. Short of some wiggling from Alice, neither of the two stirred.

Sammy stopped crying at the sight of Jarem coming through the open doorway. He reached down for her, and she looked at him suspiciously.

"Come to Daddy, Sammy," he crooned. "Let the other babies sleep."

She put her arms up and let him lift her from the crib.

Jarem turned to Meredith, and she snapped her mouth shut. She wasn't sure what he'd done, but it was nothing short of a miracle.

And sexy. Jarem was hunk in a *cu-wrap*, holding a cranky baby. *And Janice said whoever I mated with would be excused from duty immediately and freed to do nothing but help me with the babies. If Sammy likes him this much, that's gold in a* cu-wrap. She decided hunk in a *cu-wrap* was better.

"What does she need?" he asked, snapping Meredith out of her stupor.

"Check her diaper, but I'm betting she's hungry again."

He trailed a hand down her ribs, probably noting how thin she was. His brow furrowed in what she would assume was worry. "Right away," he agreed.

Chapter Six

Six weeks later

"Her punishment is *what*?" Ellwood had never looked so horrified.

"Meredith agreed to it," Jannie reminded him patiently. "We've allowed her to choose her own mate. She won't just be handed off to a man in an arranged marriage."

"But she has to...?" He waved his hand in an uncertain motion.

"Give him at least two children. They will have to be conceived *in vitro*, and they won't be biologically hers, but since Meredith has made a life of looking after other people's children, that doesn't bother her. She'll bear them and give birth to them. By Sakk law, they will be legally her own children. They cannot be removed from her, unless she commits a felony under Sakk law."

"But—?"

"Yes, it will be a sexual relationship," she answered what was probably his complaint. "She *chose* her mate. One would assume, she's chosen a male that she won't mind a sexual relationship with, since they've consummated the relationship already."

In fact, Jannie had told a little white lie of sorts to arrange that. She'd told Meredith she would start searching for willing males, but she hadn't. Based on Beldon's assessment of Jarem, she'd guessed the promise of biological children would counter Jarem's misgivings about a relationship with Meredith. She'd guessed, and had been proven right, that Jarem would lay claim to Meredith immediately to keep fictitious 'other hopefuls' from making a move.

Ellwood's voice dragged her back to the conversation.

"Chose? Consummated? In other words, she's already married to this person?"

"Mated. Yes. Remember that Meredith has been here at the consulate for more than three months. She's had ample time to meet someone she wouldn't mind being mate to, and since the male in question is willing, there was no reason not to let her choose him."

He sighed, rubbing a hand across his forehead. "And what other *choice* was she given for punishments?"

"Two, actually."

He looked up at her expectantly.

"She could have left the consulate and faced the American justice system, or she could have stayed on lockdown within the consulate, doing whatever chores we found for her."

"For how long? What would the sentence have been?"

Jannie shrugged. "For the rest of her life, of course. Leaving the consulate meant she would face American justice."

"Not if you moved her to another consulate," he pointed out the obvious.

She smiled. "Now why did I never think of that?"

Ellwood shot her a sour look. "I know you, Janice."

Too well. "I needed a long-term solution for Meredith. If I moved her to another consulate, the US authorities would try to extradite her from wherever she was."

He grumbled his agreement to that. "Off the record..."

"Yes?"

"I'm glad you found a workable solution. It's going to be a tough sell to the authorities, but how are they going to argue it?"

"How, indeed?"

"Is there any word on adoptive families for the surrendered children? You have how many now?"

"Just the three so far. They'll be leaving on the ship tomorrow with their adoptive parents."

"So quickly? I thought it took three months to get people from Sakk to Earth."

"These parents aren't coming from Sakk. Remember, we have colonies and consulates on eighteen worlds, in addition to Sakk." It was a half-truth, but she didn't want to share the news of *who* would be adopting the children unless he asked directly.

The nest parents coming in on the ship that would take Jarem and his family out *had* been rerouted on their way to a seed world. A retiring nesting pair had agreed to stay on to take care of a new set of babies, until another couple could arrive from Sakk to take on the duties of care to adulthood for the toddlers in the group.

"And you believe you won't have problems placing any children who are surrendered?"

Jannie smiled widely. "We will have prospective adoptive parents at the consulate at all times. When children are surrendered, they will be placed with parents immediately."

He seemed stunned by that pronouncement. "So you won't be using a foster system at all?"

"No. It's kindest to the children if they are placed immediately with parents."

Ellwood nodded. "That should shut the naysayers up." He waved. "Have a good day, Janice. It seems I have a lot of work to do."

"You, too. Good luck!"

He groaned and then shut the connection. Jannie laughed. Ellwood complained about his job, but she suspected he liked the challenge and protested more than was necessary.

****

Master Beldon accompanied them aboard the ship. He walked ahead of them, armored, one hand on his sword hilt. It would have bothered Meredith if Jarem and Janice hadn't explained that it was ceremonial.

Meredith and Jarem came down the ramp behind him. Jarem had Todd cuddled to one shoulder and Sammy perched on the opposite hip; Meredith carried Alice. Each of the children held a favorite toy—Todd's attached to his wrist with a soft cuff, so he couldn't throw it, and Jarem had an overstuffed duffel bag full of supplies hooked over one shoulder.

179

Meredith had started to separate which toys they should take along and which they should leave behind for the next group of children, but Jarem had corrected her. The consulate had already stocked age-appropriate toys, supplies, furniture, and clothing up to 4T in both girls' and boys' styles. Since most of the toys had been gifts from warriors, they expected the children to take them along. At that point, Meredith had resorted to separating which toys they would have in the rooms aboard ship and which would be boxed to be transported directly to Jarem's ancestral home.

She'd done the same thing with the clothing. She'd boxed clothing that was more than two sizes larger than the children were currently wearing for storage aboard ship and had the rest sent to their quarters, just in case of growth spurts.

Since she was officially a Sakk mate, Meredith had been informed she was eligible for the stipend given before a mate moved to Sakk. She'd had to use hers to purchase from catalogs and online, but Meredith didn't mind. As she'd told Janice, "Give a woman unlimited credit, she's sure to find something she wants."

They'd spent the last week switching the babies over to the Sakk form of waste wraps and training wraps. Though it had taken Meredith time to get used to wrapping them correctly, she had to admit they were more comfortable and just as useful as disposable diapers. With the laundry machine set right next to the changing table, she used it as she would a diaper pail and started the wash once a day.

They'd settled into family life with a minimum of fuss. While Sammy had distrusted Meredith for nearly a month, she'd latched onto Jarem almost immediately. Todd was an easy baby who, much like Alice, loved everyone on sight.

Right on cue, Alice patted Meredith's chest with the stuffed bunny in her hand. "Mama."

Sammy glared at her and snuggled closer to Jarem. "No. Daddy."

Jarem laughed. "And it seems you each have the parent you wish to have, so no arguing, girls."

The warriors rushed back and forth, peeking looks at them as they made their way through the landing bay. Something told Meredith that it was busy work. Just an excuse to get a look at the babies coming aboard. One stopped to gape at them, then hurried along at a sharp sound from Beldon.

An armored man met them at the far side of the bay and bowed deeply. "Welcome aboard. Your rooms have been prepared. If anything is amiss, please let me know directly. Only older, widowed warriors are allowed in the nest areas. If you see anyone else in the area, report it immediately. For your safety, of course."

"We will," Meredith assured him.

Jarem started questioning him. "The furniture was set up as I requested? And the food requirements the cooks at the consulate sent along? Are your cooks prepared to handle the children's needs?"

The captain nodded. "Just as you specified. I will guarantee the young ones and your mate will be comfortable aboard my ship."

"Good. We should see our quarters then."

Beldon turned to them, placing a hand on each child's head in turn. Then he nodded to them. "You are in good hands. Have a safe trip."

He was gone before Meredith could thank him.

They followed the captain through the corridors, and Meredith tried to remember everything he pointed out: dining halls, the medical bay, and more. She turned her head, trying to find anything she could use as a landmark to find the garden again.

Jarem leaned close to her and whispered. "You and the babies won't be allowed to leave our quarters without guards. The lecture is for me, not you."

"Oh. Of course."

The captain stopped at a set of double doors and barked out a command in Sakk. The doors slid open, and Meredith headed inside. She stopped, gaping at the size of the space.

"Good God." It slipped out without decorum.

Jarem appeared beside her, smiling, one eyebrow raised. "Only the best for our children," he quipped. "Only the best for my mate."

"How...?" The rest didn't emerge. Too many questions fought to be the first out.

"The walls are temporary structures. This is a nest intended to bring dozens of matches from a seed world. Refitting it to be home to a family of five wasn't difficult, and these structures and furnishings can be reused for future family passages."

She wandered through the rooms, stunned. They'd set up a living room, dining room, and three bedrooms. The cribs, high chairs, playpens, and changing tables had all been relocated from their quarters in the consulate, complete with the Dr. Seuss's *Cat in the Hat* mobile hung over Todd's crib. They'd created a home in the nest room. There was even a small kitchenette area.

Most likely for heating formula for Todd and storing snacks.

A squeal of delight brought Meredith's head around. Sammy was running across the room with a cookie in each hand.

"Already at home."

Jarem nodded his agreement.

****

Three months later

Meredith smoothed her dress and fussed with Alice's curls. Sammy sighed in her sleep, curled up on the padded bench with her head on Jarem's thigh. To Jarem's other side, Todd slept soundly in a Sakk carry-basket. She wished she could be as calm about meeting Jarem's family as the children were.

Or as comfortable about how I look. Alice was wearing a *cazta* in deep purple and a pair of soft black Mary Janes with white bobby socks.

Sammy wore a baby blue ruffled dress that reached her knees, white tights, and a pair of high-top tennis shoes that matched the dress. Todd wore a pair of infant dress pants with a white shirt and brown boots.

By comparison, Meredith felt more than a little silly in the Disney-style floor-length gown with matching gloves that reached her upper arms. *If it was yellow, I'd be the very image of Belle from* Beauty and the Beast. It wasn't yellow, of course. It was a rich Hunter green that complemented her eyes.

"Cup." Alice put her hands out to Meredith, opening and closing them in a 'gimme' motion. "Cup, mama. Peeze." Though she'd reached physical milestones faster than most children Meredith knew, her speech patterns hadn't evolved yet.

She's only a year. Next week, she reminded herself. If her speech patterns didn't start maturing soon, there was plenty of time to have the Sakk healers work with her to improve it.

Meredith smiled and pulled a cup of fortified almond milk out of the bag between her ankles. In the next minute, it was stuffed in Alice's mouth, and she twisted the closest curl to her face around her hand.

Nearly naptime. It was a safe bet all three children would be asleep when they reached Jarem's home.

"We'll be there soon," the man in question intoned.

Meredith nodded in response.

Her apprehension made little sense to her. The message that had arrived from Jarem's parents the month before made it seem that they weren't adverse to the less-than-customary additions to their family. Still, she worried that they were being gracious to cover their disapproval.

He reached out and took Meredith's hand. "They'll love you. All of you."

She nodded, though she wasn't sure that was true.

Jarem cocked his head to one side and seemed to consider her. "Something is bothering you."

"You're so sure they'll like us."

"Love you," he corrected.

Meredith sighed.

"They will. The only reason they didn't meet us at the shuttle was that they have no transport large enough to bring all of us to the ancestral home." He'd explained that before.

"How can you be so sure?"

"I've told you about my family."

She nodded. He was the only child of a couple who were now too old to have more children. He had two older uncles, widowers who had produced only female children, all of whom had left the nest and mated before Jarem was even adolescent. "There are no children in the house and haven't been since you were a child."

And Jarem is thirty years old. That's a long time without children. Would his parents and uncles be too old to accept the many changes children would bring into their lives?

185

As if he heard that question, Jarem shook his head. "You've agreed to carry at least two children for me. Even if we don't have a boy, Todd is able to carry on our family name into the next generation. The worst thing they can imagine is the family dying out and the ancestral home falling to ruin."

Meredith took a calming breath. "Okay. You know them better than I do." *That goes without saying. I don't know them at all.*

The miles passed in near silence, and Alice fell asleep. Finally, the transport glided to a halt. Jarem lifted Sammy to his shoulder, and she opened sleepy eyes.

"We home, Daddy?" she grumbled.

"Yes. We're home." He stood and lifted Todd's basket in his other hand.

Meredith placed the empty cup in the bag, looped it over her shoulder, and lifted Alice to the opposite one.

A knock at the double doors seemed to ask permission to open them.

"We are prepared," Jarem offered in Sakk.

The doors opened, and Jarem stepped down ahead of her. One of the warriors held out a hand to help Meredith down. She took it, self-conscious though doing so wouldn't have bothered her on Earth. It wasn't something Sakk males typically did. Only the fact that Jarem's hands were full of sleeping or sleepy children excused another male daring to touch her for any reason but an emergency situation.

A ground-shaking cheer went up, and Alice startled in Meredith's arms. Thankfully, she didn't start screaming and crying. Instead, she rubbed a fist into her eye and looked around.

One hand went out and cycled in the 'gimme' move again. Alice started bouncing up and down on Meredith's arm. "Ba-oon, Mama. Ba-oon. Ba-oon."

She looked up, stunned by the sight of not only a massive crowd but further the banners, ribbons, and...sure enough, balloons. Though Meredith couldn't identify what they were made of, they clearly resembled fully globe-shaped balloons in bright colors and marked with Sakk glyphs in contrasting colors.

Sammy snapped a look at Alice, followed her line of sight, and started making the same request of Jarem. Todd, true to form, slept through it all.

People closed on them from all sides, reaching out to touch the children. Meredith's heart pounded out a warning. This had the potential to become a mob, if things went badly.

Jarem smiled and greeted one person after another, and she reasoned that he wouldn't do that if he believed there was danger inherent in this scene.

"Clear a hole," a voice thundered in Sakk.

The crowd parted, and a slight, older woman came down the aisle, surrounded by three hulking men. Meredith didn't have to ask who she was.

Jarem's mother. Arrayanne. It was more difficult to identify the three men, since the brothers looked very much alike. Meredith offered a smile, hoping for the best.

They looked from one baby to the next, seemingly stunned to silence. Completely oblivious to the situation, the two girls continued to ask for balloons.

At last, Arrayanne said something in Sakk Meredith didn't understand. The male at her back marched back the way they'd come. He returned a few moments later, his hands behind his back. When he reached the others, he said something she didn't catch.

Arrayanne turned and accepted two balloons from him. She offered one to each little girl.

Sammy hesitated to take hers but did so at Jarem's urging. One of the brothers reached out and tied the ribbon around her wrist to avoid the usual loss of balloon catastrophe most toddlers suffered. Sammy turned and hugged Jarem, shooting shy looks at his family.

Alice started clapping and laughing. She reached for the bright-colored globe and patted it clumsily.

"It is so good to hear babies laugh again," Arrayanne noted wistfully.

Meredith dusted off the Sakk she'd been learning. *"These young ones need to laugh."*

"The whole town rejoices."

"I can see that." Who could miss it? Of course, it made sense. Two little girls meant the possibility of mates for the sons of the families gathered to meet them.

"Are the young ones hungry?"

Jarem answered that time. *"Anyone willing to offer a cake or pie will soon find themselves in favor with the girls. Todd has not progressed to more than vegetable paste, grain mush, and milk."*

Meredith laughed at the rush of people towards what she suspected were food carts. She had no doubts their children were going to be spoiled rotten.

Section Two:
Clipped Wings

Hayley and Parrin; Holly and Trabor

Chapter Seven

Hayley smoothed the layers of purple silk over her thighs, her nerves jumping. Two weeks ago, she'd been just another secretary. Then her sister had convinced her to come to the Sakk consulate in Hartford to be tested. Hayley had gone along as a lark, just one more time she would go along with Holly's flights of fancy.

Only this time, it hadn't proven to be a wild fantasy. From the moment the testing pad had turned blue, indicating that Holly and Hayley were crossbred human-Sakk females, her life had changed at a whirlwind pace.

Holly's question—spoken aloud but to no one in particular—that Hayley's 'birth defect' may have been partial wings had sent the Sakk into a frenzy, and they'd all but begged to examine her medically.

There had been no need to ask what the scans had shown. The flurry of wings fluttering in excitement had sent Hayley's stomach into a similar tizzy. Apparently, though the alien race was winged, and they'd reportedly found a winged Earth-born child, it had never occurred to them that crossbred Sakk, born on Earth, might have stubs of wings that had been surgically removed by doctors who didn't know what they signified.

In less than an hour, she'd gone from an office drone to something akin to a princess.

Whoever said fairy tales don't come true?

Reinforcing the mental image of her new status as royalty, the Sakk prince had arrived by shuttle from Arlington, Virginia within an hour of her medical scans, just to meet Holly and Hayley and to welcome them back to the Sakk race.

Of course, his visit hadn't stopped there. Plans for their 'coming out' into Sakk society had been planned meticulously. Their psychological profiles had been dissected, their preferences nitpicked into minutia, and their relationship examined in detail.

Though Holly and Hayley had never been apart, they'd agreed that living in the same town would be as palatable to them as being married...*mated* into the same household. That pronouncement had pleased the Sakk immensely, because it meant spreading the genes farther than they would with the two sisters marrying two close male relatives.

An attack of nerves had Hayley turning toward the floor-to-ceiling mirror to survey her image. She hardly recognized herself. Beauticians had pampered and primped her, leaving her feeling very much like a bride on her wedding day.

That's what I will be today...if I choose to be.

In mere moments, Hayley and Holly would be introduced to hundreds of Sakk men in the hopes that they would choose mates from among them.

As if thoughts of her younger sister summoned her, Holly bounced through the door into Hayley's quarters without so much as a knock. That wasn't a new thing for Holly; she'd been doing it since they were toddlers.

The green of Holly's dress matched both her eyes and her name. Her sister's golden hair fell in curls around her elfin face. And her heels were high enough that Hayley wondered how she could walk on them at all, let alone with such grace. Holly stopped short and spun, showing off the short, strapless confection she'd be wearing to the 'meeting day'.

By comparison, Hayley's dress was sedate. It reached to her ankles and had wide straps of wispy material that nearly covered her scars. Her shoes were moderate heels that reminded her of Cinderella's glass slippers.

They were as different as night and day. Hayley was level-headed, and Holly was prone to flights of fancy. Hayley was as dark as Holly was fair. Holly's heels brought them nearly even in height, compensating for the more than half a foot difference in their heights. And they were both supposed to find mates? Something told Hayley that would be easier said than done.

"Well...? What do you think?" Holly demanded.

Hayley made a show of her consideration. "You look great."

She only wished she felt as secure about her own appearance. When the Sakk had suggested something backless or strapless for her, Hayley had balked. A lifetime of hiding the scars on the back of her shoulders was hard to squelch. In the end, she'd agreed to this dress as a compromise. Anyone looking closely enough would be able to see the scars, but the men weren't supposed to get that close.

"You're thinking about it again," Holly chided.

"I know." There was nothing more to be said about it. There was no reasoning that the scars were a source of pride now. Hayley wasn't proud of them and probably never would be.

Holly enfolded her in a hug. "They're going to love you. You'll see."

Though Hayley doubted it, she nodded her agreement.

****

Half an hour later, Hayley and Holly entered the large room set aside for meetings of Sakk males with Earth-born females, each of them on an arm of the Sakk prince—or Sakkra, as he preferred to be called. There were fewer men than she'd anticipated—perhaps three dozen in all, suggesting they might be arranging the meetings by locality the males lived in instead of performing a mass meeting of all the males at once.

It would make both of us finding a man in the same area easier.

Men stopped speaking and turned to look at them. The hunger in their eyes stepped up the tension in the room several notches, and Hayley shivered in response.

In a flash, one of the closer males whipped the cloak off his back and offered it with a tip of his head. Hayley stopped and stared at him, wondering what it meant.

Sakkra's voice was calm and sounded of amusement. "I am certain Ms. Harrison is not chilled. Perhaps the closeness of all the males has unnerved her."

His head came up, his eyes wide, and the young man stepped back, seemingly chastised.

Hayley's face heated at the response. "It's all right. Really. Thank you for the offer."

He smiled like a teenaged boy whose crush had noticed him and tipped his head again. "Any time, Ms. Harrison."

Sakkra led them down the center of the room to the plush chairs set up for them. Sandwiches and canapés were set on a small table between the two chairs, and an additional chair was set to the outside of each of theirs.

Most probably for the men to sit in while they meet us.

There was a door behind the chairs, and Hayley wondered about it. If there was a close door, why were they walking between the two rows of men?

Maybe it's some sort of tradition. Considering the Sakk culture, that made sense.

They'd barely settled when one of the men approached Holly. "Would you like a drink, Ms. Harrison?"

She smiled widely, flirting with him already. "I'd love one, thank you."

He moved his attention to Hayley. "And you, Ms. Harrison?"

"All of you really should call us Holly and Hayley. Two Ms. Harrisons is going to get confusing, don't you think?"

He seemed stunned by the idea. "As you wish." There was a moment of silence. "Would you care for a drink...Hayley?"

"Please."

"Alcoholic or non?"

Keeping a clear head sounded more appealing than steeling her nerves. "Non-alcoholic, please."

"Alcoholic," Holly chimed in. "It is a party, I guess."

The Sakk man withdrew, leaving them momentarily alone. Heads tilted toward him as he made his way to the refreshment table.

He's passing the news that we want to be addressed by our first names. Considering Sakk mores, it had to be a monumental change for them.

The first of the men approached and whispered with the guards—armed with swords and positioned around Hayley and Holly—before he stcppcd past them. He bowed deeply to Hayley and Holly. "I am Lariam of Tracia. May I sit and meet with you, Hayley and Holly?"

Holly waved him closer, and he took the seat to her side. Hayley's heart ached at that move. Already, the men were showing a preference for her sister. Some things never changed.

There was a moment of uncomfortable silence. "Perhaps I should tell you about myself," Lariam offered. "I understand your interests are very different, and what may appeal to one may not appeal to the other."

Holly smiled in a way that told Hayley she was plotting something. Before Hayley could warn Lariam, Holly started speaking.

"That is an excellent idea, but there is something you should tell the others. It's very important."

Hayley felt a sick headache coming on, but she waited to see what Holly was up to.

His brows furrowed. "Of course. Anything that will make you at ease," he vowed.

Holly leaned toward him, showing an indecent amount of cleavage. "There is a...family tradition."

Family tradition? What family tradition?

The Sakk were eating up every word. Even the guards were paying keen attention to Holly's caution.

"The older sister marries...mates first. So, impressing Hayley is what you should be focusing on. I won't choose someone until she has, and I'll be choosing someone from the same area she does."

Hayley snapped. "That's not—"

"No complaints," Holly cut off her rebuttal that there was no such tradition. "You may only be two years older than I am, but you are older."

There was no arguing that part of what she said. *But what does she intend to accomplish?*

Lariam offered a slight nod. "I understand. Thank you for that information." He hesitated and then moved to Hayley's side.

Before he could open his mouth to speak to her, the male with the drinks reappeared. Hayley grabbed the closest glass and took a gulp of it. The burn moving down her throat and chest caused her to gasp in surprise.

"Um...that was your sister's drink," he apologized.

"I know." Hayley took another drink of it and handed it off to Holly.

Holly looked pleased with herself.

No surprise. I am going to kill her later.

****

"Would you like to dance, Hayley?" Jamil, the newest of her suitors, asked.

After an hour sitting on her backside, getting up sounded appealing, and the Sakk music that was playing in the background was perfect for a slow dance. "Yes. I would. Thank you."

He offered his hand, and Hayley took it, sliding to her feet. The Sakk parted to give them room to dance. A few of the males shot Jamil dirty looks, but none of them made a move toward him.

Hayley settled her hands on his broad shoulders, and his wrapped loosely around her waist. They started to sway together, and Hayley took advantage of his proximity to consider him.

Jamil was tall and dark-haired.

Or did they call it feathered? The Sakk didn't properly have hair, since the hair-like curls on their head were long, fluffy feathers, soft as down.

He liked many of the same things she did. Overall, Jamil wasn't a poor choice, if she was going to choose a man.

That thought short-circuited at the feeling of one of his hands massaging her shoulder. His fingers were following the line of scar tissue, which meant he was trying to confirm the rumors and stories about her clipped wings.

That was hurtful, but what was disconcerting was the arousal pooling low in her abdomen at his touch.

"Stop it." It was out before Hayley had a chance to reason why it bothered her. It was both an intrusion and an annoyance to her, and she wanted Jamil as far away from her as she could push him.

Before she lost her composure and did so, another male closed on them. "She told you to stop what you're doing," he warned.

Jamil released her, and Hayley started to ease away, the hair rising on the back of her neck in warning. Guards came from every direction, more than a few with their hands on the hilts of their weapons.

"And I did," Jamil growled back, making an expansive movement with his arms.

Her next step back was misplaced. Hayley caught her heel in the hem of her dress and pitched backward. One set of male arms caught and lifted her, while guards rushed past her. Her ankle twisted with a sharp pain that drew a shout from her.

In the next heartbeat, all hell broke loose. Wings closed partway around her, blocking Hayley's view of the commotion.

The man holding her started shouting orders. "Remove Holly. Place a guard on her quarters. Tell medical to expect us." With that, he was in motion, sprinting away with Hayley in his arms. "Clear the room," he shouted back.

Hayley held on to the edges of his *ullium* armor, her heart pounding. Every step sent little reminders of her injured ankle up her leg, and tears pooled in her eyes.

Doors parted. Shouts in Sakk followed them down the corridors. Finally, her rescuer lowered Hayley to a *bio bed*.

Her heart pounding and her breathing strangled, she looked up at the guard over her as he backed away to let the healers tend to her.

He was beautiful. In many ways, he reminded her of Holly. His eyes were a deep green and his hair a gold that was only a few shades away from the color of her sister's hair. He was one of the smaller Sakk males she'd seen, but his wings were long and graceful. His appearance was at odds with his status as a soldier. If she were meeting him out of armor, Hayley would have guessed he was a poet or an artist.

****

Parrin stared at Hayley Harrison, his lungs deliciously full of her feminine scent. Whatever male she chose would be a lucky man, and with

201

his town's meeting day with her scheduled for nearly a week away, it was unlikely she would find no one to choose by then.

That a given...and she being *not* his woman, Parrin backed away from her, mourning the loss of her in his arms already. He stopped short at the end of her arm and glanced down at the hand still gripping his armor.

"Oh." Her hand retreated, and her cheeks darkened in a demure blush, but her eyes remained locked with his.

The meek exclamation of sound matched the woman. She wasn't a 'party girl,' as her younger sister was. Hayley was a gentle female. He'd lay wagers that her likes and dislikes were more refined than Holly's were. Though Sakk males were at the whim of females, he couldn't imagine any man wanting Holly instead of Hayley.

A tear stained her cheek, and Parrin ached to wipe it away for her.

She is not my woman. That reminder burned; he backed away and offered her a soft cloth instead.

Her throat bobbed, and she thanked him in a low voice.

"Captain?" the master healer inquired.

Parrin turned to him, expecting rebuke. There was none forthcoming.

"I have secured the doors, as Sakkra requested. You are ordered to remain here until we are given the clearance to release the locks."

He straightened, recognizing the order to remain as Hayley's personal guard.

"Understood." *And it will give me time in Hayley's company.*

That was a scandalous thought, but as long as he didn't voice it publicly, no one had to know he harbored it.

****

Treating her ankle didn't take long. Even a break could be repaired in a matter of days, so a sprain was akin to putting a Band-Aid on a cut for the Sakk.

Not that they used Band-Aids, of course. Only the deepest of cuts required bandaging, and those were typically treated with pressure bandages.

That left Hayley with a lot of time and little to do but sit on the *bio bed*. They'd offered electronic amusement to her: television, Internet, movies, and eBooks, but who could relax and focus on them while there was still a lockdown?

"You're sure Holly is okay?" she asked again.

The guard who'd saved her nodded. "She was never in danger, but having females around when the males are already hot-blooded is not a good combination."

"Then why are we still on lockdown?"

The corner of his mouth curved up in a grim smile. "Sakkra is deciding on the punishment for the two males that started this. Until that is settled, the other males will be on edge."

Hayley wanted to argue that they didn't deserve punishment for it, but she knew better. With the problems facing the Sakk race, the males would have to be on their best behavior or risk a war like the one they had millennia ago.

The silence was potent. Hayley decided to break it. "Thank you for saving me."

"The males wouldn't dared have harmed you," he dismissed her.

It wasn't the answer she'd been hoping for.

As if he realized that, the guard snuck a look her direction. "It was my honor and pleasure to do so."

Her heart fluttered at the smoldering look. "So... What is your name?"

His brows went up in seeming surprise. "Parrin, Ms. Harrison."

"I thought I asked all of you to call me Hayley?" *Am I flirting? Well, why shouldn't I? He is drop-dead gorgeous.*

A slight color flooded his cheeks, and he tipped his head. "It would be my pleasure, Hayley."

"Would you talk to me?"

His Adam's apple bobbed, and he nodded. "What would you like to talk about?"

At a loss, she grasped at the first thing that came to mind. "Tell me about your town."

Parrin's eyes got a faraway look to them. "Sutrane is a lovely little town. A farming community. An artisan colony. We have live music and theatre, museums, and expansive markets with both food and cloth. Most people walk from place to place instead of taking transports. Children have ponds and fields to play in. Of course, we have a constabulary to make sure unattended children do not injure themselves."

"Close to the mountains?" Hayley's memory for every town on Sakk was weak, but she remembered that there were several farming communities near the western mountains.

His smile was warm and wistful. "Not far. Half a day's walk or less than an hour by transport."

She considered what to ask next. "Are you an artist or a farmer?"

"A little of both, I suppose. My family owns a small farm. Not one of the largest in our area. I enjoy the arts, so my free time is spent sculpting and painting."

"You have brothers and sisters?"

"One of each. Both younger than I am. My brother Jerrol is only a few *yans* younger than I am. My sister was a late addition to the family. Abia will reach puberty in a little over a *yan*."

Parrin's eyes lit up when he talked about his family. Hayley realized this was what she'd missed meeting men in that circus their laws demanded.

And it's worse on their world, where men still fight to choose mates. Parrin was someone she could like, but how could you tell that when every move was regimented and watched by dozens of other hopeful suitors?

"Have I said something wrong, Hayley?" Parrin asked.

"No." An idea occurred to her. "So your town is a small one. There aren't many Sakk males from your town here on Earth then."

"Four others, I believe."

"Perfect."

He hesitated before he answered. "Is it?"

"I believe it might be."

Parrin seemed taken aback, but before he could ask her what she meant, the doors parted, and Sakkra entered the medical bay. The prince waved Parrin away, and the young guard left without more than a bow to his prince.

One of the healers rushed to bring a chair for Sakkra, and the prince settled into it. "My apologies for this deplorable scene, Hayley."

"They were beating each other senseless. I thought that was only supposed to happen on your home world."

Sakkra winced but didn't reply.

"And now I hear you're going to punish them. I have to admit, I'm not really comfortable with that, despite what they did to each other."

"Precisely what I needed to speak to you about."

That stole whatever would have emerged from her mouth next. Hayley stared at him.

"The reason the two males got into the fistfight is that Storel believes Jamil knocked you off your feet."

"When I fell?" she inquired.

He nodded. "If it was a misunderstanding, the worst they receive will be a reprimand. If it—"

"A misunderstanding," she assured him. "The heel of my shoe got caught in my hem. Jamil didn't hit me." Hayley sighed. "Maybe I should wear a shorter dress for the next meeting day."

"You're willing to continue then." He seemed relieved to hear it.

The Sakk males were probably upset that I might choose not to.

But there were still issues to be resolved about that. "Which is what I wanted to talk to *you* about."

He tensed slightly, and the healers went quiet, shooting nervous looks at each other.

"About?"

"I figure...if someone wants something to change, someone has to talk to the head honcho."

Sakkra cocked his head to one side, then nodded. "I would imagine that is true, assuming I am a head honcho."

"You are. I met a man today."

His eyes gleamed at the news.

"Don't misunderstand me. I'm not prepared to make a choice this second."

"Very well. What are you saying...or asking?"

"Today's meeting was a zoo."

Sakkra looked around as if seeking input from the healers. "Zoo? I don't understand."

Idiom. Sakk males were often lost by idiom. "It was...too much. A smaller group might be better. Less crowded. Less stressful."

"It might." Sakkra seemed to consider it. "You want to meet the males in smaller groups?"

"I would prefer a small town anyway, and since Holly has left the choice of place to me..." Hayley leaned toward him. "Could it be arranged? Meeting the men from a small town?"

He was silent for a moment, seemingly mulling something over. "You want to meet males from small towns only?"

"For now. If I don't find someone I like there, we could move to the men from larger towns...but meeting them in smaller groups." Hayley secretly believed she wouldn't need more than one more meeting day to announce a choice, if she worded her next request well.

He nodded slowly. "If it would lessen your stress and make you happier, of course."

Hayley considered how to phrase the rest.

"Is there a particular town you would like to start with?" His smile said Sakkra knew precisely what she was after.

A knot lodged in her throat, and Hayley swallowed it. "The man I met told me about a town." *Either he approves or disapproves.*

"Do you recall the town's name? Or the male's name? I can find out what town he's from for you."

"The town was called..." The name escaped her, and Hayley wrestled with what Parrin had told her. "Soothgrain?" she ventured.

Sakkra's brow furrowed in confusion.

The master healer stepped forward. "I believe, Ms. Hayley, that the town might have been Sutrane?"

Sakkra shot the healer a smile. "Ah. Sutrane. A lovely town. Let me see how many men we have from that area."

Hayley bit her tongue to avoid admitting she knew how many men were from Sutrane, more or less. When she trusted herself not to blurt it out, she offered a smile that felt strained. "Thank you. May I return to my room now? I'd like to check on Holly."

"Absolutely. One of the guards will escort you, if that is all right with you?"

They'd never required guards for Hayley and Holly before, but perhaps the men were still 'hot-blooded'. "Sure. I'll wait here for him." On some level, it surprised her that Sakkra wasn't going to escort her personally.

He rose and smoothed his *cuzta*. "I will send him in. In the meantime, I have to change the schedule of meetings."

Her heart light, Hayley waved goodbye to him.

****

"We are *in*," Trabor announced, strutting into the barracks room he shared with Parrin and two other mid-level officers.

Parrin chuckled at Trabor's human euphemisms. "In what, *homie*? You've found a party tonight?"

"No, my friend. The schedule of meeting days for the two lovely ladies has been rearranged." He stopped at the mirror and started primping his deep red hair feathers.

"Changed? We've been moved forward?" That was big news.

"Not just moved forward. We meet the ladies tomorrow."

I've already met one of them. It was amazing that Trabor didn't already know it.

209

Trabor continued, oblivious to his hesitation. "I don't know what caused the change, but the entire schedule has been rearranged to work small towns to large."

Parrin smiled. "You know I was a guard at the meeting today."

Trabor turned and gaped at him. "I'd forgotten that." He hurried over and settled on the edge of Parrin's bunk. "Tell me about them. What are they like?"

"As different as can be from each other. The younger is like a wild bird on the wing. The elder is dark and refined."

He scowled. "Unlikely to choose our small town then. Neither sounds as if they would choose Sutrane. The younger will want excitement."

"We are close to several larger towns, capable of providing that. You visit them often enough." In fact, Trabor might be a good choice for Holly.

"True, but the elder will prefer a large town with its many refinements. Rumor has it they have never been apart."

"I've heard the idea to move to smaller towns was Hayley's idea. That's the elder," he supplied for Trabor, since it was unlikely he'd read the files on them as most of the males had. "And I have heard their nest has a tradition that the eldest chooses a mate first. Holly won't choose first and will follow the elder, wherever Hayley settles."

Trabor smiled slyly. "Then we must convince the elder to choose Sutrane."

Bitter anger welled in Parrin's gut. "I would not be overly familiar with Hayley. She took offense to one of the males she met today, and there was a brawl at the meeting." He considered that. "Perhaps that is why she asked to meet males from smaller towns." Surely she hadn't asked for Sutrane in particular.

"Really? Why weren't the alarms set off?"

Parrin waved off the suggestion. "It was two errant males. Hardly something that required more than a few guards."

Trabor's brows went up, and a knowing smile curved his lips. "But the guards there would have protected the females and broken up the fight. Which did you do, Parrin, my old friend?"

Heat worked its way up his neck and cheeks. Parrin cleared his throat. Trabor waited patiently for an answer.

"I took Hayley to medical."

"A female was injured?"

His horror at the idea was understandable. A male who injured a female could be killed for it. Even an accident that caused a female to be injured held the most severe punishments.

A male who was not constantly aware of a female, his own or not, wasn't trusted with a female of his own. Since only one in a little less than two hundred males ever got a mate, losing your slim chance at it would be a crushing blow to a male.

Parrin reminded himself that Trabor had asked a question. "Hayley tripped. I don't know if the males will be held responsible for it, since she tripped backing away from their altercation." Personally, he hoped they would, but that would be Sakkra's choice and not his own.

Trabor sighed and pushed a hand through his hair. "Perhaps being the first to meet the ladies after such a scene is not a gift." He shot a calculating look up and down Parrin's body. "Or perhaps you are in and do not know it."

"What are you talking about?" Parrin thought he knew, but it was outrageous to suggest such a thing. He'd barely spoken to Hayley.

Trabor laughed heartily. "Do me a favor, old friend."

"What favor would that be?"

"Put in a good word for me with the young...with Holly." He rose and ambled away, still laughing, while Parrin fought for the proper words to vent his outrage.

****

Hayley stood before the mirror again, surveying her reflection.

Sakkra had taken her musing about wearing a shorter dress to heart. Today's outfit was roughly based on the design of the first dress but just shorter than knee length.

It was purple, as the first had been. When Hayley asked, she'd been told purple was the color worn by females that had wings or had given birth to a winged female child.

On the orders of the healers, her modest heels had been replaced with Mary Jane-style flats. Though they'd healed her sprained ankle, the healers maintained that Hayley needed to rest it for a week.

Other than that, she was just as primped as she'd been the day before. The beauticians brought in for them had arranged Hayley's hair in an up-do and left curling tendrils floating around her face.

It was all too easy to imagine herself as sexy, and that was something she'd rarely imagined. Hayley had always envisioned herself as gawky and scarred. It was hardly a sexy image.

But the reflection told another story. Hayley's heart fluttered in excitement. She was a sexy woman, setting out to meet a man she wanted.

A knock brought her attention to the corridor door.

"Yes?" she called out.

"Are you prepared, Ms. Harrison?"

More than prepared. "Yes. I believe I am."

****

It took only a moment to spot Parrin. He was in the far corner of the room, talking to a young man with burgundy hair. Hayley tried not to stare at him, but the looks Holly and Sakkra shot her said she'd failed miserably.

As they had the day before, all the men stopped talking and turned to watch them enter the room. The redhead leaned toward Parrin, whispered something, and Parrin scowled at him.

Hayley looked away, unsure of herself again.

She settled into the chair set up for her and repeated her order of a non-alcoholic drink.

When she looked up, a dark-haired Sakk man was already approaching.

Damn. Hayley had been hoping Parrin would meet them first. *Relax. It's probably tradition. Much of Sakk culture is tied up in tradition.*

She pasted on a smile that felt strained and settled in to meet the men in whatever order was required by their tradition.

****

Parrin found himself watching Hayley avidly. Every man that approached her stepped up his frustration another notch.

What if Trabor was correct and Hayley had chosen Sutrane for him and not for his stories about the town? It was such an appealing premise, he could hardly control his arousal at the thought.

Stop it. I am not a pre-prime buck anymore. I can control myself. He stopped short of reasoning that Hayley was just another woman. There was no such thing as 'just another woman'. And if there was, Hayley Harrison wasn't it.

Korr backed away from the ladies with a bow, and Trabor started forward. Unlike the other males, he didn't sit at Hayley's side. The hot-headed young cock made a beeline for Holly and sank into the chair with a wide smile for the ladies. It was a unique entry that had the possibility of alienating them...or making a favorable impression on the ladies in question.

Let's hope he makes that favorable impression on Holly and not on Hayley.

****

Hayley watched the cocky newcomer schmooze Holly in amazement. Sakk men were usually accommodating, deferring to Earth-born women. This one was self-confident and not afraid to flaunt it.

Moreover, he'd gone to Holly's side and not Hayley's. Since Holly's announcement the day before, none of the men had chosen to sit next to Holly.

Holly seemed to be eating up the newcomer's banter. It was the usual...trying to impress her with his family's holdings, the types of things he gauged she might like to do, and on and on.

Good. Maybe she'll decide she likes him.

Hayley searched out Parrin, watching his gaze slide away as hers locked on him. A smile flirted at her lips.

"So... Tell me, Trabor," Holly purred. "Are you close friends with the blond over there?"

Hayley snapped a look of disbelief at her. What was Holly doing? She couldn't be thinking about choosing Parrin herself.

Trabor glanced Parrin's way, and his smile widened. "Parrin? You could say that. We went to school together, a *yan* apart. Our homes are very close, no more than a quarter of the way across town from each other."

"Do you think your friend likes to dance?"

"I'm not certain. Why don't we call him over here and find out?"

Trabor yelled out Parrin's name and waved him closer.

Hayley took a calming breath and looked up at Parrin as he approached.

"These lovely ladies would like to dance, Parrin. I was certain you would oblige one."

Without delay, Parrin offered Hayley his hand. She placed a trembling hand in his and let him help her to her feet.

****

Parrin swallowed hard at the feeling of Hayley's hand in his. *I have to be dreaming.* But he knew he wasn't.

Hayley took a step forward and wrapped her arms around his neck, going up on her toes slightly to accomplish it. Parrin hesitated a moment before he wrapped his hands around her waist.

She'd only protested when Jamil put his hands on her shoulders. As a guard, Parrin hadn't reacted to that move, because Jamil hadn't been moving his hands down her body to inappropriate touches. He still wasn't sure what had upset Hayley about the move, but he wasn't about to repeat it.

They started to sway together, her body enticing his to semi-readiness.

Not a good idea. I need to keep my errant body under control.

"I never thanked you for helping me the other day," Hayley breathed.

His lips quirked up. "Actually, you did."

216

She smiled a knowing little feminine smile. "I think you're right."

There were many things Parrin wanted to ask, but he was afraid he would be, as Trabor would put it, pushing his luck. Instead, he opted for a compliment. "You look lovely today, Hayley."

"Lovelier than yesterday?"

How does a man not offend? "I believe I like this dress better than the last, but the lady herself is always lovely." This dress was shorter and showed off her legs. Not as short as the dress her younger sister wore, though.

Her cheeks went a stunning shade of red. "Why thank you, Parrin."

That spelled the end of his control. His cock went hard and heavy behind his *cuzta*. Hayley gasped, and he winced, anticipating her reaction to his erection.

Her color rose another notch, and Hayley nestled closer to him. "Did you know I requested to meet men from your town next?"

He shook his head, at a loss for words.

"Do you know why I asked for that?"

"No." Parrin felt they were closer together, though he was sure he hadn't closed the distance between them.

She swiveled her hips against him, stealing Parrin's breath.

"Are you offering to be my mate, Hayley?"

Hayley went up on tiptoe, whispering 'yes' into his lips...just before she kissed him.

****

Parrin didn't waste a second; he parted her lips and made the most of the kiss. In a matter of heartbeats, her knees were trembling and her body hummed in awareness of the man holding her in his arms.

Holly laughed, and a masculine hoot followed.

Parrin eased out of the kiss, and Hayley stared up at him, her heart pounding.

Holly's arms wrapped around both of them and squeezed tight. "I knew it!" She loosened her grip and started bouncing up and down. "I knew you two would be the perfect pair. I knew it."

Hayley smiled. "Your turn," she reminded her younger sister.

"No problem." Holly turned to Trabor and all but jumped into his arms. She waved them away. "Go on. Get busy."

Hayley looked up at Parrin.

His expression was deep and considering. "That is your choice, Hayley."

Her stomach squirming, Hayley managed to gasp out another 'yes'.

Parrin nodded, lifted her into his arms, and marched from the room with a cadre of Sakkra's best guards surrounding them. Though he wasn't rushing, Hayley's head spun at the speed of events. She'd barely met Parrin, and she was fully invested in having sex with the man, followed closely by marrying him, a mating for life. If anyone had told her days ago that she would embrace this—hell, throw herself wholeheartedly into it—Hayley would have told that person he was insane.

The guards reached the door to her quarters first and opened it to let them pass. A confusing rush of Sakk words followed them through the opening, and the door closed behind them.

I have to learn the Sakk language. Of course, she had the three-month trek to Sakk to accomplish it. She'd secretly wondered how many of the first generation of Sakk-crossbred humans had been conceived during the journey.

"What did they say?" she asked, as Parrin pushed past the drape that separated the sitting and eating areas from the bedroom of her quarters.

He chuckled darkly. "They wished us many healthy daughters."

Her face flamed. "Oh. I guess they would." Though the breeding measures and Sakk-born females were lessening the strain of a male-heavy society, the Sakk still hadn't recovered from the near extinction of their females millennia earlier.

Those worries were short-lived. Parrin's mouth came down on hers, wiping away every concern, save the most immediate ones.

Hayley moaned at the sensation of Parrin following her down onto the lush mattress. Her body was in a riot, taking in every sensation at once and approaching overload.

Parrin's roaming hands weren't helping her find focus. One stroked from her knee up the outside of her thigh, delving beneath the silk of her skirt. The other worked its way up her arm, teasing at the side of her breast. She moved against him, encouraging Parrin.

He would be experienced with women, she knew. Adolescent Sakk males went through a stage where they required frequent sexual interaction. As Hayley understood it, widows and prostitutes took care of their needs.

Parrin wasn't treating her like a prostitute, of course. He took his time, stroking and exploring Hayley's body. Their mouths meshed and parted in a feast of pleasure. Her body heated, demanding more of him.

As if she'd spoken the thought aloud, Parrin turned, placing Hayley above him. She gasped at the feeling of his cock pressing to her through layers of clothing. She reached for the zipper down her back, fumbling with it.

Parrin's hand covered hers, and he drew away from the kiss. "Shhh. Let me."

Hayley nodded and eased her hand away from the zipper. Parrin slid it down slowly, his eyes locked with hers. Tremors worked their way through her body, and she gasped for breath.

The dress parted, and Parrin worked it off her shoulders. Silk stroking at her scars drew a moan from her. Parrin cocked his head to one side and smiled. His cock jerked against her body. Hayley arched against him, drowning in need.

He traced the scars with his fingertips, and her breathing hitched. Parrin shifted and took her breast into his mouth. His stroking hands and suckling mouth had her body throbbing, half-formed pleas leaving her trembling lips.

Parrin reversed their positions and knelt up between her thighs. Hayley stared up at him, watching her clothing and shoes being stripped away in a daze.

"He touched your wing base," Parrin muttered.

"What?" Her voice sounded weak and far away to Hayley.

"That was what you took offense to. Jamil touched your wing base." Parrin moved on to his own clothing, leaving them both nude. His cock nestled to his stomach, ready to stake a claim on her.

Hayley swallowed a lump in her throat, watching the slight movements of his length avidly. "I don't have wings," she reminded him. True, she'd been born with stumps of wings, but those had been removed when she'd been less than a month old in the belief that they were a birth defect.

Parrin lifted her to her knees, steadying Hayley when her balance proved uncertain. "The wings are erogenous zones for us. The wing base especially so."

Answering that was difficult. "Then...Holly?"

His smile sent a new set of butterflies winging through her stomach. "Poor girl." He reached a hand up to stroke one scar, leaving Hayley gasping against his chin. "She doesn't know what she's missing."

Parrin laid a hard kiss on Hayley's lips, then moved with lightning speed. Before Hayley's senses righted themselves, he was at her back, trailing his lips along her scars, heating them with his breath, stroking his tongue along them.

His cock lay against the base of her spine, taunting Hayley with what she wanted. His hands explored the front of her body, massaging at her breasts, pressing lightly down her abdomen, widening her stance to tease at her clit.

"I can make you come like this, Hayley. Is that what you want?"

"I want..." Truth be told, she wasn't sure what she wanted, save that she didn't want him to stop.

"Come like this and then feel my length filling you?" he tempted her.

Hayley nodded her agreement.

Parrin's groan sounded of exquisite pain. He went back to his play, raising her arousal to a fever pitch. Her legs trembled, and she nestled closer to Parrin's body.

He settled her onto the mattress again, his hands massaging at the scars that were fast becoming a favored part of her anatomy. Parrin captured her lips, the kiss hot and hard. He ground his hips against her, adding the promise of what was soon to come.

The heat between them came to a head, and Hayley grasped at Parrin's shoulders, drawing him closer, her body exploding in delight.

His head came up, and he thrust into her. Pain and pleasure warred against the backdrop of the continuing orgasm. Parrin's breathing hitched, and he looked down at her, his eyes widening.

"You were virginal?"

****

Hayley murmured something that sounded of agreement, and Parrin cursed himself silently. Human women usually weren't virgins when they came to the consulate to be tested. For that matter, unless a female was born on Sakk or came from a seed world with wings, none of them were expected to be virginal.

Parrin had never had a virgin before. During his pre-prime settling, he'd been tutored by two widowed aunts. Since neither had been related to him by blood, it had been socially acceptable for them to have a taste of pre-prime cock while working him through the fever to the control he now possessed.

That control asserted itself now. Females could be injured in a first mating. Had he done so?

Having never been schooled in the particulars of a virgin female, he wasn't certain what to expect. The faint tang of blood mixed with the sublime scents of sex. *She could be injured.* The concept of asking the healers for aid was both appealing and terrifying. He would definitely hold that as a last resort.

Hayley lifted a leg and wrapped it around him, and Parrin decided to take his cues from her. Her nipples were hard, her body moving against his as if urging him on. Clearly, she wasn't incapacitated by pain. Were she seriously injured, she surely would be.

Parrin thrust deeper, and Hayley cried out. He hesitated long enough to note her impassioned eyes, to hear her sounds of pleasure, to feel her pulling at him. That spelled the end of his control.

The rest was fast and drugging. Parrin's balls pulsed in the rush of cum up his cock and into her body. In the aftermath, Hayley held to him, pressing kisses to his chest as her sheath spasmed around his length.

Parrin's wings curved around her, a show of protection inborn to the Sakk. "Why didn't you tell me?" he asked.

Hayley smiled a sweet little smile. "Do you think I would have wanted something different?"

That was hard to answer. "How could someone as beautiful as you be virginal at nearly twenty-five?"

Her face reddened in a deep blush, and she raised one hand, touching one of her wing bases over her shoulder.

Parrin pushed the hair, disheveled and half-loosed from her fancy hairstyle, away from her face. "They may have clipped your wings, but that has taken nothing from you." She was a sensual woman, and any man who let a scar blind him to that was a fool.

Hayley's smile was brilliant, a clear indicator that he'd said the right thing. "How soon can we bind?" she asked.

His cock went from semi-erect to erect, drawing a gasp of surprise from her. "As soon as you want to, Hayley."

Section Three:
Unexpected Princess

Amy and Sakkra

Chapter Eight

"When I get to Sakk—"

Amy laughed heartily, then swallowed it at Lucy's look of annoyance.

"What?" her best friend huffed.

Oh, boy. Now she's indignant. "Luce, you haven't even gotten inside the consulate yet."

"It has to be right, Amy. It just has to. I've never felt like I fit in. This *must* be why." Her eyes pleaded for confirmation.

"Well, there's only one way to find out."

Amy refused to give her hope. It wasn't right to feed into this insane need Lucy had to find out she was secretly Sakk.

Every day, between a dozen and four hundred women came to consulates, around the world, to be tested. They drooled over hot men with wings. They spent time with whatever the testing entailed. And, according to the statistics she'd seen in *Time Magazine*, six hundred and ninety-nine in seven hundred left the consulate with crushed dreams.

There was little chance Lucy would be one of the few Sakk women the consulates located every month. Like most who came to be tested, Lucy had pinned her hopes on the result being positive. That's why Amy had agreed to come with her.

To handle to inevitable fallout. Lucy has never liked being told 'no'.

Lucy bounced on the balls of her feet, bobbing her head as if searching for a peek of birdman hunk over the heads of the assembled crowd. "It's going to be perfect, Amy. Just perfect. Have you seen the videos of Sakk? It's beautiful."

"Yes. I've seen them." Sakk was undeniably beautiful. It was the kind of place she'd like to visit. But moving to another world? The women who tested must be desperate or crazy.

"I've heard the Sakk are hung, too."

Several heads snapped around. Lucy was oblivious to her mortified and hostile audience. Amy's face burned, and she avoided their gazes.

A tone sounded, and the voice half the world recognized as Representative Janice Beldon filled the air. Amy knew it was recorded; the news had reported that Janice and her mate, Beldon, were on Sakk, anticipating the birth of their second child.

"In one minute, the shield before you will drop. You will have two minutes to make your way to the next checkpoint before the shield comes up again. Please proceed in an ordered and sedate fashion. Those requiring extra time or assistance will be met by warriors and aided into the checkpoint building."

Amy shivered at the idea of being trapped inside the shields that protected the consulate.

"No weapons are permitted inside the Sakk consulate. Ready yourself for a security check."

Lucy purred, probably visualizing a very personal strip search with one of the Sakk warriors. Amy opened her mouth to remind her that their scanners did it for them, then closed it with a snap. It was unlikely Lucy would listen anyway.

A second tone sounded, and the crowd surged toward the checkpoint. Lucy grabbed Amy's hand and dragged her along. Though they didn't run for the building, the assembled women walked double time, shouldering those who pushed too close.

It's a busy day today. There were more than three dozen women vying to be first in line at the checkpoint.

The tones counting the time until the shield would rise again seemed to come too fast, and Amy's heart raced. They came to a halt in the checkpoint building, and she took a deep breath. The final tone sounded, then a warning blare. The stillness in its wake jangled Amy's nerves. Before she caught her breath enough to focus on the murals decorating the walls, an armored male body was there, blocking her view.

"Identification, please."

Amy fumbled for hers; Lucy had hers ready.

The warrior took Lucy's driver's license. "Ms. Ferguson, what brings you to the consulate today?"

"Testing for mating." There was a blatant invitation couched in Lucy's voice that made Amy want to shake her head in exasperation.

His gaze traveled up and down Lucy's body. "Sakkan bless you with a positive result." The cock rising against his indecently tight pants was impossible to miss.

Amy averted her eyes and offered her driver's license. The warrior handed Lucy's back and took Amy's gently.

"Have you come to the consulate to test as well, Ms. Davidson?"

"No." It came out too forcefully, and she winced. "I just came here as emotional support for Lucy."

"A pity." There was no hint of offense in his tone. "Welcome to the Sakk consulate, Ms. Davidson. May your stay here be pleasant."

"Thank you." She accepted the license back and started to put it away.

The warrior didn't move immediately along, as the others were, bustling down the line. He stared at her, bringing goose bumps up on her arms Amy avoided looking at him; his proximity alone made her nervous. At last, he moved on, and she sighed in relief.

"Did you see that, Amy?" Lucy whispered excitedly.

"What?"

"He was staring at me. Do you think they can sense the ones that will test positive?"

"I don't know." *I hope not, because he was staring at me.*

****

Amy held her breath, as Lucy placed her hand on the testing pad.

It had taken hours to process in. Once they'd passed the sensors that would report all weapons, even those made of ceramic or plastic, the next shield had been lowered, and they'd been admitted into the outer ring of the consulate. The main building was a grand affair, complete with columns reminiscent of ancient Greek buildings.

There, the questions had begun. In one room, Lucy had undergone rudimentary psychological testing. In another, they'd asked for her medical history. It surprised Amy that they asked it, considering their medical diagnostic equipment.

In a third, there'd been exhaustive questions about Lucy's education, her interests, and her goals. That had set off warning bells, and Amy had asked about it, interrupting the process for the first time. The answer had been simple and elegant.

"We find it best to introduce females to males with complementary interests. A female geologist would do best mated to a male who enjoys hiking, for instance. A female sociologist or linguist, by comparison, with a male who prefers life in population centers. Music lovers would thrive with males who reside in areas with several stages for performance."

"You match that intensely?"

"A small concession to make. If the ideal group at this consulate fails, we may shuttle males from others for the female to meet. Or a female may prefer males her opposite. Some do. For a mate, a male would give up hiking...or accompany his mate to performances that are not typically to his tastes."

That was interesting, but... "You don't expect women to change their interests for their mates? Compromise?"

He offered a stunning smile. "What is it humans say? This is a female's market. The advantage is yours in negotiation."

The shifting light reminded Amy that the final test was in progress.

The warrior at the console pressed buttons. His hands went still, then closed into fists.

Amy didn't have to ask what it meant. The testing pad hadn't turned blue. The test was negative. She let out her breath in a sigh.

Lucy didn't have to ask what it meant, either. "I was so sure. Try again. It can give a false negative, right?"

"No. It cannot." The warrior at the console seemed pained by that fact. "I am sorry, Ms. Ferguson. For you. For myself. For all of Sakk." He sounded it, and Amy felt a spike of pity for all of them.

Lucy pulled her hand back and looked at it as if it was a traitor. "There has to be a way. I'd be willing to carry children that are genetically spliced, if that would work."

The warriors shot each other wary looks. The one behind the console winced, and Amy realized he was trying to find a way to gently refuse Lucy's plan.

"I will...propose it, Ms. Ferguson," he offered.

Lucy smiled. "Please. I'll wait."

He hesitated, nodded to one of the others, and left the room. One of the two remaining warriors took his place at the console.

Probably to protect it, in case Lucy attacks the automated messenger which has denied her Sakkhood.

Amy ran the math, realization making her ill. No matter how gently they refused Lucy, this was going to get ugly. All told, Amy had minutes to defuse the situation. Otherwise a full-blown 'Ferguson fit' would ensue. *That's why I really came here. To keep Lucy from getting herself arrested.*

She stepped between Lucy and the table, trying to distance her friend from the situation mentally. "Luce..." *What? What excuse can I make?* "The medical risks in this are probably extreme," she cautioned.

"Oh, I don't care about that." She waved off Amy's concerns with a flip of her manicured nails.

"You should, Luce. You should consider it."

Lucy pushed at Amy's shoulder playfully. Amy caught herself on the edge of the table, righting her balance. One of the warriors tensed to move, but he didn't interfere.

"Such a worrier," Lucy chided. "You always were."

And you've always been reckless. Amy bit back the retort.

Tapping keys behind her made Amy's heart stutter. They were probably calling in more warriors. Visions of them evicting Lucy made her head swim.

Think! "Okay. It's safe then. I'll buy that. After all, they've worked with humans before, and I doubt they killed a bunch in trial and error."

The ruffling of wings sounded like a warrior took offense to the comment.

Lucy nodded resolutely, seemingly mollified.

"But I bet the workup to see if you're even compatible enough for that sort of experimentation is lengthy." Amy looked toward the closest warrior, silently pleading for his help.

His eyes narrowed, and his jaw tightened.

They don't lie, she reminded herself. *Janice Beldon said they feel lies are unethical and beneath a warrior of Sakk.*

If I'm wrong, please let him keep it to himself instead of correcting me.

At last, he offered a terse nod of his head. "There would be many, many tests," he confirmed.

Amy bit back a sigh of relief. *Many tests. Not a lot of time but many tests. Thank you for playing along.*

"I'll take them," Lucy offered. "The sooner we get started, the sooner I can choose a mate."

Of course you will. Amy cursed herself for not realizing how obsessed Lucy was with this idea. She opened her mouth to reply.

A bark of foreign speech sounded behind her, shocking Amy to silence. She half-turned on the pivot point of her grip on the table, meeting the startled gaze of the warrior at the console. The flashing lights beneath her field of vision drew her attention down to the testing pad.

She'd inadvertently grasped it when she'd steadied herself on the table. They'd tested her.

Blue. Everyone knew what it meant when the pad went blue. *I'm a match. I'm Sakk-descended.*

Amy recoiled, her head spinning. "No." She couldn't become a Sakk mate. She was engaged to Jason. She was in love with him. Instincts to choose a mate or not, she was marrying the man she loved.

Lost in the internal horror show of having to refuse the Sakk and hope for the best—hope that they'd open the shields and let her leave without a fight—everything around her became an indistinct buzzing.

A punch snapped her mind back to the reality of her situation, and a keening wail rose around her. Arms closed around Amy and drew her to a very male chest.

No. I'm not taking a Sakk mate. That was the last coherent thought she managed. Amy started beating at the warrior holding her captive.

****

Sakkra, second son of His Majesty Sakkrel, strode down the corridor between the inner consulate and the outer. Beside him, Colonel Ezu gave his report.

The prince did his best to ignore the too-tight Earth-style pants and bare chest Ezu chose to entice the human females. Those who'd won their places on Earth had gone to embarrassing extremes to attract matches from this planet.

The clothing was the least of it, in Sakkra's opinion. Some had posed for native magazines that featured nude males or those engaged in all manner of sex acts. A few had acted in live sex vids with human women for the 'exposure'.

Sakkra winced at the unintended pun. He'd never fully understood how the warriors expected this form of baiting to work, especially considering the fact that more men than women indulged in watching the vids, he'd been told. Not to mention that women looking for a mate were unlikely to look for one in a sex vid. On some level, it would seem in direct opposition to what they hoped to accomplish.

Still, those engaged in the unconventional activities were having sex. Quite a lot of it, based on the rumors. Sakkra half-expected to be greeted one sunrise with the news that one of the males had inadvertently impregnated an unknowing match, thinking she was human.

We have a one in seven hundred chance, he thought bitterly.

And now this again. "We may have to alert the local authorities," Sakkra mused.

The colonel would know that. If it turned to violence, he would do so automatically.

"Yes, Sakkra. We may. This one is particularly...intent."

It could be worse. The religious zealots who had attacked the shields with rocket launchers had been worse, but Master Beldon had still been on Earth to handle that situation. He'd deftly countered the attack, turned the combatants and their weapons over to the American military, and had kept everyone within the shields protected.

In some ways, Sakkra would rather handle armed opponents than one distraught and unbalanced human female. *Sakkan tests the worth of every man in His own way.*

A prayer uttered under his breath, Sakkra returned to the situation at hand. "She is not at all close to what we need to find?" It wouldn't matter if she was. Ms. Ferguson was mentally unsuitable to carry young for them, it seemed. He cursed the fact that the earlier testing had missed it. Perhaps they needed to make the psychological portion longer and more involved.

"No, Sakkra. Not at all."

He nodded grimly. If she was close and not unbalanced, she might have found a male willing to accept implanted spliced young from her for the joy of a female in his bed. Or they might have been able to establish a new breeding colony with willing human females that were close stock but not close enough for true mating. Sakkra had considered both possibilities more than once. It wasn't ideal, but what was with well over a hundred males to each female?

Sounds of a struggle stopped Sakkra in his tracks. Had the female attacked his men? Had she made threats?

Not one but two shouting women prodded him to a run. Sakkan only knew what the problem was, but it was worse than he'd expected. His heart thundering, he launched into the testing room.

The two women were struggling with a warrior each on opposite sides of the room.

Sakkra looked back and forth between them, at a loss to explain it. How had this started?

Their vocalizations provided the answer for him. One was shouting obscenities and threats.

The one that hoped to be a match. We have to make the early testing more intensive. He focused on the other.

"You can't keep me here. I didn't volunteer. I didn't ask to be tested." Her voice was high in panic. Her eyes were wide and wild.

And her lip is bleeding. Sakkan, no! Please, don't let my men have done that.

Sakkra shot at glance at the test pad, confirming that it was blue. His mind worked at the problem with all due haste. The program would have started automatically, but someone would have had to order it to complete the cycle.

Or to abort, but aborting sometimes causes a fault requiring a reset of the equipment. He would have ordered it to complete the cycle to avoid that.

She hadn't asked to be tested. She'd touched the pad accidentally, no doubt. The warriors hadn't considered the possibility that she would test positive as a match.

And with an unbalanced human woman who wants to be a match in the room. He prayed she hadn't injured the other female.

And now the match is being detained by my men against her will. It was a nightmare in the making. The human governments could wage war over this. They could refuse to allow more testing. If the young female had even a single bruise caused by his men, they could—

"I'll kill you."

237

Sakkra snapped a look at the other female, just in time to see the warrior restraining her wrap a hand around her throat.

I have to move! "Stop! Remove her from the outer ring immediately. Colonel Ezu, help him."

The colonel's nod said he understood his actual job was to keep the warriors from killing her for threatening a match. Two more heartbeats, and the warrior would have managed that.

As if in confirmation, the warrior's hand wavered before it withdrew. He maneuvered the struggling female between himself and Ezu.

"Turn her over to the human authorities," Sakkra ordered. "And have her coded into the database as a threat." With that accomplished, Ms. Ferguson would be unable to approach the shields at any consulate without the human authorities being summoned.

Ezu nodded stiffly. "Immediately. You have my vow." He led the way out of the room, the surly female screaming curses and kicking at her guards.

That handled, Sakkra turned to the young match. She pummeled the major's chest with her small fists, pleading to be set free. Sakkra felt a pang of regret. The match reminded him of the first caged birds he'd seen on Earth.

She would be released. Of course she would. But first, her wound would have to be tended to. Sakkra scooped her up, the major grasped her wrists, and her screams reached an earsplitting high.

"Calm, young one," he soothed her.

She struggled against the major's grip, trying to escape Sakkra's arms. "Let me go. Let me go. Let. Me. Go!" She was screeching now.

She pulled a foot back to kick the warrior holding her wrists, and he switched both wrists into a single hand to grasp the foot in his other.

"When your wound has been tended to," Sakkra offered calmly. He moved before she could protest, into the corridor and toward the main medical bay.

She kicked with the other foot, and the major released the first to block the blow. He turned his body, walking backward to take himself out of the most effective kicking range.

"People know I'm here," she warned them. "If I don't come back, they'll make sure the authorities know you have me."

If your former friend is the 'people' you are hoping will save you, I would rethink that hope. But saying that would only alienate and frighten her. Sakkra kept his mouth shut, quickening his step.

A crowd was starting to gather in doorways along the way. As if that was too much for her peace of mind, the young match started kicking frantically and screaming. Her face went an unhealthy shade of red that made Sakkra worry her heart would give out before they managed to tend to her medically.

At the first sight of the *bio bed*, she shrieked and bucked against their hold.

Healers ran from every direction. "Sakkra, what is this?" the master healer asked.

"She has a wound that needs tended. Do so."
The sooner, the better.

The healer shot an incredulous look back.
"In this state? Perhaps I should—"

"Don't you dare!" she shouted. "I am walking
out of here, and you're opening that damned
shield to let me."

"You have my vow," Sakkra assured her.
Hadn't he already promised she'd be free to leave
when her wound was tended to? How many
times would he have to say it?

Her struggling ceased, and she stared at
him. "You're giving me your word?"

Sakkra bit back a growl of frustration with
her. "Yes. I am. Now will you allow the healers to
see to your wound?"

She looked from face to face, trembling in his
arms. Her throat bobbed, and she took ragged
breaths. At last, she nodded. "Yes. Okay. As long
as I can leave."

The major met Sakkra's gaze, waited for his
nod, and eased away, releasing her wrists. She
twisted, and Sakkra released her onto the *bio
bed*, giving her the freedom she desired.

She shivered, and one of the healers draped
a blanket around her shoulders. The skittish
young match jumped and shot a wary look at
him. When no one advanced on her position, she
pulled the blanket shut around her body and
huddled inside it, the toes of her soft boots
sticking out from beneath it.

The healers moved away to order tests on her
condition. Everyone else stayed in place, as if

unconsciously forming a blockade to any escape attempts.

Her trembling eased, and her color and breathing returned to something resembling normal. At length, she cleared her throat. "I'm not staying," she offered calmly. "I can't stay. I have a life. Please, understand."

Warriors muttered what were probably curses on their luck. They'd found a match only to lose her.

All of Sakk weeps for your loss. Sakkra held up a hand to motion for silence from his men. The last thing they needed was to frighten her worse than she already was. "No one will force you. Our warriors only meant to aid you. Not to harm you and not to capture you. You have my solemn vow. When your wound is healed, you are free to leave."

She pulled the blanket tighter around her body, and one of the healers gasped.

Sakkra turned to him. "What is it?" he whispered. *Is she ill? Injured? Sakkan forbid, already bearing a winged child?*

"The ring, Sakkra," he replied formally. "I have heard such a ring is called a...joining ring. It means she plans to become mate to a human man."

Sakkra stared at the small diamond ring on her left hand, his heart aching for her.

"I have a life," she repeated solemnly.

Sakkan, what will this discovery do to that life and those plans?

****

241

Amy sipped at the juice the healers had provided, eying the group of men across the room from her.

Only one of them had started speaking their language, and the one called Sakkra had ended that. Since then, they'd all spoken English. Amy suspected Sakkra was making sure there could be no misunderstandings about their intentions caused by the language barrier. She was glad for it.

She'd picked up bits and pieces of information by listening to them. Already, she could identify the master healer for the consulate, a general, a major, a colonel... And Sakkra, a Sakk prince.

The last one still shocked her. They'd sent a prince to talk to Lucy. A prince had carried Amy to the clinic.

A prince promised I can leave. Thank God! Even though the Sakk didn't believe in lying or other forms of subterfuge, the fact that a Sakk prince said it made her feel all the better. Who, within the consulate, was going to outrank a prince? The only one she knew who could wasn't on Earth.

The door opened, and a human man walked into the clinic. He looked around and headed for Sakkra. A body length away, he stopped and offered a sharp bow of his head to the prince.

Amy watched the interaction, trying to dissect it. She would have assumed the newcomer was a police officer sent to liaise with the Sakk consulate, but his clothing didn't support that image. He was dressed in a pair of biker boots, faded jeans, a crisp t-shirt, blue jean jacket, and had his long blond hair pulled back into a short ponytail behind his head. Any liaison with the consulate would wear a suit and tie or at least a collared shirt with pristine jeans, she was certain. So, who was this man?

"You called for me, Sakkra?" His voice was deep, calm, and collected.

The prince nodded, his light brown curls swishing around his face, half-hiding his dark gray eyes. "I have a new assignment for you."

The Sakk consulate hires human workers? It was the first she'd heard of it. Even jobs like cooking and janitorial were reportedly held by their own people. Usually men, though she'd heard a few older women worked as beauticians, styling hair and applying makeup for matches meeting Sakk men.

The new arrival's gaze flicked Amy's direction and then away. "I see."

Her mouth went dry. "What are you talking about?"

The human opened his mouth to answer, and Sakkra waved him off. The prince approached the bed.

"Your life has been threatened."

"Lucy wouldn't—"

"I can't chance that."

"Meaning what?" she demanded.

Sakkra sighed. "Rietin is assigned to your protection."

"I will be invisible," Rietin assured her. "Unless you need me, of course."

"I won't need you," she snapped. *A private investigator. They hired a sleazy private investigator to follow me around.* Amy fumed at it.

Rietin looked at Sakkra, seemingly seeking his orders and disregarding hers.

The prince took his time formulating an answer. "This...Lucy Ferguson will likely be incarcerated for tonight. We can discuss this when you've rested."

Amy slid off the table and shucked the blanket they'd given her onto the bed. "There's nothing to discuss. I am free to leave and free to live my life. Thank you, gentlemen, for healing my lip. Now, if you'll excuse me, I have a life to get back to."

She expected them to follow her toward the doors, to protest her dismissal of their plans...something. No one moved. No one contradicted her. Amy looked at the doors, challenging them.

Sakkra tipped his head. "Can I be of any more assistance, Ms. Davidson?"

"The way out?" she asked, needing an excuse to explain her hesitation. Otherwise, they might think she was reconsidering becoming a Sakk mate.

"To your right. Follow the corridor all the way to the courtyard and gardens. The warriors will open the back shields onto the street beyond for you."

"Thank you." Amy sauntered away, feigning confidence she didn't feel.

Warriors in the corridor snuck glances at her, but none of them were rude enough to stare or challenge her decision. None of them spoke to her.

The door at the end of the corridor led into an atrium with stone benches and Sakk symbols engraved into the stone pathway between the many ordinary-looking plants.

They probably weren't allowed to import their own plants onto Earth.

The sun welcomed her outside, and the breeze was brisk and clean. She wondered at that. It almost seemed that the air inside the shields was filtered and circulated, but there was no one to ask that question of.

I don't want to know it. If I ask it, I'm getting involved in their problems.

Aren't I? I'm what they are looking for, right?

No. They are looking for willing *volunteers. That's not me. I have a life here. I have a family. I don't intend to move to an alien planet for a guy I don't even know.*

Amy made her way to the other side of the atrium and nodded to the warrior standing next to a console.

"Good day, ma'am," he intoned. "Please feel free to come again any time."

Unlikely. She smiled anyway and made her way to the street at his hand motion to do so.

Her turn toward the parking garage short circuited. They'd come in Lucy's car. She was in town with no vehicle. It would take a train and two buses to get home without one.

Amy looked back at the consulate. *I bet they'd give me a ride home if I explained the difficulty.* She'd seen the vans with the Sakk crest around town.

Yes. They would give me a ride home and expect me to change my mind. No thanks. I can stop by an ATM, get change, pick up some lunch, and take public transportation home. That in mind, she squared her shoulders and reversed direction, heading toward the closest train station.

****

"What was that hesitation?" Sakkra spoke aloud. "Why did she change direction that way?"

Rietin sighed. "I imagine her *friend* drove her here, and Ms. Davidson realized she would have to take public transport to get home instead. The train station is that direction."

He grunted his agreement, though it stung that it had been something so mundane. *What am I so upset about?* It wasn't as if it was likely that she was having second thoughts about mating with a Sakk warrior. *She has a mate waiting for her at home. She has a life we have no right to interfere in.*

"What do you want me to do now that she's refused my protection?" Rietin asked.

"Protect her. Is there any doubt? The other female threatened her life."

Rietin's silence raised the fine feathers at the base of Sakkra's skull. He glared at the tracker, demanding an explanation silently.

The wingless male cleared his throat. "Humans often say such things and do not mean them, but after reviewing the vids of her reactions... I cannot deny there is a chance this one means Ms. Davidson harm. It is wise to protect her from harm."

"And your concern is...?" Sakkra prompted him.

"My concern is that Ms. Davidson may consider this an intrusion into her life. Even stalking. She may suspect we mean her some harm by it. There are human laws to protect females from those who mean them harm. Even though we don't, she may claim it and be...believed.

"Human females like Ms. Davidson are independent creatures. She lives alone, away from her parents' nest. She is not accustomed to her wishes being disregarded. Whatever I do, it must be done gently. As quietly and unobtrusively as possible."

Sakkra considered his evaluation and found it sound. *I usually do with Rietin.* There were many reasons he was their premiere tracker on Earth, and Rietin's ability to blend in with the native population was nearly the least of it. "I agree. Do whatever you need to do. Expenses are approved."

Rietin tipped his head and withdrew, off to plan his protection of a very headstrong young match.

Sakkra ambled toward his quarters, feeling worn in both body and mind. His men handed off reports of the day's activities to him, from this consulate and all the others that had finished their daily testing. Concentrating on them was nearly impossible with memories of Amy Davidson in his arms taunting him.

She cannot be mine. She will not be mate to any of our kind. She already has a mate.

Chapter Nine

Amy stared at the telephone, reached toward it, then eased her hand back again. She had to make the calls eventually. *But not yet.*

How was she supposed to tell her parents that they were both Sakk-descended? How was she supposed to tell them that any of her cousins might be so heavily Sakk-descended as to be unable to reproduce with a human man?

What if I am? That thought set off a basket of snakes in her stomach.

The other call she had to make was to Jason. How could she tell him she wasn't human? How could she even start?

I'm Sakk-descended. The barrage of questions he would fire at her made her head spin. How would she know that? Why had she agreed to be tested? Did she prefer a Sakk warrior to a human man?

I need to try something else.

A funny thing happened when I went to the consulate with Lucy today.

As if! The last thing Amy would call this mess was 'funny'. *Terrifying. Life-altering. Maddening.*

"I told you, you shouldn't have gone with her."

Amy winced at what would most likely be Jason's rebuke, imagined though it was. *He'll say it. No matter how I break the news, he'll come out with that at some point.*

249

After that, the dozens of unanswerable questions will start. Could they have children together? Would those children be sterile?

Will they have wings? God forbid! Her heart stuttered at the possibility. The reports about the breeding colonies said Sakk-descended sometimes produced winged babies with each other. *Usually with small, deformed wings, but still winged.*

Not like Sakkra's wings.

She shook away the memories of the Sakk prince, concern in his gray eyes. His wings had been long and full, strong wings that looked like they could lift him from the ground, despite the slightly higher gravity on Earth.

Not conducive. I need answers, not daydreams.

Could we have children together? If Jason was at least partially Sakk, they might be able to, but there was no way to know if he had Sakk blood without testing at the consulate.

I need answers to these questions before I call anyone. Sakkra would give her answers, she was sure. It was the least the Sakk owed her after the upheaval they'd caused in her personal life.

A heavy-handed knock at the door put a premature end to her self-righteous internal rant. Amy glanced at the clock, noting that it was after eight.

Who would come here at this time of night? And without calling? Certainly not her parents or Jason. *Maybe Jo?* Her cousin had shown up with an armload of books or a DVD and asked for a couch for the night on more than one occasion.

The knock sounded again. It was more impatient and decidedly male.

Amy pushed off the couch and padded across the floor in her fuzzy slippers. The peephole was a little high for her comfort, but she rose on tiptoe to use it.

"Jason?" She tried not to let her dread color her tone. *I probably failed.*

"Oh, so you *are* there."

Her fingers shook against the deadbolt. "It's after eight, and I wasn't expecting anyone. I wasn't going to announce I was here until I knew who was on the other side of the door." Wasn't Jason the one who kept telling her to be safe? A woman living alone and all of that?

The lock snapped open; she turned the handle and opened the door for him. Jason scowled at her, then stomped inside without a greeting. That set off warning bells.

Amy closed the door, taking her time about it. "Is there a problem, Jason?"

"Problem?" he grumbled. "This fiasco is a little more than a problem, don't you think?"

He knows? How could he? It was better to be sure than to blurt it out and shock him with more than he already thought was wrong. "Which fiasco?" *Please be referring to a problem with the caterer or the deejay.*

"Which—? You're not seriously going to pretend the little scene at the Sakk consulate today never happened, are you?"

She turned toward him, though she knew it was probably a mistake. Jason stood in the center of the room, his jaw clenched shut, his hands fisted at his sides.

"I'll assume Lucy called you," she replied wearily. *The bitch. The jealous brat.*

"From jail. I would have thought you would have had the courtesy to. After all, you *are* my fiancée." His gaze flicked to her hand, as if he was assuring himself she was wearing her ring.

"I would have, once I had the answers to the questions you're going to ask me. I didn't want to let the cat out of the bag when everything was still so uncertain."

"So you chose not to tell me my fiancée is a fucking alien?"

Amy jerked away at the warning in his voice, coming up hard against the door. The completely outrageous thought that she should have taken Sakkra up on his bodyguard settled in her mind.

That's ridiculous. This is Jason. We love each other. But he doesn't trust me, apparently. That piqued her anger. "I didn't *ask* to be tested," she protested. "Lucy pushed me onto the testing pad, and—"

"That doesn't change that you're one of them."

"For all you know, you are, too." It was out before Amy could reason herself out of saying it so bluntly. "I had no clue I was. Are my eyes an odd color, Jason? Is my hair overly fine? No."

Jason stared at her, his mouth moving as if he wanted to protest in return but couldn't form it.

She forced her voice to gentle. "Come to the consulate with me." At the very least, she'd be more comfortable walking in there if she had Jason with her to assure she could walk out again.

Sakkra would make sure of that.

Stop it! The last thing she wanted to do was depend on the Sakk prince for anything. "We'll ask our questions. Let them take their tests."

"If I'm one of them, I don't want to know it. I don't want to be one."

"You think I did?" In the hours since she'd been tested, her life had been in complete disarray.

"I don't want *you* to be one, either. Don't you get it?" There was something manic in that. "I told you not to go to the consulate. I told you, and you just had to go."

Her mouth went dry at his meaning. "I can't change what I am, Jason. But we can go to the consulate and ask—"

"And if they say I'm human?"

"You're enough for me." Was that his problem? Did he think she was that shallow?

His eyes narrowed. "It's *not* enough for me. We had plans, Amy. We planned to have a big family. A big Italian, *human* family. Remember those plans?"

The finality of his argument raised stomach acid in her throat. "You're not even going to try. Are you?"

"I don't think this is going to work."

Her hands shaking, tears pooling in her eyes, Amy pulled the engagement ring off and held it out on the palm of her hand. Jason hesitated, then marched across the room and plucked it up.

"You would have been enough for me," she repeated.

Jason didn't answer. He motioned her away from the door. Amy complied on quaking legs. He didn't even look at her. Jason pulled the door open, stepped through, and slammed it shut. His footsteps echoed down the hallway, courtesy of the hardwood floors.

The sobs won the battle, bursting free from her in a rush. Amy slid down the wall and huddled in on herself.

That morning, she'd had it all: a man she loved, a job she liked, and a calm, ordered life. Now? She'd lost Jason. Since she worked with Lucy, and Lucy had apparently set out to destroy her life, it was a safe bet Amy should plan to start job hunting in the morning.

I have some things left. My family. A few friends who aren't also friends of Lucy's.

But not Jason. And no idea what she even had to offer a man. Could she ever give a man, besides a Sakk warrior, children? She couldn't promise that. She couldn't promise that she couldn't, either.

Oh, this sucks!

Her future loomed before her. For the first time in her life, it was full of dark uncertainty. The only way she could give a man assurances was to mate with a Sakk warrior.

I don't want to go to Sakk! Amy didn't want to leave Earth. She'd never had dreams of being an astronaut. *Face it. I don't have the right stuff.*

Not to mention the fact that she didn't want to leave her family. Odd as some people found it, her mother was one of her closest friends. *The closest now.* And her cousin Jo was a close second. Leaving her family wasn't an option plan.

They have no right to ask me to, she fumed.

A rational voice in her rioting mind reminded her that Sakkra wasn't demanding anything of her.

But their testing caused this!

That damned rational corner piped up again with the truth that marrying someone as shallow as Jason and losing him when she couldn't provide those all-important children to prove his virility—*Or God forbid, I gave him winged children!*—would have been just as bad. *Or worse.*

That was sobering. And confusing. How could Amy make plans for her life when she no longer understood the rules of her existence?

I have to know.

The pressing need to prioritize, right the wrongs of her perceptions, and fill in the gaps in her knowledge sent Amy rushing to the closet to grab a jacket. Sakkra had answers she needed. *Desperately.* She intended to get them.

Amy was halfway across town before she realized she was still wearing her pajamas and slippers. *It's just one more upheaval in my life,* she rationalized.

****

It wasn't until she reached the shield that Amy realized she hadn't thought the process through to the end. *What is wrong with me? I've never been this disorganized.*

She stood at the barrier, at a loss for how to get inside. There wasn't a doorbell or an intercom. What was she supposed to do?

Amy laid a hand to the shield, certain they wouldn't be allowed to use it if it was capable of hurting someone that way. It was cool and smooth, lightly buzzing against her skin.

Frustrated, she hit it. That was a mistake. It felt like hitting a wall.

Well, it's supposed to, isn't it? She shook her hand out, wincing.

Okay. Breaking in isn't an option. Of course, she'd known that.

So what do I do now? Realization was slow coming. They would have watches, wouldn't they? Or they would be scanning the shield from inside. One way or the other, someone would notice her when they got to this point.

Amy would wait. It couldn't take them that long to spot her. Could it? That thought in mind, she turned her back to the wall and slid down the shield, using it to support her back.

She didn't question why she was doing this. Sakkra had answers she needed. *I'm not leaving until I get them.*

****

Sakkra rushed into the command center. "What is it?" He dimly noted the chamber was full of warriors, easily three times the normal for a night watch.

"She has returned."

"Who has?" Nothing the warrior at the desk said was making sense.

"The young match."

Sakkra's heart skittered in shock at the news, and he circled the desk to look at the screen, certain the warrior had been mistaken. Since there had only been one match located recently—no matter how sloppily—there was no question *which* match he meant.

"It *is* she."

To his credit, the young warrior didn't answer the insinuation that both he and Rietin might have been wrong.

Sakkra focused on Amy Davidson, trying to assess the situation. He'd fully expected never to see her again. He'd resigned himself to the loss of her. She'd been intent on marrying her human male.

Sakkan, what changed?

The young match sat on the stone walkway, leaning back against the shield, her hands tucked under her chin. She wore a hooded jacket over odd patterned pants and some sort of furry foot coverings.

"What is she wearing?" He'd never seen anything like it.

The warrior cleared his throat. "I believe it is a particular style of human sleeping clothes."

"Sleeping—? Why in the ten systems would she wear sleeping clothes here?" Sakkra didn't wait for an answer. "She'll freeze. We have to admit her." Whatever else Amy was, she was Sakk-descended and clearly distraught. What was she thinking to come here like this?

"I will send—"

"No. I will bring her in."

The warrior looked up, seemingly scandalized.

"She is not carrying weapons." He didn't make it a question.

The warrior answered anyway. "No, Sakkra. The scan is negative for weapons."

"Then there is no reason for me not to see to her condition personally. General Lea...Corporal Brak...Accompany me." Sakkra had to accept guards, or his warriors would keep him from going to her.

He pushed away from the desk and stalked down the corridors to the main entry point, the two warriors at his heels.

Sakkra didn't pause. There was no question the warrior would be dropping the shields ahead of him and raising them behind him again. The last shield dropped when he was two steps away, and Ms. Davidson overbalanced backward and caught herself on her elbows.

She must have been using the shield to support her weight.

He squatted to her side and offered his hand. She stared at it for a moment, wary.

"I have questions for you." Her voice was strained and breathy.

At this time of night? Sakkra nodded. "Come inside where it is warmer." This close, he could see that her hair was damp, and the jacket she wore was unequal to the dropping temperatures.

She swallowed hard, and her chilled, shivering hand crept into his. Amy allowed Sakkra to lift her to her feet.

"Come inside," he repeated. Clearly, she was already suffering from the weather.

"I'm not volunteering," she informed him. "I just have questions."

His heart ached at her refusal, though it wasn't personal. "As you wish. You have my vow that you can leave whenever you wish, as long as it is safe for you to do so."

She considered his vow for a moment, then nodded.

****

The wind whipped through her lounging pants, and Amy shivered. One of the warriors with Sakkra pulled off his cloak and wrapped it around her. She suspected Sakkra would have given her his own, had he been wearing one.

He came out here without a cloak? Why?

"Thank you," she whispered in the sudden realization that she was being rude.

The warrior didn't flirt with her, as she'd expected him to. His nod was stiff and formal.

They led her into the consulate, deep into the crosshatch of hallways. Sakk warriors crowded around them, and the warriors escorting them warned them back. It took her a moment to realize she'd pressed close to Sakkra, and she eased away, her cheeks burning.

A door opened, and Sakkra guided her inside. The two others followed, and the door closed behind them.

The room was a small living room with a table and chairs for eating at the far end. Her gaze strayed to the silver drapes that no doubt led to a bedroom and bathroom.

Her mouth went dry as she pieced together what this room was used for. *Mating.*

"Amy?" Sakkra reminded her.

"This is...?" Words failed her.

"It is a comfortable place. You can sleep here if you feel the need. You are safe. We are not making demands of you or assumptions about your intentions, I assure you."

"You use these rooms a lot?"

"I believe we were overzealous in planning for a dozen of them." He winced. "We rarely use more than one a month for the intended purposes. It's more likely that visiting media or dignitaries will use them, but I suppose the space is not wasted.

"Can I offer you food or drink?" he offered.

She started to shake her head, then reconsidered. "Orange juice or lemonade? Thanks."

"Colonel, if you would."

One of the two warriors tipped his head and left the room.

Amy sank into one of the plush chairs. The words wouldn't come. All the questions she'd reasoned she needed to ask him eluded her.

He settled on the chair across from her, his eyes assessing. "What is it? What has happened to send you here...this way?"

Jason's angry shouting echoed in her memories, and she grasped at a question at random. "Can I have children with a human man?"

The wings on the last remaining warrior bristled, but he remained silent otherwise. She focused on Sakkra, wringing her hands in her lap nervously.

"I cannot say for certain. Since our goal was breeding matches for ourselves, whether or not they could breed with the general population was of no interest to us." He hesitated. "Perhaps the healers can offer more information. I am...a leader, not a medical man, but I would imagine it would depend on how close to Sakk the man in question is personally."

Her heart sank. Even if he'd let her, she couldn't give Jason assurances. She couldn't give any man assurances. The only way to know would be to have any given man she liked tested and hope for the best. *What man would put up with that?* None she knew.

****

Sakkra winced at her pallor. "The Sakk genes have been spread far and wide, in males as well as females. I am sure some human-appearing men could reproduce with you. Others?" He shook his head sadly. "I regret that the best we could do would be to test individual men for you."

Amy was silent for a long moment. At last, a strange, strangled sound escaped her.

He stared at her, trying to reason what had sent her so late in the night and in clothing that was so inappropriate to the situation and the weather.

Her hand moved in aimless little fluttering motions that drew his gaze. It took a moment for him to focus on what had changed since that morning.

"The ring," he breathed. "The joining ring." She wasn't wearing it. His understanding of the tradition was somewhat lacking, but as he understood it, once a man placed his ring, a woman rarely removed it.

"I never take it off."

A female journalist with a similar ring had told him that. Sakkra didn't doubt Amy was the same with hers.

Amy focused on him. "It's called an engagement ring," she corrected him.

Sakkra nodded. "Did your...?" What did one call a human intended? "Did he remove the ring?"

Did he do it because she'd tested as a match? Had he seen it as an insult that she'd tested? Had he rejected Amy in the belief that she couldn't provide him with children?

"Jason? My *ex*-fiancé?" She laughed harshly. "Yes, he took his ring back. He said he didn't want to marry a fucking alien." She put up a hand to still his protest. "His words, I assure you. Not mine."

"I am sorry. If I could undo this, I would."

She nodded, making the attempt to smile. It was short-lived, and her throat bobbed in half-swallowed sobs.

His mind whirled. Sakkra searched frantically for anything he could do to make this right, but there was likely nothing. Even if Jason had enough Sakk in him to have children with Amy—unlikely as that was—it was nearly a given that he wouldn't allow the testing to establish it.

****

The stresses of the last day crashed down on her, and Amy started sobbing. She tried to stop it, but once the tears were loosed, the dam broke, and they kept coming.

The room went still, and she realized she was alone, even among those who claimed they wanted to welcome her. That made her cry harder. She buried her face in her hands and gave up all attempts at propriety.

Sakk moved around her, but she didn't look up at them.

"Here. Drink this." A hand touched her wrist lightly.

Her throat raw and dry from crying, she attempted to do so, but her stomach balked at the concept.

Sakkra started to move away, and she closed her hand in his Sakk outfit. He seemed stunned by the move, but he opened his wings and arms, his expression questioning.

Amy didn't consider it for more than a moment. She needed companionship, even if it wasn't romantic companionship. If her mother was here, she would hug Amy, soothe her. *I need that right now.* She pressed to his chest, sniffing and swallowing, feeling wholly miserable.

Wings closed around her, and Sakkra wrapped an arm loosely around her waist. His humming calmed her hitching breaths.

Amy closed her abused eyes, exhausted, comforted by Sakkra's attentions. Her circling thoughts slowed, and darkness closed in.

****

"Sakkra, should we—"

He shushed Brak. *The fool.*

Even in sleep, Amy Davidson was far from calm. She trembled and sniffed. Low moans of protest escaped her throat. The grip on his *cuzta* made it clear she was not prepared to abandon the pitiful comfort he offered in her traumatized state.

No one will force her to. Sakkra laid his opposite hand on her shoulder, talking himself out of rubbing at her back in what might be misinterpreted as a sexual move.

Protective instincts reared up in him. In the last day, he'd seen Amy's panic, her determination, her uncertainty, and her heartbreak. Whatever discomfort or longing it cost him, he would offer what peace he could for her.

General Lea leaned close to whisper to Sakkra, in an attempt not to disturb Amy, no doubt. "Should I call the healers?"

His meaning was clear. A traumatized match was often sedated to avoid psychological or physical damage.

"No. She has already refused sedation once today. I will not presume to take her choices from her, in any way. How can she trust us, if we do?"

Lea's nod said he understood perfectly. "What will we do?"

"Only this. As long as she requests it." If it meant holding her while she slept all night, Sakkra would gladly give her comfort. Since he couldn't make her human, it was all he had to offer.

"As you wish, Sakkra."

****

Amy drifted in a semi-conscious state, warm and comfortable. There was a chest under her cheek, and the tang of musk made her mouth water.

She tried to work her way to an explanation for it. Jason liked space in bed. Have sex, roll over, and go to sleep.

Jason! Jason was gone. He'd taken the ring back and called off the wedding.

Then who am I sleeping with? She snapped awake and pushed away from her living pillow with a gasp, coming up against a semi-rigid wall.

"Shhh. You are safe."

I know that voice. She looked up in shock. *Sakkra?*

His wings retracted slowly, and she looked around in a panic, breathing a sigh of relief that they were still on the couch and not in a bed somewhere.

And there's not a chain on my wrist, either. Thank goodness!

The two Sakk warriors from the previous night were still there, though they were lounging in chairs instead of standing.

"You will always be safe here," Sakkra reminded her.

Amy wasn't sure how to answer that. She rubbed her eyes, then patted at her jacket pocket.

No phone. "What time is it?"

Sakkra looked toward the warrior who'd given her his cloak.

The other man leaned back and looked at something she couldn't see. "A quarter before five of the clock."

"Early," Sakkra assured her.

She pushed to her feet and slipped the cloak off her shoulders. Amy handed it to the warrior who'd lent it to her with a word of thanks.

"Ms. Davidson?" Sakkra inquired. "What are you doing?"

"I have to get ready for work. I'll be late."

He pushed to his feet, his wings stretching wide.

A morning stretch? It seemed intimate to watch him do that.

"Do you have a vehicle with you?" he asked.

"Yes. It's in the parking garage one block over."

"It is still dark. Please allow my men to walk you to it. For your safety." It was closer than she'd ever thought she'd hear a prince come to pleading.

The other two took to their feet, towering over her.

"Okay. Sure." In all honesty, she wasn't happy about the idea of walking to her car in the dark in this neighborhood, so the escort was something of a relief.

Amy headed for the door, but a niggling of regret stopped her just shy of touching the handle. She half-turned to Sakkra. "I'm sorry about...about last night. It...it won't happen again. Thank you for trying to help."

He seemed pained by the pronouncement. Sakkra tipped his head smoothly. "We are at your service, Ms. Davidson. You are welcome here at any time."

Answering that was impossible. She tipped her head in return and rushed out the door, stopping cold again in the hallway.

The one who'd given her his cloak motioned to her right. "This way, Ms. Davidson."

"Thank you." She let him walk beside her, lost to find her way out of the maze alone.

Just as I can't find my way out of the mess I'm in alone.

There was little question that she would have to leave her job. Working with Lucy would become impossible within hours or days.

Then why am I hurrying to it?

Realization made her quicken her step. Amy wasn't hurrying to the job. She was speeding away from Sakkra. Waking up in his arms had been far too appealing. Falling asleep there had been far too easy.

I really don't need this in my life right now. It is just one too many complications in an already complex situation.

Chapter Ten

"I don't understand why you want to do this?" her boss repeated. Gary stood with his legs spread and his arms crossed over his chest, looking down at her while Amy packed her desk.

Defensive much, Gary? She sighed. "I don't *want* to do this, but for my sake and the company's, I don't see another choice." Amy wracked her sleep-deprived brains, wishing she did see another option, but worrying half the morning hadn't dredged up more of them.

As it was, her only reprieve from Lucy's full steam fit was the fact that the woman in question had called off sick today. Tomorrow, she would return in a snit, looking for trouble.

"If Lucy can't act professionally, we'll just —"

"Fire her?" Amy finished for him.

He grunted his agreement.

"And she'll sue. Even if you win in court and prove you had just cause, Lucy will cost you and the company a fortune to prove it."

Gary shifted as if in discomfort. Amy's heart sank a notch. She'd known he wouldn't be able to argue that.

He sighed. "I'll move her to another office."

You would have to transfer her to the moon. Or to Sakk. Why couldn't Gary understand? If Lucy went as far as calling Jason, she was intent. Amy knew from experience that Lucy was a bulldog. When someone crossed her, she didn't let go until the body stopped moving or the other person withdrew entirely from the situation.

269

He shook his head. "I could transfer *you* to another office." The resignation in his expression said he'd already anticipated her answer.

"There is no office that doesn't interact with payroll." And payroll was where Lucy hung her hat. *Damn the luck!*

"I can't convince you to stay? Can I?"

"I wish you had something I hadn't already thought of," she admitted. "Anything that would make this unnecessary."

His expression said Gary would rather risk a lawsuit than let Amy walk out the door, but in this lousy economy, he couldn't risk his own job that way. "Good luck, Amy. It's going to be hard to replace you."

"And you."

He offered his hand. "You've got a glowing reference, when you need it. I'll say...I'll say we're reorganizing, and your job is moving to another office."

She took it and shook his hand, appreciation for the lie nearly choking her. "Thanks a lot, Gary."

****

Her parents' house loomed over her. Strange how it had never felt that way before.

I've never had to tell them we're not human before. Amy wasn't looking forward to that. *In the least.*

I'm wasting time. Putting this off won't help, and it won't make it disappear.

As if confirming that, the drape in the front window moved. Her mother appeared, smiled, waved, then disappeared from view.

She's heading to the door. There's no putting this off.

Amy pushed the car door closed and started toward the door. Her mother beat her to the front porch, but only by a few heartbeats.

Diane looked as young as she'd looked when Amy was in high school. *As young as she looked when I was in second grade.* Her blond hair showed not even a hint of gray, and her lavender eyes crinkled and creased a little at the edges.

Lavender eyes... Amy had read that Sakk-descended often had oddly-colored eyes. Someone could easily guess her mother was Sakk-descended, though there was no hint in Amy's appearance. Amy looked much more like her father than her mother.

Diane pressed a hand to Amy's forehead, no doubt gauging her temperature as she had when Amy had been a child. "Good. You're not sick."

Amy managed a weak smile. "Why would you think that?"

"You've never been one for playing hooky. Naturally, I assumed you *must* be sick. I'm glad I was wrong."

"Are you?" Amy certainly didn't feel well. She was scattered, unbalanced—

"Of course I am. No mother wants to see her child sick or injured. It's the worst. There's nothing you can do about it but wait it out and treat it as best you can." She waved it off, seemingly weary at the very thought of it.

I know something worse, and there's nothing you can do about this, either. Not even wait it out.

Her mother cocked her head to one side and did a visual assessment of Amy. Then Diane hooked arms with her. "Come inside." She sighed. "And then you can tell me what happened with Jason."

Just the thought of him broke Amy's resolve, and she sobbed. The newly-erected dam burst, and the tears started flowing again.

And Sakkra isn't here this time.

That made her cry harder. Amy stumbled along blindly beside her mother, sinking to the couch gratefully when they reached it.

Diane disappeared, then returned with a box of tissues and a glass of juice. "Nothing in the world is worse than a child who is hurting," she grumbled.

I will probably never know. Amy hiccupped and let loose a strained laugh.

Diane sank into the other end of the couch. "Tell me. What has that hotheaded boy done this time?"

Amy wanted to deny that it was Jason's fault, but there was no other way to present it. *I was willing to try. He wasn't.*

Her mother sighed again. "I swear. Men always lose their minds close to the wedding."

"There isn't going to *be* a wedding."

She wrapped her arm around Amy's shoulders and hugged her. "Oh, Amy. Most of these things are nothing more than cold feet."

Amy shook her head, then blew her nose.

The pause was long enough that it could be nothing but an evaluation. "He didn't cheat on you? Did he?"

Not that I know of.

Now I'm just being snippy. "No. Nothing like that."

"Then whatever he's done—"

"He left me. Jason took his grandmother's ring back, and he left me. He's not coming back, and good riddance to him!" But the truth still hurt. *A lot.* "There won't be a wedding."

"I don't understand this." Her mother's exasperation was impossible to miss. "What is he thinking?"

Amy forced a calming breath, took a sip of the juice, and composed herself. "You know I went to the Sakk consulate with Lucy the other day."

Diane nodded solemnly. "I'll assume she isn't Sakk."

How well you know Lucy. "No. Of course she's not. I was trying to calm her down, and Lucy pushed me. Not hard. She was horsing around, but she pushed me onto the testing pad."

Her mother paled, and Amy hurried on.

"I'm Sakk. We are, I mean. I can only test positive if you and Dad do as well."

There was a moment of potent silence. "They're sure?"

"No false positives or negatives."

"This is no reason to call things off with Jason," she decided.

"*I* didn't. He did. I wanted to have testing done. I wanted to ask questions of the Sakk. I wanted to find out if we're compatible or not."

She winced. "Jason doesn't?"

"Not only doesn't he want to be tested, he can't stand the thought of me being Sakk-descended. He's a bigot, Mom."

"Oh... Oh my!" She hesitated. "What are you going to do now?"

"Cancel everything. Get as many deposits back as I can. Find a new job. Go on with my life...somehow."

"Find a new job? What happened to your *old* job?"

"Lucy?" Amy felt certain she didn't need to say more.

"Oh. I take it you'll need a new best friend, as well as a new fiancé."

"I don't *need* either of them," she groused.

Her mother wisely changed the subject. "What about the Sakk?"

Memories of Sakkra holding her while she wept shook her with their intensity.

"Amy?"

"They aren't asking for anything. Their prince apologized for the trouble they've caused me."

"But what *about* them?" Diane asked softly.

"I'm not leaving Earth."

"There's no way for one of them to stay here?"

"I don't know." *Is there a way?* Mating with one of the Sakk warriors wouldn't be a hardship if she didn't have to leave Earth for him.

I don't want another man. Certainly not yet. "I'm not ready to think about that yet."

She sighed. "I suppose we should let your cousins know."

Amy groaned. "Not today, please. I'm not ready to answer their questions." *And I seem to come up with more questions to ask every time I talk about this situation.* "Give me a few days to get back on my feet. Okay?"

"Is this weekend long enough?"

I don't think it will ever be long enough. "Sure. That would be fine."

****

Amy tossed her heels on top of the box from her office and dragged it out of the car after her. She hip-bumped the door shut and let herself into the building through the security door. It was a three story climb to her apartment, and Amy was sure the soles of her feet would be black from going barefoot up the stairs, but it was better than carrying the box in her heels.

The key slid into the lock easily enough, but it stuck when Amy tried to turn it. *Damn it!* How many times had she mentioned the problem to the manager?

Jiggling the key didn't work. Removing it and trying again didn't, either.

"Not today," she moaned. Did everything have to go wrong at once?

Amy shifted the box, trying to trap it between her waist and the door. With two hands free, maybe she could find the sweet—

The box overbalanced and toppled to the floor. Pens and papers skittered and shuffled around her feet. The coffee cup Lucy had given her for her last birthday shattered on the polished wood.

For a long moment, Amy stared at the destruction. Laughter bubbled up from inside her, and tears pooled in her eyes.

"Let me help you with that," a familiar voice rumbled out.

Amy wiped her eyes on the cuff of her dress shirt and looked around at the new arrival. It was the man the Sakk had hired to protect her.

His expression pleaded with her.

Maybe he's not such a scumbag. "He won't just send you away. Will he?"

"Sakkra? No, he won't do that, Ms. Davidson."

This is a good thing. Besides my family, it's all I have going for me right now. "Thank you. I would appreciate it."

****

Rietin took a calming breath. He'd been afraid she'd attack him at the admission that he wouldn't be leaving.

She's allowing me to help. That was nothing short of a miracle in the making.

He glanced at her bare feet and winced. "Stay where you are." Any move had the likelihood of her stepping on ceramic and cutting herself. "Hand me your keys."

"Okay." She offered them readily.

Getting the door open was the obvious first step. Rietin played the key back and forth, moving the heavy door this way and that. Finally, the lock snapped open.

That will have to be repaired. He made a mental note to have a team from the consulate do the job the next time she left the apartment.

Rietin considered lifting her inside, then rejected the idea. It would be too familiar, and Amy would surely take offense. "Step inside carefully. Do you have a broom and dust pan?"

She stepped gingerly into her apartment. "Yes. I'll get it."

He crouched down and started collecting her belongings into the box. Though it was unseemly to pry, he noted photographs of Amy with friends and family. Two of them had Lucy Ferguson in them. He moved on, collecting pens and knick knacks, cards, and—

Realization made his heart stutter. *She cleaned out her desk at work.* He'd seen her walk out with the box, but he hadn't attached significance to it. *That means she no longer has a job. But why?*

Her footsteps approached, and Rietin hurried to put the last of the items in the box. He topped it with her shoes and reached up for the whisk and dust pan Amy offered.

She reached for the box and nearly overbalanced onto the shattered ceramic. Rietin dropped the tools and steadied her. He pulled his hands back slowly.

Amy didn't comment on the move, though she moved from foot to foot for a moment in what appeared to be an attack of nerves. Rietin went back to sweeping up the ceramic.

"I'll get a waste basket for the shards." She rushed away.

I'm making her nervous. If he didn't put her at ease, he would never be able to do his job effectively. Rietin could protect a person who didn't like him or didn't notice him, but it was much more difficult when the person didn't trust him.

Amy was back a few minutes later, offering a round plastic trash can.

Most likely from her bathroom. Rietin tipped his head and took it, dumping the debris into it. He performed a second sweep, hoping he hadn't missed any shards that might injure her.

At his second deposit in the can, she reached down for it. "Here. Let me take that. Why don't you grab the box?"

The request surprised him, but he complied. Stepping into her apartment without a squad of warriors felt wrong to him, but Rietin did so at her request.

"Where would you like this?" he asked.

"The coffee table would be fine. Would you like a drink?"

He paused, the box millimeters above the surface of the table she'd indicated. "Beg your pardon?"

"I should know what your plan is to protect me. Shouldn't I?" The door clicked shut, and she turned the problematic lock.

Rietin deposited the box and straightened, trying to organize his rioting mind. "If you wish, of course." None of his charges had asked before. He reminded himself that she'd made an offer. "Nothing alcoholic. I am on duty."

"And when you're not? Coffee?"

"Coffee would be wonderful." He couldn't get enough of the human drink. "Not...what?"

"On duty." She pulled a bag of coffee from the freezer and filled an electric grinder. The whir of the blades cut off his answer. She continued as soon as it stopped. "Who will be protecting me then?" Amy filled the metal mesh filter with ground coffee.

Rietin ambled toward her. "I never go off duty. Having more than one here would draw attention I am certain you would like to avoid." He settled on a stool at the breakfast bar. That gave him an adequate vantage point to make plans for her protection. She would need an area shield protecting the outer walls and windows, monitoring...and the repairs to her lock.

Amy finished filling the coffee maker with a pot of water, drawing his attention to her again. She pressed the button to start the brewing cycle, then turned to him, her brow furrowed in seeming confusion.

"You work around the clock?"

He managed a weak smile. "I do sleep, if that's what you're asking. I simply...won't sleep until you do."

Her color dipped. "You're not staying here."

"In your apartment? Of course not. I wouldn't dream of it." Sakkra would never approve such an unseemly arrangement.

She relaxed a notch, and her color seeped back.

But she should know what the actual plan is. She asked. "I'm in apartment 2C. If you need me, I'll be there whenever you're here. I'll also give you phone numbers to my cell and the direct line to the consulate comm center. You will always have a way to reach us."

Amy turned back to the coffee maker, seemingly rattled.

Rietin ground his teeth in frustration. A floor below her and the opposite corner of the building had seemed distant enough for him. Perhaps he'd misjudged.

****

Amy forced a calming breath. "What does your ID say?"

"Pardon?"

She pulled down two mugs. "When I moved in, it took more than a week for the background and credit checks." She turned toward Rietin.

His wallet was open on his palm, and he nodded toward it.

Her heart pounding, Amy crossed the distance between them and took it. One side was a standard Virginia driver's license. The second proclaimed him an agent for the NSA.

She scanned her gaze down his clothes. "You dress to blend in."

Rietin smiled. "Anywhere I have to, whether it's black tie, California casual, or jeans and t-shirts. They spent a fortune outfitting me with everything I might possibly need."

Amy passed the wallet back to him, and he pocketed it.

"And how did you get mixed up with the NSA, Joshua Rietin?"

His eyes narrowed. "Call me Josh, if you're more comfortable with it, but my name is actually Rietin, and I am *not* a member of the NSA. I liaise with them, and they provide a cover story for me to allow me to move unimpeded."

"Cover..." She swallowed a lump in her throat. "Cover story?"

He nodded solemnly.

"Why do you *need* a cover story? And how did you end up working for the Sakk?"

"Working...for the Sakk?"

"Everyone knows they typically only use their own people. I understand why they would want a human to blend in. How were you chosen to be that human?"

Rietin winced.

Amy stared at him, trying to understand his sudden attack of nerves. "Come on. You've given me this much information." *Speaking of which... Why* is *he giving me all this information?*

"The simplest way to put it is that the Sakk *do* only use our own. Since humans would stand in my way in the same situation they would clear the way for your own government, the NSA...arranged for me to appear to be—"

"Human. You're Sakk?" *Of course. Not all Sakk have wings. I don't.*

"Yes. I am."

281

Amy rounded the breakfast bar and climbed onto another of the stools, stunned by the revelation. "You look and...and sound so human."

"Part of my cover. It took me more than a year of training with Representative Janice to learn enough idiom to pass muster, and that was after a year of learning basic American English on Sakk."

"Were you born on a seed world? Is that why—" Her face flamed. "Oh, I'm being rude. I'm so sorry."

"I don't mind. No. I wasn't born on a seed world. I was born on Sakk. My two sisters are short flight. Uh...They have small, vestigial wings. With the breeding measures, not all young are born fully-winged."

"But all the ones I've seen are."

Rietin hesitated. "The strongest genetically are given first priority in finding mates."

Her temper uncorked. "Being wingless is seen as a genetic weakness? Being part human is?"

"No!" Rietin lost his composure for the first time. "I'm not sure anyone can claim to be pure Sakk at this point. Well, besides Sa Beldon, of course."

"But you said —"

"*I* am genetically inferior."

"The men who come here to find mates are all fully-winged."

"Not all of them."

"Maybe women should know that."

Rietin stared at her, his expression questioning.

"You know. Let them know there are options."

He mouthed the word 'options' back, as if it was foreign to him.

No time like the present. "For example, are any of the Sakk warriors willing to live on Earth with their human mates?"

The silence was palpable. "If you're afraid of leaving Earth—"

"I haven't agreed to anything," she reminded him. "But the last thing I would agree to is leaving my family on Earth and moving to another planet."

Rietin nodded slowly. "I can understand how difficult that would be."

"Well?" she prompted him.

"No one has asked. If it meant a mate, I imagine a male would agree to it." But he was pensive, seemingly unsure of his answer.

"But?"

"The consulate is not currently adapted to that purpose. But it could be," he hastened to add. "Do you believe more women would agree to be tested if we arranged it?"

"Some would, I'm sure."

****

Sakkra's muscles tightened at the sound of his comm unit squawking out an urgent summons. "Yes?" *If it is not Rietin, the tracker will answer to me personally.* Evening meal had come and gone, and still there had been no word from him about Amy Davidson's condition.

"Rietin comming, Sakkra."

"Secure line to me." *He may have personal information about her. There is no reason to expose the warriors to that.*

After a moment, Rietin opened the discussion with the fact that he was connected.

"What in Sakkan's name took you so long?" Sakkra groused.

"Ms. Davidson wanted to know my plans for protecting her. We discussed it over a meal."

Words failed him, and his temper rose.

"I have no plans to seduce the young match," Rietin assured him. "I helped her when she dropped a box of her belongings, and—"

"She was leaving?" Sakkra's heart pounded at the thought of it.

"No. She..." He hesitated long enough to make Sakkra's stomach churn. "She lost her position of employment and was bringing her belongings home from work."

"Why? Was it our fault?" How much upheaval had the Sakk caused in her life?

"I don't know yet. She went to her office and left it again shortly afterward. I don't know what transpired inside."

"Yet." Sakkra added a tone of order to that.

"I will need Koebi to handle that tomorrow. It was too late to investigate today by the time I learned she'd lost her position."

"Agreed. I will have his schedule changed to put him at your disposal for the next few days."

"Good. That will help."

"What about the rest of your plans?"

Rietin didn't waste a moment. "She has allowed me to install simple monitoring...stress activated voice and panic buttons in her apartment. I have also erected a shield wall on the outside walls and windows of her apartment.

"I will need Koebi and a warrior with a background in maintenance to see to the lock on her apartment door."

"Changing the locks?" he asked. Did someone dangerous have a key to her home?

"No. I checked to be sure. Only Ms. Davidson's parents and the building manager have keys to the lock. I ran a background check on the manager. He has no criminal history, no ties to anti-Sakk groups or organizers, and there is no indication that he is at risk of accepting bribes to pay for outstanding debts. But the lock sticks. In an emergency, she must be able to get the door open quickly."

"Understood. When should I tell them to arrive?"

"When she leaves. She already feels pressured."

"In what way?"

"She is not comfortable with allowing me to escort her. Thankfully, she isn't balking at me following her."

"Good." It wasn't. It would be safer if Rietin was in the vehicle with her. Safer still if she was behind the bulletproof glass of Rietin's van. But after learning the tracker had enjoyed Amy's company, Sakkra was selfishly glad she wasn't comfortable with Rietin's continuous presence.

The tracker wisely chose not to question his response.

"How much time did you spend with Ms. Davidson, Rietin?" *How Sakkra envied him every moment of it!*

"Less than two hours. Enough to help her clean up her scattered belongings, discuss the security arrangements, set up the shield—"

"Share a meal." *Why does that bother me so much?* He denied it was jealousy. Amy wasn't Sakkra's woman to be jealous over.

Rietin remained silent.

"What is it?" Sakkra snapped. Had the tracker gleaned his interest in Amy? *Unfortunate and ill-timed though it is.*

"Ms. Davidson raised some interesting ideas, but it is hardly my place to—"

"Say it." His muscles were strung tight, and Sakkra had no idea what had been suggested or in what context.

"She believes we should arrange for matches and their mates to stay on Earth."

"Another breeding colony?"

"I don't believe that was her intent...precisely. But daughters produced by Earth-side matches could find mates at the consulate or back on Sakk."

"To what end?" Sakkra didn't understand her purpose in suggesting it.

"Two main reasons. The first would be that female young raised in the consulate would be more at ease with Sakk traditions and culture...and language, for that matter. They would be more accepting of mating and less skittish of Sakk males."

"Is Ms. Davidson skittish of our males?" The question was out before Sakkra could talk himself out of asking it.

"She doesn't appear to be, though she did suggest that we should bring in more wingless males of strong stock and tell the human women that such males are available, if they prefer it. If they are uncomfortable with the idea of mating with a fully-winged male."

"Was that her second reason?"

"No. That was a separate suggestion.

"Ms. Davidson suggested that letting women know they don't have to leave their families and friends and lives behind on Earth to move to Sakk would be advantageous and might entice women who wouldn't otherwise choose to test to the consulate and Sakk mates. As their daughters grow older and their families die off, they may be willing to relocate to Sakk, but in the meantime, they could produce daughters.

"Ms. Davidson will not leave Earth. It is her home, and her family is here. I believe she feels that accepting a Sakk mate means she will have to abandon all of that. Not that she is prepared to accept any male so soon after losing her fiancé."

Sakkra's heart sank. "I see." He'd come here as an ambassador of his people, when Master Beldon and his mate returned to Sakk. Would he have come if it meant leaving his home and family forever? *Probably not.*

His secret hopes evaporated that quickly. Amy might take a mate someday, but only if she could stay on Earth. *And only if her mate is wingless.* "I understand. Let me look into it. Be sure to report what you learn."

"As you wish."

Sakkra closed the comm and made his way to bed, weary in body and mind. Her ideas were sound, and Sakkra felt they could be beneficial. For now, he would have to figure out how to present them to Ellwood best.

Perhaps Amy could help with that as Jannie helped Beldon present their case for testing. Perhaps I should invite her to dinner.

Chapter Eleven

Amy twirled around to check her dress, her heart pounding in anticipation. Though Rietin had told her it didn't matter what she chose to wear, being invited to dinner by a prince seemed to indicate something more than jeans, even if it was a business meeting and not pleasure.

Go with it. It's not like you have any other reason to get dressed up in the near future.

I am not going to think about that tonight. I am going to enjoy myself. Period. End of subject. This is my new life.

That decided, she pulled on a long coat, picked up her purse, and headed down to meet Rietin. He met her at the security door and escorted her to her car. With a tip of his head, he went to his van and followed her across town.

In the wide drive at the back of the consulate, he pulled around her car and preceded her through the shield layers, his stops and starts letting her know when it was safe to continue on.

I should have let him drive me. It retrospect, it seemed petty to insist on driving herself, considering the fact that they were headed the same place. The van Rietin drove was a plain panel van without the Sakk seals, so it wouldn't draw unwanted attention. And... The Sakk weren't asking for anything from her, and accepting a ride from Rietin didn't obligate her.

I shouldn't depend on them. That was a hard idea to shake.

There was time to find a balance. The Sakk would likely be part of her life forever, now that they knew she was Sakk-descended.

They parked in an underground garage, and Rietin led her into the consulate and through the hallways to a door not far from the clinic. He knocked for her, tipped his head, and left without a backward glance.

"Enter." It was definitely Sakkra's voice, but he sounded distracted.

Amy pushed through the door and examined the room before closing it behind herself. It was a large office with four-foot-high screens along one wall and bookshelves lining two of the others. A large tapestry depicting a Sakk man and woman holding hands took up much of the last wall. The furnishings consisted of a conference table surrounded by ten cushioned chairs and a desk with two guest chairs and one chair behind it...currently occupied by Sakkra.

He looked up, then startled and pushed to his feet. "Oh, I am so sorry."

"You look busy."

Sakkra glanced toward the paperwork and back to her. "You have given me many things to think about."

"The ideas about mated couples staying on Earth?" she guessed.

"Among other things. Please, make yourself at home." He motioned to the conference table. "I'll call for the meal, and we'll discuss your ideas."

Amy headed to the table and removed her coat. She folded it over one of the chairs. On the other side of the room, she heard Sakkra speaking in the Sakk language.

She turned to look at him, smiling at the way he moved. He was graceful. Amy had never seen a man move the way he did. There was something nearly hypnotic about it.

He pressed a button on the board, then stood. His smile of welcome disappeared, and a heated look took its place.

Amy swallowed hard and took a step back. Maybe the choice of outfit hadn't been prudent. She'd forgotten why the Sakk were looking for mates in the first place.

Sakkra straightened, and his expression smoothed into a strained smile. "You look lovely."

She smoothed the dress over her fluttering stomach. "Thank you."

He crossed the room toward her, and Amy forced herself not to retreat. That would offend him, she was certain.

Sakkra guided the chair to her left out and motioned her into it.

Amy struggled to remember the last time a man had held a chair for her. *Certainly pre-Jason.*

I will not *think about Jason tonight.* She took her seat with a nod of thanks, and Sakkra slid her closer to the table.

He didn't join her immediately. Instead, he collected some papers and a pen from the desk.

"I thought the Sakk typically used...your version of computers," she noted.

He took the chair across from her and settled the papers in front of him. "For most things, we do. I like making notes and drawings for myself on paper."

A knock at the door interrupted them, and Sakkra shouted out an order for whoever it was to enter. Two Sakk warriors came in, pushing a cart laden with food between them. They set the table, then placed platters of food and pitchers of drinks between them. The two didn't serve the food. They were gone with a quick snap of a bow, closing her in with Sakkra again.

****

Sakkra didn't question that Amy Davidson was discomfited, but he wasn't sure precisely why she was.

Quantifying his own discomfort was easy enough. The sight of her in the skimpy little black dress and the memory of her sleeping in his arms had rendered his cock hard and ready for a sexual encounter she wasn't going to offer.

He started describing the types of food on the table. It was an innocuous enough discussion that he hoped would cause his cock to subside in disinterest. It didn't.

Amy chose the rice dish and sautéed baby vegetables with a side of dark bread.

"I apologize that there are no meat dishes," he offered.

"I don't eat much meat. Mostly beef and fish." She paused with the fork halfway to her mouth. "I suppose that makes sense, all things considered."

Sakkra swallowed a mouthful of the vegetables. "It does, actually. Very few of the Sakk-descended we've found on Earth have been big meat eaters, and even those matches typically lose the taste for meat when they are carrying young. They may still eat fish, but rarely land animals or fowl."

"Do you serve any fish or meat in the consulate?"

"Typically fish. We do occasionally serve beef or pork. We do not serve winged animals...for obvious reasons."

"Well that makes sense." She took another bite of the rice.

"We farm several types of Earth fish—at the consulates, aboard ship, and on Sakk itself—for the Earth-born matches. Introducing cattle and pigs to Sakk is more problematic, so we transport a small amount of frozen meat from Earth every month."

She seemed to consider that, stirring her food idly with her fork. "This is another example of things I think the women need to know. There is the assumption that women who go to Sakk won't have the things they like available to them when they leave Earth."

"Like the fact that there are males without wings available to be mates." He didn't question it.

"Honestly, I never knew it, until I met Rietin. I naturally assumed that all men from Sakk were winged. All the advertising you do to entice women in shows *winged* men."

Sakkra placed his fork on the table, his appetite waning at the wriggling apprehension in his stomach. "It was an oversight. We consider the fully-winged form ideal...beautiful. Not that we find those without wings lacking," he hastened to add. The last thing he wanted to do was offend her.

"I think I understand. At some times in history, a well-rounded female was most attractive. At others, women who were thin to near emaciation was. The art from those times reflect whatever the preferred standard for beauty was at the time."

"This is why we need your help so desperately. We make choices that match our sensibilities...our arts, but those choices have inherent messages to Earth-born that we do not intend to send."

She pushed her plate away and reached for the paper and pen. "May I?"

Sakkra pushed them toward her. "Please."

Amy turned a piece of paper to landscape orientation and started sketching. He rose and circled to her side of the table, watching the rough outlines appearing.

She started speaking. "You find the fully-winged form most appealing, so put two of those men center. Partially-winged—"

"Short flight," he corrected her.

Her hand stopped sketching for a moment, then continued. "Sorry about that. Short flight. I didn't mean to offend you."

"It's not offensive. My apologies. It is simply the correct terminology."

Amy turned to look at him. She offered a nod, then went back to drawing. "Short flight men further out. Then those with no wings. I would also choose men with a variety of hair...feather colors and eye colors. You tend to choose blond men. I hadn't realized how varied they really were until I reached the consulate."

He leaned closer to her. "To what end? Do women really choose men based on physical traits?"

"In part. You have to find something appealing in more than just shared interests. We want to impress upon women that there is a man to fit any given tastes."

"I think I understand." He hesitated before asking his next question. "And you believe allowing matches to stay on Earth would be advantageous as well?"

She didn't hesitate. "I think it would. In more ways than one."

"Because they won't have to leave their lives and families," he parroted back to her what Rietin had told him.

"That's one advantage."

"And the other?"

She set the pen down and looked up at him. They were close enough to kiss, and Sakkra's mouth watered to do so.

This is a business meeting. A move like that would alienate her, and considering her tenuous relationship with the Sakk, that was the last thing he could risk.

"How many countries do you have consulates in?"

"Ten. We are in negotiation with seven more."

Her smile made his heart thud against his ribs. Would that the smile was intended for him, he would consider himself lucky.

She has just lost her intended mate. She is not seeking another at this time. Who knew how long it would take a female to recover from such a loss? Widows often chose not to take males to their beds for more than a *yan* after losing one.

"You're already aware that some women might want to mate with a Sakk warrior to have a new world to explore."

"Of course. Jannie made it very clear that linguists, botanists, biologists, archeologists—most types of scientists, healers, and sociologists—would find Sakk a treasure."

"Some women have a similar ache to explore Earth."

Sakkra considered that. "It is nothing to us to send shuttles from consulate to consulate. A matter of an hour or two of flight time. We do it often."

"The countries you have consulates in today?"

"The United States, the United Kingdom, Germany, France, Italy, South Africa, India, the Ukraine, China, and Bermuda."

Bermuda had been incredibly easy, compared to other agreements they'd made. With Sakk technology for purifying sea water or waste water into potable water, they'd only had to promise to produce two million liters of potable water a day and supply it for free to the Bermudan government for distribution to their population. With the Sakk providing more than a tenth of the daily water used on Bermuda, the little island had been most accommodating.

And that was before tourism increased by fifteen percent in the wake of the improvements the Sakk offered.

"You don't realize what a gold mine you're already sitting on." Her tone was wistful.

"We are?" In truth, he wanted to hear her talk about a subject she was clearly so taken with.

"Have you ever heard of a honeymoon?"

"I am afraid not."

"When humans marry, they often take a trip to celebrate. If you allow the human mates to travel anywhere you have consulates, it is an incredible gift. Some people never manage to travel as they would like to. Not to mention, nearly every country you named is a popular travel location for people in other countries.

"You're not even limited to those locations. If you issued passports to the Earth-born Sakk-descended and their Sakk mates, you could make agreements to use the landing strips at military bases of Sakk allies on Earth or airports, and allow them to take day-trips by shuttle to other locations where you don't have consulates. It would be a dream come true for some women."

She stopped talking, her color high, her dark eyes glittering.

Sakkra was momentarily struck mute by the sight of her. At last he managed a nod and rushed to his side of the table. "I need to make notes. There is so much to be done. Sakk stationed locally who speak the languages could act as translators and guards for those stationed in other areas who don't." He realized he was rambling.

Amy sat, her arms crossed under her breasts, smiling widely.

"Would you care for a drink while we talk? Wine?"

She hesitated, her expression guarded. "One. I still have to drive home."

Sakkra bit back the reminder that Rietin could drive her. "As you wish, of course."

****

Amy paced the floor, fleshing out the idea of honeymoons on Earth with Sakkra.

The wine he'd offered was sweet but strong. It went to her head, and she'd decided walking the room was a good idea.

Amy looked over his shoulder, settling one hand on his back. The feathers on his wing teased her nerves, and memories of those wings wrapped around her brought completely inappropriate musings to mind.

Sakkra stiffened, then looked over his shoulder.

She backed away with a gasp, her cheeks burning. "I apologize. I take it touching your wings is...against some rule?"

"It is only done in certain circumstances." He didn't elaborate on what those circumstances might be.

He rose to his feet, facing her fully. His scent was far too appealing. Amy considered asking him what cologne or soap he used, but she suspected that was his natural scent.

I don't need to know that. If I know it, I'll want to investigate it.

"Have I made you uncomfortable, Ms. Davidson?"

"No." *Far too comfortable.* "And please... Call me Amy."

"Amy."

His voice rumbled against her mouth, and visions of his lips closing on hers made her go weak in the knees.

"You seem tired," he noted.

Not tired at all. Energized. But what she wanted was something she shouldn't even be considering, especially not four days after losing her fiancé. "Yes. A bit."

"Will you come again?" His gray eyes pleaded with her.

She swallowed hard, the double meaning hitting her full force. Amy didn't doubt it would be easy to come with Sakkra. The man would doubtless be one hell of a lover.

Better than Jason ever was.

He means meeting to discuss the changes they'll be making. She nodded. "Yes. I will."

Sakkra raised her hand, laying a kiss on her knuckles. She gasped, and their eyes met.

The urge to kiss him was more than she could stand. Amy pulled her hand away and turned toward her coat. The moment she had it in her hand, she rushed toward the door.

"Can I walk you out?" he offered.

She stopped with her hand on the door handle. It wasn't smart. *Not smart at all.* "Yes."

****

Sakkra watched Amy pull out of the bunker, Rietin's van trailing in her wake, his heart aching.

His cock wasn't faring much better. The woman was enough to drive any man to madness.

And I'm inviting her into my company again? A woman who is determined not to choose a Sakk mate at all, let alone me?

Oh, but her scent and reactions said she might someday change her mind about that. Was it worth being driven half-mad if there was a chance of her choosing him? Or of her not changing her mind about leaving Earth?

"Yes. It is." Sakkra didn't question it.

Instead, he went back to his office and looked over the notes he'd made with Amy's assistance. The surest way to make an impression on the lady was showing her he took her suggestions seriously.

He would order new advertisements immediately. Sakkra intended to have them in distribution before Amy visited the consulate again.

Chapter Twelve

The sound of Amy's cell phone ringing dragged her from sleep.

Since she'd blocked Lucy's cell phone, her home phone, her father's home phone and cell phone, and every phone number associated with their formerly-shared employer—save Gary's personal cell number, and since Amy didn't pick up calls with 'unavailable' incoming numbers, the worst that could happen was that Lucy had purchased a disposable cell phone and was disturbing Amy's sleep with it. She wouldn't make it through to Amy, at any rate. If it came to Lucy playing those sorts of pranks, Amy would turn off her cell phone at night. *Simple.*

As if anything about this was simple.

She fumbled the phone from the nightstand and fought to focus on the caller ID on the screen, noting that the tone wasn't an incoming call. *It's a message.*

The ID came into focus slowly. "Jason."

Her heart thudded against her ribs. *Maybe he's thought about it. Maybe he's decided to go with me for testing.*

Maybe he's texting me to demand some other gift he's given me back. Maybe he's drunk and feeling spiteful.

There was no way to know but to open the message. Her hands shaking, Amy punched the button to do so. It wasn't a text; rather it was a video message.

She considered closing it without watching whatever the video was.

No, it's better if I know. Even if it was just more hate from Jason, it was better that she get it over with and write him off completely.

Amy muttered a curse and pressed the button.

It took a few heartbeats for what she was seeing to make it through the protective veil of disbelief. Jason was in his bed, on his back...naked. Lucy sat astride him, riding him.

Fucking my ex-fiancé. Less than a week after he dumped me! You bitch. You bastard. Damn you both!

She exited out of the video, cutting Lucy off mid-scream of 'YES!' Deleting the message wasn't enough for her. She blocked both of Jason's numbers, then his parents' number. Amy threw the cell phone across the room with a sob.

"We're done, fuckers. No turning back from here."

That stated to the empty room, Amy curled to the bed, but now there was too much adrenaline in her system for her to sleep. She sighed, pushed from the bed, and made her way to her desk and the laptop. If she couldn't sleep, she might as well look for a new job.

And block Jason through email as well. She'd already taken that step with Lucy. *Might as well finish the job.*

****

"We're done, fuckers. No turning back from here."

Amy's voice coming from the speaker next to his bed snapped Rietin awake. He threw back the blanket, then jumped from the mattress, wearing only a pair of knit shorts, cursing aloud at the fact that the speaker had gone silent.

"Replay last five minutes," he ordered the security board's voice recognition software. "Vocals and possible security risks only." That would allow him to get an idea of the situation without wasting time with dead air. Hopefully.

A tone that could only be her cell phone sounded once. Then again.

"Jason."

"Shit."

The sounds that followed could have been a hard-core pornography video. Male grunts and shouts overlapped with a woman—not Amy—screaming out a litany of *"Yes! Yes! Yes! Y—"*

The sob that followed was likely Amy. A sharp sound that might have been her cell phone hitting the far wall of the room echoed it. The lack of separation between the sounds indicated that they were that close in reality as well.

Definitely Amy.

The curse that had woken him repeated.

Silence fell, potent in the stillness of the room. Before he could move, Amy's muttering reached him over the speakers.

Real time. It took only a minute to decipher that she was talking to herself. *About finding a new job and moving somewhere Lucy Ferguson can't find her.*

Fuck me! I have to see whatever Amy saw. He rushed to the keypad and called up the scans of Amy's comms. Since they were deleted unless he called them up within an hour and he never eavesdropped on them, save in an emergency situation like this one, he hadn't mentioned to Amy that he could do this. *And I won't. Unless I have to.*

The video came in from a cell phone registered to Jason. *Her ex-fiancé.* It was as graphic as he'd guessed and showed Lucy Ferguson engaged in a torrid affair with the...

Can one call such an unfeeling beast a man? Rietin wasn't certain about that.

I have to do something about this. I have to protect her.

But how? Routing all her calls through the consulate would be an invasion of her privacy.

What about messages to her cell phone and email communication? That was possible. Such communications were often delayed. She'd already placed blocks on both methods of communication, and Rietin could take on the screening process personally, via his own cell phone.

He didn't question the wrong or right of it. In moments, he was coding in the necessary information. As an afterthought, he allowed messages and email from her family to pass directly to her without his intervention.

As his final move, he had all the pertinent information about this incident—the audio and video from Amy's apartment and the video message—saved in a locked and time-stamped file. If Lucy Ferguson escalated this, he would have ample proof to use against her with the human authorities.

If I don't get to her first.

Chapter Thirteen

Amy made her way down the stairs, her head fuzzy and eyes aching from too little sleep. She had no real reason for going out, but staring at the walls was likely to drive her insane.

She'd done what she could and sent off her resume to a half dozen companies that were hiring. It would be a waiting game until someone replied.

Rietin beat her to the security door by several steps, opened it, did a quick scan for security, and then held it open for her to precede him into the garage. As usual, he offered a tip of his head but didn't speak to her unless she spoke first.

But this time, his gaze lingered.

I look that bad, don't I? She didn't ask it.

Amy made her way to her car and stared at the keys in her hand.

Rietin's footsteps toward his van slowed, then stopped. There was a heartbeat of silence. "Ms. Davidson? Do you need anything? Are you all right?"

A wry smile pulled up at the edges of her lips. "You know I'm not. Don't you?"

He didn't reply for a long moment. "Yes. I do."

"You know what? I don't feel like driving today. Would you mind?" Since he'd told her that was his preferred way to protect her, she guessed he wouldn't balk.

Enough of this. I've spent nearly a week looking at all the things the Sakk have cost me. I should take advantage of some of the things they are offering.

"Of course."

She turned toward him, biting back a laugh at the sight of him rushing to the passenger side of his van to open the door for her. "Are you a professional driver, too?"

"When the situation calls for it, but it's not my primary function."

Amy knew well enough what his primary function was. She crossed the garage to his van and slid inside, reaching for the seatbelt with a whispered word of thanks.

Rietin closed the door, went to his side, and got in. Once he'd started the van, he turned to her. "Where do you need to go?"

That was still the question she didn't have an answer to. "Need to? Nowhere, I guess?" *Now I feel like shit. I'm making work for Rietin for no good reason.*

"I understand."

"Do you?" Why she bothered to ask was beyond her.

Rietin went red-faced, and his hands gripped the steering wheel so hard, his knuckles stood out in stark contrast. His jaw was clenched tight. "Maybe a visit to your mother might be in order today?" he suggested carefully.

Realization sank in slowly. "Do you listen to all my calls?" It didn't have the bite she wanted it to have. Even though she should be furious with him, it was a relief to have someone to talk to.

"No! Of course not!"

"But?" she prompted him.

"I explained the stress sensors."

Amy nodded. "Something I said or did when the video came in set them off," she guessed.

"Yes. There is an automatic buffer of an hour to let me see a precipitating event, to be used as evidence, should that become necessary—"

"So you scrolled back." She didn't question it.

"Voice only." He winced. "Do you feel that was wrong of me?"

"Thank you, Rietin. I'm...glad you're here to protect me."

His relief was impossible to miss. "Your parents' home?" he suggested again.

She nodded. "I think my mother should meet you. In fact, if Lucy is this far down the warpath, it might be a good idea if my mother knows how to reach you in an emergency."

"You haven't told her about me yet?" He seemed shocked by that concept.

"I wasn't sure how to."

He nodded his agreement and put the van in gear.

While they were on a roll, Amy decided that discussing her concerns with him might be a good idea. He was her bodyguard, after all. "I didn't expect Lucy to use Jason that way."

Rietin snorted.

"What?"

His cheeks darkened a few more shades. He pulled onto Main Street and headed west, before he answered. "It is not appropriate for me to—"

"I'm not a virgin, Rietin. Whatever you're thinking, I might have already thought it." The thoughts circling in her head all night had made her weary.

"If you wish—"

"I do."

He offered a tense nod. "I was thinking that it looked like Jason was *using* Ms. Ferguson more than a little."

That wasn't one I thought of. Before Amy had a hold on herself, she was laughing.

"Are you all right?"

That made her laugh harder. At last, Amy managed to stop. "I think I needed that." She sobered a bit. "Now I have to figure out how to keep her from escalating this."

"If you wouldn't be very angry—"

"If it's an answer to it, I'm all ears."

"My job is to protect you," he reminded her.

"That goes without saying, but you're saying it."

He shot her a sideward glance before he continued. "I have already taken...measures to protect you from Ms. Ferguson."

Her stomach twisted a bit. "Like?"

He sighed. "Phone messages and email from your family will route directly to you. All other messages... With your permission, I will see them before you do. If they are not an attempt to harm you like...last night was, I will allow them to come to you."

Answering that was hard. "But you've already done it, so you did it without my permission."

He winced again. "I will *un*do it, if it distresses you. I have no wish to—"

"No. It's a good solution." A smile pulled up at her lips again.

His eyes narrowed at the sight of it. "Yes?" It wasn't quite a challenge.

"I don't suppose you'd just delete spam messages while you're doing it." Amy expected Rietin to refuse. After all, he was her bodyguard, not her secretary.

He shrugged. "It would not be overly difficult."

****

Rietin shifted uncomfortably. "I should wait in the van," he suggested. He turned to make his way back to it.

Amy grasped him by the arm and pulled him to a halt. "No you don't. I want my mother to meet you."

Right on cue, the door opened, and Diane appeared. Rietin hastened to turn to her, thankful that Amy released his arm before her mother could see it and raise a protest of some sort.

The older woman smiled widely, though the creases in her forehead made it clear she was confused. "Well, this is a surprise. Come in." Diane cleared the way and waved her welcome.

Rietin let Amy go first, guarding her back. He tipped his head respectfully to Diane as he passed her. "Thank you for your welcome, Mrs. Davidson."

The idea of walking into her home when her husband wasn't there put his nerves on edge, even more so than entering Amy's apartment had, since Diane was a mated woman. On Sakk, this simply wouldn't occur.

They weren't born on Sakk. Their sensibilities are more American than Sakk. But he'd rarely dealt with Earth-born Sakk-descended who didn't have a Sakk-born male hovering over them. Though he'd had no problem treating human women as their own men would— respectfully so, it was a very different thing to treat a Sakk-descended woman as he would a human. Certain mores were ingrained into him, and they were hard to shed.

Diane launched right in. "Would you like anything? Coffee? Lemonade? Iced tea?"

"I wouldn't want to put you to any trouble."

Amy sighed. "Rietin likes coffee, though he's too polite to say it. I know there's always a pot on."

Her mother turned smartly and made her way to the kitchen, Amy in her wake. Rietin hesitated, then followed them.

"Rietin. That's an interesting name," his hostess commented.

"A Sakk name," Amy informed her.

Diane took a slow inventory of him. "Earth-born?"

"No, ma'am," Rietin replied. "I'm afraid not."

She made a non-descript sound.

"I should wait in the van," he repeated.

"Don't be ridiculous," Diane ordered. She turned and placed a mug of coffee in his hand.

"The sugar is on the table and the half and half is in the fridge."

He hesitated, uncertain whether he was welcome or not.

"I won't take 'no' for an answer, young man. Move." She raised one brow in challenge.

"Yes, ma'am." A smile flirted with his lips.

Mother and daughter shared pleasantries while they prepared their own drinks. As a group, they moved to the living room; Diane and Amy settled to the sofa together, and Rietin took a chair.

Diane looked at her daughter over her coffee mug. "As I said earlier, this is quite the surprise." She took a sip, patiently waiting for an answer to the unasked question, Rietin was sure.

"It's not what you think," Amy replied. "Sakkra assigned Rietin as my bodyguard."

Her mother nodded. "He's intelligent then. That's good. Since their misstep got Lucy on the warpath, the least he can do is protect you from her."

Amy didn't hesitate. "I wanted you to meet Rietin, just in case Lucy causes problems for you."

Rietin fished out one of his business cards and leaned across, offering it to Diane. She took it and examined it closely.

"If you have any problems, I can assign men to you. For that matter, I can assign one to you now, if you feel so strongly about the danger Ms. Ferguson poses." Sakkra might question that, but considering Diane's reaction, he felt certain the prince would err on the side of caution.

She waved him off. "Lucy tends to fixate on a target. I would be surprised if she decided to focus on me when Amy is so visible a target."

I've heard that before. Usually before the worst happens. "I would appreciate it if you would put my number in your phones. In case of emergency, I can have a squad of warriors to your position in between five and ten minutes. Unlike the human authorities, you will be a priority for us."

Diane nodded. "I'll do that. Thank Sakkra for us."

He tipped his head. "I will certainly do that." *When I tell him I've made this offer. I hope he isn't too angry about it.*

The discussion moved to other topics: Amy's search for employment, a discussion of Jason that Amy begged off on, and the fact that several of her cousins had already arranged time to be tested by the Sakk.

Rietin sent up a prayer to Sakkan that at least one of them would test positive. It would take away the sting of Amy refusing them. *Perhaps if one of her cousins tests positive, Amy will agree to choose a mate and go to Sakk.*

Or perhaps they will both refuse to leave Earth, which will force Sakkra to take action on Amy's ideas for matches living at the consulate or another secured location.

He pushed to his feet, excusing himself to refill his coffee mug. Halfway across the room, motion from the direction of his van stopped him cold.

Rietin parted the drapes a bit and looked out, his heart thundering in warning at the sight of Lucy Ferguson lurking around his vehicle. He thought quickly, dredging up a reason to go out there without alerting Amy or her mother to the situation.

Inspiration struck, and he set his mug on the small table. "I'll be right back in. I left my phone in the van." It wasn't precisely a lie. Rietin carried one phone, but there was always a spare in the vehicle in case the one he carried was damaged or lost.

A faint word of agreement came back his direction. As he'd hoped, it seemed Amy and Diane were deeply engrossed in their discussion.

He didn't waste time. Rietin left the house and made his way directly to the interloper.

Lucy didn't try to hide herself. She turned and leaned against the van, smiling as Rietin approached her.

"Any reason you're messing around with my van?" he inquired.

"Didn't touch a thing," she replied, her hands up as if to appease him.

Rietin crossed his arms over his chest, issuing a silent challenge.

"You're a friend of Amy's?"

"I wouldn't say friend." The presumption of claiming such a thing would never occur to him.

Her smile faded, and her expression went hard. "Well, she moves quickly, doesn't she?"

"Excuse me?" She couldn't be insinuating what he thought she was. Even if she was, considering her assignation with Jason the night before, Lucy had no moral high ground to speak from.

"None of my business," she conceded.

No. It's not. Rietin waited to hear what her game was.

"Just so you know, Amy isn't what you think she is."

"And just what is she?"

Lucy smirked and sauntered away. "You'll find out soon enough."

Rietin watched her get in her car and drive away. He made a note of her vehicle and license plate number. Then he pulled out his phone and dialed the comm center at the consulate.

It took only a few moments for the patch to Koebi. Rietin greeted him with a grumbled "This is priority."

The other tracker didn't question it. "Go."

"I require three men. Now. The first will locate and follow Lucy Ferguson. She is driving a black Mustang convertible with personalized plate S-X-Y-G-R-L."

"Has she accosted the young match? Uh...Ms. Davidson?"

"Not today, but she has been harassing Ms. Davidson in stealth."

"You want to know where she goes and what she does."

"I want to be sure she is nowhere near Ms. Davidson or her family."

"Done."

"The second man will watch Ms. Davidson's mother."

"For what reason?"

"Ferguson was lurking about Mrs. Davidson's home." Since he wasn't certain what Lucy's aim was in being there, it was better to be safe. "Though Mrs. Davidson believes Lucy means only to cause Amy harm, her concern is reason enough to protect her, and her mate is not in the home to protect her."

"I agree. And the final man?"

"I want the van I'm driving replaced. Now. Full diagnostics run on the vehicle."

There was a moment of tense silence.

"She was lurking around my van. Considering what I know of the female, I would not put sabotage past her."

"Done. The vehicle will be replaced within half an hour. Should I report this to Sakkra?"

He hesitated a moment. "Yes. Please do. I do not trust this woman, and the more I hear about her, the more I believe preemptive measures are best."

"Done. And...Rietin?"

"Yes?"

"Be safe." He disconnected.

Rietin took one last look the direction Lucy had gone and started back for the house. A tone from his cell phone brought him up short on the edge of the curb, and he punched up the message. It was a text message on hold in his queue for Amy. And it was from an unknown cell number.

He opened it, his blood boiling at the contents.

Nice new boyfriend. I'll be fucking him next. Enjoy while you can.
Luce

So that was the way she wanted to play it? Rietin bit back the urge to answer her challenge. Instead, he saved the message as he had the earlier attack on Amy.

He went back into the house, trying to school his expression, though he raged silently. Whether it would harm Amy or not, Lucy Ferguson had *no* chance of bedding him. Rietin had never been lonely enough or horny enough to bed a viper like her.

Amy looked up from the coffee machine, her smile fading. "Problem?"

He closed the cell phone and pushed it back into his pocket. "Just erasing spam." *When did I start lying to my charges?*

"I *was* joking about that," she responded, but she laughed.

It was good to hear her laugh.

Chapter Fourteen

Amy trudged up the stairs toward her apartment, exhausted. It would be all she could do to get a meal down before falling into bed. It was strange, but they never seemed to eat much when Sakkra invited her to the consulate for a business dinner.

Tonight was the third meeting she'd had with Sakkra about the proposed changes in as many weeks. He'd even hinted at the idea of giving her a job as their Earth-born representative...complete with world-wide travel to every country with a Sakk consulate and additional day trips to countries with proposed agreements.

Amy wasn't sure how she felt about that. She was sure the money would be more than adequate, but working in close quarters with Sakkra was guaranteed to drive her crazy. She hadn't come to terms with being Sakk-descended herself, let alone the idea of mating for life with a Sakk-born man, so the idea of entering into any relationship—business or pleasure—with a Sakk prince she was undeniably attracted to was too much for her mind to handle right now.

She rounded the last corner and headed for the door with a sigh. The key fought sliding into the lock, and Amy cursed aloud. It had been too much to ask that Rietin's men had permanently fixed the problem. She made a mental note to talk to the manager about it in the morning.

In the meantime, she had to get in.

She focused on the keyhole and gasped in surprise. It wasn't that the lock was fouled. There was something inside the opening. Realization that it was some sort of hardened glue made her heart race.

Rietin. Amy turned back toward the stairs, pressing and holding the number five, the autodial she'd set to his cell phone.

She stopped short, her breathing going strangled at the sight of Lucy holding her father's sawed-off double-barrel shotgun. Though she'd often mused over what irony it was that someone as irrational as Lucy was trained in using and had access to firearms, the irony was no longer, in the least bit, amusing. *I never thought she'd use one on anyone else, let alone me.*

There was no question Lucy intended to use it now.

Amy dropped the phone, hoping the autodial had gone through. If Rietin saw her calling, he'd come up to investigate, open line or not.

Please let him investigate.

"Home from your *date*?" Lucy asked.

"What?" What in the world was Lucy talking about.

"Or don't you feather-heads call it dating?"

"It wasn't a—"

"Let me get this straight. You have a whole world full of men who would lay at your feet for a kiss, let alone a fuck or a wedding ring, and you want to steal *our* men. Pathetic, Amy. Really pathetic."

"He's a *friend*. I have no interest in Josh." *No offense, Rietin.*

319

Not to mention, after that stunt you pulled with Jason, you have no room to talk. Of course, saying that could win her a prize of buckshot before Rietin could arrive to save her.

"That's not what *he* says."

"What?" What had Rietin said? And in what context? For that matter, when had he talked to Lucy?

"You took him to the consulate."

"You're *following* me?"

"Were you having him tested as a match? Did he want to test?"

Her anger threatened to uncork. "No and no," she offered calmly. Her mind worked fast. What other reason could she have for going there with Josh? "He has an interest in Sakk culture. The consulate seemed like the perfect place for him to learn more."

Her smile was slightly manic. "In other words, he wasn't Sakk-descended."

"I wouldn't know," she lied. "I'm not privy to Josh's medical—"

"It's just one disappointment after another, isn't it?"

Amy bit back the urge to reply to Lucy's wild delusions. Out of the corner of her eye, she saw Rietin creeping up behind Lucy. She forced herself to look at her former friend. Amy had to keep Lucy's attention on herself.

The shotgun came up, and Lucy grumbled a curse. "The least you can do is answer me." Her finger tightened against the trigger, a not-so-subtle warning.

Lucy has never liked being denied or ignored. And she's never excelled at subtlety.

Words stuck in Amy's throat. It wasn't just Lucy's outburst. Nor was it the shotgun pointed at her chest. It was Rietin's lunge for Lucy leaving her breathless.

"Answer me!"

He knocked the weapon up and aside, and Amy dropped toward the floor. If it was pointed up, down was the direction she needed to be moving.

"I'll kill you!"

Overlapping with Lucy's shout was the roar of the shotgun. Trails of scorching pain ripped through her. Amy's head hit wood. Hard. Starburst of colors blinded her, then everything went black.

****

Rietin wrestled with Lucy Ferguson, setting off the other shot into the ceiling in the process. It wasn't as easy as he would have imagined. *Insanity makes one strong.*

Strong but not skilled. Whatever training she had, it didn't match *yans* of military training. *Not to mention, she would have to reload to use the weapon again.*

With one hand wrapped around her weapon, he used the other to lay blows. Admittedly, he laid the first two with less force than he should have used, but the idea of striking a female, human or not, was against everything he believed.

The woman is trying to kill me. She is trying to kill a match.

That was all he needed to spur him into motion. Rietin laid a blow against her skull with the power to kill. She crumpled, and he let her fall. Self-preservation demanded he know if his adversary was alive or dead before showing her his back, so he checked for a pulse.

Alive. Rietin cursed himself for his disappointment. The last thing the Sakk needed was the death of a human at Sakk hands.

But the time to worry about that was later. Rietin wrenched the weapon from Lucy Ferguson's hands. Then he turned toward Amy.

Her stillness caused his heart to stutter in fear. Rietin was at her side in a heartbeat, cursing at the blood trailing off her face and soaking through her shirt.

He scooped her up and bolted down the stairs to his van, using the remote to open the side door when he was still a floor away. With Amy laid on the floor of the vehicle, Rietin dragged out the medical kit. Battle bandages were necessary.

Thankfully, they were also fast. Meant to be used in the heat of battle, the bandages would apply pressure and slow bleeding chemically after application. Rietin had them in place in moments. Then he wrapped Amy in blankets and wedged folded ones around her. He tossed the weapon in the back, trying to keep it from sliding against Amy on the way.

He slammed the door as he heard the first sirens approaching. There was no time to deal with human authorities. Amy needed the Sakk healers.

She needs the safety of the Sakk consulate and its shields.

Once they were out in traffic, he contacted the consulate. In addition to having the healers ready for Amy's arrival, the warriors at communications would liaise with the human police. The last thing he wanted was Lucy Ferguson escaping punishment for her crimes.

****

"Sakkra!"

He dropped the spoon next to his plate, grumbling sacrilegious oaths. Was it too much to ask that he be granted a meal in peace? When he'd agreed to take this post, Sakkra hadn't realized the problems he would have to personally attend to would be non-stop.

I have to answer them. There will be no peace until I settle the latest disaster. "Yes?" He didn't bother to mask his irritation.

"Rietin has contacted us, Sakkra. It is most urgent."

His heart stuttered, and he knocked his chair over in his scramble to his feet. "What is the situation?"

"The young match has been injured. Rietin is bringing her here for medical attention."

"*Zhick,*" he cursed. "Comms, follow me."

He rushed into the corridor and shouted an order to clear a path in Sakk. Warriors pressed to the walls, and the order passed in a thundering wave in every direction.

Sakkra ran for the tunnel entryway, warriors falling in behind him. "Direct Rietin to the bunker entrance. Have the medical team meet us there."

"Yes, Sakkra," the same warrior who'd been briefing him replied from the nearest overhead speaker.

In the background, other warriors coordinated Rietin and the medical team, repeating Sakkra's orders.

"How soon will Rietin arrive?"

"He has reached the inner marker."

"*Zhick!*" Sakkra nearly doubled his speed, going from a jog to a sprint, and still he reached the bunker door only heartbeats before Rietin's van squealed to a halt in the underground bunker.

In the distance, the metal blast shields closed them into the secure level of the consulate. Though it was protocol and not a sign that they were under physical attack, Sakkra shuddered.

Rietin wasted no time. He launched from the vehicle without shutting down the thundering engine, dragged the sliding door open, and lifted a blanket-wrapped bundle that was surely Amy out of the back. He turned with her in his arms, and Sakkra's gaze locked onto the crimson on the tracker's hands and clothing.

"*Zhick!*" Sakkra pushed a hand through his hair. "How severe is it?"

The tracker didn't meet his eyes. He hurried by Sakkra. "She will live, but there is no question this will leave scars." Rietin shouldered past gathered warriors on his way to the tunnel, stopped, and barked out an order for a hole, just as Sakkra had earlier.

His stomach a wriggling mass, Sakkra followed him. By the time his tongue unglued, Amy was on a transport cart. The battle bandages on her face were dotted in blood, attesting to deep wounds beneath. He let loose a series of curses.

The warriors lining the walls were less restrained. Grumbled promises of death for those responsible had Sakkra thanking Sakkan that the blast shields were closed. In this state, it would be far too easy for his men to become an unruly mob.

Had he been thinking clearly, Sakkra would have called a lock-in for his men the moment he learned what the emergency was. Now that every male within the consulate likely knew, it would cause more harm than good to lock them away from the injured female.

The cart started moving. One healer held Amy's head still to avoid jarring her wounds. A second ordered tests on the keypad and read off results. A third pushed the cart and shouted a list of supplies and procedures to the comms., which would relay them directly to the master healer preparing for her care.

Murmuring in the ranks announced the warriors passing updates on her condition along the line, forward and back. There were more than a few protests when they learned she'd been shot with a native weapon.

Warriors peered around the healers at her. Some bowed their heads in silent promises of protection. Others raised their heads and hands in prayer and hummed Sakkan's healing song for her. At med call, the warriors were closed outside while Rietin and Sakkra accompanied Amy in.

The healers pulled a drape around her. Sakkra started to protest, then calmed himself with the fact that they likely had to remove her clothing to treat her wounds. It was unavoidable that the healers would see her unclothed. It would be unacceptable for Sakkra and Rietin to see her in such a state.

Updates came in over the comms, and Sakkra attended to them all, though always with an ear to what the healers were discussing behind the drape.

Reports came in that the human authorities had collected Lucy Ferguson and transported her to medical aid.

The healers worked at removing pellets of metal from Amy's face and shoulder.

Rietin explained the entire fiasco, from beginning to end.

Representative Ellwood demanded a meeting by vid-comm at Sakkra's earliest possible convenience.

Sakkra ordered a team of warriors to Amy's family. The last thing he could conscience risking was injury to her family. Though Lucy Ferguson was imprisoned, there were others who hated the

Sakk, and an unprotected Sakk-descended family was easy prey.

Comparisons of Amy's wounds to battle damage sent a sick swirl through Sakkra's stomach.

At last, the healers opened the drape. Amy was dressed in an ornate sleeping gown, and the linens on the bed had been changed, but the healers' surgical wraps had enough of her blood on them to turn Sakkra's stomach in worry.

He went to the *bio bed*, assessing the damage to her with a wince. A series of wine-colored lines and dots marred her cheek. Another peeked from beneath the neckline of the sleeping gown, racing away toward her shoulder. A few of the wounds were stitched, indicating that they would leave scars.

"How many will scar?" Sakkra asked.

Gabin, the master healer, traced the longest line along her cheekbone. "This one." He motioned to the one on her shoulder. "This. And those that are knitted manually." He hesitated for a hand of heartbeats. "It will likely never be as it was, but I am certain it will not affect her desirability."

Sakkra rattled his wings, furious at the tactless handling. "And what of her sense of self?" he demanded. "Females are fragile like that. Things like scars, especially such visible scars, make them self-conscious."

Gabin tipped his head. "I meant no offense. You are correct, of course."

Rietin groaned. "I should have realized Ferguson might find a way through the security door. I trusted that she had no way into the building. When I saw her pull the trigger, I had no choice but to act. I should have reacted faster...earlier perhaps."

"Don't be ridiculous," Sakkra snapped. "You did all you could, considering the circumstances. You got her here in time to save her life."

Gabin cleared his throat. "I have been reading human medical texts. If the humans would aid us with the reconstructive surgery...what they call plastic surgery—"

Sakkra glared at him.

The master healer shifted as if in discomfort. "We have not developed the skills in eradicating scars they have."

"At this moment, we face the very real possibility of war with the humans. Though it pains me to admit it, securing their help is not our most immediate concern." He didn't add that it was unlikely they would reach any human medical professionals with expertise in this field tonight.

Gabin sighed and nodded. "As you say, Sakkra."

Rietin leaned against an empty *bio bed*. "You realize our most immediate concern," he stated wearily.

Sakkra ground his teeth at the truth. Their best intentions and safeguards aside, he was about to make a decision that courted war. "She cannot leave when she wakes. Not until she's safe, and that may not be soon. I will have to convince her this is in her best interests."

Silence fell around them. A half dozen pair of eyes stared at Amy. Sakkra didn't doubt that none of the others envied him his position.

I would gladly hand it over to someone else. But he owed Amy more than that.

"Healers...Rietin... Clean up. Command!" he ordered the comms to the command center open.

"Yes, Sakkra?"

"Order every warrior to battle readiness. I want the corridors clear and every man armed and armored. Two watch sections, until the all-clear is called."

"Yes, Sakkra. And...and the young match?" he chanced asking.

"She lives and will continue to live, thanks to Rietin."

Gabin spoke up. "You three go first. I will remain with—"

"No," Sakkra corrected him. "I will watch over her. Clean her blood off of you. I can't stand to see it."

Their voices overlapped in a chorus of: "Yes, Sakkra."

The others filed out of the room. Rietin looked back at Sakkra and offered a tip of his head before he disappeared into the crowd of warriors and started issuing orders.

Sakkra took Amy's hand and pressed his lips to the back of it. "Please understand. I only mean to protect you. It wasn't Rietin who failed you. It was I."

Chapter Fifteen

Amy stretched, closing her hand on the silky sheet. She recognized the Sakk material and worked on the puzzle of why she was covered in it.

Lucy. The memory was so stark and shocking, she jerked.

The shotgun. The sharp explosion seemed to echo in her ears. Her cheek ached and she shied, trying to escape the full bloom of pain she knew was coming.

She came up hard against a warm wall of muscle. Words she didn't understand encroached on her muddled mind. Hands closed on her arms and she jerked awake, a scream escaping her lips.

"Shhh, Amy. You are safe here."

Sakkra knelt beside her on the *bio bed*, his hair feathers disheveled, his expression concerned.

Her mind was muddled, and words fought emerging. Amy pushed herself up to sitting, and his hands retreated. Seeking the solid reality of him, she grasped Sakkra around his waist and buried her face in his chest. Her fingers tangled in his wings.

"Something for the pain," someone else whispered.

She nodded, and a pinch and hiss of air announced them administering their version of a shot. The ache in her cheek faded away. Once that happened, she was free to enjoy being back in Sakkra's arms.

His musk was rich and heady, and Amy bit back a moan. Her libido kicked into high gear. Her nipples peaked and ached for his touch. Her slit wept lubricant that would ease him in. Images of them entwined in the silky material taunted her.

How many times had she dreamed that? How many times had she woken, aroused, taunted by dreams of Sakkra telling her she was safe as he drove into her ready body?

Enough to make me consider coming here in the middle of the night to offer it.

Yes, she was safe in his arms, and Sakkra seemed always ready to hold her when she needed it. Wasn't that what every woman wanted in a man?

I'm alive because of Sakkra. Because he wouldn't take 'no' for an answer. "Safe. Yes. Because your man saved me," she breathed.

****

Sakkra wanted to put his fist through something. Amy was clearly aroused, in his arms...and talking about another man.

"Rietin." At best, the tracker would be sent to another consulate...or a seed world where Sakkra could 'reward' him with fucking genetically weak young matches into their early broods.

If she chooses him, she'll stay at the consulate willingly. He had to allow it, though only if she knew and accepted that Rietin could not give her young. Perhaps Rietin's lack of wings appealed to her. *And she could carry with donated sperm, if it came to that.*

She raised her head, a purr escaping her lips. It took a moment for Sakkra to recognize that she was nibbling at his jaw line.

His cock came up between them, and his breathing went rough in arousal. "Amy..." He didn't know what to say. If she wanted him, Sakkra wasn't about to stop her. *I'll kill any man who thinks he has a reason to object.*

One soft hand delved beneath his *cuzta*, trailing up his thigh.

She has to choose. Tell her! "Amy, if we do this, you are choosing to become my mate."

Her hand stroked the length of his cock through the under-wrap. "Oh, yes."

"Say it." Despite his best intentions, it came out a plea.

"Yes."

"Say it." He'd never wanted anything more than her. He'd give up Sakk for good, if it meant a life with this woman.

"Your mate. Yes...I'll be your mate." She came up on her knees, her lips closing on his.

Sakkra backed off just enough to avoid her lips. "Give me the *bio chains*, code the bed, and leave us."

No one argued with him. The chains settled in his outstretched hand, and Sakkra motioned his order to leave with a jerk of his head.

Amy's hand left his cock and started working at the clasp at the waist of the sleeping gown she wore. He let her, certain that she wouldn't figure out the mechanism before they were alone.

Gabin stopped at the doorway. "Sakkra, do you require—"

"I require you to leave," he snapped.

The silence was broken only by the sound of the doors opening and then closing again. A tone announced that they had been secured.

Sakkra closed his mouth over Amy's, working the fasteners on his *cuzta* while she investigated the one on her sleeping gown. When the fasteners were opened, he dropped the *cuzta* away.

At last, she tried squeezing the tabs together, and the clasp on her sleeping gown came open in a rush, spilling her breasts against his now-bare chest. Amy's hand went to his under-wrap, and she repeated the squeeze maneuver to open the sides. She pulled the fabric away, leaving them body to body, with only his *Kieta* between them.

Her mouth left his, and Amy raised her wrist, offering it to him. "Now. Please, Sakkra."

"Soon. I must be inside you first."

Her eyes dilated, and she arched against him in offer. Sakkra pushed the sleeping gown off her shoulders and cupped one lush breast in his hand. He lowered his head and sucked her nipple in.

Her hand closed in the back of his hair, and sounds of pleasure filled the air around them. Amy parted her legs for him. Whispered pleas for him to fill her made his head spin.

Since he was the second son, Sakkra could have any woman he wanted as his own. Even so,

Sakk princes typically chose virginal women as their mates. Amy wasn't virginal. Of that, there was little doubt. Far from being off-putting, Sakkra was sure mating with a woman who knew what she liked would be more than he'd ever dreamed of.

Sakkra took the time to show the other breast similar attention, but putting off what they both craved was too maddening. He'd wanted her practically since he met her, and Sakk princes were not well versed in waiting for anything they wanted. He straightened and captured Amy's lips again, groaning at her attempts to lever herself onto his ready cock.

Her hand brushed his wing, sending pleasant tremors through his body. She looked up at him, hesitated, then did it again, purposefully stroking him, learning what he liked by trial and error.

He positioned himself and thrust into her body, and her short fingernails dug into his shoulders. They parted minutely, and Sakkra started pounding into her body, staking a claim on his woman...his princess. To his delight and surprise, she was a tight fit for him.

Her sounds went sharp, and her hot breath bathed his mouth, promising dozens of delights. Her legs tightened around Sakkra's waist, pulling his cock further inside her.

Amy didn't last long. Her body clenched hard at his length, encouraging him to climax with her. Sakkra indulged, his heart hammering in excitement the likes of which he'd never felt with one of the women provided for him.

Of course not. Those women were paid to make sure I was sated well. Amy is sharing sexual fulfillment with me. The two were vastly different.

"Sakkra?" Amy questioned.

That has to end now. "Labtrayel," he corrected her.

****

Amy fought to make sense of whatever Sakk word he was using. "I don't understand."

"The mate of a prince or emperor does not use her mate's title when they are intimate. That is for public appearance."

"Then...Your name is..."

"Labtrayel," he reminded her. "Only you and my family may use it."

She repeated it several times, trying to commit it to memory. "It may take me a while to remember that," she admitted. Her cheeks heated. "It's just...I already know you as Sakkra."

His smile let her know he wasn't offended. "It is often thus when a Sakk prince takes a mate."

Sakkra...Labtrayel eased out of her body, and Amy tried to make sense of it.

He cupped her chin in his hand. "Is there a problem?"

"You said you had to be inside." Why was he pulling out if he had to be inside to put the *bio chains* on?

"My...essence had to be inside," he explained.

Aftershocks wracked her at the reminder.

Sakkra raised her hand and kissed the knuckles. "Now we code the *bio chains* and then seal it with another mating."

"Again? Don't you need time to...recover?"

He chuckled darkly. "Let me lay the chains, and you will understand."

Amy nodded, her heart tripping in excitement.

Sakkra raised one of the chains from the mattress and placed it around her wrist. Once he'd locked it on, a light humming raced up her arm, making her gasp.

"Now mine." He looped the matching chain around his own wrist and fastened it one-handed.

At the first stroke of his fingertips over her unmarked cheek, the arousal rocketed. His half-erect length went hard again, and realization struck.

"The *bio chains* act as an aphrodisiac?"

"Closeness brings awareness. Touch brings pleasure."

He stroked a fingertip along her lower lip, and she trembled in need.

"Sexual touching brings more."

More was an understatement. The drive to have him inside her again was mind altering.

"Not yet," Sakkra whispered. "The chains must code first."

He kissed her, a slow, deep kiss that made her head spin. His wings closed around her, enveloping her in his scent and touch.

Just when Amy thought the anticipation would be too much for her, a tone sounded.

Their lips parted, and she opened her mouth to ask if it was time for the promised mating. Sakkra's cock sliding home answered the unasked question.

The second time he made love to her was even more delicious than the first. The sensation of being stretched around his length and girth was more pronounced. Her mind registered every thrust and withdrawal in a series in individual nervous impulses that sent shockwaves through her system.

His hands stroked up her back, holding Amy tight to his body. Her climax skyrocketed, and starbursts of pleasure washed over her. The rush of Sakkra's cum pushed her past all conscious thought.

Little things came into focus again, one at a time: their sweat-soaked bodies rubbing against each other, the scratch of the medallion he wore, the sound of their breathing, the tickle of Sakkra's wings against her spine.

"Labtrayel," she reminded herself.

"Yours to use," he replied.

Exhaustion weighed her down, and Amy wrapped her arms around him.

"Tired?" he asked.

She nodded.

Labtrayel slid free of her body and arranged Amy on the *bio bed*. Once he'd covered her with the silky sheet, he laid a kiss on her forehead.

"Sleep, Amy."

Even if she'd wanted to stay awake, she didn't possess the energy to do it. Consciousness drifted away.

****

Sakkra smiled at the sight of his princess sleeping. Considering the amount of blood she'd lost, the other physical and emotional traumas of her day, and the mild pain relief he knew the healers had administered, he was mildly surprised that she hadn't succumbed to sleep during or just after the *bio chains* coded.

She is mine now. My princess.

He dressed, mindful to the noise he was making. Though he doubted Amy would wake easily, the last thing he wanted to do was interrupt healing sleep.

That accomplished, he went to the comm board by the door, turned down the volume, and asked for Gabin.

"Is your Sakku in need of me, Sakkra?" he asked urgently.

"Is it safe to move her to our quarters?"

"I will bring everything you need."

"Quietly. Sakku Amy is resting," he warned in reply.

"Yes, Sakkra." Gabin closed the comms from his side.

It didn't take long for a light knock to announce the master healer's arrival.

Sakkra coded him in, and Gabin entered with a bow to Sakkra and then the sleeping Amy.

The healer wasted no time. He threaded the royal *Kieta* over Amy's head, then coded the *bio tracker* to her. When that was complete, he offered a *tova* sleeping gown and sheet in royal *ullium.* The fabric didn't simply have the coloring of the protective metal. Threads of it were woven in, making it akin to Kevlar fabrics humans used.

Sakkra took them with a raised eyebrow, challenging Gabin to explain why there were women's clothes in the royal colors on hand in the consulate. The sheet was expected. Sakkra had such sheets on his bed every night, but there was no call for such clothing.

The master healer cleared his throat, his face darkening. "They came on the same ship you did, in a variety of sizes. But only sleeping gowns," he hastened to add.

"In the event that I found an Earth-born female I wished to make my own?"

"I would imagine that is always a concern, Sakkra."

A smile pulled at his lips. "I suppose so." It certainly was now that he'd mated with Amy.

The healer pulled the drape closed and left Sakkra in peace to dress his mate in royal vestments. She moaned a protest, then settled back into sleep. When she was properly dressed and wrapped in the *tova* sheet, Sakkra pulled the drape back and lifted Amy in his arms.

"All is prepared?" Sakkra inquired.

"Of course."

The healer trailed Sakkra to the doors and followed them out into the corridor. At the sight of them, the warriors lining the corridor went to one knee.

Sakkra made his way between the columns, whispered prayers for their health, safety, and fertility rising around them. Corridor to corridor, the reaction of his men was the same.

And many yans *in the future, each of them will be able to brag that he was there when Sakkra claimed Sakku Amy as his own.* It was an event few were blessed enough to witness.

At their quarters, Sakkra settled Amy in their bed and covered her with a quilt.

Gabin waited in the main room. Sakkra left Amy behind and went to see what the healer had to say.

"We do have only sleeping wear in the royal *ullium*," he noted carefully. "And we have no daily wear in pure white, either. Of course, Sakku will not be up to public appearances for at least a week. Possibly longer." He didn't add that getting either white *tova* or *ullium*-weave *tova* from Sakk would take much longer than that.

Sakkra considered that. "My Sakku is Earth-born. Especially while she heals, she may be more comfortable wearing clothing she is accustomed to."

"Should we purchase more like those destroyed by the attack?"

He considered that, remembering the clothing she'd come to the consulate in after her fiancé had abandoned her. "No. When she wakes, I will ask her permission to have warriors move her personal belongings here to the consulate for her. When she feels up to it, she can purchase whatever she likes on the consulate account. Dressed as a human or dressed as the Sakku she is, my mate will have a princess's closet."

"As you wish, Sakkra."

"No. As Sakku wishes." He hesitated, another thought occurring to him. "Are you familiar with the human custom of rings for mates?"

"Of course."

"I understand there is more than the engagement ring involved."

"Yes. The engagement ring and the mating band worn on the female's third finger on the left. The male wears a matching band on the corresponding finger."

"I wish rings in *ullium* with what the humans call a teardrop diamond for the engagement ring."

"Decoration for the bands? Humans often decorate the bands."

He pressed a hand to his *Kieta*. Amy wore a ring that she called a *Claddagh*. There was a tradition about placement of the design. "The royal *Kieta* at half-turns. The *Claddagh*, facing opposite the *Kieta*, at the other two quarters."

"I do not understand. You wish one design to always be upside down?"

"It is a human tradition. Wearing of the *Claddagh* in that manner *means* a female is mated. I want a symbol that no one, Sakk or human, can mistake."

"I quite understand. It will be as you wish. I will give the jewelers at the consulate the proper measurements and orders."

Sakkra nodded. He looked toward the corridors and all the problems awaiting him. *My mate needs me.* Instead, he went back to the bed and stripped off his clothing. Beneath the *ullium-*

laced *tova* with her, Sakkra gathered his princess into his arms.

Chapter Sixteen

Amy came to consciousness slowly, trying to make sense of where she was and why. She wasn't wearing her favorite fleece pajamas. Instead, she was surrounded in something that felt like silk but was as warm as her winter blankets.

She yawned, wincing at the pain in her cheek. That brought the rest back in a rush. She was at the consulate. Lucy had shot her. And Sakkra...

Amy sat up with a gasp, looking down at the delicate chain ringing her right wrist. Her heart pounded in a mixture of excitement and surprise.

It wasn't a dream. I'm really mated to Sakkra.

"May I enter, Sakku?" a strange voice called out from the other side of a golden drape.

Sakku? She worked at that. *Sakkra means prince. Maybe Sakku means...princess?*

"Sakku Amy? Are you well? May I enter?"

She straightened the nightgown, self-conscious. "Yes."

The healer passing through the drape was vaguely familiar; that put her at ease. She recognized him from her previous visits.

He bowed to her, then reached to the panel above her head and started pushing buttons.

"What are you doing?" she asked.

"A few tests. Your *bio tracker* says your heart rate is elevated."

Her cheeks heated. "Just memories. For a moment, I didn't know where I was." *Then I remembered.*

His eyes went soft in some emotion she'd like to deny was pity. "You are safe here, Sakku Amy. I guarantee that. Six of Sakk's best guard you, and you are within the shields. Nothing can harm you here."

"What about my family? Those nutcases out there have attacked Sakk-descended before."

He raised his hands in a calming motion. "Sakkra has taken care of it. Your family have guards and temporary shields. Eventually, they will be moved here or to somewhere they feel comfortable and safe."

"He did all of that?"

"Yes, Sakku. Of course he did."

Amy didn't know how to interpret it. Instead, she focused on the more pressing issues. "I take it Lucy is in jail again?"

"A hospital jail room, I am told. She will recover well."

Her cheek twitched again. "Will I?"

His hesitation told her more than he intended it to, she was sure.

"We are consulting with human plastic surgeons. I am certain they will be able to heal your injuries fully, and with our healing measures, the recovery period from the surgery will be much lessened."

Amy nodded solemnly.

"In the meantime, your *bio tracker* will help us monitor your condition."

He'd mentioned that before. "*Bio tracker*?"

He motioned to a heavy medallion strung around her neck on a chain. "All members of the royal family wear them."

Amy fingered it. *Sakkra wears a similar one.* "I see." She looked around, struck by the silence in the room. "Where is Sakkra?"

"Attending to the details of this situation. I can send for him."

"That's okay. If you could just direct me to—"

"You really shouldn't be up," he dismissed her.

"I'm fine, I'm sure." She didn't feel dizzy or sick.

The healer looked toward the comm board, seemingly torn.

"I am fine. Please, I'd rather walk."

He bowed deeply. "I must insist you take your guards with you. If you feel ill, they will bring you here."

But not call for him. Oh! The bio tracker will do that. She nodded. "Of course."

The healer took a step backward and offered his hand to help Amy from the bed. When she was on her feet, he gathered more golden silk from the chair and held it up for her to slip her arms into.

When she hesitated, he spoke again. "Would you rather dress, Sakku? I am afraid I would have to call for clothing from our storeroom. Your own were ruined."

"No. This is fine." She turned and eased her arms into the sleeves.

The healer released it onto her shoulders and took another step back. Amy belted the robe around her and faced him again.

"Well then... I suppose I should find Sakkra."

He nodded and led the way to the door.

Amy took the time to look at the rooms they passed through. They were large, and there were offshoot rooms that proved to be an office and library. This certainly wasn't the type of room Sakkra had given her before. She suspected these were his personal quarters.

Our personal quarters. That thought sent a shiver of delight down her spine.

In the hallway, six hulking Sakk warriors went to one knee in a bow.

Amy took an involuntary step back, shocked by their actions. She composed herself. "Can you show me where Sakkra is?" she managed.

One rose and tipped his head. "Of course, Sakku. If you would?" He motioned for her to accompany them.

She walked to his side, self-conscious for reasons she couldn't put a name to. The others took to their feet and arranged themselves to all sides of her.

"Is this really necessary?" she asked.

The healer erupted in a spate of Sakk speech.

The leader of the guards nodded. "Yes, Sakku. It is necessary."

"Then lead on."

****

"Your tracker put a local woman in the hospital, Sakkra," Ellwood argued. "Don't you realize what the media is going to do with this?"

"That *woman* nearly killed one our females. If it had been any of my *other* men, I assure you Ms. Ferguson would not be drawing breath. She has a lump on the head, perhaps a concussion. We had to render emergency aid to —"

"I know that. You know that. You don't understand the media circus we'll be dealing with."

Sakkra bit back the protestation that he didn't care about their media. He'd never understood human fascination with the subject, the obvious undermining effect due to libelous or substandard reporting being celebrated, and the unconscionable effects it had on human behavior.

The only thing that mattered now was Amy's condition. He wouldn't even be here now if it wasn't for the fact that Ellwood had insisted it was an emergency.

The human in question continued speaking. "We have to release a statement for you, Sakkra. We have to explain why your man reacted—"

"Because she's one of our females." Why was that so difficult for them to understand?

Because they don't lack females. They don't prize them as we do.

Something told him to hit Ellwood with everything at once, though he didn't know if it would make a difference. "She's more than *any* Sakk female, Representative Ellwood. Amy is *my* mate, and any of my men will die or kill to protect her, as they would any woman of our kind. All the moreso because she is Sakku...what you would call a princess."

The human sat back in his chair, seemingly stunned. "She's your...?"

"Mate. Yes. Amy. Is. My. Mate." How clear could he make it and have the human still misunderstand him?

The sound that escaped Ellwood's lips spoke of a sick headache coming on. "Now we're dealing with an international incident of a *much* higher order."

"Is that good or bad?" One could never tell with humans. *It doesn't sound good.*

"Good for you. Bad for Ms. Ferguson. Attack on or attempted murder of a member of a foreign royal family is an act of terrorism."

"Should I care?"

"Knowing Lucy, no," Amy spoke up from behind him.

Sakkra whirled around, then launched toward her. Stunned by the sight of her in the command center when she should be in bed. Amy stood tall and proud, wrapped in an ankle-length robe of royal *ullium.* She looked every millimeter the princess she was.

He rushed to her side, running a hand over the dark red lines of healing tissue on her cheek. "You should not be up. You are healing."

She smiled weakly, though slightly crookedly.

She needs more pain medication.

"The healer gave his permission, as long as I take the guards with me." Amy glanced at one of the six warriors surrounding her.

Ellwood's voice reminded him that they had an audience which consisted of more than Sakk males. "Will those heal without scarring?" he asked bluntly.

Amy blushed, and she averted her eyes.

She knows that is beyond us. I will have to speak with the healers about telling her such things.

Sakkra turned and shot a warning look at the human. "Our healers are conferring with yours. We understand there is...human surgery of a sort that may help eradicate them."

"You don't have—?"

"Our males accept their scars. Our males would die before allowing our females to come to harm this way, their own woman or not. We have never had need of such healing before." He stopped short of comparing Sakk culture to human in an uncomplimentary fashion.

Ellwood hesitated. "I'll send your medical team the names of the best we have in the field. They will be in touch before lunchtime. You have my word on it." He tipped his head. "Ma'am...Sakku, take care. Sakkra...I will issue a preliminary report for you. I know how to phrase this. Good day to you both."

With that, the screen went blank.

Sakkra placed his fingers under Amy's chin and urged her face up so he could see her eyes. Thankfully, she wasn't crying. That would have shredded him.

"I will never allow you to be harmed again," he vowed.

She shot him that same lopsided smile. "I'm sure that's true."

"And I will eradicate every sign that this has happened to you."

Amy wrapped her arms around him, whispering her thanks into his chest. As appealing as it was to have her in his arms, it wasn't right to show such affection in front of his men.

"Are you hungry?" he offered. She'd slept through breakfast, and he doubted she'd had enough time to eat since he'd been gone.

"Ravenous."

He wrapped an arm around her and led Amy toward their quarters, her guards and his falling into step around them. Sakkra ordered two away to see to food for them.

The walk passed in comfortable silence. At last, they entered their quarters and left the warriors behind. Amy headed for the table, and Sakkra guided her toward the bed.

"Sakkra..." She looked toward the door and lowered her voice. "Labtrayel, I can sit up. Honestly."

He laughed. "Are you saying you don't want to be in bed with me?"

Her face went an enticing shade of red, and she didn't respond to that.

"I suspected as much," he teased her. "We have much to discuss."

"Do we?"

He steadied her onto the mattress and tucked Amy in. "We do."

She bit at her lower lip. "We're going back to Sakk soon, aren't we?"

Sakkra sighed. "No, and we can come to an agreement about the time we spend on Sakk and the time we spend on Earth at a later time."

"On Earth? You mean... We won't be moving to Sakk permanently?"

"Do you want to?"

That seemed to confuse her. "Well...not permanently, but that was the agreement. I knew that when I accepted becoming your mate."

He leaned down and laid a gentle kiss on her lips. "As I knew you had reservations about it when I claimed you as my mate. Beyond that, I thought my Sakku had instituted new policies that allowed for matches to stay on Earth."

That seemed to confuse her. "I can't ask you to give up Sakk permanently. It's not right."

"Neither is making you leave your world permanently, which is why I propose a compromise. I have been told that many Earth marriages are built upon healthy compromise."

"This isn't exactly an Earth marriage, and... You are a Sakk prince. You cannot tell me your father will be happy with you compromising."

He shrugged. "I am the younger son, and my brother has already produced an heir to the throne. I hear his mate is carrying a second. There is no reason for me not to take on the post of ambassador to Earth on a semi-permanent basis."

"What do you propose? Six months each?"

Sakkra took her hand, shaking his head. "That would be problematic, at best. The trip to Sakk takes nearly three Earth months. We would spend half the year in transit to spend three months on each world."

Her expression crumpled. "Oh. I didn't realize how long the journey was."

"My idea is simple. It is tradition for the young of mated couples to be born on Sakk. The young are safe to travel at three *sa-sen*."

"So go to Sakk when I'm pregnant and come home with a young baby?"

He could see the concern in her eyes and guess its cause. "Your parents are more than welcome to travel with us, if that would ease your worry. No grandparent wants to miss the early days of a new life, and as Sakk-descended and mated, there is no reason for them to be denied passage to Sakk."

Amy scrambled to her knees and kissed him. The arousal was blinding in its intensity.

Sakkra pulled away from the kiss regretfully. "Not yet. The food will be here shortly." Even though the cooks would be making their food separately from that of the men, there would be little delay in its arrival.

She groaned in complaint, but she allowed him to tuck her back into bed.

"One more thing we should discuss," Sakkra reminded himself.

Amy perked at the announcement. "Yes?"

"Would you permit my men to bring your belongings here? The healers wish you to remain here for the next week, and I am certain you would like your own clothing, electronics, and... Anything you might wish."

She hesitated long enough to make Sakkra nervous. Just as he would have apologized for the idea, she started speaking.

"Can Rietin lead the team? It's not that I don't trust your men," she hastened to add.

"But you *do* trust Rietin?"

She nodded. "I do."

"I believe he should be your personal guard then. You will need a team of men for your protection, and a wingless tracker like Rietin would be a good liaison with any human authority figures you might encounter."

A smile pulled up at her lips.

"What is it?" he asked.

"Just imagining Rietin in a tuxedo," she imparted.

Sakkra laughed heartily at the mental image. "I believe we should accept an invitation to a formal affair." He sobered. "When you feel up to such a thing."

Chapter Seventeen

An assault on Wednesday evening left two women hospitalized and has blossomed into an international incident.

When twenty-six-year-old Amy Davidson returned to her apartment to pick up some belongings, the last thing she expected was an unbalanced woman with an illegal sawed-off shotgun, waiting for her inside the secured building.

Lucy Ferguson, aged twenty-five, was apparently so distraught over being told she wasn't Sakk-descended that she decided to kill off Sakk-descended Davidson. She tricked one of Davidson's neighbors into letting her through the security door and disabled the lock on Davidson's door, laying her trap for the other young woman.

Unfortunately for Ferguson, there were a few things she didn't know about the situation. She didn't know Davidson carried a comm device, that she had a group of Sakk warriors guarding the entrances to the building...or that Davidson was a Sakk princess, thanks to her mating with Sakkra, the younger son of Sakkrel, the Sakk emperor.

In the resulting altercation, Ferguson fired two shots, wounding Davidson. Davidson's guards subdued Ferguson and rushed Davidson to the Sakk consulate and appropriate medical aid.

Ferguson faces federal charges for terrorism, as well as local charges for assault with a deadly weapon, aggravated assault, and attempted murder. She remains in guarded condition in the lockdown wing of Heaven's Mercy Hospital.

No official statement has been released about Princess Amy's condition, though unnamed sources report her condition as guarded but stable.

Sakkra's snort said he didn't appreciate the sensationalism and errors any more than Amy did. He cleared the screen and turned to Amy. "I suppose we must make an *official* statement," he noted.

"I suppose we should. I do like one thing in that account, though."

One brow went up. "And that would be?"

"Princess Amy. I like it."

"My men will call you Sakku or Sakku Amy. It is tradition."

"Of course. They're Sakk. But for the humans? It makes sense for them to have a name they understand for me, and it sounds...refined. Like Princess Di."

He wrapped an arm around her and laid a kiss on her lips. "Then our *official* statement will use that name for you."

A light tap at the door announced that their moment of peace was over.

"Yes?" Sakkra called.

"Your guests, Sakkraas," one of the warriors replied.

Amy looked down at the fleece pants and t-shirt she'd been lounging in, then started to rise. It was probably best for her to disappear behind the curtain and dress in something more suitable.

Sakkra pulled her back to the couch next to him with a smile. "For *these* guests, you need not dress further."

That shocked her to silence. Sakkra was typically overprotective about what people saw her wearing.

"Send them in."

The door opened, and her mother came in, followed closely by her father and her cousin Jo. Amy launched across the room, and hugged Diane, tears misting her eyes. She pulled away a moment later, cursing herself for being so childish.

As if reinforcing that, her mother pressed a hand to Amy's forehead and smiled. "They're taking good care of you, I see."

Amy nodded. "Sakkra wouldn't stand for less."

Her father leaned in and pressed a kiss to her unmarked cheek. "Princess Amy?" he teased.

Jo took up the chorus. "Does that make me a Duchess?"

"Have you been tested yet?" Amy countered.

Her cousin shook her head. "No. Rae and Tracy tested negative. Guess there's no reason to."

Amy nodded, and she glanced at Sakkra, certain that he would be disappointed her cousins hadn't proven close enough to test as compatible.

To her surprise, he was on his feet and striding toward them. He tipped his head to

Diane. "Mother, thank you for coming. I know it means a lot to Amy to see you well and safe."

She enfolded him in a hug, and Sakkra's shock was impossible to miss. He shot a look of near-panic at Amy's father.

"While I don't mind you calling us Mom and Dad, Diane and Steve will be fine if you're more comfortable with it."

Diane released Sakkra, and Steve offered his hand. Sakkra took it awkwardly and shook it.

"Welcome to the family," her father intoned. "Thank you for taking such fine care of our daughter. And of us."

"Thank you for coming," he repeated. He released her father's hand and tipped his head to Jo. "And you, Jolene."

"Jo is fine," she responded.

He waved them toward the sitting area. "Please, come in and make yourself at home. Refreshments will be along shortly."

Amy went back to her place on the sofa, smiling at Sakkra tucking the blankets around her again. "I told you that I'm not an invalid."

"Yes. I know." But he finished tucking her in, then settled next to her.

Her mother laughed. "You should have seen me trying to keep her in bed or on the couch when she was sick."

Amy sighed. "The healers hover constantly. It's not as easy to sneak past them as it was to sneak past you. And that's before you take my personal guard into account."

"Complaining?" Sakkra asked.

"No. Just commenting."

"Good."

Her father leaned toward them, his elbows planted on his knees. "What is the plan now?" he asked carefully.

"We're not moving permanently to Sakk," Amy informed them. "We will make some trips there, of course. Anytime we make the trip, we'll be gone for about a year, since it takes about three months to reach Sakk and the same amount of time to make the return trip. While we're there, we should spend some time there before we return."

"And when will the first trip be?" Diane inquired.

"Royal children are born on Sakk. It's tradition."

"You're not!" Jo's eyes went wide, and she waited for a response.

"No. Of course not." Amy's face flamed in embarrassment.

Sakkra entered the conversation. "We've arranged for plastic surgery for...repairs. And I believe Amy would like to take a honeymoon...or a series of them. It would not be unexpected for a new princess to tour the consulates and meet the military leaders at each base."

Her heart skipped in excitement. "Bermuda? Italy? Germany? The UK?"

He smiled. "Of course. I will leave the details up to you. The healers will not allow us to travel for at least two weeks, I'm sure, but we can visit wherever you wish. Now or later."

"We won't be seeing much of you," her mother noted.

Amy took Sakkra's hand. "Actually, we were discussing a few things."

"Like?" Her father raised an eyebrow in silent demand.

"You used to joke about wanting to land a big contract that would require travel."

He nodded. "Few of those accounts exist, though."

Sakkra tipped his head. "One does. Amy tells me she learned about marketing and promotions from you."

Her father's jaw dropped in understanding. "But you already have a contract with Patterson for that."

Amy shook her head. "I've read the contract. It's not comprehensive. It is for specific advertising services. What we have in mind is completely separate...a publicist like you more than an advertising agency."

"What *do* you have in mind?"

Sakkra took over again. "Amy suggested several changes to the way we reach out to the people of Earth. What we show people. How we present it.

"Among other things, we need someone Sakk-descended to travel with us, someone with an eye to putting together the type of materials we require. Interviews. Documentaries. New advertising. We need someone who can choose locations and who knows how to present the information to our best advantage. Someone who can liaise with Patterson to make them more effective. Someone who knows how to phrase the requests we make. You, Steve, would be ideal.

And..." He squeezed Amy's hand. "It would give you the opportunity to travel and to be with Amy when our children are born."

Silence fell in the wake of his offer.

Sakkra broke it. "If you are not interested, I under—"

"No," both of her parents shouted together.

The door opened, and one of the guards poked a head in, seemingly assessing the situation. Sakkra waved him away, and he retreated and closed the door.

Her father took a moment to compose himself. "Of course I'm interested. What man wouldn't be? But..." He glanced at his wife.

Sakkra's wings ruffled. "We would never ask a mated man to leave his...wife. Diane is most welcome whenever you travel on Sakk business."

In the next heartbeat, her father was on his feet, offering Sakkra his hand again. "I'd say you'd just made my career, but the truth is you've just made my life."

Sakkra took her father's hand but shot Amy a questioning look.

She laughed. "It's a good thing."

His shoulders relaxed, and he offered them a stunning smile.

"And I know just the way to start," he continued.

"You do?" Sakkra seemed confused by that.

"Exclusive first pictures of the local royal couple? Maybe from their honeymoon tour of the consulates? The bidding war would be formidable, and the proceeds could be donated to a charitable cause of your choice."

Amy pressed a hand to her scarred cheek, trying to reason herself out of being self-conscious. It was a lost cause.

Sakkra squeezed her hand again. "Only from her unmarked side?" he suggested. "Until the surgeries are done."

She wrapped her arms around him, nodding her agreement.

"Scarves are in this year," her mother offered. "You could wear a large pair of glasses and a scarf wrap for a while."

"And there are cosmetics that can hide scars, once they've healed," Jo added.

"I know a fabulous photo journalist who has been trying to get an interview with Sakkra for months. She'll agree to only photograph Amy from one side...if we give her dibs on the first full-face shots after the surgery."

Sakkra was silent for a long moment. "I believe, as humans say, you have a deal, Steve."

Chapter Eighteen

Gabin waved Amy toward the waiting *bio bed*, and the human surgeon crossed the room to offer his hand to Sakkra. They'd been through this twice in the six months since Lucy's attack on her, so there was no instruction necessary.

They'd done the repairs to her face first, and the first full-face shots of her had graced the cover of *People Magazine* within weeks of the second repair.

This would be the least of them, eradicating the scar on her shoulder. At least, if anything went wrong with this one, it wouldn't show much unless she wore a strapless dress.

Nothing has gone wrong so far. Nothing will go wrong this time. Labtrayel won't stand for it.

"Your healer has informed me about the changes to the process," the surgeon assured Sakkra.

Amy turned to them, confused by the pronouncement. "What would be different?" Why would it be?

Gabin offered his hand to help her onto the *bio bed*. "It is nothing to worry about," he soothed her.

Amy levered herself up, but the discussion still bothered her. "Why would the process have to be different this time?" She insisted on an answer.

Gabin looked to Sakkra, a sure sign that her mate had ordered the healer not to tell her. She shot a look demanding an answer at him, and Sakkra sighed deeply.

He came to the bedside and raised her hand for a kiss. Her rings shifted, and she smiled at her mate.

"You know the *bio tracker* monitors you constantly."

She nodded. "Of course." It was part of Sakk tradition. The royal family was never unguarded.

"Two days ago, the *bio tracker* picked up a subtle change in you, and test scans were ordered."

Gabin had told her the scans were simply in preparation for the coming surgery. "What kind of change?" What had they been looking for?

He kissed her hand again. "You are bearing my daughter."

Her heart stuttered. "If this isn't safe, it can wait."

Sakkra opened his mouth to speak.

"I mean *completely* safe. If there's any chance at all—"

"Completely safe," he assured her. "If there was any chance of harming our daughter, Gabin would not allow the surgery to happen. As it was, he simply made a small change in the medications."

Amy took a calming breath. "Okay. If you're sure..."

"We are," Gabin assured her. "The medications will sedate you further than they have in previous surgeries. You will sleep longer. We will use a different type of pain relief and for a longer period of time, so we do not stress your system."

She nodded, taking it all in.

Sakkra guided her back to the mattress and laid a kiss on her forehead. "And you will be the most beautiful woman at the President's holiday ball."

She smiled, then laughed. Sakkra had said that more times than she could count, and she still didn't believe it.

It's still good to hear it.

"And Rietin will be very unhappy about wearing that tux."

Sakkra winked at her. "I hear he is cursing already."

Section Four:
Genetically Inferior

Jolene and Rietin

Chapter Nineteen

Rietin panned his gaze up and down the little temptress's body, his cock pressing against his jeans. As if she felt his gaze, she turned, performed the same assessment of him, and smiled.

She sauntered toward him, her musk rising. "Friend of Sakkra and Amy's?" she asked.

"You could say that." Rietin wouldn't presume to, but it explained his presence at the princess's family holiday party without exposing his true purpose. Amy had been adamant about playing down the sheer number of guards they'd brought with them. At least half of them were wingless males who could pass for human.

Being circumspect about his relationship to Sakkra and Sakku had another benefit. His interactions with Lucy Ferguson had taught Rietin well that either confirming or denying himself as a friend of the Sakkraas could result in unintended consequences.

Two of her fingers walked up his thigh between their bodies. Rietin glanced around, assuring himself that they were unobserved.

He smiled. "My room is upstairs."

"So is mine," she purred.

"Even better."

Sakkra and Amy had retired to their room more than half an hour earlier. That meant he was free to enjoy himself while the winged warriors stood guard overnight.

"When?" he invited.

"Now works for me."

He nodded and led the way up the stairs.

A glance back at the turn revealed two more buttons open on the little temptress's blouse. His cock took immediate interest in that, and he started unbuttoning his shirt in response. Whatever happened next was going to be a heated encounter.

Good. It's been too long since I've had one.

She led him to her room—which was conveniently across the hall from his, halfway down the guest wing. Rietin closed the door behind them and turned to look at her. Her blouse was opened to her waist, and an appealing little wisp of lace covered her breasts.

He pulled his shirt off over his shoulders and pitched it across the room. Hers came off slower, and she dropped it to the floor.

Delicious anticipation scented the air. Rietin went to work on his jeans, and she did the same with her pants. She gasped as he slipped the jeans down his legs.

He cocked his head to one side. "Problem?"

She shook her head, swallowing hard. "I just like..."

"Like?" he prompted her.

"Commando." Her cheeks darkened in a flush.

That broke Rietin's self control. He pushed his jeans off, toeing the soft leather shoes off ahead of them, then strode across the floor to her, completely naked.

She didn't back away. In fact, her hands released the pants and cupped his face. They met in a kiss that made him ache for more.

He guided her toward the bed, taking mincing little steps in deference to the clothing ringing her lower legs. He was hungry. Beyond hungry. Ravenous for every sensation of her he could experience before daybreak.

She unfastened the bra and slipped it off between their bodies. It hit the floor with a whisper of sound.

At last, she was pinned between his body and the mattress. A moan escaped her lips, and she pulled back from the kiss.

"I'm on the Pill," she gasped out.

"I'm disease free." Even if she wasn't, there was nothing the humans carried that Sakk medicine couldn't cure, on the off chance he was able to be infected. Still, Rietin knew that might not matter to her. She could still insist on a condom.

I'll wear one if she does. Though Rietin rarely indulged in a female, he always carried a few condoms with him. He preferred not to wear them though, so he didn't mention it unless the female requested it.

This one didn't. She pushed down at her panties, circling her hips against him in the process.

Damn, I need this. Rietin went to one knee, laying kisses on her lightly-tufted mound as he worked the panties down.

She pulled at the elastic holding his hair back and released the short ponytail behind his head. His hair feathers cascaded around his face, springing into their natural curls. She combed her fingers through them, moaning again.

He slipped off her flats, taking the pants and panties off of each foot as it was raised for him to remove the shoe.

She spread her legs minutely, and he took advantage of it to stroke her ready body with his fingertips. She widened her stance more, and Rietin started working her with his mouth, savoring her feminine taste.

Her hand fisted in his hair, urging him on. She gasped out a request for more.

Gladly. Rietin doubled his efforts, drinking in every sound and squirming movement.

She shimmied in a way that told Rietin her balance was uncertain. He closed his hands around her waist and lowered her to the mattress where she sat, trembling and gasping for breath.

"Are you okay?" He reminded himself to keep his accent steady.

She nodded. "That was...Wow! You have skills."

Rietin smiled at the compliment. "Well then... What *will* we do now?"

She shot him a look of disbelief. "I suggest we test the limits of our endurance."

"I have quite a bit of it."

A smile pulled her lips up. "Prove it."

"Gladly." Rietin crawled up between her thighs and lifted her at the hips.

His first thrust had her arching her back from the mattress, her nipples hard little nubs.

Oh, yeah. Just the sight of that will keep me hard half the night. The taste and scent of her would keep him hard longer than that.

They moved in violent motions, both of them pursuing a shattering climax. Rietin couldn't have recounted which of them came first. Sounds overlapped with sounds, her body milking his spasming cock until he felt as lightheaded as she had when he was eating her.

They held to each other in the aftermath, sweat soaked and shaking. She wiggled against his cock, setting off aftershocks.

Rietin half-withdrew from her heat in order to take one glorious nipple in. Her body reacted to the added stimuli with more tight contractions of her inner muscles.

Oh, yeah. This isn't ending anytime soon.

"What is your name?"

Her question came without warning, bringing a sense of guilt with it. He was going to lie to her. He always lied to women he bedded.

"Josh. Josh Rietin."

"I'm Jo. Jolene Williams, but you can call me Jo."

"A lovely name, Jolene." How he managed to say it without choking was beyond him.

Rietin's heart beat out a warning. This was Sakku Amy's favorite cousin. He'd heard the name many times, though he'd never met the lady before.

It doesn't matter. She's a willing human woman. There's no reason for me not to take what she's offering.

****

Jo stretched in bed, coming up against cold sheets on the other side of the mattress. She raised her head, squinting in the sunlight streaming around the slatted wooden blinds she'd forgotten to fully close the night before.

"Josh?"

He didn't reply, and she dropped to her back on the mattress.

Pleasant little aches reminded her that she'd met her perfect match sexually. Josh knew precisely what she liked and offered it tirelessly.

Why didn't I meet him a year ago? Or two?

Why? A year earlier, she'd been fresh from a breakup with Carl. She wouldn't have noticed a guy then, even if Josh had grabbed her and laid one of those toe-curling kisses on her. *Well, maybe then,* she conceded.

Earlier than that, she'd still been neck deep in a relationship with Carl and tying the noose around her neck by believing his lying ass.

Maybe he's not gone. It was possible that Josh had gone back to his own room to change or gone down to breakfast. If he had a room, it was a safe bet he was invited to breakfast.

That in mind, she jumped from bed, grabbed one of the outfits she kept in the closet in her room at her aunt and uncle's house, and rushed into the three-quarter bath that she shared with her sister's room.

Memories of the two of them in the shower sent shivers down her spine. The sounds he made when she sucked him were sinfully arousing.

Move. Don't give him time to leave without offering to meet him again.

She rushed through a shower, dried off, and pulled her clothing on. That accomplished, she hung the towel and bathmat to dry and made her way downstairs.

Uncle Steven and Aunt Diane sat at the table, chatting over plates of pancakes and cups of coffee. Jo went to the sideboard and filled a plate, then slipped into the closest chair.

She looked around at the empty table, her heart aching. "Looks like everyone got an early start. Is anyone else still here?"

Jo tried to keep her tone light. Based on her aunt's non-reaction, she guessed she was moderately successful at it.

"Just the three of us. Amy and Sakkra had an early shuttle to Bermuda. Their men left with them. Others ate an early breakfast and went off to whatever their plans were for the day."

She nodded and started eating, trying to hide her disappointment. There was no way to ask if Josh would be invited to the Easter celebration without her entire family scenting that she might be falling for someone again.

Besides, if he's a friend of Amy and Sakkra, there's no saying Aunt Diane invited him.

She sighed and tried to cover it with a sip of juice. Aunt Diane's questioning look let her know she'd showed her hand...just a bit.

****

Rietin stood on the beach outside the small security shield, conspicuously dressed in jeans and boots, in contrast to the bikini-clad beach bunnies and the tourists in their t-shirts for the Frog and Onion Pub or Bone Fish Bar and Grill. His hair blew free around his face; he'd considered putting it up this morning, but—for a reason he couldn't name—he decided to leave it down today.

Inside the shield, Sakku Amy wore a one-piece maternity swimsuit in the royal white and *ullium* with a white sarong, and Sakkra wore a matching pair of men's trunks. The slight swell of her pregnant womb was the subject of many of the pictures being snapped, Rietin was sure. A full dozen of Sakkra's finest held position inside the shield, keeping watch on the tourists and paparazzi on the other side.

Bermuda was one of Amy's favorite places in the world, and she and Sakkra visited often. Though the day had started off with a meeting with the Bermudan government, they never failed to make a visit to the island a mini-vacation if they had the chance.

Though Rietin was consciously scanning the area for any threats to Sakku Amy and Sakkra, he'd resigned himself to the fact that his subconscious was intent on torturing him with memories of Jolene. Her face at climax. Her body begging for him with signs of arousal.

Watching her sleeping before he slipped out of her room and to his own had nearly broken his resolve. He'd considered waking her for one more round of what was undeniably fantastic sex. He'd never met a woman he meshed so well with before.

Reality had stayed his hand, of course. It would be unkind to wake her, both unkind to her and to himself.

What can come of it? He wasn't capable of giving a human woman children and probably wasn't capable of giving a Sakk woman children, either. *I've known that was the case since I was fourteen* yans *old, and the healers made it clear I would never be approved to take a mate.*

There are women who can't have children, due to their own medical conditions. I could marry one of them. We could adopt children.

He wondered if the Sakk would allow him to raise a surrendered child. Maybe a male who was genetically sound and could save his family line.

You know they won't. Not as a single male and not with a woman who isn't Sakk-descended. Since I can't mate with a Sakk-descended woman, I will never have a Sakk-descended child.

And considering the bias against Sakk in other circles, the human authorities will not allow me to adopt a human child if I marry a human woman.

Not to mention, any woman I marry or mate with wouldn't be Jolene. It was enough to drive a sane man to madness.

Rietin sighed and focused on his prince and princess again. His job was to ensure their safety.

My job is all there will ever be for me.

Chapter Twenty

"Your cousin to see you, Sakku," Colonel Muuzo announced from the doorway to the lounge in Sakkra and Amy's quarters. Before an answer came from inside, he turned, bowed to Jo, and backed away to let Jo pass.

Amy looked up from the book she was reading, her smile fading at her first glance Jo's way.

Jo felt her cheeks heat. *That's it. Amy will know something's wrong. I've never had a poker face.*

Right on cue, Amy said Jo's name, a question couched in it.

Her knees quaking, Jo made her way to one of the other chairs and sank into it. "I need to talk to you."

She didn't *want* to discuss this with Amy today. This was the last thing she *wanted* to do.

Amy set her book aside. "Go on."

She glanced at the colonel. "Alone?" she requested.

He waited long enough to see Amy's wave of dismissal, then retreated and shut the door behind him. Jo sighed in relief at that. This was going to be hard enough without an audience.

"What's wrong?" Amy asked. A smile curved one side of her lips. "What is your mother furious about this time?"

Jo winced. Furious described her mother's current mood well enough.

Her cousin's smile faded again.

"I need your help." *That's the understatement of the century.*

"I can't imagine I'd turn you down, but I need to know what the problem is to figure out what kind of help I can offer." She wasn't teasing. Amy had gone deadly serious, as if she'd grasped the gravity of the situation already.

Tears pooled in Jo's eyes. "I'm pregnant."

Amy's jaw dropped. "You?"

"Yes."

She nodded, seemingly stunned. Jo supposed that made sense. It wasn't a situation anyone who knew her would have expected to find Jo in.

"And before you ask... No, I don't want to abort or to give the baby up for adoption."

"Oh, your mother is going to uncork."

The blunt statement drew a weak laugh from Jo. "Tell me about it." She sighed. "She already has. You know my mother. You're only twenty. Halfway through college. No husband. You're ruining your life. You're ruining *my* life." *I won't be responsible for raising this kid, you know.* "Uncorked is too kind a term for it."

"If you're asking for a place to stay until this all blows over, you're welcome. We have tons of space here at the consulate."

Jo stared at her clasped hands, at a loss for a moment. "That might help, but..." The rest stuck in her throat. She tried to calm her rioting heart rate and started again. "What I really need your help with is something altogether different."

Amy cocked her head to one side. "I'm listening."

377

"I need your help to find the father."

Words seemed to fail her cousin. "You don't know who—?"

"Of course I do. You know me better than that." Jo fumed at the insinuation. "The one time in my life I have a one-night stand, and the contraception fails. I hadn't been with anyone since Carl." *More than a year ago, but Amy knows that. I was crying on her shoulder the night I caught him with that slut.* "And I haven't since, so...there's really no question who the father is."

"But you don't know how to find him again?" she guessed.

"It was a one-night stand, Amy."

"You can't go back to where you met him and ask around to see if he's a regular customer?"

Jo swiveled her head in a negative response. "I met him at the family Christmas party, and we...sort of...uh... Well, I guess it's obvious what we did."

"Then someone in the family must know him."

Jo shot her the standard 'duh' look. "You and Sakkra do, which is why I'm here." She waved off Amy's move to answer. "Please, Amy. He's not listed in the phone book. I can't find him on the web. I need to find him to let him know."

"He's not Sakk?" Amy asked, seemingly perplexed.

"Of course not. Don't you think I would have told you if he was?"

"But he said Sakkra and I invited him to the party?"

"Yes. He did." Was Amy being dense?

"To a *family* Christmas party?"

Jo dusted off the 'duh' look again.

Amy put up a hand asking for calm. "Okay. I believe you, but I don't remember us bringing or even inviting anyone along who isn't Sakk." Before Jo could protest, she continued. "What did he say his name was?"

"Josh. Josh Rietin."

Amy's eyes went wide. "Rietin? You're *sure* he said his name was Rietin?"

"That's what he said."

Her cousin didn't respond, and Jo's blood ran cold.

"Oh, God. He's married. Is he married?" Josh wasn't wearing a ring and didn't have a pale band where he *should* be wearing one, but that didn't mean he was single. There was a reason behind Amy's shock, and Jo couldn't come up with another one.

"No. If it is Rietin, I guarantee he's not married." She rose and went to the screen in the wall. "Display a likeness of Rietin," she ordered the computer.

His picture appeared, surrounded by Sakk glyphs.

Jo breathed a sigh of relief. "That's Josh. Now...will you help me find him?"

Amy's intended answer never emerged.

Sakkra opened the door and breezed through the room to his wife. "Ah. Two and a half of my favorite ladies." His hand covered Amy's midsection. "And what brings Jo here today? Just a visit?"

Something told Jo that Sakkra's presence here wasn't a coincidence. Most likely, one of his warriors noticed her upset and called for him.

Before Jo could open her mouth to repeat the request to find Josh to the Sakk prince, Amy answered him.

"Jo has some news. She's pregnant."

Sakkra smiled widely. "Such a blessing. Who is the lucky sire?"

Amy cleared her throat, and Sakkra raised head to meet her gaze. She jerked her head toward the screen, and he followed her line of sight.

His smile disappeared. A rapid-fire series of sounds in the Sakk language left his lips.

Amy darkened. "Speaking in Sakk in this situation is incredibly rude, Sakkra. And, yes, she is absolutely certain it's Rietin."

Jo pushed to her feet, stung by the predictable male response. "If you're not going to help me find him—"

Sakkra was at her side that quickly. "You don't look well."

Though her heart was pounding and her stomach churning, though tears burned at her eyes, Jo straightened and offered a bald lie. "I'm fine."

"You're not." There was a note of alarm in his response that stopped Jo cold. "Amy, I believe the healers should give her a thorough check over."

Amy seemed to consider that. "That sounds like a very good idea. You are really pale, Jo."

That's going too far. "I'm fine," she insisted.

Amy took her arm. "Humor him. It's ingrained in Sakk males. Pregnant women are coddled." She raised a beautiful *ullium* medallion with Sakk glyphs on it from her chest and showed it to Jo. "They monitor me all the time. One bad burp will set off an alarm in medical."

Jo wanted to argue that she was joking, but something told her Amy was being serious. *But still...* "It's not...dangerous, is it?"

Sakkra's expression of offense taken was answer enough.

"Okay. They can check me over. *Then* you'll help me find Josh?" she asked. Even if it was some underhanded paternity test, Jo knew how it would turn out, and she didn't doubt that Sakkra would do everything possible to make sure a pregnant woman had her baby's father around to help her. It was part of the Sakk mentality about child rearing.

"Of course," Amy assured her, but there was an unexplained tension in the air.

****

"Rietin, you are relieved," Eli informed him.

He checked the watch on his wrist. "You're not due to relieve me for two hours."

Five yards away, the newest match was shopping with her mate, purchasing candies and toiletries to take to Sakk with her.

"Sakkra requested your presence. It is likely Sakku wishes to dine out or has an event to attend."

Rietin grunted his agreement and left Eli in charge of the security detail. He started his van and headed for the consulate, deep in thought. Though Amy typically arranged things like that further in advance, it was possible that was the case, and one never kept royalty waiting, even if that royalty was as laid back and unassuming as Amy was.

In all honesty, it was a relief to leave the detail he'd been assigned to. Protecting a newly-mated couple was a bitter reminder of what he would never have.

Too weak genetically to be awarded a match—on Sakk or on Earth—Rietin had long since resigned himself to bachelorhood and had petitioned for work as a warrior guard on a seed world. With the treaties on Earth, the need had arisen for wingless guards who could blend in with the native population.

Blending in wasn't enough. Rietin wanted more. Though human women were willing to share a bed with him on a regular basis, nothing more could come from it. It would be dishonorable to marry one and not tell her what he was, to let her hope for young that could never be between them.

Rietin swallowed down the familiar dull ache and maneuvered into the bunker tunnel. The van had been outfitted with sensors that would release the sections of shield for him, as long as only he and members of the royal family were inside the vehicle. If there were any others aboard, it would be handled manually by the command center, and a full scan of the vehicle would be carried out between the first two shields. Since he was alone in the van, there were no delays in him passing through.

Alone. Why did it seem everything was a reminder that he was and ever would be alone?

The parking space closest to the doors was designated as his, thanks to Amy's request for Rietin to act as her personal bodyguard on her outings. Rietin parked and left the vehicle behind, glancing at the white limo in the opposite spot. If Amy's outing involved shopping or visiting her family, they would take the van. If it was a formal affair or dinner out with Sakkra, they would travel in the limo. They were the only two land-based vehicles Amy used.

More than one warrior sneered at Rietin's clothing, and he studiously ignored them. Blending in meant he could usually choose human clothing he found comfortable. In Rietin's case, that meant jeans, t-shirts, a jean or faux-leather jacket, and cowboy or hiking boots.

The others either wore *cuzta* or stripper wear. While the former was comfortable, the latter couldn't be mistaken for it. A smile pulled up at the corners of his mouth at the undeniable truth. It was jealousy that made them sneer.

He stopped at Sakkra's office door and knocked.

"In!" The reply was curt and without humor.

Rietin winced. There was nothing worse than a prince having a bad day. He entered quietly and waited for acknowledgement.

It didn't come immediately, putting his nerves on edge. If Rietin was a general, he might be so impertinent as to remind Sakkra he'd been summoned, but he wasn't.

At last, the prince looked up...and scowled.

Rietin's heart skittered, and his mouth went dry. The copper tang of fear tainted his tongue, and he retraced the last week of his life. The last month. *Sakkan, what have I done wrong? What will the punishment be?*

"There you are, Rietin."

"Yes, Sakkra. As ordered." He always followed orders. *Then how did I run afoul of the prince?*

Sakkra sat back in his chair and raised an eyebrow. "You act as guard to my mate often."

"I do." Since he'd saved Amy's life, she trusted him. "If I have offended her somehow —"

"No. No offense."

Rietin breathed a sigh of relief. Since offending Sakku Amy could mean his head, it was good news that he hadn't.

Sakkra continued. "Did you enjoy her family's holiday celebration?"

"I suppose I liked it well enough." Her family had provided meat-free dishes for the Sakk in attendance, and it was a joyous night full of color and scent and sound.

Have I offended her family? That was unlikely. The event had been more than two months earlier.

"And after Amy and I retired to our room?" he pressed.

Visions of Jolene were potent, bringing his cock to life. Anger that the prince was interrogating him about his sexual exploits followed close on its heels.

"I see." The prince's comment sounded like a condemnation.

Rietin bit back four unkind remarks and two attempts to explain himself. There was nothing to explain. He hadn't been on duty, and there were no rules against bedding willing human women. Jolene hadn't been wearing an engagement or wedding ring, all of Sakku Amy's cousins had reportedly failed testing as matches, and she'd been more than willing.

"Did you *enjoy* Jo?" Sakkra challenged him.

"Has the lady made some complaint?" he countered.

"Not...precisely."

Rietin opened his mouth to offer the opinion that nothing else entitled the prince to this highly-inappropriate discussion.

"She *has* brought something to my attention that demands...handling."

"And that would be?" *I have broken no laws.*

Sakkra hesitated. "You may want to sit for this."

Something in his tone unnerved Rietin. Or perhaps it was something in the prince's expression. "Sakkra?"

"By Sakkan, sit!"

His mind spinning at the change of mood, Rietin did so.

Sakkra took his time. "The lady...Jo is bearing."

Another reminder of what I will never have. "You know very well that—"

"I know she is Amy's mother's brother's child, which makes her close family to my own mate. I know that, while all Amy's other cousins tested negative as a match, Jo never tested. She believed her sister's and cousin's failures meant she would also fail. I know you are more human than most Sakk males." He put up a hand to still Rietin's protest. "Most of all, I know the *bio bed* has cross-matched the babe she carries to your genetic code."

His heart pounded hard against Rietin's ribs, and his breathing went harsh.

"Jo carries your daughter, Rietin, and there is a fair chance the young one is at least a short flight, based on her genetics."

He could hardly take it in. A female was bearing for him, and the child was of strong stock.

"She came here looking for you," Sakkra continued.

"Why?" The question was out before Rietin could censor himself.

"That is something only Jo knows for certain. I suggest you ask her."

Sakkra rose from behind his desk and ordered Rietin to follow him. In a daze, he did so, leaving Sakkra's office and making his way to the main medical bay in the prince's wake.

The hostility of the other males drew his attention, and Rietin came to a startling realization. *They are jealous, but not of my clothing.*

****

The door to the clinic opened, and Sakkra stepped through. Jo opened her mouth to ask him about his search for Josh, but only a squeak emerged.

Josh loomed in the doorway, only inches shorter than Sakkra stood, his deep golden hair pulled into a ponytail behind his head. His fists were stuffed in his pockets, and his gaze didn't quite meet hers. If she had to name his expression, she would choose either shell-shocked or discomfited.

Jo eased her mouth shut, at a loss to tell him what she'd come here to say. If he'd seemed happy to see her at all, it would be easier.

"You came to see me?" Josh asked softly.

"I shouldn't have," she blurted out. *This was a mistake.*

His head snapped up, and he stared at her, his face going an unhealthy color. "What do you mean?"

Jo slid off the *bio bed* and pulled her tennis shoes back on. "This was a mistake. I shouldn't have come here."

"But—but you're carrying my child."

His confusion made it through her panic, and she stared at him, her sweatshirt in hand. He knew. That's what she came here to do...to tell him.

Her heart said that wasn't what she'd come here for.

What? You expected him to be overjoyed that a one-night stand got you pregnant? You expected that he'd say he missed you? That some romantic fantasy would unfold, where he whisked you off your feet?

None of that was forthcoming. Jo pulled her sweatshirt on, fighting with the stubborn zipper, trying to avoid crying in front of him.

"Jo? The *bio bed* says the baby is mine." He paused. "Ours, I mean." That sounded like a concession.

Her hair still trapped inside the sweatshirt, she looked at Amy, pleading for answers.

Amy offered a weak smile. "Sakkra had them check."

"And you didn't tell me. My own cousin didn't trust me." Today was turning out to be one heck of a disappointment.

"I did. We both did, but..." She glanced at Sakkra. "You don't tell a Sakk male he's about to be a father without being certain."

Jo grasped at the edge of the *bio bed*, her senses reeling. Her eyes slipped shut, and strong arms encircled her. She didn't question that it was Josh lifting her onto the bed and tucking the silky blanket around her.

A cup of cold water touched her lips, and she swallowed a sip.

"Healer?" Josh asked, his voice rough.

An extended period of discussion in Sakk followed. Jo opened her eyes, focusing on Josh.

She hadn't been imagining it. He was speaking Sakk.

"Josh?" *He really is Sakk? That isn't possible.*

His jaw tightened a notch, and he stopped speaking. "My name is Rietin."

Words failed her. His name wasn't Josh? He lied to her? She supposed he wasn't the first man who had, and he wouldn't be the last.

He sighed and met her gaze directly. "Working among humans, I needed to disappear in a crowd. I adopted a name humans would accept. My *name* is Rietin."

"You're... No, you can't be. You don't have..." Jo looked at his shoulders, though she knew he didn't have wings.

"Neither does Sakku Amy. Neither does Representative Janice. With the breeding measures, not all Sakk have wings."

"But the Sakk men do," she insisted.

"Most of the ones who win the right to come to Earth to seek mates do," he corrected her. "I never thought it was possible." He shook his head, his expression unreadable.

"Thought what was possible?"

"That I would be blessed with a mate and a child."

Her heart skipped a beat. "M-mate?"

"Of course. We must."

"Mate?"

"Rietin," Amy called out, clearly warning him off.

He ignored her. "You carry my child, Jolene. Our daughter. We must mate."

That was it, the blunt instrument that tore her heart out. Though it pained her to say it, there was only one answer she could give to that. "No."

****

Ice raced through Rietin's gut. "What?" She was refusing him? She couldn't! *Can she?*

The solid fact that accepting the *bio chains* was always the female's choice hit him hard. She could choose to refuse him, child or no child.

"Jo, you don't understand," Amy pleaded.

"I understand just fine," she countered. "It's J—Rietin who doesn't. I am not a Sakk woman."

"Obviously, you are," he pointed out, employing the last of his strained patience.

"No. It's my choice. Just as it is for any woman who comes here to be tested."

"It's a little late for that," he offered bitterly. *How did I offend Sakkan so grievously? How could he bait me with what I want and steal it away?*

"You Sakk men." It sounded like a curse when she said it. "One woman is just like another to you. As long as you have one, you're happy."

Rietin was too shocked at the accusation to protest it.

"Jo," Sakkra offered in a soothing tone.

She continued on, venting at Rietin as if the prince hadn't spoken. "I am not an accessory you get to pick up in town and claim as yours just because you got me pregnant."

"I never said—"

"Didn't you?"

"It may have *sounded* that way, but..." She confused him. Rietin had never been so tongue-tied. "Don't you want to be my mate?"

She didn't reply. The confusion and hurt in her expression gave him hope she didn't know what she wanted. Perhaps she was speaking in anger.

I suppose I am as well.

Sakkra interrupted them before she formed a definitive answer. "I believe the healers have more tests they wanted to run. Perhaps we should let Jo eat and rest before we continue this discussion."

"Is there a problem?" Rietin asked. "With the baby?" Terror as he'd never known it assaulted him. What if he couldn't give Jo viable young?

She tilted her head toward the healers, her expression frustratingly vague.

"She seems healthy enough," Gabin replied.

"She?" Jo's answer was little more than a breath of air. "So it is definitely a girl?"

Sakkra nodded. "Absolutely."

"Will she have wings?"

What difference does that make to her? Did the idea of a winged child frighten her? Perhaps enough to terminate the pregnancy? *Sakkan, no. I beg of you. Not that.*

"We cannot be certain for at least six more Earth weeks," Gabin stated.

"Six. Okay...six weeks."

Her distraction set off alarms in Rietin's head. "Please let me speak to you," he requested formally. "When you've rested."

Jolene stared at him for a long moment. At last, she nodded.

Rietin leaned down and pressed a kiss to her forehead. "Take care."

He left her, resting in the *bio bed*, seemingly stunned by something he couldn't name.

At the comm board in his quarters, Rietin checked his schedule, intent on cancelling a few days of it. It was blank, and a note that he'd been removed from duty by Sakkra flashed an ominous warning.

Suddenly, he wasn't certain how he would survive the empty hours without assignments.

Chapter Twenty-One

"A girl." Jo swallowed a sob and then hiccupped. She paced the guest room Sakkra had given her, her mind rioting.

Before she'd found out Josh—*Rietin,* she reminded herself—was Sakk, she'd daydreamed about having a girl. In that awful moment, when she'd learned he lied to her, she'd considered aborting. Jo still wasn't sure why she'd considered it.

But a girl. Their world was struggling because they didn't have enough women. The thought of aborting one that was guaranteed to be a match for them was inconceivable.

A match. The thought of her daughter being given no choice, as the Sakk-born females were, made her stomach clench. She had to talk to Amy. There had to be rules about this, rules that granted her daughter the same freedoms human women enjoyed, even though the father was Sakk.

That firmly in mind, she went to the comm board and searched out the purple button that would open a general channel to ask questions of. Sakkra had promised it would answer her questions...and locate Amy and Sakkra for her.

"Where is Amy? Princess Amy?" she corrected herself.

"Sakku Amy is in dining area two." To her surprise, the voice seemed to be live and not computer-generated.

393

"How do I get there?" *It couldn't be somewhere I knew. Of course.*

"A guard has been dispatched to—"

"What? Why can't you just give me directions? Or post a map here on the screen for me?"

His tone remained cool and calm. "A guard has been dispatched to escort you, Ms. Williams. Can I be of any additional assistance to you?"

"I suppose not." *Calm down. He's probably following orders.*

"Good day, ma'am."

"Thanks."

No sooner had the word left her lips than a polite knock came from the door. Jo crossed the room and opened it to find an armored warrior on the other side.

He stepped back and motioned to her right. "Dining area two, Ms. Williams."

"Thank you."

Jo stepped into the corridor and reached to slide the door shut. His hand was there first, and she cleared the way, allowing him to shut the door for her.

One thing you can count on with Sakk men: lack of women has bred impeccable manners into them.

He walked at her side, silent, nearly brooding. All in all, it made her distinctly nervous.

When the other warriors started appearing from side doorways and corridors, Jo understood why they'd assigned a guard to escort her. There was something wild in the air, nearly feral. If her guard hadn't been so nerve wracking, she might have moved closer to him.

The wing extending around her shoulders startled her, and Jo elbowed a lower joint in surprise. That seemed to be the breaking point for the rising tension.

Two of the other males stepped in front of them, clearly ready to fight. One addressed her guard. "Move your wing. You can see she doesn't accept your *familiarity*."

Her guard didn't back down. "What she doesn't accept, *boy*, is the attention she's forced to endure from the likes of you."

Ruffling wings and sharp sounds in the Sakk language, coming from all sides, sent her into a panic. "Don't," she whispered. "Just let me pass."

The one who'd challenged her guard reached for her. Something in his expression told Jo not to allow him to make contact. She dodged him, and her guard dragged the interloper away and shoved him against the wall.

The other male between her and the direction they'd been traveling grabbed her guard by the shoulder and laid a punch across his cheek. That gave Jo the opening she needed, and she bolted through it and down the corridor, ducking attempts at other men grabbing for her, ignoring calls for her attention.

The fistfight turned into what she was sure was a full-blown riot behind her. Males started rushing around her and into the fray instead of trying to engage her. Alarms blared.

I don't know where I'm going. The realization brought her up short.

At the next corridor, a young warrior waved for her attention. "The dining area. Come."

She had no reason to trust him, but it was a concrete direction, so Jo went that way. He didn't wait for her to reach the corner. He didn't try to touch her. By the time she made the turn, he was halfway down the corridor and shouting something in Sakk at the comm board.

He yanked the door open and waved her in. Jo took a moment to register the trays of food on the tables before she complied. It was a dining area. The door closed behind her, and the lock clicked.

The men in the room came to standing in a rush, and she shied from them. Something hit the door, and Jo focused on Amy, sitting at the far end of the room. With the warriors standing, there was no direct path to her cousin.

At a loss for something better to do, Jo used the closest chair, thankfully empty, and launched up onto the table. She ran down the length, wincing the few times she caught the edge of a tray and flipped it.

Sakkra reached up and scooped her to Amy's side when she reached the end, and Jo sank to the floor, exhausted by the last few minutes. Amy joined her, their backs pressed to the wall behind them.

"Are you okay?" Amy asked.

Jo nodded. "Just...tired."

Warriors snuck glances their way, then focused elsewhere.

At last, Sakkra started giving orders. "Eat while you can, and clear the mess. Once they've broken the fight, you will likely have to take up quarters."

Jo looked down at her jeans, groaning at the food staining them. She'd *caused* much of the mess.

"We have clothes you can use while they wash," Amy assured her.

Jo nodded, swallowed a lump in her throat, and started crying. Maybe staying here at the consulate wasn't a good idea after all.

****

The sound of the general alarm brought Rietin out of his chair and to the comm board. There were few things that required such an alarm. The reports streaming across the screen made his blood run cold.

"Jolene." *Jo and our daughter are at the center of this?* He punched the button to connect him with the command center. "Where is Jolene?" he demanded of the warrior on comms.

"Tracking, Rietin."

Seconds passed, and he ground his teeth in frustration. It would do no good to head off in the wrong direction, so he was stuck waiting for directions to her. "Command!"

"Dining area two," he replied. "She is locked inside with Sakkraas."

"On my way." Rietin grasped his sword and headed that direction without his armor. Chances were, his opponents would be no more armored than he was. Even if they were, lack of armor would allow him agility they would lack.

There was no mistaking the sound of hand-to-hand battle.

Rietin screwed up a vicious smile. *I've brought a sword to a fistfight. Good.*

The warring males didn't see him coming. Rietin raised his sword and called a halt.

Several of the closest males stopped to gape at him. Others followed.

"You dare brawl with a woman and child in the midst of it?" he challenged them.

For a moment, no one answered him. Rietin was starting to believe it would end that simply, with them shamed into ending this insanity.

Then a large male pushed his way through the crowd toward Rietin. "After how shamefully you treated her, you dare offer counsel to others?" he countered.

"I am going through you to find my daughter and her mother. If you stand in my way, I will cut you down where you stand. If I find they have been injured in any way, I will see all involved lose their heads."

His laughter was dark in the promise of a hard fight. "Come try me, bare back."

If he was hoping to goad Rietin into attacking in anger, he was doomed to be disappointed. Instead, Rietin walked toward him, daring the other male to stand his ground.

The fool made a swing for Rietin's head, and he ducked it. It was a mistake many Sakk warriors made. They thought their "superior genetics" made them better fighters. From what Rietin had learned in life, the only things that made better fighters were skill and drive to win. He had both in abundance.

His punch rocked the larger male back several paces, and he followed it up with a boot to the wing. The snap of bone was somewhat satisfying.

"That is your last warning," Rietin informed him. "I *will* win this fight, if you persist."

Proving he had more bloodlust than brains, the fool rushed him.

I did say it was his last warning. Rietin brought his sword up in a slice to the chest, and the other male's forward motion, drove it deeper.

He went down with a howl, pressing his hands to the blood flowing down his abdomen and staining his *cuzta* a deep red.

"Call the healers for him," Rietin ordered. He would probably live. *A pity for him. After this pathetic display, it is likely Sakkra will remove his right to choose a mate. For most males, death would be preferable.*

In the distance, a young male turned to the comm panel.

Rietin readied his sword again. "Anyone else intend to stand in my way?"

The other males parted to make a hole for him.

He nodded solemnly. "Report to the audience hall. All of you. Sakkra will deal with you at his leisure."

They turned away, leaving only the injured man, squirming on the floor. There was little question that the men would do as he'd ordered.

Failing to do so meant Sakkra finding them unworthy of taking a mate.

He rounded the downed man without comment. Anything he had to say he'd already said with his weapon.

At the dining area, he called for the command center.

"Rietin at dining area two. Release the locks."

"But the men..."

"I have sent them to the audience hall. Release the locks."

"We have orders."

"Unless you want to be the next to taste my weapon, release the locks so I can check on my daughter and her mother." That stung more every time he said it. *My daughter and her mother. I have no right to call Jo anything but that.* Oh, but he wanted one.

"As you wish, Rietin."

****

The speakers came to life, and Sakk language filled the air around them.

"What is it?" Jo asked.

Sakkra stood, offering his hands to help Amy and Jo up. "The riot has ended. It is safe to leave. Command has ordered everyone to lockdown, for the moment. It would be safest if you joined Amy in our quarters."

Jo pulled herself to her feet with Sakkra's help. "I came here to speak to Amy anyway, so staying in your quarters is a good idea." She looked down at her stained jeans. "As long as there's something for me to change into there."

Amy laughed, shimmying her way to her feet with Sakkra's help. "Most of my pre-pregnancy clothes will fit you. You're welcome to them, since I can't wear them for a while."

The doors opened, and the warriors filed toward them. The lines of men parted, and Rietin stalked between them. His blond hair was loose and fell in curls to his collarbones. His expression was hard in challenge.

And there's blood on his sword. Her stomach roiled at the sight. "He killed someone?"

Sakkra shook his head. "No. There have been no deaths. I imagine someone refused to give up the fight."

Rietin didn't hesitate. He made his way to Jo, and all of the other warriors gave him a wide berth.

As if he realized it bothered her, he set his sword on the edge of the table. "Are you all right?" he asked.

Jo nodded, at a loss for words. He was beautiful, powerful... Raw sensuality poured off Rietin in waves that made her dizzy, and his potent scent wasn't helping matters.

She weaved on her feet, and he scooped her up in his arms. His proximity and strength made him all the more appealing.

"I knew it," he grumbled. "You need a healer."

Sakkra's voice made it through the haze of her muddled thoughts. "Bring her to my quarters. The healers can check both women at once."

They were in motion that quickly. Jo held to Rietin's jacket, her senses in a spin.

****

"All is well," the healer announced. He shot a look of exasperation at Rietin.

Jo bit back a laugh. Clearly, the healer found Rietin as overbearing as she did personally.

But cute, she admitted ruefully. His overprotective nature wasn't as possessive as it had come off earlier. The way he badgered the healer, the way he paced and worried came with true concern.

For me or for our daughter?

My daughter. She couldn't allow herself to let down her guard yet. Rietin had made himself clear earlier. *He wanted to marry me—mate with me—because I'm pregnant.*

No other reason. Jo wanted to cry.

"It would be best if we did continuous monitoring for a few days." Rietin's tone said he was insisting on it.

The healer sighed. "I would have to concur with that. Such high levels of stress are not healthy for a bearing woman and her child."

Jo gaped at them. "I promise not to burp. Okay?"

Both men stared at her, and Amy started laughing. She waved the two men off.

Apparently, that didn't mean they weren't going to continue with the farce. The healer strung a plain metal disc around her neck and worked at the comm board.

"You really should relax, Ms. Williams," he offered in what Jo could only assume was his most patronizing voice.

She adopted a sugary sweet tone for him. "If you and Rietin weren't so overbearing, it would be easier."

"That's okay," Amy settled on the mattress beside her and patted Jo's hand. "As soon as the *bio tracker* is coded, they will be leaving."

"But the lockdown—" Rietin started to protest.

"Will continue if you are in your quarters, in the corridor, or anywhere else in the consulate. A dozen of Sakkra's best are stationed outside that door." Amy motioned to it.

A tone sounded, and the healer picked up his tools and bowed to Amy. He turned smartly and headed for the door.

Rietin stood there, red-faced, seemingly deciding whether or not to argue the order.

Amy crossed her arms under her breasts, a move that accentuated her pregnant form. Something told Jo that was her intent.

"Females with decisions to make talk to other females. *Smart* males allow them privacy to do so."

He tipped his head to Amy, shot a look of longing at Jo, and stomped out.

Jo collapsed to the pillows, biting back a groan. *If he hears that, he'll be back at the bedside in a flash.*

Amy stretched out beside Jo, running her hands over her womb. She was a little over four months along, but the baby was big enough to make it look more like six months and moved in ways that made Jo wince in sympathetic discomfort.

Her baby is definitely winged. Sakkra practically called for a public holiday when it was confirmed.

"So... What did you need to talk to me about?" Amy asked her a full minute after the door closed behind Rietin.

"I want my daughter to be allowed to choose a husband. When she's old enough, I mean. Just because Rietin is Sakk, I don't want her choices taken away."

Her cousin smiled. "I thought that might be a concern. You don't have to worry about it. Sakkra has already agreed that daughters raised on Earth will be given the same choice Earth-born Sakk descended are."

Jo took a calming breath.

"You like Rietin. Don't you?"

She didn't know how to answer that.

Amy turned to look at her. "Sakk men don't always express themselves well."

That broke the dam. "He wants to mate just because I'm pregnant." Misery and rage fought for supremacy.

She sighed. "I doubt that."

"You heard him."

"Yes, but I have the benefit of knowing Rietin."

Jo tried to argue that she didn't want to know him, but curiosity won out. "Then tell me about him, because he's not making a good impression right now." Part of her wanted to believe he wasn't what he seemed.

Amy settled back on the pillows. "Rietin thought he would never be allowed to take a mate. He's what the Sakk refer to as...inferior stock or genetically inferior."

Jo winced. "Because he doesn't have wings?"

"Haven't you watched *any* of our new commercials?"

She shook her head. "Didn't think I needed to," she grumbled.

"I guess so." Amy hesitated for a moment, then continued.

"No. A lot of strong Sakk-descended, both male and female, don't have wings. What matters is certain key gene sequences. Rietin doesn't have them. He picked up too many genes from the non-Sakk members of his ancestry.

"That meant the Sakk didn't want him to reproduce. Or maybe they thought he *couldn't* reproduce with a match from a seed world. I've never been clear on the distinction. At the same time, he thought he was too Sakk to reproduce with a human woman."

Realization made her stomach clench. "He thought he couldn't have a child with anyone?"

Amy nodded. "You could say finding out you were pregnant to him was more than just surprising. It shattered his beliefs about himself and his future. For the first time in his adult life,

Rietin dared to dream he could have what he'd been told he could never have."

"A child."

"Not just a child. A mate. A woman he is compatible with. Other Sakk have a one in one hundred and eighty some odd chance. Sakk who come to Earth have a chance with one in seven hundred women willing to be tested. Until today, Rietin thought he had no chance at all. Do you know how...?" She winced. "Pardon the pun. How astronomical it is that the two of you are compatible?"

Again, she wasn't sure what she wanted to say. "I don't even know where to start making sense of all this," Jo admitted. The stark reality of the situation made her groan. "And you're leaving for Sakk soon."

"Come with us."

Her heart stuttered. "What?"

"To Sakk. My parents are coming. You could come, too. There's plenty of room on the ship. Look at it this way. You'll be far away from Earth, outside your mother's communications range. You can take a leave of absence from college. You'd probably have to do that anyway. Believe me, carrying a Sakk baby isn't easy. Naps are essential." She shot Jo a hopeful look.

"I don't know. Running away from Rietin won't help me work things out with him." But she wanted to go. Badly.

"Well, of course he has to come. Today proves the only way to keep you safe without a brawl is to assign Rietin as your guard. No Sakk male with a brain would try to argue his right to protect his child. Or argue his familiarity with you, for that matter."

There were too many choices to make, and Jo was exhausted already. It seemed Amy's prediction of a nap in her future was about to be fulfilled.

"Come on, Jo. You know you want to see Sakk."

"Yes. I do." Spitting out the rest was more difficult than she wanted to admit. "Okay. I'll come with you to Sakk." Another thought occurred to her. "But my daughter is being raised on Earth."

"Of course. Who else would my daughter play with?"

Jo managed a weak smile in answer. Then she closed her eyes with a sigh.

****

"You six may return to your quarters. There is no question you were trying to hold back the men to protect Ms. Williams's escape."

They tipped their heads, whispering their thanks to Sakkra, before they turned to leave the audience hall. The youngest was pale and wide-eyed, no doubt thanking Sakkan that they weren't among the four stripped of the right to choose a mate entirely.

The two who'd attacked Jo's guard, a third who'd made a lunge for her—and by the grace of her duck alone had avoided tackling her to the floor beneath his bulk, and the one who'd refused to stand down at Rietin's order had all faced that penalty. They would have their choice of donation of their sperm and death, or duty on a far-flung station.

And they have a week to choose their punishment.

The others involved in the riot had been punished with extra duties and suspension from meeting matches for two Earth months. Even that had stung.

But it is supposed to. Any man not mindful of a woman, especially a bearing woman, is not worthy of being responsible for the protection of a mate and children of his own.

On the other hand, the final six had been excused of all punishment, and the male who'd led Jo to the dining area had been awarded honors by Sakkra for it.

And he didn't touch Jo in the attempt. That meant Rietin wouldn't have to *discuss* his future boundaries with him.

Sakkra turned to General Lea. "No matter their choice, they are not to leave on the same ship my mate and I do."

He bowed stiffly. "Understood." With that, he took his leave. Lea had a lot of work ahead of him, since he'd been named Sakkra's voice on Earth, in the absence of the prince.

His exit left Rietin alone with Sakkra. The tension in the air was impossible to miss.

"You realize you presented yourself badly this morning," Sakkra informed him.

"I know it. Now I have to find a way to undo it." That went without saying. He had to have Jo in his life. *And our precious daughter.*

"Walk with me." Sakkra rose and started moving. Since there was no question Rietin would obey, he didn't look back to confirm it.

The silence was thick and potent.

"My Sakku and I spoke at length about the situation before this deplorable scene."

Rietin didn't question what they'd decided. The prince would get to it in his own time.

"Amy is inviting Jo to go to Sakk with us. I am allowing it."

His heart ached at the loss of her already; he had to find a way to change Sakkra's mind. "But you said no woman could leave Earth without being mated. That has always been the rule, even in Representative Janice's time as liaison."

"Jo will not be going alone."

Rietin shook his head, confused by the conflicting messages he was receiving.

"You will be accompanying her as her personal guard."

His mouth went dry. "I take it there is more to this," he guessed.

Sakkra didn't answer immediately. He stopped at the kitchen and picked up a cart of food for Amy and Jo. With the commotion, it was a safe bet neither of them had eaten much of their lunch.

If anything. Jo likely didn't eat at all. No wonder she was faint.

They were well on their way to Sakkra's quarters before the prince returned to the subject. "You will have three months before we reach Sakk. If you fail to convince Jo that you should remain in her life by then, I will encourage her to meet other males and will ask if she wishes you to remain in her life at all. Am I understood, Rietin?"

Three months to convince Jo to become my mate, or I lose the right to ever approach her. "Perfectly."

Corporal Brak opened the door for them, and Sakkra made his way across the large front room to the drape at that shielded the sleeping area from view, Rietin in his wake. He stopped short, halfway through the drape Sakkra had parted for him, a smile pulling up at his lips.

Amy and Jo were both asleep, facing each other on the wide bed. It was a peaceful scene, one he would not disturb for any reason.

Jo has always been lovely when she sleeps. Leaving her the first morning had strained Rietin's control. *This is why.*

Chapter Twenty-Two

Two weeks later

Jo straightened her backpack on her shoulders, her heart hammering. *I'm in space. How the hell did I end up in space?*

She was training to be a teacher, not an astronaut. *Christa McAuliffe I am definitely not!*

Jo winced at the comparison. Sakkra had assured her that there hadn't been a disaster aboard a Sakk ship in well over six hundred years. Yans, she reminded herself. *Maybe that means we're due for one.*

Or maybe it just means they're good at what they do and don't use the lowest bidder.

"Please, let me carry your bag," Rietin requested again.

She started to argue that it wasn't the bag making her wince. Amy caught her attention and motioned to Rietin behind the tracker's back. Jo sighed, stripped off the bag, and handed it to him. Amy and Sakkra had tried to explain that Sakk males would be distressed to see a pregnant woman carrying things for herself.

That's silly. It's sexist. Then again, considering the lack of females in their culture, she supposed the pampering they showed them was only to be expected.

Rietin smiled at her and shouldered the bag. Jo looked away, rattled. His smile made her feel things she had no right feeling. *I can't trust him.*

411

Can I? She shot a sideward look at him, questioning what she knew about him and what she was assuming about him.

The only way I can know is to talk to him.

Men lie. Oh, but she knew that well enough.

That doesn't mean all men do.

Time for an olive branch. Jo managed a strained smile. "Thank you."

His smile widened. "Anything for you, Jo. Anything."

Butterflies erupted in her stomach, and she focused on Amy.

Gabin appeared at her side, his expression issuing a warning.

"I know. Be calm, Jo. Be calm."

He disappeared without a word.

The shuttle door opened, and Jo took a calming breath.

****

Rietin bit back a series of curses. At every move he made, every offer of comfort or support, Jo reacted with upset or hostility. She was volatile, much moreso than he'd attribute to simply bearing.

The door opened, and Jo moved to follow Sakkra, Amy, and Amy's parents. Rietin took her hand, determined to make his place in her life as clear as he could without *bio chains* binding them together.

Jo looked as if she was about to balk. Out of the corner of his eye, Rietin saw Amy mouth something that looked suspiciously like "Let him." Jo's muscles eased, and whatever protest she'd intended to make never emerged, though her color stepped up several notches.

Rietin wound his fingers through hers, and Jo let him. She shot him a questioning look, then took a step toward the opening. He matched her pace, letting her comfort take precedence.

He heard the Sakk warriors drop to one knee nearly in unison before they'd cleared the doorway.

Two came to their feet again and bowed deeply to Sakkra and Amy. Both were silver-haired, though only one wore the ornamentation of command.

"Welcome aboard, Sakkraas. Your quarters and those of your...guests have been prepared."

"As I ordered, I assume." There was a warning in Sakkra's voice.

The captain's wings stiffened, as did his spine. "Of course." He motioned to the male standing beside him. "I present to Sakkraas Master Healer Dravil. He is the preeminent birth healer on the planet and has presided at the birth of both Sakkriel's young heirs. He has been hand chosen to see to Sakku's needs by Sakkrel."

Dravil tipped his head politely. "I will see Sakku for an initial examination before we leave orbit, at Sakkraas' convenience, of course."

"And my cousin, Jo," Amy corrected him.

His brow furrowed. "Sakku may bring whomever she wishes with her, of course."

"You misunderstand me. You will be treating Jo as well."

He hesitated a moment, and he and the captain exchanged a potent look.

The captain found his voice first. "If Sakku's cousin requires medical aid, I am certain my personal healer would be available to—"

Amy cut him off smartly. "Jo is bearing. Dravil *will* care for her as well, I hope?" Though she'd made it a question, Rietin didn't doubt that everyone would take it as an order.

Dravil's smile widened. "As Sakku wishes. I normally treat several females at once. Two for the duration on the journey is akin to a holiday for me."

His gaze trailed from Amy to Diane, then focused on Jo. His smile faded away. "I am not well-versed in human births," he informed them.

That snapped Rietin's patience. "It is not a human birth, and there is no reason not to tend to my daughter."

"But she is not..." The healer cut himself off mid-sentence, but his meaning was clear.

Mated. Yes, I know it. Rietin glared at him, challenging the healer to make a comment about it.

He didn't.

Wisely.

But that didn't stop the gathered warriors from peeking up at her unchained wrist.

Sakkan damn them. I'll gut the next one who approaches her with more than the most common courtesies on his lips.

As if in agreement, Jo shifted closer to him.

****

Jo glanced toward their joined hands again. Part of her wanted to shake Rietin free. The other—more vocal but less welcome—part admitted that holding his hand was nice.

"This will be your room, Ms. Williams." The captain's translated voice snapped her attention up.

The Sakk glyphs on the door made no sense to her. *I should take a picture of it with my cell phone, so I can find it again.*

Oh, who am I kidding? I won't be allowed to leave my room without a guard, just as I wasn't allowed to at the consulate. How am I going to get lost?

Rietin will be that guard. Her hands started to sweat, and she hoped Rietin wouldn't notice it.

"Thank you. I'm sure it will be perfect."

"Yours is there, Captain Rietin."

Jo took note of it. It would be to the left of hers, as she entered the corridor.

She expected him to continue on to pointing out Diane and Steve's room, then Amy and Sakkra's room. He didn't. He waited patiently for something she couldn't name.

"He won't move on until you are safely in your room," Amy informed her.

"Oh, but... Isn't your...?"

"No," Sakkra informed her. "The quarters we will share are for mated couples, dignitaries, and ranking officers. We will be available to you, any time you wish to see us. Rietin can escort you to us, or we can come to you."

She swallowed hard and looked up at Rietin. Her nerves properly jangled, Jo released Rietin's hand, then made her way to the door to her room. She turned to shut it behind her and found Rietin looming in the doorway.

"Allow me to bring your pack in?" he asked. His eyes pleaded for something she couldn't name.

"I'll take it. I really should... I think I need a nap."

Rietin took the backpack off his shoulder and offered it, his smile strained. "As you wish, Jo. Always as you wish."

She took it, words sticking in her throat. He stepped back and closed the door for her.

Jo stood there, uncertain. She wasn't really tired, but she wasn't sure she wanted to unpack either.

Boxes were stacked neatly against the far wall. Most of her belongings were in storage at the consulate. They'd only packed the things she'd proclaimed she couldn't do without for a year.

And maternity clothes they claimed she would need before they reached Sakk. Jo admitted she'd probably brought too much with her, but she'd never faced being away from home for a year at a time.

She went to the stack closest to her and started to shift one of the boxes. It wasn't too heavy, but Rietin would have a fit if she tried to move them without assistance.

Jo looked at the wall that separated his quarters from hers. Why was it that she didn't want to upset Rietin? Her head spinning in confusion, she made her way to the bed. Maybe lying down wasn't such a bad idea after all.

Chapter Twenty-Three

Six weeks later

"Just a few more moments," Dravil soothed Jo.

"Can you tell yet?" She'd asked that question at the sixth week after she came to the consulate—their fourth week aboard ship—and the seventh. It was the eighth week, and Jo still didn't know if her daughter was winged.

Dravil smiled warmly and went back to work. She reminded herself to be patient. The healer was one of the royal healers; he'd delivered both of Sakkra's nephews, and he'd been hand-picked by the Sakk emperor to deliver Amy's daughter.

He's treating me, because Amy asked him to. Dravil could have told the ship's healer to tend to me instead.

"Fully-winged or nearly so," he reported.

Tears pooled in her eyes. Jo had dreamed of a winged daughter...and she'd dreamed of one without wings. Now that she knew, there were so many things she had to plan for.

Dravil appeared at her bedside, clearly assessing her condition. "Are you well, Ms. Williams? Should I summon your mate?"

"I don't *have* a mate," she reminded him bitterly.

He straightened at the rebuke. "Of course. Should I summon...your daughter's sire?"

She shook her head. She wasn't sure how she felt about the fact that their daughter was winged. The last thing she needed was Rietin's excitement about it.

"Would you like me to call for Sakku?"

Jo nodded and managed a shaky "Thank you."

"As you wish, Ms. Williams."

He went to the comm board and relayed the message that Jo wanted to see her cousin. She didn't understand everything he said; her grasp of the Sakk language was still weak.

It didn't take Amy long to arrive. She rushed through the door, looking harried. "Is something wrong?" she asked urgently.

Dravil shook his head, then went back to packing his tools. "They are both healthy and strong, Sakku." He slid a sideward look at Jo. "Your cousin is...upset, I believe."

Amy dismissed him, and Dravil left Jo's room.

He's probably off to report to Sakkra that the baby has wings. It seemed the entire ship was on pins and needles, waiting to hear if her daughter would be winged.

Amy went to the tray of frozen juices in sealed containers and poured herself a glass of the frozen lemonade. "Want one?" she offered.

Jo pushed up from the bed, sighing at the size of her womb already. "The berry punch?"

Her cousin poured one for her, then held it out for Jo. She took it; they went to the sitting area and took two of the soft chairs.

"It's the fact that the baby is winged. Isn't it?" Amy asked bluntly.

"It's everything."

Her cousin shot her a knowing look, one eyebrow raised for effect.

Jo sighed. "Okay, the fact that the baby is winged does limit my choices."

Amy took a drink of her lemonade. "In what way?"

Putting it into words was difficult. At last she grasped on a concrete example she could use. "When I'm trying to start my career, she'll be starting school."

Amy nodded. "So will mine."

"Well, I'd always planned to teach at the school my kids attend for preschool and elementary school, if possible."

"Who says you can't?"

"What? Of course I can't. She'll be bullied. Someone might break her wing without even really meaning to. I've heard they are very easy to break." Dravil had been answering her questions about the particulars of dealing with a winged child, just in case Jo's daughter was winged.

Amy smiled. "General Lea is setting up the first two colony compounds while we're gone."

Jo took her time, drinking down a quarter of the glass of berry freeze before she answered. "I heard about the plans, but I don't understand what that has to do with anything."

"Assuming at least a woman or two each year wants to stay on Earth, we will need a school system soon."

"I could teach there?" Jo hadn't considered it before.

"I was actually thinking of you running the program. You could teach, of course, especially

420

while there are only a few children to deal with. Later on, when you would naturally move into an administrative position, you could give up the classroom and do that."

"Amy, I'm not even a licensed teacher yet." And her heart ached at the idea of leaving her baby to go to school every day. "I might not be for a long time," she admitted.

"The Sakk government decides what makes someone a licensed teacher. We'll be on Sakk for a full six months. We'll have three more months on the trip back and as much time as we need afterward to have you trained."

"As a *Sakk* teacher?"

Amy swallowed another sip of her drink. "More a melding of Sakk teaching methods and European, I would think. If we got a retired master teacher from Sakk, we could have you qualified to teach within a year of returning home to Earth. You've already got two years of college for a teaching degree in that would license you in the state of Virginia...which you don't need to teach in a consulate school, of course, but it will allow you to handle a cross-cultural program. You could take some additional college classes if you think you need them, but you would be a foreign graduate student, for all intents and purposes. We have the benefit of being able to accept all of your existing credits."

"Wow." Jo set her glass down, her head spinning in new possibilities.

"You and the Sakk master teacher would set up the program together."

"Me? I've never done anything like that before."

"There's a first time for everything. This is the first time we've ever set up a school system on Earth."

"Wow." It seemed all Jo was capable of verbalizing.

Amy laughed. "Think of the other plus-side."

"Which is?" Jo continued on without letting her answer. "I'll have to teach both Sakk subjects and the usual ones we do on Earth." It was a lot to teach a child.

"It won't be as difficult as you think. Remember that the parents can teach both languages at home. The consulate already has software designed to teach other Earth languages, which children could use for home study. Children could be trilingual or even more before they reach high school. Not to mention, you'll be able to take the best field trips in the world."

"We will?"

Amy motioned around at the room. "You can bring children aboard Sakk ships and shuttles. Not only can you visit the world, the ships can do weekend trips through the solar system. The children won't be able to go to the surface, but they can see high definition live video of the surface or the atmosphere."

Jo considered that. "Can I see the ship?"

"Now?" Amy seemed shocked by the question.

"Can I?"

Amy pushed to her feet and retrieved her glass. "*We* can go anywhere we want, as long as we take my guards. Well...anywhere but the engine rooms and other machine areas. Too hazardous for pregnant women."

Jo vaulted to her feet and grabbed her own glass, already making plans for field trips to come.

****

The comm board toned, and Rietin tensed. *Damn Dravil for noting that Jo was more relaxed when I'm not hovering.* It wasn't simply the fact that the healer had banned Rietin from attending checks on his daughter that upset him. The fact that Rietin made Jo nervous, after all this time, stung more than he wanted to admit.

Sakkra invited whoever was contacting him to speak. Rietin's heart went into overdrive at the sound of Dravil's voice.

"Ms. Williams requests an audience with Sakku."

Amy made it to her feet and slipped on a pair of flat shoes. "I'm on my way."

"Do you need me?" Sakkra asked.

Dravil continued. "No, Sakkra. I believe this is...a female request."

"Very well."

Amy was already halfway out the door. Rietin rose, intending to follow her.

Sakkra intercepted him halfway. "Dravil will come directly here. Whatever it is, you will know as soon as possible."

423

"What if Jo needs me?"

"She will decide if she needs you, when she needs you, and if she wants you."

Rietin wanted to argue it, but there was no winning an argument against a prince. He stalked back to the chair he'd abandoned and dropped into it with a series of grumbled curses.

The wait was nerve wracking, and a light knock at the door sent Rietin to his feet again.

"Enter," Sakkra called out.

The healer strode into the room as if he owned it, tipped his head to Sakkra, and offered his report smartly. "Ms. Williams and her daughter are healthy and strong." He slid a glance at Rietin. "The babe is also winged. Fully or nearly so."

Rietin smiled. A laugh bubbled up from inside him. They'd done it. He, a 'genetically inferior' male, had produced a fully-winged daughter.

"Why did Jo ask to see Amy?" the prince inquired.

"I do not understand it, Sakkra. Ms. Williams seemed distressed by the news that the babe was winged."

Rietin's smile disappeared that quickly. She was upset that their daughter was winged. Perhaps Jo wouldn't want a winged child. Would his daughter be enough, if Jo decided to deliver the baby and walk away?

No. He wanted Jo in his life. His daughter would be special, but not as special as having Jo's love.

Worse, after his misstep with Jo, he wasn't sure Sakkra would let him keep his daughter, if Jo rejected them both. Would they place her in the care of one of the adopted families that took in surrendered children?

Dravil and Sakkra continued speaking, but Rietin didn't hear any of it. The only thing that mattered was finding a way to convince Jo to choose him, their daughter, everything they could have together.

He rose, dimly noting that Dravil had left.

"Where are you going?" Sakkra asked.

"To see Jo."

"You'll have to wait."

Rietin glared at him, wagering his life on the chance that the prince would understand his frustration. "Why?" What roadblocks were being erected between them now?

Sakkra smiled. "Apparently, Jo and my Sakku have decided to tour the ship. They are well guarded, but I guarantee they need the time alone to discuss...female matters."

He nodded. "They tend to do that often."

"Females with decisions to make talk to other females. Smart *males allow them privacy to do so."*

I suppose I should be a smart male. But the idea of Jo making decisions without him made Rietin distinctly nervous.

"Yes. They do. I'm glad that my mate has her mother and cousin along. Females thrive in the company of other females."

****

425

Jo handled the tiny outfit, trying to follow the directions Dravil had given her. The winged doll and outfits were supposed to prepare her for dressing her daughter in all manner of Sakk clothing without harming her tiny wings.

She tried the simplest form of infant *cazta* again and managed a sloppy wrap. *Not nearly as well as Amy does it.* Then again, her cousin had been practicing it for three months, and Jo had been at it for a little more than an hour.

Jo practiced it twice more and then decided to take a break. Her mind was on dozens of other things, not the least of which was what she was going to name her daughter.

Why she'd chosen to wait until she knew if the baby had wings or not to name her was a mystery to her, but she had. Jo had looked up baby names and made a full list of names, separated by babies with no wings and those with wings.

She went to the bedroom and pulled the tablet she'd made notes in from her backpack. Jo ripped out the page of baby names for babies with no wings, crumpled it, and tossed it at the trash can. She poured a glass of frozen lemonade, took it to the bed, and curled onto the mattress with the second page of baby names written on it.

The first few names held no appeal for her at all. *I honestly thought those were good? Why?* Jo scratched off one after another, whittling the list down to five names in a single pass.

Working it down from there was more difficult. In the end, one name stood out from the rest. *Daya Arianne.* She smiled and circled it, then set the tablet aside.

Jo took a drink of her lemonade and settled back into the pillows, content that she'd accomplished something important. *I've named my daughter.*

Speaking of the little angel, she started kicking. Jo set her lemonade on the bedside table and started rubbing the sides of her womb.

She actively tried to avoid rubbing the front, but—as per usual—she managed to hit the sensitive line that ran from just beneath her breasts to the top of her pubic curls. Jo winced at the sharp influx of sensation. It wasn't that it was painful, but it put her nerves on edge.

How many times had she considered asking Dravil about it and chickened out? Too many to count. If it was something to worry about, she wasn't sure she was ready to hear it. If it was nothing to worry about, she wasn't comfortable wasting the master healer's time with it.

Maybe I should ask Amy. Why hadn't she considered that before? *It was too simple an answer.* Her cousin could tell her if this was something related to Sakk pregnancy Jo didn't know about. At the very least, she could ask Sakkra, without raising alarm. God forbid it was something to worry about, Amy could get Dravil involved before whatever it was got worse.

She levered herself up off the bed and made her way to the comm board. They'd arranged a direct line to Amy and Sakkra for her, and Sakkra responded promptly.

"Good evening, Jo. Do you need any assistance?"

"Is Amy around?"

"She's napping. Is it something I can help with?"

The words stuck in her throat. "Just a question for Amy. It can wait."

"Are you certain? You sound distressed. Can I summon Dravil for you?"

"There's no need to bother him." *I hope.*

"Still, you sound as if you should have someone check on you. I'll send Rietin."

"That's not—"

"Dravil or Rietin." His voice held a note of warning.

Jo debated that. Though she wasn't sure she wanted to talk to Rietin about this, she *really* didn't want to bother Dravil unless it proved to be an emergency. "Rietin."

"He will be there promptly."

The comm connection closed, and Jo sighed. Rietin had been inside her room many times, usually to deliver food and drinks to her or to help her move boxes, but she'd avoided talking to him about her plans for the baby so far.

That's because I didn't know what my plans were. She conceded that she still didn't. *Not entirely.* But she was closer than she'd ever been to a concrete plan.

Rietin knocked and was through the door before she got an entire word out in answer. He closed the door and made his way to her, scanning his gaze up and down as if searching for some injury she'd managed.

"I'm not hurt," she informed him.

"Sakkra said you were in need of me."

"Sakkra warned that he was either going to send you or Dravil here. It was my choice which."

A smile flirted with the corners of his lips. "At least I am the lesser of the two evils."

She sank into the closest chair. "I didn't really *need* either of you, but there was no reason to bother Dravil for nothing."

His smile widened.

Jo re-ran her comment, coming up at a loss for what would amuse him. "What?"

"I don't mind you calling me for no reason. If it means I get to spend time with you, call anytime."

Her heart raced, and her cheeks flooded with heat.

Rietin didn't comment on it. He ambled to the closer of the two chairs left and sat. His gaze strayed to the winged doll, and he lifted it gently from the table, cradling it like an expert.

"You've been around babies before," she guessed.

"Only the ones surrendered at the consulate. There haven't been many. After the initial influx, there have only been four."

The next question fought emerging and finally escaped as a comment instead of a question. "You like babies."

He met her eyes. "Yes. I always have. I considered being a teacher once."

"Why didn't you?"

His smile faded a notch, and he didn't answer it.

She worked her way to one possibility. "Because you thought you couldn't have children?"

Rietin nodded. "I thought it might kill me to care for the children of others as a profession, so I chose the other skills I possessed instead."

"Tracking."

"Tracking. Fighting. Using my wingless state to liaise for the Sakk." He lifted one shoulder in a shrug.

"I think you would make a good teacher." Something about the way he held the doll told her he possessed a gentleness that some children required. The way he handled problems told her he had the grit to keep order in a classroom.

His smile returned. "Perhaps I should. Perhaps we could teach together."

She hadn't considered that. "Maybe. It's possible. Amy is arranging for a master teacher to work with me on Sakk and return with us to Earth. We'll need more than one teacher on Earth, even when we have only a few children to teach."

He shot her a look of disbelief, then returned to his examination of the doll. "I suppose so. I wasn't aware that Sakku Amy had arranged that."

"We decided it today."

Rietin unwrapped the doll and rewrapped the *cazta* one-handed. The wrap was smooth and even.

Inspiration struck. "That's one thing you can teach me."

He shook his head slowly. "What is?"

"How to wrap one of those things." Jo motioned to the doll.

"It's not as hard as it seems at first." Rietin moved his chair closer to hers and demonstrated how to wrap the clothing. He offered the doll to Jo.

She took it and tried to do it. The results surpassed previous attempts, but it wasn't even.

"Try again," he suggested.

Jo unwrapped the doll and started wrapping the cloth.

"Looser there." He pointed out the left shoulder.

She did as he'd suggested and moved on to the next step.

"A little more to the right."

The instructions went on. In the end, her wrap was nearly as perfect as his.

"Do you want to learn the other wraps?" he offered.

She set the doll aside. "Maybe another time. I should practice that one first."

His smile widened.

"What?"

"If I'm going to teach you—"

"That means I'm inviting you back to teach me." She stared at him for a moment. "I guess I am." That wasn't such a hardship.

****

Rietin bit back a wider smile. He was making progress.

Jo started to rise, and he waved her back.

"What do you need?"

"I left my lemonade in the bedroom."

He nodded and made his way to it, plucking the glass from the table. The open tablet on the bed caught his attention, and Rietin stopped to look at it.

His heart stuttered at the contents. *Names.* One was circled. *Daya Arianne. Our daughter has a name.*

His fears that she was shying from the idea of a winged child faded away.

"Rietin?"

"On my way." He pushed through the drape and handed her the glass. It had warmed and was nearly melted. "Would you like me to refresh it?"

"No. It's good." Jo drank down half the glass and set it on the table next to the training doll.

He examined her, noting Jo's preoccupation. Sakkra had said she seemed distressed. Rietin still had no clue what caused her upset.

"Why did you call for Sakku Amy?"

Her cheeks darkened in a blush. "It's nothing. Really."

Rietin squatted to her level, trying to meet her gaze. "If it's nothing, share it with me." It seemed she didn't want to share important things with him. Maybe she would share something unimportant.

Jo hesitated, looked at him directly, and cleared her throat. "I have a...sensitive spot."

"Painful?"

She shook her head in a negative response.

"Show me?"

Her hand traced a line from between her breasts to the lower curve of her womb.

Rietin realized his mouth was hanging open and snapped it shut. *Dame's down. She has dame's down.* According to the medical reports on Amy, even the princess hadn't displayed that pregnancy sign.

"It's dangerous. Isn't it?" Her tone made it clear she was on the verge of tears.

"No. Not at all." Rietin placed a hand over the center of her womb, and she gasped in response. He rubbed lightly at the line, his cock coming up in excitement.

"What is it?"

"It's called dame's down. It is a Sakk pregnancy sign."

"Why didn't Amy warn me about it?" she huffed.

"I don't believe she exhibits it." He knew she didn't, but it wouldn't be proper to admit such intimate knowledge of another male's mate.

Jo nodded solemnly, no doubt forgiving her cousin for the presumed oversight. "What does it do?"

Oh, this is flirting with impropriety. He decided to simplify it for her. "Have you heard of *Kahdi?*"

"Yes. Amy warned me about that one. She said—" Her blush went crimson. "Well, she said you would be the best person to soothe it if it occurred, but I don't believe it's supposed to happen for another month or so?"

"Not typically, but it can occur anytime after the fourth month. Dame's down, when it does appear, appears at about the same time as an early *Kahdi*."

"So they're connected?"

"Not...quite."

Jo's brow scrunched in confusion. "I don't understand what you're saying."

Rietin tried to order his thoughts. "There are certain things that help minimize *Kahdi*."

"Okay. I assume you mean avoiding it instead of treating it after it occurs?"

He nodded.

"Maybe I should know how to do that."

His heart ached in the possibility that she wanted to avoid it just to avoid his touch to treat it.

"Rietin?"

I started this conversation. I should see it through. "Sakk females and young are...most comfortable with a male's touch."

She sat back a bit, her eyes narrowing.

"A male she trusts," he clarified for her. *If she doesn't trust me, that's her way out.*

"You mean...?" She rolled her hand in the suggestion of more.

"In the correct circumstances, the dame's down becomes quite stimulating." He phrased it as gently as he could.

"An erogenous zone, you mean." She didn't question it.

"Yes. I've been told it's quite potent."

Jo looked at his hand, still cupped around her womb. Rietin withdrew his touch. After such a pronouncement, it was wrong to assume she would welcome the intimacy.

"I will not. Not unless you want me to," he assured her.

"Trust," she repeated back.

"Yes. Trust." *Would that Sakkan would bless him with Jo in his bed once more.*

A knock at the door brought his head around. "Yes?"

"Jo?"

Amy. Rietin raised Jo's hand and kissed her knuckles. "I will leave you to speak with your cousin. I fear I have given you more to think about, when I meant to ease your mind."

She hesitated a moment, then leaned toward him and brushed her lips against his. "Thank you, Rietin. Maybe... Would you come again tomorrow for lunch? I'd like to learn how to wrap one of the other styles of *cazta*."

He tipped his head, in shock that she'd kissed him. "Of course."

"Jo?" Amy called out again.

Rietin went to the door and let her in. He tipped his head to Amy and made his way past her guards, his heart light.

Chapter Twenty-Four

Jo paced the floor of the sitting room, her nerves jumping. *I'm crazy. Why am I considering this?*

It was a nonsensical question. She knew precisely why she was considering going to Rietin's room. *Sex. My God, the man is the best lover I've had.*

Rationally, she knew women often turned into well-rounded—*Damn the puns you could make about a pregnant woman!*—nymphomaniacs while they were pregnant, but she knew she'd want to have sex with Rietin, pregnant or not. He could turn her on with a look, and what he could do with the rest of his body was worthy of a sex god.

It wasn't smart to jump into a sexual relationship with him again. If they mated, Jo wanted a relationship based on more than that.

Well, we do have common interests. Teaching, for certain.

Technically speaking, she wasn't jumping into this blind. He'd been coming to her room to help her learn to wrap the *caztas* for three days, and she'd been arguing this, day and night, for nearly as long.

Should I do it? Shouldn't I?

"Oh, damn this." *A person could drive herself crazy arguing where she should go from here.*

She made her way to Rietin's door, shutting her own behind her. The eight steps between her door and his felt like eighty meters. Jo took a calming breath and knocked.

Rietin appeared in the doorway, a book in his hand...wearing a *cu-wrap*, his chest and legs deliciously bare. He stood there, mouth opened wide, seemingly stunned by her arrival.

I'm not backing down now. Jo went up on tiptoe, tunneled her hands in his hair, and brought her lips to his.

It took him only a heartbeat to take her up on the offer. His mouth meshed with hers, and a sound that was probably the book hitting a wall followed.

Rietin guided her into his room and shut the door. He lifted her into his arms and pulled away from the kiss, his breathing rasping.

"Are you sure?"

That kiss had erased all her doubts. Jo nodded and leaned toward his lips again.

The second kiss was even more involved. Rietin moved them across the living room and shouldered the drape across the front of the bedroom away.

He lowered her to the mattress and started working her robe off, his breathing rasping. Jo covered his hand with hers, and he snapped a look at her.

"We've got all night," she reminded him. And if he dared disappear on her again, he was going to pay for it.

Rietin slowed. He unknotted the robe and slipped it from her shoulders, revealing the short Sakk-style nightgown she wore beneath. What she guessed was a Sakk curse escaped his lips.

He glanced up at her and managed a strained smile. "All night?"

His cock tented the front of his *cu-wrap*, proving he was as naked beneath as she was. Words stuck in her throat, and she nodded.

Rietin trailed his hand up beneath the nightgown, stroking at her heated slit. "Commando," he breathed. "I like it."

She liked it, too.

"Remove the nightgown."

Rietin didn't wait for her to comply. He worked two fingers in and out of her, driving Jo toward a shattering release, while she unclasped the nightgown, unwrapped the front, and dragged it off her arms.

She didn't doubt it was his intent to drive her over, but she wanted more.

"I want you inside me," she demanded.

Rietin's shock melted into a hungry look. "Far be it from me to deny a lady what she wants."

Her protest that he certainly wanted it too came to an abrupt halt at the sight of him unfastening his *cu-wrap* and dropping it away. Her mouth watered at the sight.

It's been way too long since I've touched him.

Jo wrapped her hand around his cock and started stroking. She leaned toward him and worked her mouth down his length, moaning at his taste firing her arousal. She massaged his balls, and they filled with semen, testifying to how long he'd been without a woman's touch.

"I thought..." He gasped. "...you said you wanted me inside you."

She released him. "I didn't say *where* inside me," Jo teased in return.

His expression challenged her. "I know where I want to be," he informed her.

"Are you saying you don't want me to suck you?"

"I don't need to come that quickly. We have all night."

In the next heartbeat, Rietin was lying across the mattress beside her. He lifted Jo astride his body and buried the length of his cock inside her.

There was nothing frantic about the sex.

Not like our first night together.

He moved slowly. Not so gently that she'd call it careful, but unrushed. Jo had been prepared for a wild ride. She hadn't been prepared for this.

Every stroke sent her higher. Every touch reminded her why she'd dreamed of him for more than a month after the Christmas party.

Climax crashed over her, and she pushed down onto Rietin's length with a series of little cries. He followed her over with a groan, his heat making her body tremble in delight.

He looked up at her, his eyes pleading. "Don't leave yet."

Jo shook her head, swallowing a laugh. "I believe you promised me the night."

****

I'll promise you more than that. But she wasn't offering more. *Take what she offers, one*

439

step at a time. Just keep praying there will be another step offered.

Rietin stroked a thumb up the dame's down, smiling at her demure little shiver. "Do I have permission to teach you?"

She nodded and gasped out a "Yes."

He pushed himself to sitting under her, used one arm to support her back, and arched her over it, giving himself room to work without removing his cock from its snug home. The move drew new moans from Jo's lips, and her eyes slid shut.

Rietin brought his head down, blowing puffs of air over the nearly-invisible hair feathers starting just between and below her breasts. Jo's hands fisted in the blanket, and her inner muscles clenched tight on him.

He exhaled a long, slow breath along the length of the line he could reach. The reaction was more pronounced that time.

Every moan urged him to more. Within minutes, Jo was moving against him, driving down on his cock while he stroked at the wispy threads of feather.

Jo levered herself forward, leaving the support of his arm. Her hands closed in his hair, and she parted her lips against his, inviting him into another heated kiss. It was nothing short of a carnal promise he intended to take her up on.

Her shouts of climax escaped into his mouth, and Rietin added more touches along the dame's down, driving her further. When her lips left his, she collapsed to his chest with a gasp.

Rietin smiled, then sobered. She was bearing and clearly tired.

"Do you need to sleep, Jo?" he offered.

"You're not getting off that easily," she informed him. "I've waited a long time for this."

"How long?" He had to know. How long had she wanted him?

She pressed a kiss to his chest. "Since the morning after the Christmas party."

His cock jerked in excitement, and she swiveled her hips against him.

Rietin nibbled at her earlobe, then laid kisses from there to her mouth. "Then I suggest I show you all the other things a man can do with dame's down."

Her answer whispered against his ear. "What, for instance?" She bit lightly.

Rietin envisioned pretty little love bites on her nipples. He'd heard it made them sensitive and the woman receptive, as a result.

"I suggest we turn you to your hands and knees and experiment."

Her next bite was slightly harder. "I imagine there are more ways than that to use it?"

He nipped at her lips, parting them with his own to mute her groan in a deep kiss. He pulled away minutely. "Yes. There are."

"Enough to last more than a night?" she hinted.

"Possibly."

"Bring a *cu-wrap* to my rooms with you tomorrow. After we practice wrapping a *cazta...*" Her short fingernails raked at his back. "I have plans for you."

"Wouldn't miss it." Rietin brought his mouth down on hers, ravenous for more of her.

Chapter Twenty-Five

Rietin opened his eyes, smiling at the sight of Jo in his bed. He considered trailing his fingers through the light dusting of dame's down, then dismissed it. She was bearing and needed her sleep. They'd gotten precious little of it the night before.

Not that I'm complaining about it. If it meant Jo still saw him as a potential mate, Rietin would go light on sleep every night of his life she allowed him to.

Sounds of rushing feet in the corridor brought his head up off the pillow. Rietin waited a moment and then relaxed. Whatever the problem, his only duty was to the woman in bed with him.

The door to his room opened, and he came to sitting, pulling his sword from the sheath at the bedside. He had just enough time to make sure Jo was properly covered with blankets before the curtain parted and Sakkra marched through.

"Rietin, Jo is—" His eyes widened, and his jaw dropped.

The lady in question snapped awake, scrambling to Rietin's back, the blankets held to her chest. Her breathing rasped in and out, and one hand closed around his ribs.

Sakkra's gaze went to the sword, and Rietin took his time, sheathing it with a prayer to Sakkan.

"You could have knocked," Rietin informed the prince.

Sakkra seemed to recover his wits. "Jo didn't show up for breakfast with Amy and wasn't answering comms. When she wasn't in her quarters, we assumed the worst."

Jo groaned. "I slept in." That sounded like an apology.

Rietin stroked her hand. "Everything is at the leisure of a bearing woman. If you need sleep, you sleep."

Sakkra sighed. "Unfortunately, we are dealing with *two* bearing women."

He isn't saying Amy's comfort is more important than Jo's, is he? Rietin prepared to protest such an impertinent assumption, prince or no prince.

Sakkra beat him in the race to words. "I will inform Amy that you will meet her for lunch instead, Jo. You need sleep."

She whispered her thanks, and her grip on Rietin's ribs eased.

The prince looked toward the drape. "When you are awake, have breakfast delivered here. I will leave a guard on the door." He didn't add that he was doing so, because the other males would now view Jo as a sexual woman but still unbound.

Rietin tipped his head. "Thank you, Sakkra. We appreciate your concern."

Sakkra made his way out and shut the door behind him. Sounds of him giving orders filtered back toward them.

Jo didn't emerge until the sounds of men moving in the corridor faded away. She tucked the blankets under her arms, her face flushed.

Rietin offered a smile. It widened at her gaze moving down his body to the blankets pooled at his waist. His cock hardened, and her breathing hitched.

"Should we order breakfast?" he offered. Duty demanded he see to her well-being, no matter how much he wanted follow through on his arousal.

She licked her lips, and Rietin's mouth went dry.

Please let her want something more. Please.

"I don't think I want to be out of bed yet," she informed him.

He waited for her to expound upon what she was insinuating. Did she want sleep or did she want him?

As if in answer, Jo pushed the blankets away, drew his hand to the line of dame's down, and dragged him into a kiss.

****

"So... Rietin." Amy didn't have to make it a question.

Jo swallowed hard and looked around for Sakkra. He was nowhere in sight. He'd disappeared halfway through the meal and hadn't reappeared.

"I told him we needed to have a female talk. You wouldn't believe how quickly most Sakk men will scram when they hear that."

"You know I've been spending time with Rietin." She didn't doubt that Sakkra knew where they were almost every moment of every day. How her trip to Rietin's room had escaped his notice was beyond her.

"Learning to wrap a *cazta*. Yes, I know."

"And talking about his dreams for the future."

Amy raised an eyebrow. "You and the baby?"

"Not exactly. Did you know Rietin wanted to be a teacher? Before he became a tracker, I mean."

Her eyes widened a bit. "He did? I never would have guessed that."

"Is it possible for the master teacher to train Rietin, too? I know he would love to follow through on his dream."

"And you two would be able to work together."

Jo took her time, drinking down several sips of her berry freeze. She set the glass on the table. "Yes. I guess we would."

"You don't expect me to believe you've never thought of that." Amy smiled a knowing little smile.

"Well, of course I thought of it. He suggested it, and I... Well, I wouldn't argue that holds appeal for me. Why else would I be asking you to let him train?"

"Of course he can train. He's an adult male. If he wants to give up his position as my personal guard, I can't very well stop him. Nor would I want to."

She breathed a sigh of relief. Though she doubted Rietin would ask for it, it meant a lot to him, she knew.

"What do you intend, Jo? Do you intend to give Rietin the *bio chains*? By resuming a sexual relationship, you know that's what he hopes you intend."

She bit at her lower lip. "I think...I think I will. Not today or anything. Maybe... It would be nice to do it on Sakk. Just because my mother isn't interested doesn't mean his father should lose out on any ceremony that goes along with mating."

Her cousin's eyes narrowed. "From what I've heard, you may not like Rietin's father."

"He won't approve of me, will he?"

"If you were carrying a boy, he would...care more. A female can't carry on his family name. The old man... According to Sakkra, he's bitter and mean."

Jo's heart ached at the idea of Rietin being raised by such a man. "I guess I have to meet him, though."

Amy nodded. "Meet him. If he's too overbearing..."

"What?"

"There will be quarters set up for the two of you at the palace. Guards will accompany you to Rietin's ancestral home. I doubt you'll need them, but you'll have them."

Jo took her hand and squeezed. "Thanks, Amy."

Her cousin smiled widely. "Will you be having dinner with us?"

She knew 'us' meant Amy, Sakkra, and Amy's parents. Thoughts of Rietin changed her answer from acceptance to refusal. "No, thanks. I think I have plans tonight."

Amy laughed. "Have fun."

"Oh, I will."

****

Rietin launched for the door at the unmistakable sounds of Jo returning from lunch with three of Amy's guard in tow. He composed himself for a moment before he opened the door and waved to her.

Her cheeks went an alluring shade of pink, and she waved in return. He started to step out into the corridor, and her words stopped him short.

"Give me ten minutes?" she requested.

Rietin tipped his head with a smile and retreated. As long as Jo was inviting him to her quarters—for sex or to spend time talking or learning to wrap the *cazta*—Rietin would gladly bend to nearly any request she made of him.

The time passed slowly, and Rietin glanced at the clock on the comm board no less than twice every minute. His jeans felt a size too tight, and he considered changing into the *cu-wrap*.

No. That would be presumptuous. Walking into her quarters in sleeping clothing speaks of intent to bed her.

His jeans and t-shirt would have to do.

Finally, the moment arrived. Rietin made his way to Jo's door, nodded to the last remaining guard, and knocked. The guard's sideward look said the *cu-wrap* nestled under the book he held

448

hadn't escaped the other male's attention. Before Rietin had a chance to remind him of his place, Jo's voice reached him through the closed door.

"Come in, Rietin."

Her voice sent pleasant shivers up his cock. He let himself in and closed the door.

She wasn't in the sitting or dining area. "Jo?" Though she'd invited him in, she hadn't invited him into her sleeping area.

The curtains parted minutely, allowing him a brief glimpse of what he suspected was a bare breast.

"I thought I told you to come in," she teased.

The curtain closed, and he stared at the swinging fabric for a moment. Rampant need sent him to the curtain and through it.

Jo lay on the bed, stark naked, her legs slightly parted. Rietin surveyed every millimeter of her luscious body, his cock complaining at the delay already. He licked his lips at the sight of the love bites he'd left the night before, darkening her nipples and portions of the areole. Perhaps the tales about their aphrodisiac effect weren't exaggerated.

She didn't move. She didn't speak. Just as he was about to ask what she wanted from him, Jo tipped her hips in mute plea.

Rietin pulled his t-shirt off and dropped it to the floor. He knelt on the mattress, pushing her knees wide. He brought his head down, biting back a groan at the hand cupping his head down to her core.

She gasped at the first suckling motion against her clit, and her fingers closed into a fist around his hair feathers. Rietin moved from sucking to licking at her wet slit. When she started squirming against him, he thrust his tongue inside, mimicking the moves he intended to perform with his cock before the afternoon was through.

It didn't take long to send her over. Jo came against his sensitized tongue, venting a shout of pleasure against the walls.

Rietin knelt up between her knees, stroking his fingertips up and down the length of his cock through his still-buttoned jeans. Jo came to sitting, spread around him. She nibbled at his throat, her hands working the jeans open.

I'll be inside her in no time.

As if she agreed with that thought, Jo dragged his jeans down his thighs to his knees. Jo shifted, bringing her legs back and folding them to one side of her body. Before Rietin could question it, his cock was deep inside the heat of her mouth.

A half dozen Sakk curses escaped his lips.

She backed away. "I will assume that was complimentary?"

"Yes. Yes, it was." Forming a sentence taxed his mind to its limits.

Jo sucked him in again, scattering his thinking mind. Their first night together teased at his memories. He'd forgotten how good at this she was. As much as he wanted to come inside her hot, little pussy, he wanted this more.

The combination of suction and depth propelled him toward bliss.

Still, it's only fair to warn her. "I'm going to come, Jo." *Hard.*

She doubled her efforts, and the pressure built in Rietin's balls. A strangled curse escaped through gritted teeth, and he released up the length of his cock and into her mouth. Jo's mouth muscles moving in a swallowing motion ripped a roar from his mouth.

He threw out a hand and lowered himself to his back on the mattress, his breathing fast and shallow. Jo snuggled to his side, her fingers making little designs on the underside of his cock. Aftershocks assaulted him, and a small amount of cum splashed onto his abs.

Jo moved, bathing him with that wicked little tongue. She sucked his length in, performing a few brutal little vacuum pulls that had him arcing up off the mattress in pleasure.

Then she released him and worked his jeans down his legs to his feet. When they slipped off, she pitched them toward the curtain.

"I think you need to move in here," she breathed.

His heart stuttered at that pronouncement. "Are you offering to let me share your quarters?"

"Removing your jeans takes too long." She trailed her hands up his legs, causing his cock to twitch in excitement. "I want you naked or in a *cu-wrap* unless we have to leave the room."

She straddled him, bringing his half-erect cock to its full length and girth again.

"You like the *cu-wrap*?"

"Don't you?"

Not particularly. Since he had a choice of wearing human clothing, Rietin found he preferred it. He only had *cu-wrap*s for walking to and from the showers at the consulate and aboard ship. He'd only had one on the night before, because his shorts had been in the clothing sanitizer. *But...* "If you like it, I'll wear it." He would order more of them, wear wingless *cuztas*, if she wanted to see him in one.

She settled across his lap, rubbing his newly-recovered cock with her ready heat. "I like it. Next time, I'm not sure I want you to remove it."

A vision of them entwined on the bed, wrapped in the *tova* sheets, his cock working her hard, had him imagining her in wingless *cazta*. "Do I get to make love to you in a sleeping *cazta*?" he teased.

Jo levered herself up off the bed and sauntered to the closet. She pulled down a nursing *cazta* and pressed it to her shoulders, as if showing it off. A sly little smile graced her lips.

Rietin put his hand out to her, plans unfolding. Jo came back to the bed and sank to his side.

"We may not come up for air until dinner," he breathed.

"I did tell Amy I had other plans."

"Did you?" Hope welled in his chest.

She nodded. "We have a lot to talk about over dinner."

His smile felt brittle. *Not what I'd hoped for.* "Do we?"

Jo dropped the *cazta* in her lap and started counting off the subjects on her fingers. "We have to discuss our daughter. We have to discuss if you're going to train with me to be a teacher."

"I will." There was little in life that held more appeal for him than that. *Beyond Jo and our daughter.*

She nodded. "And we have to talk about what happens when we reach Sakk."

"I thought it was decided that we both wanted to return to Earth?" Jo didn't want to leave Amy any more than Amy wanted to leave her parents and Jo.

"Yes, but..." She seemed troubled by something.

"But?" he prompted her gently.

"I want to..."

"Anything you want." He'd promise her anything. Didn't she know that?

"I think we should get married...mated, I mean, on Sakk."

The answer to that stuck in his throat. "We can do that anytime you want to." *If you're offering the bio chains, I'm not going to refuse you.*

"Then...I want to do it on Sakk."

Rietin leaned toward her and feathered a kiss across her lips. "Anywhere you want. Anytime you want."

Jo launched into his lap, seemingly relieved that he'd agreed. She started laughing, tears pooling in her eyes.

He cupped her face in his hand, wiping away one that rolled down her cheek. "What is it?"

"I always wanted a destination wedding. This just wasn't the way I envisioned it."

Rietin's chuckle turned into a laugh. "Sakk mating doesn't usually include it, but I am certain Sakkra would be willing to officiate a human ceremony, if that would make you happy."

Her gaze focused far away. "Pink."

"What?" What did that mean?

"I've always wanted a light pink dress. Baby pink."

Rietin considered that. "I will need to comm ahead, but that can be arranged." In fact, he knew just the thing.

In the meantime... He lowered his head and sucked at her decorated nipple. Jo's breathing degraded into harsh gasps.

"You are so using the trick with the dame's down while you're behind me again."

He released the first nipple and moved to the other. "It will take me longer to teach you all of the ways it's used," he reminded her.

"I don't care."

Chapter Twenty-Six

Seven weeks later

Jo had never felt more out of place in her life. She was hugely pregnant and wearing a slinky, ankle-length pink dress with matching gloves that extended to her upper arms and disappeared beneath the cap sleeves of the dress. Her shoes were a lovely pair of silver flats that matched the flowered band holding her dark curls in check.

"You look beautiful," Rietin assured her.

He certainly looked handsome in dress pants, collared shirt and tie. His hair was loose around his face, falling in golden waves she wanted to bury her hands in.

Jo offered him a strained smile. Though she didn't want to admit it to him, Sakkra's warning about Rietin's father—on top of the one Amy had given her—had put her nerves on edge.

A light knock at the door let them know it was time to disembark. Rietin took her arm and led Jo through the door.

Amy had told her they would have a few royal guards. In reality, they had eight of them. Jo swallowed hard.

They made their way out of the ship, warrior guards to the sides and back. Rietin panned his gaze around and escorted Jo toward a lone male standing at the far end of the shuttle bay.

There was no smile of welcome for them. The older male stood, his arms crossed over his chest, staring down at them from a height of almost a foot taller than Rietin stood. Something about his stance and expression put Jo's nerves on high alert.

They came to a halt an arm's length away from him. Neither father nor son reached out toward each other. There was a moment of tense silence.

"Gomen," Rietin intoned. "It is my honor and pleasure to present my mate, Jolene."

Gomen's gaze flicked toward Jo's hand. "Mate?" he challenged.

She spoke up. "I asked Rietin to wait until we reached Sakk. I wanted to have a *marriage* celebration. I thought...I thought you might wish to attend."

He made an indeterminate sound. "Human traditions. She looks human." Gomen raked a sneer up and down his son's body. "As do you. It's pathetic. You embarrass me."

Rietin took her hand. "Has he impressed you enough with his courtesy, Jo?"

"Not quite," she ground out. "I want to ask him something."

Rietin waved her on.

She took a step toward Gomen. Jo rubbed a hand over the swell of her womb. "*This* is your granddaughter. Your only son's child. She has wings, you know. Full, beautiful wings. She's genetically superior, in all ways. She's your flesh and blood and bone and feather. And you really intend to turn your back on that." She didn't question it.

"A daughter." He snorted in seeming disgust, then glared at Rietin. "Not a son to carry on the family name, but a daughter. You have always been useless."

Jo snapped. She reached out to smack Gomen across the face, grumbling curses in English.

His hands came up, and all hell broke loose. Rietin yanked Jo behind him, shouting a warning to Gomen to stand down. Six of the eight warriors shot past them and piled on Gomen; the other two hustled Jo and Rietin toward a waiting transport.

"In," one of them ordered.

Rietin launched inside and lifted Jo in after him. The doors slammed shut. Outside, sounds of shouts and fighting ramped up.

"What will happen to him?" she asked, switching back to English now that she wasn't addressing someone who spoke only Sakk.

Rietin pulled Jo onto his lap, then pressed a kiss to her forehead. "Prison, most likely."

"Prison? He didn't even touch me."

"He raised a hand to a bearing woman. That's all it takes on Sakk."

"But...I was trying to hit him."

Rietin smiled. "Bearing women are known to be emotional. Any Sakk male who crosses a bearing woman expects to taste her fury. But you never...*never* raise a hand to her."

Jo's protest died in her throat at the sound of Gomen arguing with the warriors.

"I would not have harmed her. You expect a man to let a little..."

"Sakku Amy's cousin," one of the warriors snapped over whatever insult Gomen started to make.

"What?"

"Before you insult Jolene, you should know she is close cousin to Sakkra's mate. I suggest you choose your words carefully, Gomen."

All struggle stopped. The stillness was deafening.

Gomen said something she didn't catch. Footsteps moved away.

After a few moments, the doors opened, and two warriors tipped their heads. "Are you well, Jolene? Do you require a healer?"

She shook her head, at a loss for words. Jo sank to Rietin's chest, needing his comfort.

He wrapped his arms around her. "Just take us to the palace."

"As you wish, Rietin. We will inform Sakkra of the situation."

"Please do."

The doors closed them in again.

Jo snuggled to him, exhausted by the turn of events.

"Just rest," Rietin soothed her. He started humming the tune he used when she had *Kahdi.*

Before he finished the song the first time, she was asleep.

Chapter Twenty-Seven

Amy smiled at Sakkra's mother. She'd felt instantly at home with the emperor of Sakk and his mate, and the comfort foods and drinks provided for her had been plentiful and delicious.

The business between them had been a simple matter of Sakkrel bestowing his confidence in whatever choices Amy and Sakkra made for Earth.

A warrior rushed into the room and bowed to Sakkrel. He went to Sakkra's side and leaned to whisper something in his ear.

Sakkra shot a look Amy would qualify as horrified disbelief at the messenger. He rose and tipped his head to his father. "If you would excuse me."

"Sakkra?" Amy called out. Something was wrong. Something was *very* wrong.

He hesitated, then held his hand down to her. "You should come."

She pushed to her feet awkwardly. "What is it?"

"It seems Gomen raised a hand to Jo. She may need you."

Her heart stuttered at the pronouncement. *"Is she okay?"* Amy forgot to use Sakk in her shock.

"She is well. Adding the extra guards was strategically sound."

"Where is she?"

Amy turned toward Sakkrel and his mate, shocked that they had risen from their thrones and joined the conversation.

"They will arrive here at the palace in a few moments."

"Order Dravil to their quarters," Sakkrel instructed.

The messenger bolted away.

"Take us to them."

Sakkra led the way to a door with a circular drive beyond. Two transports pulled in before Amy had a chance to ask for an ETA.

The first transport stopped past the doors. The transport's doors opened and six warriors emerged, trotting toward the second transport. They opened the rear doors and reached hands in, aiding Rietin out of the back.

Amy left Sakkra's side and bolted for them, her heart pounding at the sight of Jo cradled in Rietin's arms.

Rietin didn't wait for her to ask a question. "She is simply tired," he assured her.

"Dravil is waiting to check her."

The man in question loped from the palace and arrived at their sides. Instead of going to Jo's side, he came to Amy's. A dizzying rush of Sakk language left his lips.

Sakkra scooped her up in much the same way Rietin carried Jo. He started walking, leading the procession back into the palace.

"Sakkra? What are you doing?"

He didn't answer immediately. He and Dravil kept talking. At last, Sakkra focused on her. "It is time."

"What is—?" Realization made her blood run cold. "You're joking." *But she knew he wasn't.*

Dravil smiled. "The *bio tracker* picks up the changes in your body before you note them."

"But I'm not due for more than a *month*." In her shock, Amy couldn't call to mind the corresponding Sakk term.

He tipped his head. "The release of adrenaline may spur the release of the hormones that spur labor. That is why we endeavor to keep heavily bearing women calm."

As if in agreement, their daughter started battering at the walls of her womb.

Sakkra winced at the implied rebuke.

Or maybe at my gasp? Amy took a deep breath, as Dravil had taught her to in labor.

Another male came running, and Dravil tipped his head toward Jo. "The *bio tracker* shows she is well but stressed. Give her a mild sedative. She should be well tomorrow morning."

He pulled out a small hypo kit and selected one. The shot was in Jo's arm in seconds.

Dravil drew Amy's attention back to her own situation. "Do not concern yourself, though. A babe at this stage of development is perfectly able to live outside the womb. And it will be easier for you to deliver her, since she will be slightly smaller than she would have been at your planned labor date."

Amy nodded. Even human children at thirty-four weeks weren't considered overly premature, and Sakk medicine outstripped human in most respects. "Okay then. Let's get this babe born."

461

****

Jo woke in a bed and reached for Rietin automatically. He sank to the mattress beside her and pulled her to his bare chest.

She took a moment to evaluate the situation. He'd removed the gloves, her shoes, and the headband, but she still wore her gown.

"Oh, no. It's completely rumpled," she moaned.

Rietin chuckled. "Our wedding will be held in three days. We have plenty of time to have the dress cleaned and prepared again."

"It will?"

He nodded.

"I missed something, didn't I?"

Another nod.

"Would you mind sharing?"

"Sakku Amy went into labor. Their daughter was born a *ses-time* ago. Sakkra requested that we put off our ceremony for three days, to allow your cousin and their new babe to attend."

"Of course!" She smiled. "I guess that means we have nothing else to do today."

His expression lit in interest. "I suppose that's true."

"We have plenty of time to have the dress cleaned."

In the next moment, his mouth was meshed with hers.

Section Five:
Homeless

Sandy and Darm

Chapter Twenty-Eight

"And why are you visiting the consulate today?"

Her hand shaking, Sandy offered the sonogram picture.

The huge Angel-like man stared at it in confusion, then took it. His eyes darted this way and that so long, she considered pointing out what he needed to see. Her move to do so ended at his gasp.

He sees it. But what would he do?

There are no unwanted children on Sakk. They even took on strong Sakk-descended orphans and surrendered babies.

That didn't mean they'd accept unwed mothers and their bastards, though. Her own family and Zeke hadn't wanted anything to do with her and her baby. Why would they?

"Please... Come with me." He motioned Sandy out of line and escorted her to a door between the checkpoints. On the other side, people milled in a thick stream down the hallway.

"Make a hole," her escort thundered.

Other Sakk men scrambled to do so, waving a handful of wingless women and men along with them. They all stared at Sandy as she picked her way between the rows.

Her face burned in embarrassment. She was clearly pregnant and just as clearly wearing second-hand clothes instead of the finery Sakk women wore. They were already making judgments, she was sure.

They probably think I want to give my baby up to the Sakk.

Oh, man. What do I do if that's the only help they'll offer? There has to be another way.

As if in confirmation, whispers raced down the line of soldiers, and their scrutiny intensified. Sandy tried not to meet their gazes.

She glanced up at the sonogram picture still clutched in the warrior's hand. Every few steps, he looked down at it as if he was in shock. Turn after turn, they walked in silence. He stopped abruptly, and she did likewise, jerking to a halt.

"This way... What is your name, young one?"

"Sandra Vick."

"Ms. Vick." He bowed his head. "If you would?" He motioned to the door to her left.

Her stomach clenched. "Please call me Sandy. Only teachers and doctors call me Ms. Vick." Not that she had teachers anymore.

"As you wish, Sandy. This way, please." He opened the door for her and waved her through.

She ambled into the room beyond, backpedaling at the rush of men coming toward her. The chest at her back didn't help, and Sandy squealed in alarm.

"Stop," the warrior at her back ordered. His hand came up, motioning the others to a halt.

The closest man's feathers ruffled. "They said it was an emergency."

"Emergency?" Sandy asked. *What emergency?*

"No emergency," the one at her back stated. "But the young one does require...evaluation."

"She has tested as a match?"

The sonogram picture changed hands. "No. But there is little question that she is one."

The doctor—at least Sandy assumed he was a doctor—stared at the picture for only a moment. "This way, young one."

The warrior who'd escorted her answered before she could. "Her name is Sandra Vick, but she prefers to be called Sandy."

The doctor nodded. "This way, Sandy."

She whispered her thanks to her escort.

He tipped his head. "I will take my leave now. Good fortune, Sandy."

In the next heartbeat, he was gone.

****

Yet another Sakk warrior came into the clinic room. It seemed a steady stream of them found reasons to visit while she was there. This one came with a female and a winged baby in tow.

"I have been told you prefer to be called Sandy," he greeted her.

She swallowed a mouthful of the sweet cornbread they'd brought her on the tray of food. "It's my name. What's yours?"

He smiled and executed a slight bow. "Sakkra."

Sandy took a drink of the apple juice, trying to hide her shaking hands. "The prince?" Who was she that a prince was coming to visit her?

466

Sakkra pulled up a chair for the woman with him, got her situated, and pulled one up for himself. He settled in it with a flourish. "Yes."

"What can I do for you, Prince Sakkra?"

"Just Sakkra. It translates as 'prince'."

She nodded to the woman. "Your wife?"

"Mate," he corrected her.

Sandy took another bite of the cornbread.

The woman smiled. "My name is Jo. Sakkra's mate is my cousin Amy. She would be here, but she's at a meeting in DC right now."

"Okay," she mumbled around the last of the food in her mouth. Roll call was complete. Time to get down to business.

"If you'll tell us the name of the father, we'll help you find him."

Sandy coughed on the mush in her mouth, and two of the doctors rushed to assist her. She forced a breath. Then a second. They stopped short of touching her, though they seemed indecisive.

She focused on Jo, trying to find the words to protest. "Find *him*? I know where he is, but who *wants* him?" *Certainly not me. If that's the help they're willing to offer, I don't need it.*

Jo and Sakkra shot unreadable looks at each other. Finally, Jo spoke.

"Where is he?"

"At his shitty little apartment across town, of course." What did that matter?

Sakkra's brow furrowed, and he leaned forward on the chair. "He's not one of my men?"

"Not unless you've had men without wings hanging around Earth for the last few decades."

She seriously doubted it, and she'd known Zeke since they were in Kindergarten together. It was unlikely he'd been recruited that young.

"No. Nothing like that, of course." He stared into space. "Your... The sire thought he was human, as you did yourself?"

She nodded. "If it takes two Sakk-descended to make a winged baby, then he must be Sakk-descended, too."

There was another potent moment of silence. "What *precisely* did you come here for, Sandy?"

She fisted her hand in the silky sheet, her heart pounding so hard and fast she went lightheaded. The doctors shifted and shot looks between themselves, as if deciding whether or not to approach her again.

Probably my heart rate. She made a conscious effort at calming it.

"Sandy?" Jo prodded her.

"They said... In the interviews, Janice Beldon said there were no unwanted babies on Sakk."

"Do you want to give your baby up?"

"No! Absolutely not."

Sakkra motioned for her to calm. "It is true that there are no unwanted children on Sakk, but what do *you* want from us, Sandy?"

She fought for any reasonable request she could make. "To stay here. I'll earn my keep...room, board, medical... I promise."

Sakkra stared at her, then nodded slowly. "Welcome home."

Sandy's muscles relaxed at his agreement. "I don't have a lot of experience. I can cook and...file and type. I'm sure we can find something of value I can do."

Sakkra gaped at her, momentarily stunning her silent. "There will be time to discuss that later."

"I don't understand," she admitted. They had to discuss how she would pay her way.

"Bearing women do not..." He glanced at Jo.

The other woman smiled widely. "Pregnant women don't work on Sakk. The warriors won't stand for it. For now, consider yourself our guest."

Sandy nodded, at a loss for words. *I don't want to be in their debt. I want to earn my keep.*

I have no choice. It seemed they weren't going to let her earn her keep.

"Sandy?" Jo called out.

She forced herself to pay attention to the conversation. "Yeah?"

"Do you need an escort to pick up any of your belongings?"

Swallowing the laugh was difficult at best. Sandy motioned up and down her body. "Everything I value, I carry with me."

Jo paled a notch, and Sakkra shot her a look that said he didn't understand the inference.

Chapter Twenty-Nine

Darm filed into Sakkra's office with two dozen other warriors, wondering at the strange request for his presence in this company. He would have suspected they were searching for the one who'd impregnated the new young match, but their features and coloring varied too much for that.

"Men," Sakkra greeted them. "You have all heard we have a match who is bearing among us."

She doesn't know what the sire of her babe looks like? Darm screwed up his lip in disgust. It was likely a drunken sex act, then. *But why are they not cross-matching the babe to the sire with the bio bed? It is capable of that, and all of us have samples on file.*

The prince continued. "The sire is..."

Sakkan! Not dead. Or matched to another female in the months since this one conceived.

"There is no curse appropriate to describe the Earthling," Sakkra imparted. "He refuses responsibility for his young and for the match bearing his son."

Son. Darm winced. It would be easier to find her a mate if she carried a daughter, winged or not.

"Because the babe is winged?" one of the other men chanced asking.

"He doesn't know the babe is winged. He rejects the very idea of being a sire and of having a mate."

Darm gaped at him. "What a... You are correct, Sakkra. There is no word strong enough. The glut of females on this world, and he has no appreciation for the gift they are." He tipped his head to the prince. "My apologies for the interruption."

"Excused." Sakkra hesitated a moment. "There was a time when we were not as appreciative," he reminded them.

"As you say, Sakkra."

He nodded, then continued. "The young one did not come here searching for a mate. Her son's sire has made her wary of males and their motives."

"Why *did* she come?" someone at the far end of the room asked.

"She felt she had nowhere else to go."

She has no family? No ancestral home?

"Her mother's current mate banished Sandy from the nest when he learned she carried a babe without a mate."

Shock nearly folded Darm's knees. Were there any responsible, caring males on Earth?

"She lived in what the humans call a shelter. It is...a barracks for those who have no homes. They only allowed her to stay so long because she is bearing.

"This...shelter offers a modicum of food and medical care, but when Sandy learned her young one was winged, she fled. She doesn't trust healers who work for the government with a Sakk child. She fears they would injure her son...or use him for testing...or take him from her with their laws."

The silence in the room was absolute.

"Ideally, Sandy will choose a mate. All of you test as primary matches for her likes and dislikes."

The males scanned the others in the room, sizing up the competition for her attentions.

Sakkra continued. "But Sandy *is* a female from Earth. She is not a match from a breeding colony."

What does that mean? It sounded like a caution, warning of a twist, a deviation from the norms they expected for even Earth-born matches.

"Whatever man she chooses must agree to raise her son as his own, as he would a fully-winged female born on a seed world." Sakkra paused, seemingly letting them consider it.

"Your families may balk at this, I know. You may have to take nest parent duties on a seed world or guard duties here on Earth to remain with Sandy and your young, if your family persists."

Darm weighed his options.

"If any of you cannot live with such an arrangement, I suggest you leave now."

A trickle of warriors headed for the door...then a flood. Darm shifted to join them, paused, and planted his feet. The sire hadn't appreciated what a prize a female and young were. Darm did, and he wouldn't shy from a complication or two in claiming one.

The door slid shut, and he glanced around, meeting the gaze of the single other male who'd

472

chosen to stay. The odds of becoming mated were better than he'd ever dreamed.

If she chooses to mate.

Sakkra grunted. "Two. Less than I'd hoped for but better fewer than more, I suppose." He turned and headed for the door. "Come along. It is time to meet Sandy."

"Now, Sakkra?" Darm asked. "You said she wasn't seeking a mate."

He paused, halfway through the door, then continued. "She isn't, but my mate and Jo both assure me that human women often form an attachment to males who are in close contact with them, especially in trying times. You two will be Sandy's guards."

"Guards?" the other questioned.

"Her personal guards. Each will have half a turning. Based on evaluations of her sleep patterns, the changeover will come at two of the afternoon and two of the morning. That grants each of you roughly half of her waking hours."

"Equitable," Darm agreed.

Sakkra motioned to him. "You will take first shift with her."

Which means I am cut short this turning. "I am honored." Part shift or not, he would still be first.

The prince stopped at a door in the match living quarters and knocked lightly.

"Come in," Sakku Amy called out.

Sakkra opened the door and entered, waving the two competitors in after him.

The three females looked up. Darm dismissed the princess and her cousin—both carrying their young daughters in slings—and focused on the third.

Her hair was the color of the sun behind a mist, with just a hint of orange in the mix. Her eyes were the blue-gray of the feathers on an American Jay.

The swell of her pregnancy was very pronounced, making Darm wonder how far progressed she was. He would have to check with the healers at another time. By Sakkan, it made her all the more beautiful.

"These are your personal guards, Sandy. If you leave your rooms, the one on duty at that time will escort you. If you wish to leave the consulate for some reason, he will lead your security detail."

"Is that really necessary?" she asked.

Jo grimaced. "Believe me, it's best."

Sakkra continued as if the interruption hadn't occurred. "If you wish food brought to you, the one on duty will do so. If you wish privacy, he will retire to his own room. They will have the two rooms bordering yours. If you wish company, they both have interests compatible to yours."

She nodded weakly. "What should I call you?"

"Zave," the other hastened to offer.

"Darm."

Her lips moved, probably repeating their names to commit them to memory. At last, Sandy nodded.

****

The two warriors stared at her intently, making Sandy self-conscious.

Sakkra continued. "Darm's shift will be from two of the afternoon to two of the morning. Zave's will be the opposite hours. Any comm board or comm unit will summon them...or summon aid."

"How do I use it?"

He stepped to the comm board and pointed out a large, round, yellow button. "In a medical or...any other kind of emergency, press this button and state your emergency." He pointed out a small blue button next to it. "If you wish to summon Darm or Zave, press this one. It will automatically connect to the correct guard for the time of day." He pointed out the purple. "This button will contact a comm station. They can connect you to Amy or Jo...or anyone else you may need to contact."

"And...I can't leave my quarters without a guard."

"You should not," Zave attested.

Darm shot him a sour look, then focused on Sandy. "It is not overly dangerous for you to leave your quarters. It is an honor to have you here and our happy duty to escort you. We will carry items for you, reach or lift for you, and protect you, should that be required."

She pointed to Jo. "Then why did she say it really is necessary?" Something told her she wasn't being told the whole truth.

"Sometimes...warriors are overzealous in trying to aid a female. Having a single male responsible for her reminds others to keep their distance."

Sandy found it hard to find the words to respond to that. Finally, she stammered out a 'thank you' to Darm. He executed a bow in response.

She stared at him a moment longer. All the warriors had been kind and polite, but Darm moreso than the others. There was something indefinable that drew her to his bright green eyes. It warranted another look, she reasoned.

His hair was in long, golden waves that reached his shoulders, and he was fully the tallest man she'd encountered so far. If Sandy were to guess, she'd place him at more than six and a half feet. But it wasn't an oppressive height.

Realizing she was staring, Sandy shifted her gaze to Zave. His expression was hard and fixed on Darm. There was a warning in that look, an air of violence held barely in check.

Sandy tarried only long enough to note his dark hair and deep blue eyes that reminded her of Zeke's. *Too much like Zeke. Especially his anger and the way he orders me around.*

She looked at Sakkra, intent on asking for Zave to be reassigned.

No. I'm a guest here. They'd been assigned for a reason. The work schedule wasn't something a guest should interfere with.

"Is there a problem, Sandy?" Amy asked.

"Just tired, I guess."

Sakkra extended a hand to aid Amy to her feet. "Decisions can wait for another day. If you wake hungry, comm one of your guards."

"What time is dinner? Is there a way to set an alarm for it?"

Jo laughed heartily. "Pregnant or nursing women eat whenever they're hungry. Rietin brings me snacks in the middle of the night."

The spike of envy was inevitable. *Zeke would never be a husband like that.*

But now she had guards to act the part. It was a duty to them, which was rather depressing, but they would still cater to her every whim.

That puts me in their debt. Maybe I shouldn't overuse it.

"Okay." She rose and headed for the curtain that separated the living room from the bedroom and bathroom.

At the threshold, she looked back. Darm was ushering everyone out into the hallway.

Chapter Thirty

Three weeks later

The lurching of her son left Sandy gasping for breath. She started to lever herself up, and it happened again. Her hands shaking, she reached for the emergency button on the closer comm board, then veered to the blue button. She pressed that one instead. Whatever this was, it probably wasn't an emergency.

If it is, he'll call for the doctor.

"Darm?" she managed, hoping it was still his shift. *I haven't slept enough for it to have changed over yet.*

"You need something, Sandy?" His voice was clear and strong, indicating she hadn't woken him.

"Help. Please..." The baby moved so abruptly, she saw her abdomen undulate. Sandy moaned.

Before the sound faded, the door slid open. Darm shot through the curtain and to her side. At first, she thought he was nude, but he was wearing something that looked like a towel wrapped around his waist.

"What is it?" he asked urgently.

Her son answered for her, another rolling wave that brought tears to her eyes.

"Something...wrong, I think."

"No. Easily remedied," he soothed her.

Darm cupped his hands around her womb and made cooing noises. The lurching became a light kicking. Darm lowered his head and laid a

478

kiss against her womb. A lullaby left his lips and whispered against her.

Sandy sighed. Exhaustion overwhelmed her. Her eyes slipped shut, and Sandy reached down and stroked his hair feathers.

Another kiss feathered against her womb.

Sandy turned toward him, and Darm's hands retreated. The song started again, and Darm stacked small pillows around her womb, creating something of a soft nest.

The soothing sounds and lack of sleep caught up with her, and she slipped toward oblivion.

****

Darm smiled at Sandy, reveling in pride that he'd calmed the babe for her and allowed her precious sleep.

Kahdi was a common complaint among their bearing women. It wasn't inherently dangerous to mother and child, as long as it was treated promptly, but exhaustion was never good when a female carried.

"Heed me, young warrior," he whispered. "Your mother needs her sleep. I suggest you do the same, so she can rest."

There was no answering thump. Still, he tarried, humming Sakkan's Night Song a third time.

****

Sandy stretched, then burrowed her face in the pillow that still held Darm's scent. Her room was quiet...peaceful. For the first time in the three weeks she'd been at the consulate, it felt like home to her.

Memories of Darm brought a smile to her face. It felt like home because of him.

Sandy considered having breakfast, but sleep was too alluring.

It wasn't just the baby's restless nights that convinced her to sleep longer. If she was awake now, she would spend half the day thinking about Darm. Even if he was awake now, Sandy couldn't order the comm board to call him. Though they hadn't specifically said it, she'd gleaned that it was considered inappropriate for her to knock on their doors directly.

Maybe if I sleep in, I can spend more time with Darm later.

A smile on her face, Sandy rearranged the pillows Darm had stacked the night before. The song he'd hummed echoed in her memories, and she hummed what she could remember of it.

In her dreams, Darm joined in.

****

The pacing in the corridor grated at Darm's nerves. At last, he pitched the *Zuda* cards on the table and pushed to his feet.

Zave whirled around as the door opened and glared at Darm. That was enough to put Darm's neck feathers on edge.

"Is something amiss?" he inquired.

"Sandy has not started her day."

Darm glanced at the time plate on the comm board across from them. "It is nearly twelve of the day." That was a full five hours later than she typically called for a morning meal.

"I know it. She has not eaten. I heard her use the water room earlier, but nothing more."

Darm's muscles tensed at that. How close was Zave to hear such a thing?

The competitor to Sandy's attentions didn't notice his response. "Did she retire late last night?" He seemed desperate for an explanation.

Memories of calming her son heated his blood. "No, but she did suffer a mild bout of *Kahdi.*" *Not severe enough that I would expect her to sleep for an extra five hours.* "Perhaps she has suffered it several times and not asked for—"

The door opened between them, and Sandy looked from Zave to himself.

Darm felt his cheeks heat. He tipped his head to her. "My apologies for waking you, Sandy."

Zave grumbled the same.

"Oh, you didn't," she replied brightly. "I was awake already."

"Are you well, Sandy?" Zave inquired, shooting Darm a look that said he should withdraw.

It is Zave's time with her. Though it made his heart sink, Darm forced himself to turn away.

"I'm fine. I just wanted to—Darm!"

He stopped and turned back, stunned that she'd called for him. "Yes, Sandy?"

"Thank you for helping me last night."

He smiled. "An honor and a pleasure, I assure you."

Zave's eyes narrowed.

"Call us if you have need again. *Kahdi* is a common complaint among our bearing women, especially in the latter half of their pregnancies."

Sandy peeked at Zave out of the corner of her eyes and nodded solemnly. Her next question was directed at the other warrior. "I've heard there are movies and games in the meeting rooms?"

Zave smiled widely. "There are. Would you like to go there?"

She glanced down at herself. "If you could get me a tray of food while I shower—"

"Of course." It was clear that Zave saw this as a step toward claiming her as his mate.

"Thank you. I won't be long." Sandy wiggled her fingers at Darm in parting and glided into her quarters.

Though she was going to the meeting room with Zave, Darm couldn't help but feel there was something significant in the wave. He retired to his game of *Zuda* with an unaccountable happiness lightening his mood.

****

Sandy looked around at the sitting room, evaluating her preparations. She just hoped Darm enjoyed them. A glance at the clock showed that it was two minutes after two. She waited until ten minutes after to push the button.

"Yes, Sandy?" Darm replied.

"I was wondering if you might want to join me for a game or a movie." Her heart pounded in apprehension. *What if he says 'no'?*

"Of course. If you wish company—"

"Only if you want to," she hurried to add. Him spending time with her as a duty would be worse than him refusing outright.

There was a moment of potent silence. "I would enjoy spending time with you very much."

She bounced on the balls of her feet. "See you in a few?"

"Yes." There was something tender in that, something completely at odds with the several hundred pounds of muscle, bone, and wings that made up the man in question.

A few heartbeats later, he knocked softly on her door.

"Come in."

He entered her room, seemingly hesitant. After a moment, Darm shut the door and offered a grin.

Chapter Thirty-One

Four days later

Sandy woke with a start, groaning at the lurching baby. Her son seemed to have a fondness for the middle of the night, that was sure.

She reached up and punched the button to summon Darm.

"Yes, Sandy?"

Damn! It's Zave. She peered at the clock, cursing the fact that it was nearly four in the morning.

"Sandy? Are you well? Do you need me?"

The baby lurched again. *It's Zave or no one.* "The baby...again," she gasped out.

"On my way."

He came through the curtain, fully dressed. Zave knelt on the edge of the mattress and started stacking pillows. Trills and coos left his lips, but the baby wasn't calming as he usually did.

"Try...the song," she pleaded.

He did, and he stroked at her womb, but her son thrashed harder. Sandy went lightheaded, and spots danced before her eyes.

"Call Darm."

Zave shot her a hard look and continued with his ministrations. Sharp pains ripped through her abdomen.

"Call Darm!"

He hit the emergency button instead.

Damn him! Why won't he listen?

****

The alarm from the comm board next to the bed snapped Darm awake. Disoriented, he stumbled to the board and tried to identify the emergency. There was no announcement for battle stations or for fire suppression.

The comms were open.

Zave's voice was tense...strained. "The *Kahdi* is not easing."

In the background, he heard Sandy murmur, "I just need Darm."

That sent him bolting her direction. Sandy looked up as he pushed through the partition. She was panting, and beads of sweat coated her face and hands. She cried out as the babe rolled again.

"Move aside," he ordered Zave.

His competitor scowled at him.

"Darm," Sandy pleaded.

"Move aside." Darm added a glare that promised a fight, if it came to that.

Zave abandoned the bed with a string of foul Sakk curses. Darm settled beside her and started the calming ritual.

The babe's struggle subsided slowly. The battering became a fluttering as the young one calmed. Still, Sandy winced with nearly every movement. A tear tracked down her cheek.

"You are in pain?" he whispered.

"Yes." She sobbed.

The medical team rushed through the door.

Darm didn't waste time. "The young one has been calmed, but the pain persists."

He didn't need to say more. Unchecked, *Kahdi* could cause bruising or tearing.

It can kill a babe if uncontrolled. It can kill or injure the mother. It can leave her unable to bear, in the worst of cases.

The healers crowded around her. At their first touch, she grasped Darm's hand. He made soothing sounds and brushed the hair from her face.

One of the healers' touches drew a whimper from her. Another drew a sob, and her hand tightened. "Ow. Ow."

The babe lunged, and Sandy shot upright into Darm's arms with a shout. He whispered soothing noises and stroked circles over her womb.

Gabin gave her an injection, and Sandy relaxed against his chest.

"Is it serious?" Darm asked.

"I think not," the master healer replied. "Still, no good will come of letting it continue."

There was a moment of silence.

"Captain Darm?" the healer prompted.

He stroked Sandy's hair. "Yes?"

"The transport cart?"

"Of course." He lifted her from the bed and settled Sandy on the transport cart, then backed away to let the healers work.

Zave's voice was cold and clipped. "I will accompany Sandy."

The unspoken reminder that it was Zave's shift made his heart sink. "Of course. I should retire now." But he knew he wouldn't sleep. Not until he knew Sandy was well.

They guided Sandy away, and Zave bumped past him.

In the wake of their departure, Darm glanced at the timer. *After four o'clock. Nearly ten more hours until my shift. "Zadek bajou." Damn it all!*

****

Sandy shifted beneath the blankets, then winced in pain. Her groan brought a flurry of movement.

"She is in pain," Zave complained.

She levered her eyes open and stared at the doctor hovering over her. It was the 'master healer' at the clinic. *Gabin,* she recalled.

"It will pass," he assured one of them. Whether he meant to assure her or Zave was unclear. Gabin smiled. "Are you hungry?"

The ache in her lower ribs made her want to answer in the negative, but Sandy knew that would be a lie. "Starving."

Zave chuckled. "Good sign. I will bring you food." He rushed out the door and turned toward the kitchens.

The doctor checked the readings on the screen.

Sandy rubbed her womb, fighting for a deep breath. "Why do I still hurt?" They'd healed cuts in minutes with their technology, but she still felt like she'd been hit by a truck.

He sighed. "The young one makes using the usual methods...problematic."

She nodded. "Is he... Is he okay?" Her hands were fisted so hard in the blankets, her knuckles ached.

"Fine. He's strong."

"I know," she grumbled.

"We will be lightly sedating you both for a few days." He pushed more buttons on the console. "I would like to see you rest in bed for at least that long."

Her gaze strayed to the clock, and she sighed. *Nine o'clock. Five more hours until Darm comes on duty.*

"I assure you it is for the best," he continued.

"It's not that. After last night, I trust you're right about bed rest."

He paused and met her eyes. "What is it then?"

Oh, hell. Why did I start this? Might as well finish it. The worst they can say is that I'm stuck with Zave. "The company could be better."

The doctor glanced toward the closed door, then focused on Sandy again. "You dislike Captain Zave? Has he offended you?"

Answering that was difficult. Something told her that claiming he'd offended her would cause a stir, so she aimed for something less problematic. "I certainly didn't appreciate when he refused to call Darm for me."

His eyes narrowed. "You asked for Darm, and Zave— Why *did* you ask for Captain Darm?" There was an intensity in his gaze that sent chills down her spine.

I said the wrong thing? "The...Kandi..."

"*Kahdi,*" he corrected her.

"*Kahdi.*" She nodded, trying to commit the term to memory. "Zave couldn't make it stop. It just kept getting worse and worse. Darm can always stop it."

He sank into a chair at the bedside, seemingly deep in thought. "You asked for Darm, because you were suffering."

Sandy hesitated a moment. "It hurts. Sure." They knew that, since she was still here in medical.

"Zave refused your request?"

In for a penny... "Yes."

The doctor muttered something unintelligible.

"I don't understand."

"If you would excuse me?"

"Sure."

He hurried to the clinic doors and started pressing buttons on the comm board there. When he started speaking, it was in the Sakk language.

Sandy sighed and let her eyes drift shut.

****

Two sharp trills snapped Darm awake. Given his schedule with Sandy and the night's events, he couldn't imagine who would hail him now. Short of an emergency—which would mean an alarm—he should be left in peace.

He fumbled for the comm button. "Yes?" There was an edge of violence in his tone, he knew.

"Sakkra wishes to see you immediately." The reply was curt and warned of a prince who was less than pleased.

"I will dress—"

"Immediately, Captain Darm."

"As Sakkra wishes." If the prince wanted Darm standing before him in the *cu-wrap*, it was his choice, he supposed.

Darm pushed up from the mattress and made his way blearily to the corridor. Along the way, he finger-combed his hair feathers, trying to look presentable for the prince. By the time he reached Sakkra's office, he was awake enough to walk straight and tall, but only just.

He knocked on the door and pushed through it at the order to enter.

His move to greet their Earth-side leader short circuited at the sight of Zave under guard. "What?" The word slipped out without decorum.

Darm comforted himself with the idea that he would have been dragged from bed by a similar group of guards if he were the one facing the prince's anger.

"Ah...Darm," Sakkra offered by way of greeting.

Zave glared at him, as if he blamed Darm for his incarceration.

How did I cause this? I've made no complaint against him.

Sakkra started speaking. "Did Zave refuse to call for you when Sandy asked for you last night?"

He replayed his memories of the alarm. "I cannot say for certain. I know she was asking for me while Zave was speaking to the healers, and I went to her, as she asked."

Darm felt his face heat in renewed anger. "He did refuse to move aside. Sandy was clearly asking for me then."

"I was already performing the rite," Zave protested. "Who performs it does not matter."

Before he could reply, Sakkra did...and with nearly the same words Darm would have blurted out.

"And yet it did."

Zave nodded, his expression full of misery. "We were never told it could."

"The healers were on their way," Sakkra counseled. "Whether it would have made a *physical* difference aside, Sandy was frightened and in pain. Keeping Darm from her when she asked for him was cruel. Why did you choose to do it?"

He moved his mouth as if to speak, but nothing emerged.

"Come now. I'm certain you know why you did it."

Zave ground his teeth, his face going deep red. "I wanted to be the one to give her ease. It had always been Darm before. I wanted..."

"Go on," the prince drawled, as if he was speaking to an errant toddler.

"I wanted her to see it didn't have to be Darm."

That snapped Darm's patience. "There was nothing underhanded in my soothing her *Kahdi*."

"I know it," Zave conceded.

Sakkra nodded. "Had you refused to admit you'd been selfish and short-sighted, I would have stripped your right to seek a mate for it."

Darm swallowed a sour wave. Though the warning hadn't been meant for him, it was the thing every male feared to hear.

Zave's look of horror was his only reply.

"As it is..." The prince hesitated. "My mate is speaking with Sandy. No one will disregard her wishes again."

As a nest mother would speak to a match about a claim maker's concerns.

****

Sandy chewed the mouthful of vegetable pie, weighing Amy's question. She swallowed. "I don't understand."

The princess patted her winged daughter's back through the sling. "It's very simple. Your guards have always been at your whims. You simply didn't know it. So, I'll repeat the question. Do you wish Captain Zave to be dismissed?"

"They were assigned to me."

"You do need guards." A smile lit her eyes. "Or...at least *one* guard. If you aren't comfortable with one...or both, you can ask for them to be moved to another duty. Or if you care for a guard in particular—"

"Are you saying I could ask for Darm to be my only guard?" Her heart leapt in excitement.

"Is that something you're likely to ask?" she teased.

Sandy peeked at the doctors huddled in the far corner of the clinic. She was certain they were only pretending not to hear their discussion. "Yes. It is. Should I ask Sakkra for that?"

"You like Darm. Don't you?"

Flames of embarrassment licked up her face. Sandy picked at the blanket over her very pregnant mid-section.

"Believe me, that man loves you. If you want him, Darm is yours for the asking."

Misery ate at her shaky confidence. "How could you know that?"

"Do you know that Darm requested four updates on your condition in the first three hours you were unconscious?"

"No. I didn't know that." Sandy peeked up at her. "So...what do I do next?"

"If you're interested in my ideas—"

"Oh, I am." Amy and Jo were like the older sisters Sandy had never had.

"First, I'll tell Sakkra to reassign Zave."

"But don't get him in trouble," Sandy hastened to add. "I don't want to do that."

Amy seemed to consider that carefully. "We'll need a reason that is not his fault. We could simply say you are interested in Darm?"

Her stomach clenched, and she pressed a hand to the shooting pains. "No. I don't think that would be... I know. The reason he makes me so uncomfortable. No. That would sound stupid."

The princess cocked her head. "What will?"

"He looks like..." Sandy rubbed circles on her aching womb. "He looks like Zeke."

"The baby's father?"

"Yes."

"I'd buy that. It doesn't sound stupid at all, and it's not his fault that he resembles another man who treated you badly."

Sandy nodded, relieved.

Amy continued. "The doctors want you on bed rest."

"I know. If Zave is reassigned, can Darm spend more time with me?" She hoped so.

"I can tell Sakkra you want Darm as your only guard. Since you'll be on bed rest, we could arrange for a travel bed in your room for him."

So he won't want to share my bed. That was depressing.

"Of course, there are other things Darm can do to ease the *Kahdi*. There's more than just the calming rites."

"Like what?" Why hadn't they been using them so far?

"Massage, warm baths..." Amy leaned toward her, whispering the last one. "Sex."

Sandy's heart skipped a beat. "What?" What was she suggesting?

"The only reason your *Kahdi* is so severe is because you don't have the constant touch of a Sakk male."

"You're not suggesting I play on his sympathy to—"

"No. I'm telling you that *when* you indicate an interest, he won't hesitate long. Any reservations about taking advantage of you will be offset by what good it will do you and what he desperately wants from you."

Sandy stared at her. "You mean...?" She pointed at the *bio chain* on Amy's wrist.

"Yes. I do. The choice is yours. Darm won't ask you. He won't dare."

"How do you know he wants to then?"

She smiled a secretive little smile. "Why do you think Zave and Darm were chosen as your guards?"

"I don't kn—" Sandy gasped. Amy couldn't be saying what she thought she was.

"They were interested in you, and I don't think there's any question that Darm wants you to choose him. Not after last night."

On the money. Words failed her. Sandy forced breaths in and out slowly, trying to stop the spinning in her head.

"Only a woman can release the lock on the *bio chains.* When you're ready to ask him, go to the comm board beside the bed and press red, red, green, blue. The drawer will open. Remove the chains. When they are locked on, the bio scan to code them will begin automatically. Darm will show you what to do."

"I have to ask him to marry me?" *What if he refuses?*

Amy smiled and patted her hand. "Are you sure you want to do this?"

No. What if he isn't interested? "Yes."

"Then it's time for me to go talk to my mate."

****

Darm and Zave straightened at the sight of Sakku Amy entering her mate's office with two generals at her heels. Both men bowed reverently.

The princess glided to Sakkra's side, laid a soft kiss on his lips, and settled in the chair he'd vacated for her. She took a moment to rearrange the *Sakku Yalu* in the sling, then offered her mate a smile.

"What does Sandy want?" Sakkra asked.

Darm forced his breathing to even and his fists to uncurl. It wasn't he facing termination of rights.

Sakku Amy leveled a look of pity at Zave. "I am afraid nothing you do can put Sandy at ease with you. In fact, I am regretful that I never asked these questions of her before."

Zave winced at that pronouncement. The warriors guarding him moved closer, their expressions hot in anger.

The princess waved them off and continued speaking. "It is no fault of yours, Captain. You have the *supreme* misfortune of closely resembling the man who sired her son. Every time Sandy is near you, she is ill at ease. She sees his face in the place of yours, and that will likely not change anytime soon."

Darm groaned. "That explains why you couldn't calm the young one. If Sandy was tense, the babe would naturally be as well."

He nodded. "I will withdraw. I must." Zave turned and tipped his head to Darm. "You care for her. I know you do."

Darm didn't reply to that. It wasn't something males spoke about.

"Good luck to you."

"And to you." Darm sincerely hoped Zave attracted a match soon.

That settled between them, Zave took his leave. The guards bowed to Sakkra and Sakku, then left Darm with the prince and princess.

Sakku Amy turned her attention to Darm. "Sandy will be lightly sedated for several days. She will need your assistance with much of her daily routine, and she is not to be on her feet more than a bare minimum."

"I understand."

"Good. Then you will move your belongings into Sandy's quarters."

"Sakku?" He had to have misheard her.

"A travel bed will be moved into her sitting room for your use."

And I will content myself with it.

Unless she asks for more. His mouth went dry at the possibility, but it wasn't the appropriate thing to voice in front of either another male or the princess.

Sakku Amy opened the discussion for him. "If she invites more..."

Maintaining a steady stream of air was difficult. His cock was hard and complaining. "Yes, Sakku?"

"I believe you will respect her limitations and needs."

Needs? There were many things Sandy might be in need of. *Each more appealing than the last.* "I will endeavor to do so."

"Then I highly suggest you move into her quarters before you transport her back from the medical bay."

"Without discussing the move with Sandy first? She may—"

"I discussed it with her already," the princess imparted. "She is more than content with the arrangement."

Answering that was a minefield. "Yes, Sakku. As you say."

She rose and departed, leaving Darm stunned.

Sakkra settled in his chair again, his expression grim. "You realize what Sandy needs from you, I am certain."

His face heated at the thought of discussing such personal and intimate details with another male, mated or not. "Bathing. Feeding. Massage."

"All beneficial to her and the babe, but you know what I'm saying." Sakkra stared at him, challenging Darm to avoid the true message.

He nodded. "I do." Sex eased the *Kahdi*. Sakkra was ordering Darm to bed with Sandy if she proved willing. *Perhaps he expects me to seduce her.* "Yes. I understand."

****

Sandy smiled at the sight of Darm coming through the clinic door. He'd taken time to bathe and dress, and though she'd rather see him in the *cu-wrap*, he still looked good enough to eat.

As if he heard that statement, his grin widened. "Are you ready to return to your quarters?"

She pulled the blanket back, and Darm rushed to her side.

Bed rest. "I don't have to ride on the gurney again, do I?"

"Gurney?"

She pointed out the rolling bed they'd used to bring her to the clinic.

Darm chuckled. "I take it the transport cart is distasteful to you."

"Sort of."

"Very well." He scooped her arms under her and lifted Sandy from the bed.

She wrapped her arms around his neck, her heart hammering.

Chapter Thirty-Two

Sandy handed off the dinner tray to Darm, searching for any way to move them toward what she was increasingly convinced they both wanted. For two days, she'd been hinting that she was interested, but it seemed hinting wasn't doing the job.

When Darm massaged her and soothed the *Kahdi*, he was erect, his breathing ragged. But, as Amy expected, he wasn't making a move toward her of his own accord.

He doesn't dare.

An idea struck, and she cleared her throat, drawing his attention. Darm straightened and looked back at her.

Saying it was harder than she would have believed.

"Do you want something from me, Sandy?"

Yes, I do. "A...a bath? I could use a bath."

His gaze went hot in interest. "I will draw it for you."

He left the tray on the small table just inside the curtain and went into the bathroom.

The sound of the tub filling raised butterflies in her stomach, and Sandy rubbed at her womb, whispering to her son. "Oh, no you don't. Not this time."

"Did you call for me, Sandy?"

Her bid to deny it ended at the sight of him in the bikini-style underwear and nothing more. She swallowed hard, and managed a nod.

Sandy raised her hand, and he crossed the room to her and took it, helping her up from the mattress. He squatted slightly and lifted her into his arms, then carried her to the tub.

For a moment, he stood close to her, his breath heating her lips. "Do you need my help?"

"Can you...wash my back?"

He nodded and turned off the water.

Sandy stripped off her nightgown and panties. She slipped into the tub, sighing at the soothing heat.

Darm returned with a rag in hand, stared for a moment, and knelt toward the back of the tub. A moment later, he started spreading the soap over her back.

Sandy closed her eyes, licking her lips at the reality of Darm touching her. He stroked her through the rag, then without it, his fingers kneading at the muscles of her back and hips. He hesitated a moment, and then moved lower, massaging at the globes of her ass.

She opened her eyes and stared at him. Darm hesitated, seemingly unsure of what she wanted. Sandy pulled the bar of soap from the dish and placed it in his closer hand, then guided his hand to her breast.

He gasped for breath, then nodded. Darm rubbed the soap from her shoulders to the lower curve of her womb. He deposited the soap in the dish and returned, bare handed, stroking and massaging her shoulders.

He reached her breasts, and Sandy arched into his touch, her body on fire for more of him. Darm breathed what was probably a curse and continued. He moved lower, and Sandy marveled at how sensual she found him stroking her womb.

He paused, and she looked up, meeting the intensity of his gaze. Sandy didn't question what he was asking. She guided his hand down to her core, moaning as he made the first tentative touches against her clit.

"Yes. Please, Darm."

He whispered a mixture of English and Sakk in her ear, working her into a frenzy. Climax crashed over her, and Darm pressed his lips to her cheek.

After a moment, he pulled his hand from between her legs. "Do you need anything, Sandy?" he asked.

"More of these baths," she teased.

He nodded. "We should get you into bed."

Darm stood, then pulled down a bath sheet. Sandy stared at the length of his cock, the head peeking from the top of his underwear. Her mouth watered at the sight. He would feel so good thrusting inside her, she was sure.

"Sandy?" he reminded her.

She nodded and grasped his hand, letting Darm help her to her feet. He hesitated a moment, then started drying her with the bath sheet. Sandy consoled herself with the fact that his touch was nothing resembling perfunctory.

****

Darm stood beneath the water wall in Sandy's shower, every muscle strung tight.

502

Memories of her expression as she stared at his cock at the end of her bath haunted him.

The fantasies of her taking him into her mouth had nearly goaded him into pressing for that...or more. The last of his common sense had stayed his hand. Whether Sakkra wanted Darm to seduce Sandy or not, he would not press her to anything she didn't want from him.

But he needed. Touching her had put him in an arousal that rivaled his pre-prime settling. If he didn't take care of himself, he would be aching all night.

Darm took his cock in hand, but in his mind, it was Sandy stroking him off, her breath trailing over the sensitive tip, her mouth engulfing him.

He kept stroking, ruthlessly driving himself to completion. He stood under the water, weak and exhausted...and still needing.

At last, he got out on shaking legs. He dried himself and dressed for the night.

The slim hope that she'd heard him bringing himself to climax died a quiet death at the sight of Sandy already asleep. He consoled himself with the thought that she might sleep peacefully in the aftermath of her own climax.

But I won't.

Chapter Thirty-Three

The *Kahdi* started again, and Sandy bit back a groan. What she wouldn't give for one night of unbroken sleep!

"Darm?" she called out, hoping he wasn't sleeping.

It took only a moment for him to appear, striding through the curtain to her side. He didn't ask what was wrong. In a heartbeat, he was busy soothing the twitching and jerking.

He lowered his head and laid a kiss on her womb, and she gasped in arousal. Darm raised his head and met her gaze. His look was potent, needing.

He needs me? It hardly seemed possible.

Sandy pulled at his shoulder, and he rose up over her. Darm didn't question what she was offering. His lips covered hers, and she parted for him.

The kiss went from exploratory to heated in heartbeats. Sandy unfastened his *cu-wrap*, and Darm went still.

His lips parted from hers, and he looked down his body. He met her gaze again. "Are you certain?"

Forming words was beyond her. Sandy nodded.

Darm tossed the *cu-wrap* away, leaving himself dressed, yet again, in only the bikini underwear he wore beneath. He eased her nightgown up her body, uncovering her panties.

Then he reversed direction and worked them off, kneeling on the bed to accomplish it.

He teased his fingers between her legs, using her fluids to massage her hood. Sandy rose against him with a moan. She needed this. Oh, how she needed him inside her.

As if he took her tipping her hips as a suggestion, Darm spread her thighs and lowered himself between them. Sandy started to deny she'd asked for this.

His tongue flicking at her seam stilled any thought of protest. Oh, yes, she wanted this. Gasps escaped her lips, and Sandy tangled her fingers in his hair, urging him closer.

Darm didn't waste a moment. He went from careful tracing of her body with the tip of his tongue, to swirling the length, inside and out.

"Oh! Oh, yes, Darm!" Sandy begged him for more in half-formed sentences.

He seemed to understand her just fine. There was no question that he intended to drive her to climax, even less question that he was going to succeed admirably.

Her gasps turned to groans, then to screams of delight. That seemed to encourage Darm. In heartbeats, pleasure bloomed and raced from her core to the furthest reaches of her body.

Her eyelids suddenly felt too heavy, and keeping them open was too much work. Sandy sank to the mattress, too muddled to order her thoughts.

The mattress shifted, and she reached for Darm blindly. Her fingers tangled with his. "Don't leave," she invited.

There was a moment of stillness. Then the mattress shifted, and the length of his body heated hers. Sandy turned toward him, settling her head to his shoulder with a sigh.

Chapter Thirty-Four

Sandy opened her eyes to the sight of feathers. She was pressed to Darm's chest, his wings closed around her. It was warm, comfortable...safe.

His chest moved in a smooth, deep rhythm that made her want to go back to sleep. Being this close to him—and in such an intimate embrace—made her want to explore.

Exploration won out.

The skin of his chest was surprisingly soft, and the hair feathers were like chenille. His wing feathers were stiff but smooth and soothing against her hands.

Darm groaned and shifted his hips. She gasped at the rigid column of his cock pressing against the lower curve of her womb.

His eyes opened, and he raised a hand to stroke her cheek. His gaze shifted to the hand buried in his wing. "What are you offering, Sandy?"

Realization that his wings were an erogenous zone left her momentarily speechless. Sandy covered her confusion by laying kisses on his chest. He seemed interested in sex with her, and the last thing she was going to do was let him think she'd made a mistake by touching his wings.

He trailed one hand down her back and buttocks, then up, delving beneath her nightgown. Since he'd removed her panties the night before, undressing her took a few heartbeats. His gaze trailed over her with the intensity of a physical caress. Darm guided her astride him, so she could feel his cock stroking against her.

How long has it been for him? Something told her it had been longer for Darm than it had been for her. Considering she hadn't had sex in more than five months, he hadn't had any in more than twice the time she'd known any man over the age of seventeen to go without willingly.

Sandy reached for the bikini underwear he wore, and his breathing hitched. Encouraged, she tried to work them down, but they had little give.

One of Darm's hands left her buttocks, and he squeezed at the edge of one of the silver inlays at the hips. The clasp popped open. Her heart pounding, she did the same to the other side and eased the cloth away from his body.

His cock was only slightly longer than Zeke's had been, but Darm was much thicker. Sandy wrapped her fingers around it, testing the feel of him in her hand.

A moan emerged from deep in his chest. It sounded like he was in exquisite pleasure.

Her body was hot, wet, and acutely empty. Still, he was waiting for something she couldn't name.

He won't ask. He won't dare. Amy said that. I have to offer or take what I want.

Asking beyond her current capabilities, Sandy pushed up on her knees and started easing down his length.

His next groan was deeper, and his eyes dilated in pleasure. Darm shifted further up the bed, seating himself fully inside her. Then he levered himself to sitting beneath her. One large hand tangled in her hair, and he brought his lips down on hers.

Sandy parted for him, offering Darm anything he wanted. If his exploring mouth was any indication, he would be taking her up on that offer.

He levered his hips up, stroking his cock into her. Sandy gasped. Darm thrust again, releasing her mouth to push deeper. His hands closed on her hips, but rather than guiding her up and down his length, he held her still while he took charge.

He progressed from careful little movements of his hips to more aggressive ones, and his wings closed around her. That ramped up the sensory input; sounds were more immediate, scents more potent, and the only thing she could see clearly was Darm. His sounds overlapped with hers in a tapestry of pleasure.

"I can't hold off." It sounded like he was apologizing for it.

His heat flooded her, setting off her own climax. His groan chopped off mid-sound, and a roar escaped his lips. His hips shifted in little jerking motions, setting off aftershocks.

Sandy trembled, her entire body aware of Darm. If this was what matches felt, it was no wonder they mated for life.

"You're chilled." His wings started to part, and he gathered the blankets against her body.

She shook her head, and he stilled, cocking his head to one side as if he was questioning her.

I know how to answer that question. Sandy pushed to her knees, moaning as his cock slipped out of her body. She cupped Darm's face in both her hands, and met him with parted lips.

His hesitation didn't last long. His tongue danced against hers, and one big hand stroked at her womb, finding a sensitive line down the center.

He broke off the kiss and smiled, his eyes glittering in mischief.

"What is it?" she chanced asking.

Darm stroked the sensitive line again. Realization that it was a Sakk erogenous zone made her heart skip in excitement, and she gasped.

"I have so much to teach you," he breathed.

Chapter Thirty-Five

Four days later

Darm groaned in pleasure, spilling his cum into Sandy for the twelfth time in less than half that number of days. He raised his head, levering himself off the *tova*-covered pillow, and savored the taste of her lips. Their mixed scent was drugging within his closed wings.

She broke from the kiss, her breathing ragged. "You're still hard."

"Is that a complaint?" he asked.

Her head swiveled back and forth in a negative response, and his heart rate eased.

"Does it shock you?"

Sandy seemed to struggle with an answer. Just when he would have questioned her, she found her voice.

"I know you're...attracted to me, but do you...? I mean...do you want...?"

"Oh, yes." Darm traced the line of her lips with a fingertip. "Anything you would allow me. If you were interested in mating, I would claim you and your son as my own this instant."

Her eyes pleaded for something he couldn't name.

"Sandy?" Had he misinterpreted her question? Had he assumed too much?

She slid off his rigid length, and Darm let her go. He retracted his wings, and Sandy moved to the far side of the mattress.

His move to question her retreat ended at her reach toward the comm board. His breathing hitched in the certainty that she was about to have him removed. Sandy didn't press the emergency button. Nor did she press the appropriate sequence to call for one of the other women or for information from the desk.

Darm opened his mouth to ask who she was calling. The words died in his throat at the sight of the small drawer opening.

Bio chains. Darm hadn't even known she knew the code to ask for them. Who had she asked? When had she?

She wants *to call for them.* The concept stunned him. Sandy hadn't been asking an offhand question. She'd been offering to allow him to bind her to him.

Sandy turned and offered the chains to him, her hand a little unsteady. "If...if you want to," she whispered.

"If you want to mate and are offering to, I certainly want to," he countered, praying this wasn't some feminine test of his earlier comment.

She nodded, and he lifted one of the chains from her hand. Her nipples peaked as the first locked around her wrist. Sandy hurried to lock his on.

Sparks of light played before his eyes, and his erection was painfully pleasurable. Proving she was affected as well, Sandy straddled him and brought her mouth down on his, her body heating and inviting him in.

Darm wrapped his hands around her hips and stopped her attempt to take him in. "Not yet. The *bio chains* need to code before we make love again."

The process would have started automatically when she asked for the chains. Medical would have been notified to oversee her vital signs, especially since she was bearing. Like all rooms designed for matches, her bed was the most basic sort of *bio bed*, capable of accomplishing the necessary tasks involved in coding the *bio chains*.

Sandy nodded her agreement, and Darm set her aside and knelt to face her. The wait was maddening, and Darm started trailing his hands up and down her body.

She brushed her lips along his chest and throat, and she moaned. Sandy closed a hand around his cock.

No. I have to stop her. He eased her fingers open, and moved to her back, resuming his touching to keep her from turning toward him again.

Visions of the end of coding taunted him. In this position, he would certainly fill her from behind, her beautiful breasts in his hands.

Darm touched them, massaging the ample globes and playing at the tips. Her nipples were hard and begging for his mouth.

If I do that, I'll be inside her too soon.

Her slit was hot and ready. Darm stroked lightly at it, hungering to thrust inside. Sandy cycled her hips against him, her body trembling.

Her sounds went sharp in need, and Darm considered moving away. He'd thought he could do this. He'd thought he could keep her at the edges of climax until—

Sandy cried out harshly, and Darm started to curse himself for allowing her to climax without him. The thick, tacky cream flowing over his fingers and down his thighs stopped him mid-syllable.

Sakkan, no!

She doubled over and pressed a hand to her abdomen, venting an agonized cry. Darm eased her to the mattress and wrapped the blanket around her.

He reached for the emergency button, and the tone signaling the end of coding sounded. Muttering curses, Darm slammed the emergency button.

"Yes, Sandy?" Gabin asked promptly.

"Coding the *bio chains* set off her labor. We need you. Now!" He wiped her fluids onto the sheet and started pulling his clothing on.

"Comms follow my position!" Sounds of confusion filtered through the speaker.

"It's too early," Sandy sobbed.

Darm paused in the process of fastening his *cuzta.* "The healers will be here in moments. They will make this right." He wasn't sure that was true, but Darm had to soothe her somehow.

"How serious is the labor?" Gabin's voice made it clear he was at a run.

"Her waters have spilled."

Several harsh Sakk curses came back to him, and he winced.

"What did he say?" Sandy panted out.

"He wishes you to be calm." *It is undoubtedly true, though it's not what he said.*

He lifted Sandy into his arms and headed for the corridor, intent on meeting them along the way. The door thumped open, and the healers rushed in with a transport cart.

Darm settled her on it, and they started moving the other direction. Healers tapped at the consoles and tossed updates back and forth.

Sandy grasped Darm's hand and squeezed down tight, her other hand pressed to her womb.

Warriors on late shift took notice of the commotion, and more started gathering.

"Lock-in!" the master healer shouted, and the alarm ordering it blared.

Darm took a calming breath. The last thing they needed was to be slowed down by well-meaning males trying to offer support.

Most of the warriors disappeared into doorways. Those who were left were those on duty, and late at night, there would be a minimum of them.

Medical staff came from all directions, some joining their group and some rushing ahead of them to prepare what they needed. Gabin grabbed a passing young healer and shouted out an order to bring up equipment Darm didn't recognize.

When the other healer bolted the opposite direction, the master healer met Darm's questioning gaze. "We thought we had months before we needed the equipment for a new babe," he explained.

He nodded, though he suspected there was more to it than that. *More he isn't saying, because it will frighten Sandy.*

Darm moved Sandy from the transport cart to a full-sized *bio bed*, and the healers gave them a moment of privacy to dress her in a *tova* nursing gown. In the next moment, Gabin was between her legs, his hands deep inside her, his expression grim.

"He's coming fast."

"No. It's too early," she repeated.

"Look at me, Sandy," he ordered. When she complied, the master healer offered her a tip of his head. "Remember that you are dealing with a race who had interstellar travel when Earthlings were living in caves and forging simple metal tools."

She nodded.

"Children are vital to us, and more research has gone into the saving of them than you can imagine. We have the ability to aid your son, but not until he is out of your body. Do you understand me?"

"You're telling me to push?" she guessed.

He tipped his head. "When you feel the need to. Yes."

The healer Gabin had sent away rushed in, pushing a small clear box, loaded with medical tools. Gabin nodded and ordered a sterile field. The shield came up, and the air within smelled of uba leaves.

A natural disinfectant. Often used in sick rooms for those with immune problems or communicable diseases. Darm wanted to ask if the babe would suffer lowered immunity, but he didn't want to stress Sandy. Nor did he want to waste the healers' time.

It seemed there was no time to waste. Sandy curled her head toward her womb, squeezing down hard on Darm's hand, her scream echoing off the walls. Her legs shook in the effort to bring their son forth, small as he must be.

"That's good, Sandy," Gabin encouraged her.

One of the other healers handed Darm a wet cloth and tipped his head toward her. He nodded in understanding and started bathing her face and neck with soothing herbs.

Words emerged, though he hardly knew what he was saying to her. Promises that their son was strong and would fare well overlapped with praise for her efforts at bringing him forth.

At a momentary break in her need to push, Sandy leaned against his chest, gasping for breaths. A smile curved her lips.

"What is it?" he asked.

"You're calling him *our* son."

"Well...he is. Isn't he?"

Sandy nodded and started pushing again, her face contorting in pain.

At the next break, he asked the question he'd been thinking of asking for days. "What is his name, Sandy?"

She shook her head. "Shouldn't we...discuss that together?"

"I know you have your heart set on one," he countered.

"How could you know that?"

Darm pressed a kiss to the top of her head. "I know *you*."

Sandy moaned and started pushing again. Another shout of pain left her.

She collapsed against his chest at the next break. "Darren."

"Our son's name?" he guessed.

"Yes. That's the name I..." Sandy started pushing again.

"I like it. Darren, it is."

It didn't take long for her to deliver him into Gabin's hands. Sandy sank to the pillows, and Darm went back to bathing her with the herbal water.

The silence was nerve-wracking, and Sandy noticed it. "Is he okay? Why isn't he crying?"

Darm looked over his shoulder, watching Gabin administering an aerosol medication to Darren by way of a tiny face mask. "They're checking him." *Sakkan, please. Let him survive and thrive.*

She struggled to sit up, and Darm blocked her way. "You need to lie still for a bit, Sandy. You..." He looked to the closest healer, pleading for help.

The healer tucked a blanket around her. "Your blood pressure is a bit low, due to the labor. Stay here for a moment, please."

"But our son! I want to hold—"

Darren let loose a piercing wail, and Sandy startled. In the next instant, she was crying hard.

Darm didn't have to ask why she did. She'd been terrified that their son wouldn't survive, that everyone was hiding the fact from her. Hearing him alive was too much for her to bear in her fragile state.

He hugged her, whispering assurances that Darren had the best possible care on Earth.

At last, Gabin brought the *tova*-wrapped babe to them. He was small enough to fit in Darm's hands, held fingertips to fingertips, but Darren was kicking and beating his fists, his face screwed up in fury and deep red.

The master healer produced a small tool and showed it to Sandy. "This will help you feed your young one. It will allow him to eat breast milk, which is best for him."

"How do I use it?"

One healer raised the head of the bed, while Gabin showed her how to attach the adapter to her breast. Darm passed their son into Sandy's hands, and he took to eating like a young bird to his mother's beak.

Tears rolled down her face, and she laughed at Darren's expressions.

****

A knock at the doors brought Darm's head up. He glanced at Sandy, smiling at the fact that she was finally getting much-needed sleep.

Gabin went to the door and opened it, waving someone in.

Sakkra strode into the medical bay, smiling weakly at the sight of Darren in the *bionette*. "I take it your son is doing well?" he inquired.

"Very well, thank Sakkan."

"Good. Good." He glanced at Gabin and raised an eyebrow. "Then perhaps our master healer will see fit to release the lock-in before change of shift?"

Gabin went red-faced, mumbled apologies, and set to work releasing it from his work station. Darm chuckled at the oversight. In the rush of the birth, none of them had been concerned with anything but the most pressing concerns.

Sakkra ambled to the shield, peering at Darren through the light antiseptic mist within. According to Gabin, he would require nearly three months of isolation time within the sterile field and daily medications to build his fledgling immune system and respiratory system for longer than that.

But Sakkra's concerns were more mundane. "We have no *cuzta* or training wraps for a babe so small. I will see if we have any warriors skilled in fabrication on Earth. If not, I will send for smaller *cuzta* from Sakk, and we'll use the human equivalent of training wraps."

Darm nodded. "My thanks for your help."

"I will make a general announcement this morning, when I tell the men your good news."

A smile pulled up at Darm's lips. *I have a mate. I have a son.* He would be the envy of the consulate.

"The main medical bay is yours for the duration. The consulate will be using the battle bay."

"Is that necessary?" The battle bay was smaller and less equipped for everyday use.

Sakkra sighed. "It is prudent. As it is, everyone will want to offer gifts and prayers for the young one. We will have to keep order by insisting on medical lock-in for the three of you and high sterilization protocols for everyone and everything moving in and out."

Darm nodded. "I understand."

"Good. I should get going then."

Chapter Thirty-Six

Darm hesitated, then erased the fourth message he'd started to compose. He'd tried issuing an ultimatum, but the thought of his mother reading it had been more than he could bear. Pleading for their acceptance made him seem weak, and that would never do. A dismissal of his parents' opinions before they were fully formed was hurtful and presumptuous. A clinical recitation of the facts had proven no better.

How do I do this? Now that Sandy and Darren had been properly claimed as his own, he couldn't put this off any longer.

He'd never had difficulty speaking to his parents before. That thought made him reexamine his approach to telling them about the choices he'd made.

They are my parents. I should speak to them as I always have.

That in mind, Darm turned to the console and started typing a new missive.

My dear mother and sire,

My life has taken a wondrous turn of late, and I hope you will accept this blessing as I have.

A young match came to the consulate. She'd encountered an Earth-born Sakk-descended male, and they'd conceived a young one between them. Like many human males, the sire has no appreciation of the gift of mate and young. Rejected by the sire and by her own nest, Sandy came to the consulate—unprotected and bearing, seeking shelter in return for whatever work we would offer her.

Over the several sa-sen *she has sheltered in the consulate, I have been her personal guard. I have protected her, soothed her* Kahdi, *and won her affection. She is a beautiful and loving woman, and we mated only yesterday.*

Being late in her term, mating sent Sandy into early labor, and she delivered a fully-winged son. Though he will require close observation of the healers for an extended period of time, he is strong and determined. In many ways, he reminds me of you, father. I have claimed Darren as my own, as we both love him dearly.

I realize you may not accept these choices. If you can, I would like to bring Sandy and Darren to our ancestral home on Sakk when our son is old enough for such a journey.

If you cannot accept them, I will grieve your loss and remain on Earth with my beloved family. My place is with my mate and son.

May Sakkan keep you in health and safety, always in good cheer.

Darm

Darren fussed from his *bionette,* and Darm let out a soothing coo.

My place is with my mate and son. He sent the message to the ship leaving comm range and hurried to his son's side.

****

Three and a half months later

Darm entered their quarters with the tray of food and slid past the partition. He smiled at the sight of Darren noshing at Sandy's full breast.

"Would you like me to feed you?" he offered. *Again.* Darren ate often, and it coincided with meals with regularity.

"No. He's nearly done."

He set the tray on the bedside table and fluffed Darren's hair feathers, whispering a prayer for his strength and health. They'd only been released to their quarters a few days earlier, and Darren was still under constant monitoring.

"Oh, there's a blinking light on the comm board. I don't know what it means."

Darm looked up, his heart stuttering at the blinking blue light. *A message. It must be my parents' reply.* It surprised him that it came so quickly. They must have had luck in sending a message back on a far-flung vessel nearly the moment they'd received his.

"Darm? Is there a problem?"

"Not at all. I just have to check the message queue."

She made a faint sound of agreement, and he took his leave to the main console in the sitting room. His hands sweating, he punched up the message.

My dearest son,

Mother. Was it bad news? His mother rarely wrote missives.

Your sire and I were most surprised by your message. We wish you would have trusted us with news of your mate as you grew to love each other. I only hope you avoided doing so as not to raise the family's hopes for your happiness without return. It would pain me to think you feared our rejection so completely.

Oh, but his mother did know how to chastise him. Thankfully, he could honestly tell her he'd been unsure if Sandy would ever choose to mate.

He went back to the missive.

Preparations have begun to welcome Sandy and young Darren to the ancestral home, with your sire's usual military precision. We await news of your arrival.

May Sakkan bless and keep you all.

Impatiently,
Your sire and I

He commed the healer in charge of Darren's care.

"Is there a problem, Captain?" he asked urgently.

Darm switched to Sakk for his reply. *"How soon will my mate and son be able to travel to Sakk?"*

"I was not aware Sandy had made that decision." His voice was guarded.

"I mean to ask her, but I need to know when they will be allowed to travel before I do that."

The healer hesitated. *"On the next monthly transport, I should think."*

"That soon?" He'd expected a longer wait.

"Is that a problem, Captain?"

"No. Simply surprising."

The healer chuckled. *"As always with a young one, Captain. Good day."*

"Good day." Darm closed the comm and hurried back to Sandy.

****

Darm came through the curtain, smiling widely.

"Good news?" she asked, settling Darren back in the *bionette* that monitored him, day and night.

"I believe so."

Sandy settled on the mattress and lifted the plate of food into her lap. "Tell me while we eat?" She was ravenous and had been since Darren's birth.

Darm settled beside her, but he didn't reach for the food. Sandy took a slab of the sweet cornbread off the tray and added it to her plate. She loved it, and it seemed the cooks made a batch every day, whether the men were eating it or not, just for her.

"What would you think about going home with me?"

She was abruptly glad she hadn't started eating yet. She might have choked at that question. "To Sakk?"

"That would be home," he teased, but there was something sad in his eyes.

"You have family there," she guessed. Strange that they'd never discussed that before.

"We all do. Yes." He didn't add that she didn't have family on Earth. Darm didn't need to. As her personal guard, he'd probably read her file in detail.

It's true. Then why did the idea of leaving Earth bother her? "When will we be leaving?" *I have Darm and Darren. That is home.*

But Darm had family and friends on Sakk. Was that why she was afraid to go with him? Was she afraid his interest would wane if there were competitors for his affections?

Or maybe that his family wouldn't accept her and Darren?

"We can leave as soon as next month, but I thought the month after might be more prudent. For Darren, of course."

Sandy nodded, relieved that he didn't mean an immediate departure. "Tell me about your family."

His smile was soft and wistful. "My sire is a gruff old feather beater. Uh...master general. Retired."

She nodded and took a bite of the bread.

"My mother has the voice of Uumae...Sakkan's most beloved wife."

She swallowed the food. "She's a singer?"

"Not as a profession, but it is an interest of hers."

"Any brothers and sisters?"

"An older brother and an older sister."

"So you're the baby of the family?"

He scowled at her.

Sandy found she enjoyed teasing him. "If your sister is older, that means she's already—"

"Mated? Yes. For seven years now."

"Is your brother?"

He sighed. "No."

"I thought men typically... They said the older men had first...choice."

"Not on Earth. A few older males are chosen to come here, but the majority are young men. Daff wasn't one of the older males chosen to come to Earth. He won't be eligible to take a prize match on Sakk for at least five more *yans*. Knowing Daff, only a prize match will do for him. Or at least a level two match, if he mellows a bit."

Sandy worked at that. "Will he be jealous that you have a mate?"

"Very jealous. Insanely so. Why would you ask that?"

She smoothed the nursing *cazta*. "I don't think..."

He waited patiently for her to finish her thoughts.

"I'm not exactly a prize match."

His cheeks darkened, and his jaw tightened down a notch. "Any man would be honored to have you on his arm."

"I notice only two were interested."

His eyes widened.

"That's why you and Zave were assigned as my guards. I suspected it might be something like that, but Amy confirmed it for me."

His gaze flicked to Darren and away again. "Any man here would have gladly been your mate."

"But not with Darren." Tears stung at her eyes.

"They are selfish cowards. That is no fault of yours."

"Will your parents be upset about Darren?"

"They're already preparing for our arrival."

"What?" He wasn't serious, was he?

"The blinking light was their reply to my announcement of our mating. They are preparing and waiting for news of our arrival. If I know my sire—and so well I do—he has already requested a full report of Darren's condition and his needs. He may have already arranged for a *bionette* or *bio crib* to safeguard him at our home. He has also probably requisitioned a continuous monitor."

"Like the one Amy wears?"

"Precisely." A smile pulled his lips up into a bow. "All children are precious gifts."

"Then why would the other men be afraid to accept him?"

Darm sighed deeply, and his smile faded. "Not all parents are as accepting as mine are."

"So...you knew they'd be okay with this?"

"Not at all. I hoped they would be, and I was correct."

Forming words to answer that was difficult.

"Sandy? Is something wrong?"

She shook her head. "I was just thinking..."

"Yes?"

"That was incredibly brave of you."

He laughed heartily. "I told you they were cowards."

Chapter Thirty-Seven

Five weeks later

"You're crazy."

Darm smiled. "I'm serious. You can have anything you want. Not just for Darren. For you."

"What do I need? Honestly, Darm."

He sighed. He wished he could understand why she so resisted the concept of her mate stipend. "I didn't ask what you needed," he reminded her gently. "What do you want?"

Sandy looked around at the store, seemingly stunned. Her hair had been tamed into presentation curls, and she looked glorious in the floor-length nursing *cazta* and *tova* gloves.

"Toiletries?" He waved the way to them from memory of the store plans he'd studied.

"I like the ones at the consulate. Are those available on Sakk?"

Darm nodded. "They are imported monthly from Sakk. Clothing?" He motioned toward women's clothing.

"But *tova* is so comfortable."

"Candies? Delicacies?"

She smiled. "Unlimited chocolate? I'd get fat."

He laughed. "I doubt it, but I would not mind if—"

"Well, well, well... Knew you had to be lying about that brat being mine."

Darm turned toward the strange male's voice, tensing as Sandy dropped back a step.

Taking her lead, the guards closed on their position.

The male wore a faded pair of jeans with scuffed boots, a studded leather belt, and a button-down collared shirt with the sleeves cuffed to the elbows. His black hair feathers were cut short in the back but long enough to partially cover his bright blue eyes.

Darren's eyes. Sandy was correct. He does resemble a wingless Zave.

"You have something to say to my mate, human?" Darm knew the male's name, but he had no respect for the man. Why act as if he did?

Zeke scowled. His gaze trailed from Darm to Sandy and then down to Darren. She moved a step to the left, hiding Darren behind Darm's wing.

How quickly she has come to adopt a Sakk female's behaviors.

"The kid isn't yours, either," Zeke announced.

He would have believed Darren was Zave's, but that is immaterial. "The son of my mate is *my* son." *And I will protect him as such. Try me, human.*

The young warrior at Darm's right shifted to a battle stance, a subtle threat that any trained soldier would be sure to note and respect.

Heedless of it, Zeke continued. "Probably thought she couldn't get knocked up by one of yours. Joke's on her. Glad I didn't fall for the little slut's game."

Wings ruffled around them at the insult.

Darm calmed himself. Nothing could be gained by him ending up in a human jail cell. "Ravon, take the detail with Sandy and our son. Find her chocolate. I will join you shortly."

Sandy touched his back with a shaking hand, then retreated, surrounded by Sakk warriors. One of them stayed, despite his command. Darm shot him a questioning look, and the warrior tipped his head. Ravon had likely ordered him to stay to keep Darm out of that jail cell.

When Sandy was too far away to hear them, Darm addressed Zeke. "Were we on Sakk, I would kill you for calling my mate a wanton. As it is, I will tell you something you need to know."

Zeke curled his lip in disgust. "And what would that be?"

"You sired my son. You are a strong Sakk descendant, just as Sandy is. It is the only way to produce a winged babe, as you have."

His eyes narrowed. "I don't buy it. I want DNA tests before I cough up one thin dime for the brat."

Darm couldn't have stopped his wings from ruffling if he wanted to. And that was the last thing he wanted. "*I* support my son. Your...assistance is not required."

"Then why tell me this?" he challenged.

"I find it amusing that you are now in the same position I once was. You are unable to reproduce with a fully human woman. Less than one in seven hundred on Earth are compatible with you.

"You *had* a compatible woman that loved you and her son for the asking, and you threw them away. Now they are mine. Such a gift comes rarely in life. You may never find it again."

Zeke's face went crimson. "Hundreds of women come to the consulates every day."

"They do. And they come to find honorable, attentive mates. By Sakk law, your actions have labeled you unsuitable to take a mate. The Sakk will test you, if you wish. They will not help you find a mate.

"Of course, since you threw away one child, the loss of more may not matter to you. You may feel I have done you a favor by—"

"But I *have* a son. You said so yourself."

"No. *I* have a son. You have nothing." Saying it brought a fierce satisfaction. "Go find women to fill your bed. Maybe luck will favor you twice."

"I have rights," Zeke protested.

"To my mate? No. Sandy has made her—"

"To my son!"

"He is a Sakk child, born at the Sakk consulate, to a mated Sakk woman. By Sakk law, he is my son."

"That consulate is on American soil, buddy."

"Not really. The consulate is Sakk sovereign soil."

"I'll file an injunction."

Darm scowled, his brow furrowing. "A what?"

"Legal papers, asshole. I'll ask for custody or...or visitation. Yeah, visitation. I don't want the brat all the time. Let his mother take care of the kid, but they won't let you keep him away from me."

"And you wish this for what reason? You suddenly feel the pressing need for a son in your pathetic life?" Darm doubted it.

Zeke's smile was cold in challenge. "I'm not in the same position you were. I have rights you never will have to them, and I'll prove it, too."

A wild need to shelter his mate and son welled in him. "That depends."

"On?" Zeke asked warily, no doubt believing Darm intended to kill him.

"On how fast you are." Darm left him standing there without further explanation. It would be a race to the prize, but Darm had no intention of losing.

He found Sandy in an area full of sweet-smelling treats. "Have you found what you want?" he asked.

She glanced around his body and flinched. Darm didn't have to ask what she saw. If Zeke was skulking around, Darm could use that to his advantage.

He cupped Sandy's head in one hand and leaned in for a kiss. It wasn't something Sakk males typically did around other unmated males, but he felt certain the security detail would understand his game.

Zeke snorted, and Sandy started to pull away. Darm followed her retreat, and she gave herself up to the passion between them. When he drew away, she let out a little whimper.

Darm smiled at that. "Have you found what you want?" he repeated. He had two meanings, and her answer to either would be acceptable.

A smile blossomed on her lips. "You said anything?" A little bounce of excitement had her presentation curls swaying around her face.

"Anything your heart desires."

Sandy led him to a display of mostly gold-wrapped confections. Here and there were spots of bright colored wrappings in the mix. They shared a maker's mark of *Lindt*.

"Which ones are your favorites?"

She blushed. "Anything they make."

"Ravon."

The Captain appeared at his side. "Yes, Darm?"

"I wish every package of this maker delivered to the consulate within the hour."

Ravon smiled. "As you wish. May I leave one man behind to accomplish it while you continue to shop?" His eyes shifted to Zeke and back, indicating that he wanted to get Sandy away from the unpleasant male as soon as possible.

"Precisely my thought." Darm turned his attention to Sandy. "Is there anything else you would like?"

She started to shake her head, then nodded. "Yes. There is."

That's my woman. He offered his arm. "Lead on."

She took it and glanced toward the warrior speaking to the clerk. "What did you order Ravon to do?"

Davon smiled. "Collect a sampling of what they offer."

Sandy would probably be appalled at his actual order, but that would fade with time. Now that he'd met Zeke, it was clear she'd never been pampered as a female should be, until she came to the consulate, and she'd been actively avoiding letting Darm do that to his fullest ability.

****

Sandy looked back, her heart pounding at the sight of Zeke trailing them. As if he understood her upset perfectly, Darm extended his wing around her to block Zeke's view.

Or to block my view of Zeke. Relax, Darm. The last thing I want in my life is Zeke.

Sandy led the warriors and their unwelcome tag-along to lingerie. By the grumbling and whispering of the warriors, she guessed that this was unacceptable to them. It was unkind to taunt a Sakk male with what he couldn't readily have, she knew.

Darm squeezed her arm lightly. "Whatever you want. Our guards can turn their backs to give us privacy."

They did so as if it had been an order, and the sounds of upset diminished.

It might have been an order. Sakk men are a jealous lot. The idea of another male fantasizing about his mate is intolerable to Darm.

Sandy moved from rack to rack, picking out teddies, baby doll nighties, peignoirs, and wraps that appealed to her. Darm offered his hands to carry them. She added on some lacy underwear and bras, then some fancy stockings and high-heeled slippers.

A glance at Darm made her swallow a lump in her throat. His expression was potent, proof positive that his cock was rigid and ready inside his under-wrap.

"You want to pick the first one I wear?" she offered.

To his credit, Darm didn't groan. She was sure it was a Herculean effort not to.

"Absolutely." Clearly, he had a favorite.

"I can't wait to see."

"Neither can I."

At the counter, Darm told the clerk to put it all on the consulate account. There was no question that she was a Sakk mate. She didn't doubt Darm wouldn't let there be confusion.

Amy had told her that every warrior mated on Earth was granted a generous stipend to outfit his mate with whatever she needed or wanted before she went to Sakk with him. Some professional women chose expensive tools of their trades. Some women chose jewels and fashion clothing. No matter what they chose, no woman had exceeded the limits set for them.

Maybe there is no limit. The money being poured into Earth's economy was staggering, though she'd heard that precious metals had taken something of a dive on the stock market at the addition.

All of her purchases in the lingerie department fit into two large bags, and Darm took both in one hand.

"Anything more?" he asked.

She hesitated.

"Sandy?" he prompted her.

"You said it will be winter on Sakk?" She'd originally come here to get things for Darren.

"Yes. It will be." That seemed to confuse him.

"Okay. I need a few more things."

His smile widened. "Lead on."

Their last stop was baby clothing. Most baby clothes wouldn't fit over Darren's wings, but some things would. She picked out a hooded bunting big enough to fit over the appendages, socks and soft shoes that would last a year or more, and crib blankets.

Two of their guards took those bags, and the entire entourage—including the guard they'd left behind in the candy department—escorted her to the Sakk consulate's limousine. Most new mates rode in the consulate vans, but Sakkra and Amy had insisted she use their limo, complete with the diplomatic seal and flags, because of Darren.

Ravon addressed Darm. "The van is a bit full. Would it be possible for me to ride in the car with you and your mate?"

A shiver of awareness worked its way up Sandy's spine. It was a fifteen man van. The chances of it being full enough that their seven man detail wouldn't fit was slim.

She started to look back to search for Zeke, but Darm's wing closed around her.

He's here. "Yes. Please." Though she didn't doubt Darm could handle Zeke alone, three warriors sounded safer than two. *I'm a wimp.*

Darm raised her hand and kissed the back through the ceremonial gloves she wore."As you wish, my love. Ravon may join the driver. Darren may need to eat on the way back."

And that isn't something he wants Ravon seeing.

In short order, they were on their way back to the consulate, and Zeke was left far behind.

Where he belongs.

****

"I believe we should leave on this ship. There is plenty of room for us. There may not be on the next." That last part wasn't strictly true, he knew. To his knowledge, no ship leaving Earth had ever been full, but there was a possibility that one might be someday.

"Really?" Sandy's excitement was infectious.

It was a relief as well. "Really. My family is anxious to meet you. The transport leaves tomorrow."

"We'll never be packed in time." But the thought seemed to depress her.

"On the contrary, my belongings and our purchases can be packed and transported aboard by other warriors within two hours. I can pack your belongings in an hour longer, even if Darren demands your undivided attention."

She hesitated only a moment.

A lifetime.

"Yes. The sooner we go, the better." Her eyes were haunted, a sure sign that Zeke caused her unease.

Darm laid a soft kiss on her forehead. "The sooner, the better," he agreed. "A new life awaits us."

He took his leave and gave the orders to relocate them to the departing ship.

Then he informed medical, so all information about Darren's condition and needs could be communicated to the ship's medical crew. To his amazement, Gabin replied that he would travel with them to ensure continuity of the young one's care.

Out of courtesy, Darm informed Sakkra about the trouble headed their way. As he expected, the prince gave the order to have them off planet before evening meal. Much to Darm's surprise, Sakkra ordered everyone leaving the planet to do the same.

By midnight GMT -5, the ship would leave orbit. When a woman and child were threatened, the Sakk could move very quickly indeed.

****

Sandy watched the Earth disappearing on the shuttle's screens, her muscles easing. No matter what Zeke tried to do now, they were beyond his reach.

I hope. There were treaties between the Sakk emperor and the American government. There might be clauses in the treaty that would apply to this situation.

Darm reached his free right hand to the console and pressed buttons to change the view. "This is the ship that will take us to Sakk."

A shuttle entering the landing bay gave her perspective. "It's huge." It was. The shuttle they were in was thirty feet wide and four times as long, but the entrance to the bay looked like the mail slot on the front of a ranch-style house.

He chuckled darkly. "Yes. It is indeed."

Darren wiggled against his shoulder, and Sandy looked up at him, waiting for the complaint that he was wet or needed a feeding. The baby settled again with a sigh.

"He is fine," Darm assured her.

"Should I carry him?"

"No. When we enter the ship, as when we enter my family's ancestral home, I should carry Darren."

She suspected it was a Sakk tradition and nodded her agreement.

One of the pilots spoke in the Sakk language and Darm answered in the same.

"What did he say?"

"We dock in a few moments."

"I have to learn to speak Sakk," she conceded. She'd only picked up a few words her entire time at the consulate, since Darm and Zave—as well as the doctors and royals—all spoke English for her.

He smiled. "I will teach you, but the ship's translators will allow you to interact aboard ship...when we leave our quarters."

"Why don't they use them on the shuttles?"

"I have no idea. When Sa Beldon came aboard ship, translators were set one way...Earth languages translated to Sakk. Now they work both directions, but the shuttles have not been equipped. I suppose... We spend so little time on shuttles, it didn't seem as important."

"So I'll know what you're saying when you speak Sakk?"

His smile disappeared. "I will have to keep that in mind."

"There's something you don't want me to hear?"

"No. But I often use the Sakk language to arrange surprises for you."

Something told her he wasn't being completely honest with her.

The docking was so smooth, the pilot announced their readiness to disembark without Sandy noting the slightest change.

Darm stood and helped Sandy to her feet. He reached across her body and threaded his fingers through hers. Then he closed her in with his wing, surrounding Sandy on three sides.

They made their way down the ramp, and the Sakk warriors at the base stopped to stare. A bark of command made Sandy jump. The warriors dropped to one knee and bowed their heads.

An older male with silver curls and gold ornamentation on his *cuzta* approached them. He bowed deeply and started speaking.

It was difficult to focus on the translated voice instead of the man's natural one, and the dichotomy of his mouth moving and the overlapping sounds made her head spin. Somehow, she managed to make out the words.

"We are honored by your presence. You have my vow. You are all safe aboard my ship."

Darm tipped his head. "My thanks, Sa Biren. If you would be so kind as to have your men unload my mate's belongings and take them to our quarters, I should get my family settled."

Biran waved a group of older warriors toward the shuttle. Sandy looked at the group, then at the younger men kneeling on the floor.

"Is there a problem?" Biran asked.

"I don't understand." She looked from one group to the other again. "Shouldn't the younger men carry heavy loads?"

Biran smiled. "Only older, widowed warriors are permitted in the nest areas, but I assure you, we are able and strong enough to carry heavy loads."

"Oh." Realization stopped her cold. "I am so sorry for your loss."

His smile went brittle. "I had fourteen wonderful years with my Judia. She presented me with three beautiful children. Both of my daughters have mates and have started families of their own. I cannot regret that."

Sandy didn't know how to reply to that. She nodded, tears stinging her eyes.

Biran said something in Sakk that didn't translate.

Darm's arm muscles tightened a notch. "You may."

The older man stepped toward them, reached a hand out, and laid it on Darren's tiny head. After a moment, he withdrew his hand, a faint smile on his face. "My crew has never been honored with transporting a babe so young before. My thanks for allowing me to offer my prayers."

The other widowed warriors left the shuttle, each with a small box tucked under an arm, reinforcing how few belongings Sandy had amassed at the consulate. They peeked up at Darren, longing on their faces.

"Let them," Sandy whispered.

Darm shot her a questioning look.

"It means so much to them."

He nodded. "The masters may offer well wishes for our son. My mate is correct. Such an event should be fully appreciated."

One by one, the old warriors approached, touched Darren's head or back, and offered their thanks. When they had all done so, Biren led them to spacious quarters.

At the door, he bowed deeply. "We leave Earth's gravity in a *ses-time*. Call for meals when you have need."

Sandy worked at that. "But a *ses-time* is just over an hour. I thought the ship didn't depart until tomorrow."

He offered a sly smile. "All the passengers are aboard. Why should we tarry longer?"

Something told her there was more to it, but Sandy nodded her agreement and slipped inside the room.

Chapter Thirty-Eight

Sandy looked up from Darren's dressing at a knock on the door. She nodded, and Darm went to it.

It was Biren. He kept his eyes averted while he spoke in low tones.

"Just a moment," Darm replied. "Our son is nearly ready."

He bowed and withdrew, closing the door behind him.

It had taken her weeks to learn how to wrap a formal *cuzta*; she'd been terrified she'd break one of Darren's tiny wings. Now that she was at ease with it, it seemed the easiest way to dress a baby she'd ever seen.

Darren's current outfit was one Darm's parents had sent aboard for him. It was a deep blue that matched Darren's eyes, with the family *Kieta* embroidered on it in silver. Sandy had added a slightly darker pair of socks and soft, black baby shoes.

Darm had assured her they would be disembarking through a tunnel and into a heated reception bay, so she'd opted to carry his bunting in the wrap bag until they needed it.

At last, she decided their son was perfect. At her nod, Darm cuddled Darren to his shoulder and offered her his hand. He adopted the same stance they had when they'd entered the ship. Sandy decided it must be ceremonial.

Biren waited for them in the hallway and led them out of the ship.

Sandy looked around at the nearly-deserted hallways, her head reeling. She'd never seen them so devoid of life. "Where is everyone?"

Their captain smiled back at her. "We let the others disembark first. Young Darren does not need to be exposed to such a crush of people for no good reason."

She nodded. In other words, the healers had ordered them to minimize the crowds of new people Darren was exposed to. Sandy reversed that determination a moment later, when they stepped into the reception bay.

The crowd of people stole her breath. She'd been expecting Darm's parents...or perhaps guards who would transport them to Darm's ancestral home. There were easily more than a three dozen people in the huge bay.

An older winged Sakk warrior with silver curls escorted a short flight female that could be no one other than Darm's mother toward them. The *Kieta* at his neck confirmed their identities, and Sandy dipped her head to them in greeting.

Darm's mother didn't leave it at that. She released her mate's arm and gathered Sandy into a hug. Sandy hesitated a moment, then returned it.

When the older woman released her, Sandy looked over at Darm, smiling at the sight of his father's big hand covering Darren's lower back.

Darm's mother crowded in. "May I hold my grandson?" she asked in slow, smooth Sakk.

Darm probably warned them that I'm still learning their language.

Darm chuckled. "Sandy, these are my parents, Elenna and Daragan." He turned Darren and settled him in his mother's arms.

She cooed to him, and Darren smiled widely in return. Tears pooled in Elenna's eyes. Daragan wrapped an arm around his mate, seemingly content.

Movement to one side of the room drew Sandy's attention. She looked around at the approaching group, wondering at them. The central couple were dressed in pure white clothing with gold accents and surrounded by armored warriors.

Darm looked that direction and froze for an instant. His smile faded, and he dropped to one knee, his head bowed deeply.

Sandy started to curtsey, stopped, and tried to dissect what she'd been taught about situations in which Darm would kneel. Realization made her blood run cold. *He's never mentioned it.*

More confusing than that, Darm's parents had turned to look at the newcomers and tipped their heads politely, but neither of them bowed or went to one knee.

What am I supposed to do?

"May I?" the male asked in a tone that sounded of some sort of ceremony.

"Yes. We would be honored," Darm hastened to reply.

He reached his hands out, and Daragan transferred Darren from his mate's arms to the newcomer's. The female at his side trilled to Darren, smiling at his baby laugh.

The silence around them was absolute. Sandy forced her breath in and out, questions rising in her throat.

At last, the male holding her son met her gaze. "He will make a fine *appamora* someday."

"*Appamora?*" Sandy had never heard the term before.

Darm took her hand in his, looking up at her. "Sakkrel is offering Darren training in his chosen trade at the palace. The best of all tradesmen practice their trades there."

"Sakkr—" Her head swam at the pronouncement. This was the emperor? And his mate?

Darm vaulted to his feet and caught Sandy as her balance deserted her. Shouts rose around them, and Darm eased her to a cushioned surface.

She opened her eyes to the sight of all three of the men staring down at her. Gabin motioned for space. He read the glyphs on something that resembled a tablet computer.

The readouts from my bio chain. Darm had told her it would give baseline medical information.

At his snap of order in the Sakk language, there was dizzying motion in the crowd. A glass was passed hand to hand, and Gabin nodded to Darm.

He helped her to sitting and slid behind her on what she now recognized as a wide lounge. Gabin held the glass for her, and Sandy managed a few mouthfuls of it.

"There," the healer soothed her. "That should help. Just rest for a moment."

Sandy sank to Darm's chest, her emotions in a riot. "I don't understand what is happening here," she admitted.

The emperor returned Darren to Daragan and sank into a crouch next to her. He switched to English, stunning her with his mastery of her language. "You are aware of the threat to your son, I am sure."

Threat? "His health? But Gabin said he was doing well."

"No. Not his health. He is hearty and growing well." He shot an unreadable look at Darm.

Realization made her ill. "Zeke?" *But what danger could he pose here on Sakk?*

The emperor nodded grimly. "Sakk will not relinquish our claim on you or your son."

"He wants Darren?" *Not a chance. I won't allow him anywhere near Darren.*

A hand came up, a clear request for silence. "That will not happen. There are formalities to be observed, of course."

"There are?" Every exchange raised more questions than they answered.

He motioned to Daragan, and Darm's father started speaking. "You are both already part of our family, by Sakk law. Sa Beldon's mate, Janice, and Sakku Amy have suggested that we fill out formal adoption paperwork, as they use on Earth, securing Darm's place as Darren's sire, by human laws.

"Sakkrel—with your agreement to such, Sandy—will be named Darren's..." He seemed to search for a word. At last, he muttered something in Sakk.

Darm gasped.

"What does it mean?" Sandy asked. Since they'd said they were securing Darren's place as part of Darm's ancestral home, it couldn't mean something that would remove her son from her care.

Darm cleared his throat. "It is our equivalent of a godfather."

"The Sakk emperor will be Darren's godfather?"

"Yes. He would."

"I have no problem with that." Since she had no one else in mind for the job and knew no one but Darm's parents and the healer on the entire planet, how could she choose another?

Realization made her heart stutter. She turned her face to meet Darm's gaze. "Is there any reason I shouldn't allow this?"

He smiled. "None I can conceive of. The benefits to Darren would be immense."

"Including the benefit of protecting him from Zeke."

"Including that."

She turned and nodded to Sakkrel. "I agree. Thank you for offering this."

He tipped his head and rose. A warrior approached and offered Sakkrel a pristine white box. The emperor opened it and removed a *Kieta* cast in what she suspected was *ullium*. He slipped the monitoring device that Darren typically wore off and replaced it with the piece of jewelry.

Darm whispered to her. "The seal is a more advanced monitor. All the royal family wear them."

She nodded. Now that he'd mentioned it, she remembered that Amy never removed hers.

Sakkrel leaned down, laying a kiss on Darren's forehead. After a moment, he stepped back and addressed the crowd in a gruff tone and in the Sakk language. "Let all on Sakk be aware. This child is my *Sakkrettieff*. He is under my personal protection and care. Anyone foolish enough to injure this child injures me, and Sakkan alone have mercy on their souls for it."

No one made a sound, as if such a thing would be seen as a challenge to that claim.

He nodded curtly and met Daragan's gaze. "My healers will arrive within a turning."

"Our thanks, Sakkrel."

Sakkrel offered a tip of his head to Sandy and Darm and marched back the way he'd come, the rest of his entourage in tow.

An uneasy silence fell in his wake. Sandy swallowed hard. "His...healers?" What had she missed?

Elenna settled to the lounge beside her and squeezed Sandy's hand. "One does not take on the position lightly. Sakkrel promised to be personally responsible for Darren's protection and care. That means he will supply the best healers on Sakk for your son's care, the best food, the best of everything, as he would for one of his own children."

"And his education as well." Sandy marveled at it.

Darm's mother chuckled. "Darren need never be a military man, unless it pleases him to do so."

Her heart stuttered at that pronouncement. "Then how will he find a mate? Does he have to return to Earth to do it?"

Darm wrapped an arm around her waist. "This association will even help with that. Never fear. Darren will have nearly any unmated woman he wants, just for the asking."

The concept stunned her.

Daragan spoke up. "Are you well, Sandy? Perhaps we should get her to the nest, where she can relax in peace."

"I was just thinking," she mused.

"Yes?" Darm's father prompted.

"I never would have guessed when I walked into the Sakk consulate."

"Guessed?"

"That my son had a chance of anything noteworthy in his life, let alone being godson to the Sakk emperor."

Darm chuckled in response. "With the Sakk, he would have had a chance to pursue his dreams, no matter what. Even males who are forced by circumstance to become soldiers or priests are trained for their choices of trades."

A niggling of unease assaulted her. "Will Zeke cause problems for the Sakk?" She wouldn't put a social media campaign against the Sakk past him. If it would hurt her, she wouldn't put much of anything past him.

Daragan snorted. "There is little he can do. Who would think it right to drag a child back and forth between worlds for the vanity of one man who denied his part in the child's creation? To take a child away from stable medical care, family and friends, schooling? Even a visit every *yan* would be highly disruptive to Darren's existence, since it would mean half of every *yan* spent in transit between worlds."

Elenna continued for him. "Even if that beast of a male wished to come here to visit, he would find it not to his liking."

Sandy worked at a question that refused to emerge.

Darm explained his mother's comment. "It would take someone like Zeke very little time to find himself on the wrong side of Sakk law. He would insult you or Darren, raise a hand to one of you... If he tried to approach a Sakk woman... He would be escorted off planet very quickly. If he lived that long."

Sandy laughed at the mental image of Zeke fuming his way onto a shuttle, under heavy guard.

"It is good to hear you laugh," Elenna commented.

"There was a time when I thought I might never laugh again," Sandy admitted. She looked at Darm. "Then the most unexpected man came into my life."

He smiled widely. "I never expected to find a mate like you either," he admitted. "The males who walked away from the chance to get to know you were fools."

She couldn't find the words to respond to his praise.

Elenna shattered the moment. "Darren is asleep. I think we should return to the nest, so Sandy can sleep while he does."

"Most prudent," Daragan intoned.

Darm nodded and scooped Sandy into his arms. He pressed a kiss to her forehead.

She shot a look around, noting the males averting their eyes. "Darm, we shouldn't. I can walk."

"I was told once that you believe in carrying what you value."

Her cheeks flamed. "That was another life," she argued weakly.

"But no less true today." With that, he followed his parents to the far side of the bay and the waiting transport.

The End

About the Author

Brenna Lyons wears many hats, sometimes all on the same day: former president of EPIC, author of more than 100 published works, owner of Fireborn Publishing, columnist, special needs teacher, wife, mother...and member in good standing of more than 60 writing advocacy groups.

In her first ten years published in novel-length, she's won 3 EPIC e-Book Awards (out of 15 finalists) and finaled for 3 PEARLS (including one Honorable Mention, second to NY Times Bestseller Angela Knight), 2 CAPAS, and a Dream Realm Award. She's also taken Spinetingler's Book of the Year for 2007.

Brenna writes in 26 established worlds plus stand-alones, poetry, articles and essays. She's a bestseller in indie/e fantasy and horror, straight genre and cross-genres thereof. Brenna has been termed "one of the most deviant erotic minds in the publishing world...not for the weak." (Rachelle for Fallen Angels Reviews) Milieu-heavy dark work is practically Brenna's calling card, with or without the erotic content.

She teaches classes in everything from POV studies to advanced editing, networking to marketing. Brenna enjoys hearing from people who read her work and can be reached by e-mail.

Website: http://www.brennalyons.com/

Facebook: http://www.facebook.com/brenna.lyons

Email: brennalyons4168@live.com

Also by this Author

Available from *Fireborn Publishing*

KEIF'S DEN AND PACK
Keif's Pack
Mother of the Keif
Keif's Den (Coming Soon)

PROPHECY
Prophecy: Revelations
Prophecy: Rapture
The Prophet's Mate
Prophecy: Rampage - Meet Gavin
Prophecy: Rampage (Coming Soon)

RENEGADES SERIES
TYGERS
Renegade's Run
Max Sec

THE FANTASY CLUB
The Consort

INSTINCT SERIES
Animal Instincts

KEGIN SERIES
Earth-Born Lord
Graham: Training the Earth-Born Lord

NIGHT WARRIORS
Claiming a Lady
Stone Lord
Mother's Son
Night Warriors
Will of the Stone
Bearing Armen
Hunter's Tales

Maher Men
The Blutjagdfrau Chronicles
Veriel's Tales I: Crossbearer Turned
Veriel's Tales II: Losing Regana

URBAN GRIMM
Catch Me, If You Can
Three Wishes
Temptation of Eve

WEREWOLF U
Werewolf U
Younger Daughter
Alpha Son
Never Alone
Her Christmas Wolves

ANGEL-WING SAGA
Sons of Heaven: Beldon
Sons of Heaven: Unexpected Mates
Daughters of Man: Prize Match
Daughters of Man: Claiming a Princess

COLOR OF LOVE
The Color of Love

KEGIN SERIES
Conquest
The Last of Fion's Daughters
Last Chance for Love
Rites of Mating
In Her Ladyship's Service
Matchmaker's Misery

KIELAN SERIES
The Lady's Lowborn Lover
Time Currents
Cubed

STAR MAGES

Bride Ball
Undead in Blue
Mama's Tales
Unexpected Daddy
We Shall Live Again
May the Best Man Win
Marked
And It Was Good
Monsters of Myth Anthology

Available from **Under The Moon**

Evil Overlords Union Issue #1 Anthology
Undead Embrace
"*Playing Games*" in *Forbidden Love: Bad Boys*
"*Marked*" in *Forbidden Love: Wicked Women*
"*The Master's Lover*" in *Forbidden Love: Sacred Bands*

Available from **Logical Lust**

"*Mine for the Night*" in *The Cougar Book* Anthology

Available from **Coming Together Charity Anthologies**

INSTINCT SERIES
"*Foundling*" in *Coming Together: Into the Light*
Anthology

"*Claim Mate*" (available separately and as part of the
Coming Together: Against the Odds Anthology)
"*The Fire God's Woman*" in *Coming Together: Under Fire*
Anthology

Available **self-published**

Snapshots from a Poet's Life

Award-Winning Books

EPPIE/EPIC eBOOK AWARDS WINNERS
Coming Together: Against the Odds- 2010
Time Currents- 2010
Coming Together: Into the Light- 2011

EPPIE/EPIC eBOOK AWARDS FINALISTS
Fion's Daughter- 2004
Collected Poems: Book One- 2005 (now titled *Snapshots of a Poet's Life*)
Renegade's Run- 2005
Rites of Mating- 2006
All I Want for Christmas- 2006
Phaze in Verse- 2008
"The Fire God's Woman" in Coming Together: Under Fire- 2009
Three Wishes- 2010
Matchmaker's Misery- 2010
The Cougar Book- 2011
The Master's Lover- 2011
Bride Ball- 2011

DREAM REALM AWARDS FINALIST
Last Chance for Love- 2003

PEARL HONORABLE MENTION
Night Warriors- 2004

PEARL FINALISTS
Schente Night- 2003 (now included in *The Last of Fion's Daughters*)
König Cursebreakers- 2004 (now titled *Will of the Stone*)

JOYFULLY REVIEWED BEST BOOKS OF 2010
Written in the Stars- 2010

SPINETINGLER'S BOOK OF THE YEAR 2007

NOBODY: An Anthology of Dark Fiction- 2007 (Brenna's pieces of the anthology can be found in *Beyond the Veil*)

TRS's CAPA FINALISTS
Ultimate Warriors- 2004 (Brenna's portion is now available as *With Great Power*)
Written in the Stars

LOVE ROMANCE AND MORE CAFÉ BOOK OF THE YEAR RUNNER UP
Last Chance for Love- 2008

ROAD TO ROMANCE REVIEWERS' CHOICE AWARD
Prophecy: Revelations- 2004

LOVE ROMANCES REVIEWERS' CHOICE AWARD
Black Sail- 2003

ROMANCE JUNKIES BOOK CLUB STAFF PICK
TYGERS- 2003

FALLEN ANGELS ROMANCE RECOMMENDED READ
Devon's Price-2005 (now available in *Bearing Armen*)

JOYFULLY RECOMMENDED READ
Fairy Dreams- 2008
The Last of Fion's Daughters- 2009

TREBLE HEART FINALIST
Prophecy: Revelations- 2003

www.ingramcontent.com/pod-product-compliance
Lightning Source LLC
Chambersburg PA
CBHW020455020726
47493CB00001B/43